D0856307

CITY
OF
TIME
AND
MAGIC

ALSO BY PAULA BRACKSTON

The Garden of Promises and Lies

Secrets of the Chocolate House

The Little Shop of Found Things

The Return of the Witch

The Silver Witch

Lamp Black, Wolf Grey

The Midnight Witch

The Winter Witch

The Witch's Daughter

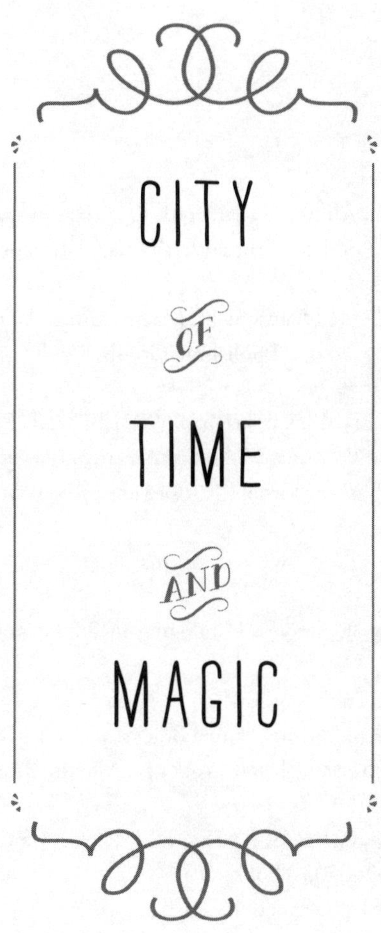

Paula Brackston

ST. MARTIN'S PRESS
NEW YORK

This is a work of fiction. All of the characters, organizations, and events portrayed in this novel are either products of the author's imagination or are used fictitiously.

First published in the United States by St. Martin's Press, an imprint of St. Martin's Publishing Group

www.stmartins.com

Library of Congress Cataloging-in-Publication Data

Names: Brackston, Paula, author.
Title: City of time and magic / Paula Brackston.
Description: First Edition. | New York : St. Martin's Press, 2021. | Series: Found things ; 4
Identifiers: LCCN 2021027561 | ISBN 9781250260697 (hardcover) | ISBN 9781250260703 (ebook)
Subjects: GSAFD: Fantasy fiction.
Classification: LCC PR6102.R325 C58 2021 | DDC 823/.92—dc23
LC record available at https://lccn.loc.gov/2021027561

Our books may be purchased in bulk for promotional, educational, or business use. Please contact your local bookseller or the Macmillan Corporate and Premium Sales Department at 1-800-221-7945, extension 5442, or by email at MacmillanSpecialMarkets@macmillan.com.

First Edition: 2021

10 9 8 7 6 5 4 3 2 1

FOR CATHY - A GIFTED PHOTOGRAPHER,
A TALENTED ICE SKATER, AN EXCELLENT
TEACHER, AND A LOVELY FRIEND

X

CITY
OF
TIME
AND
MAGIC

1

XANTHE STEPPED FORWARD ONTO THE SMOOTH, FLAT STONES WHICH WERE ALL THAT remained of the ruined castle walls. She registered the resistance of the ancient sandstone through the worn leather soles of her boots. After the springy grass of the hill it felt unyielding and solid. The April sunshine was not strong enough to warm it, the hilltop breeze whipping away the warmth of the fading day. She waited, closing her eyes against the distraction of the far-reaching view, holding herself still and quiet, listening, hoping. Yearning. She could hear skylarks whirring a ways off, and the chatter of small children as they were led back down the footpath toward home. She was aware of the light wind tugging at her loose ponytail. She could detect the aroma of the peaty soil in the air. She could feel her own heartbeat thud against her eardrums.

But nothing sang to her.

No lost souls cried out to her.

No time-distant injustice called to her.

A shadow, broad and cool, came between Xanthe and the sunshine. She opened her eyes to find Harley standing close, watching her, concern etched on his grizzled features.

"Anything, hen?"

She shook her head.

Harley rubbed his beard, looking thoughtfully at their surroundings. "Not even here?"

"I was so certain this would be the place. I really thought . . ."

"Aye, it has all the ingredients, right enough. Ancient settlement with evidence of inhabitation from 3000 BC; ruined castle and cathedral; fortifications refortified by William the Conqueror his very self; fine views of three counties for fifty miles or more; and sitting right bang slap on top of one of the strongest ley lines in the whole of England." He looked at her again, bushy brows raised. "Not even a whisper? A tingle? A tiny snatch of song?"

"Not so much as a note," she said, trying hard not to let her disappointment show. She had to stay focused. Without her, Liam was lost forever, it was as simple and as terrifying as that. It was because of her that he had failed to make the journey home. It was up to her to find him and bring him safely back. It had been her idea to visit the ancient hill fort of Old Sarum. For two weeks since her solitary return from Corsham Hall in 1820, she had searched fairs and markets for something that might sing to her and lead her to Liam. Something that would trigger her unique sensitivity—the psychometry that enabled her to detect the long past stories of those objects—so that she could travel through time again. Her skills as a Spinner were growing, as was her success at using the *Spinners* book to move through time, but before she stepped into the blind house again she needed to be sure. She needed to know for certain that she was traveling to the right place, and as crucially, the right time, to find Liam. A found thing, one that sang strongly to her, would be the surest sign, she believed, the surest way, to help her make the right journey. But all her searches had been fruitless. Trying a different tack, and with Harley's help, she had turned to the part that ley lines played in her ability to spin through time. The old lockup in her garden sat upon an intersection of two strong lines of the mysterious energy that connected ancient and sacred places. She had reasoned that another powerful location might spark something. Was it possible for a place to sing to her in the same way a precious object could? The complete lack of so much as a whisper was a crushing blow.

Harley was sensitive to what this failure meant to her.

"I'm of the opinion a person's thoughts flow easier with a full belly," he told her.

She hesitated, reluctant to abandon the day's mission, yet knowing there was nothing further to be gained by staying on the hilltop.

"Pub?" she suggested.

"Pub," he agreed.

A mile from the earthworks, The Soldier's Arms was set back from the road and offered a fine selection of local ales. She chose a corner table, the weather not quite warm enough to tempt her outside to the beer garden, and Harley fetched the drinks. The pub clearly catered to tourists, but managed to do so without entirely losing its charm. She found the low murmur of their fellow drinkers' conversations familiar and comforting. Harley returned with a brimming pint glass for himself and a smaller measure for her.

"Here ye are, designated driver." He set the drinks on the little round table between them and eased himself onto the high-backed wooden seat, which creaked in complaint at his not inconsiderable weight. "According to yon barman"—he nodded at the skinny man serving—"interest in ley lines has had something of a renewal in these parts lately. Lots of visitors haul their backsides up that hill in the hope of sensing the special energy of the place."

"Well, I hope they have better luck than we did."

Harley drank deeply, wiped his beard with the back of his hand, and let out a happy sigh. He picked a menu out of the holder on the table and handed one to her. "Food, lass. And after we've eaten and drunk, we'll bring our minds to bear on the matter in hand once more, but not before. Deal?"

She was happy to agree. After the initial shock of finding Liam had been separated from her as they had traveled to their own time, she had put all her energy into discovering a way to find him. And yet, despite her best efforts and input from both Harley and her mother, nothing had worked. She felt no closer to knowing what time he had gone to. Or rather, what time he had been taken to. It still hurt her to accept how Mistress Flyte had betrayed her. The *Spinners* book had revealed the fact that the old woman harbored secrets, but she would never have thought her capable of doing something so awful. What possible reason could she have for snatching Liam in the way that she had? Xanthe had spent restless nights trying to make sense of it. There were times when a few moments of normality to recharge and reset her tormented thoughts were extremely necessary. She and Harley chose beer-battered fish and chips for their lunch and ate in companionable silence, serenaded by the gentle noises of the pub. She watched people at the other tables, wondering what secrets their own lives held, feeling a separation from the normality they experienced. A distance from a life of straightforward challenges and obstacles. Her gift as a Spinner was something to be grateful for, something that humbled her and filled her with wonder. It was also, however, something that came at a price, and at that moment, the price was too high and was being paid by someone she cared for deeply. After their meal, feeling fortified, she and Harley returned to the topic of Old Sarum.

"How can somewhere so ancient, so full of past lives and important events . . . how can it *not* speak to me?" she wondered aloud. "I mean, on another level it does, of course. Like anyone else, I can appreciate the history, imagine what the settlements would have been like . . . but as a Spinner, I find nothing."

He gave an expansive shrug, the leather of his biker's jacket stretching over his broad shoulders as he did so. "It's your first-rate ley line location, no doubt about that, connecting Stonehenge and Salisbury Cathedral. The story goes that some ambitious bishop decided the original cathedral, up on yon hill, was too wind-blasted and remote for his needs."

"Can't have been fun slogging up there in the winter."

"Right enough. So, he got one of the king's finest archers to stand on the highest point and shoot an arrow into the valley below. He decreed that wherever the arrow fell, that is where the new cathedral would be built. Most likely hoping for a bit of soft meadow down near the river, close enough and cheap enough to rebuild on."

"So how come we ended up with Salisbury Cathedral, miles away? Must have been quite an archer."

"He was good, aye, but not that good. Legend has it he loosed his arrow but it struck a deer, somewhere not instantly fatal, apparently. Said deer hoofed it south, only to expire on the location of the current and spectacular cathedral. Bishop was so pleased with himself he only went and built the tallest spire in the whole of the country. Still is, matter of fact."

"Fascinating, Harley, but not helpful, I'm afraid. No, if Old Sarum isn't going to give me the clues I need, I think we have to accept that ley lines are not the answer. Or at least they are a part of it, but not the most significant part. Which, if I'm honest, I think I always knew."

"It was worth a try. And the fish here is superb." He smiled at her, trying hard to keep the mood light.

Not for the first time, she was grateful for her burly friend's support. With Harley and Flora now aware of her astonishing ability, at least she no longer had to face the challenges of being a Spinner alone.

When she arrived back at The Little Shop of Found Things it was nearly closing time. Having dropped Harley off at The Feathers and parked up her trusty black cab, she hurried through the front door, calling above the clanging of the brass bell.

"Mum? I'm back." As always, the smell of beeswax polish and old leather in the main part of the shop was welcoming and familiar, speaking to her of a childhood spent surrounded by antiques, and now the excitement and hope she shared with her mother for their new venture.

Flora appeared in the hallway, stepping out of the room that was her workshop, wiping her hands on a rag as she leaned on her crutches. "You're home in good time, love. Any luck?" she asked.

Xanthe shook her head. "Nothing. Ley lines are not the answer. I'll have to spend more time reading the *Spinners* book. There's got to be something in there I'm missing."

"Or another found thing to call to you."

"Well, yes, that," she replied, instantly regretting the slight sharpness to her voice. "Sorry, Mum . . . it's just that I know it's a found thing I need, but what? Where? Why can't I find one? I feel completely stumped, to be honest."

Flora smiled and stick-stepped forward. "Here," she said, holding out a scrap of paper with an address scrawled on it, "maybe this will lead to something. A man downsizing from a house just outside Devizes. Wants us to give him prices on some of the things in his collection."

"Antiques or bric-a-brac?"

"I couldn't tell over the phone." Flora put a hand on her daughter's arm. "Something will find you, Xanthe, love. And you will find Liam. Now, go and put the kettle on. While you and Harley have been stomping about on hill forts, some of us have been serving customers and stripping lacquer off a nest of tables. I'm parched."

Xanthe pulled her mother into a long, warm hug. "What would I do without you, Mum?"

Before Flora could answer, the sound of scrabbling claws on the wooden staircase announced the arrival of Pie. The little black-and-white whippet was excited to see her friend home. Xanthe bent down and scooped the wriggling dog up into her arms. "Looks like someone's forgiven me for not taking her. Come on, pooch. Tea and biscuits all round."

In the upstairs kitchen she leaned against the sink as she waited for the kettle to boil, while Pie trotted around the small room, stirred to further excitement at the sight of the biscuit tin. Xanthe unfolded the scrap of paper and looked at the address written on it. The Pines sounded more like a retirement home than a grand house, and she found it hard to be optimistic. What she hoped for, every time they received a call for a house clearance or for a valuation for possible sale, was an old manor or tiny thatched cottage, either would do, so long as they were filled with lovely old curios. What was more likely was a great deal of midcentury furniture, random junk from a long life, all of which mattered greatly to the person parting with it, but was probably of little value or use for the shop. Nor was it likely to be of sufficient age to take her back in time to whenever it was Liam waited for her. Still, business was business. The shop needed stock. They had to maintain their reputation for giving fair prices for good items. And maybe, just maybe, something in the old man's collection of treasures would sing to her.

—

Liam opened his eyes. He was lying on a narrow bed with a worn iron frame and thin mattress. The light in the room suggested dawn or dusk, he could not be sure which. There were no curtains at the window and the floorboards were bare. Sounds of the street drifted in; horses' hooves upon cobbles, carriage wheels, the shouts of hawkers and barrow boys. There was a familiar smell. Was it the sea? No, not salty, but definitely water. A river, then, close by. He tried to sit up but the movement made his head spin and his vision blur. Gingerly, he raised himself up onto one elbow, taking time to allow his senses to readjust. He could see now that although the room contained a bed, it was otherwise empty. Dust lay fairly thick on the windowsill, and there were cobwebs in the exposed beams and rafters above him. He swung his legs over the side of the uneven mattress. He was wearing the clothes he had been dressed in when he and Xanthe had started their journey through time toward home, which meant he was still clothed in the cheap hire costume he had obtained for their mission.

The fabrics of the Regency outfit were synthetic and scratchy, and the warmth of the day made him pull at the collar to remove the purple cravat, allowing him to take deep breaths of the musty air the room provided. He dropped it onto the bed, not bothering to retrieve it when it slipped off and landed on the dusty floor. He took a moment to try to work out what had happened. The last thing he clearly remembered was slipping his arms around Xanthe's waist, holding tight to her as she worked her magic as a Spinner to move them through the centuries again. Beyond that, everything was confused and fragmented. He could recall snatches of sounds, of her calling his name, of other voices from far away. He thought he remembered flashes of light but they were too vague and too fleeting to tell him anything useful. One minute he had been with her, heading home; the next he had been wrenched away, held by unseen hands, and then thrust in another direction altogether. The rest was darkness.

He rose shakily to his feet and walked the few strides to the window. The glass was opaque with grime. Using his sleeve, he was able to clean a small patch so that he could peer outside. Had he not recently traveled through time to the 1820s, what he saw would have shocked him. As it was, he accepted quite readily the fact that he was clearly not anywhere in the twenty-first century. There were no cars, no traffic lights, no wires connecting the houses. Carriages and carts of all shapes and sizes traveled up and down the street, which was at least three storeys below him, broad and cobbled. The building he was in was part of a long, high terrace, flat fronted and redbrick, without adornments, porticos, or railings, but with doors opening straight onto the road. Opposite there were no houses or shops. Instead, beyond a low wall, ran a river, broad, slow, and gray, the soft light skimming off its calm surface. Small boats were tied to moorings in the quay, while larger ones moved up and down the river in a dangerous dance against the tide, the currents, and each other. There were enormous barges, heavy with cargo, sitting low in the water; smart sailing ships heading out to sea; smaller vessels taking passengers across the river or upstream to another part of the city. For a city it certainly was, that much was plain to see. The far bank showed a similar picture to the one where Liam found himself, with buildings to the foreshore, warehouses, tenement blocks, workaday dwellings, and stores and places of trade. Farther back, set away from the noise and commerce of the river, he could make out loftier, grander constructions. There were church spires and the high roofs of mansions and hotels and important buildings too many and various to be identified from his distant viewpoint. The shouted greetings and snatches of conversations he could discern from the street confirmed that he was in England. Could this be the Thames? He scanned the cityscape for a landmark he might recognize but found none. Surprising himself, he felt an excitement at the thought that he was most likely in London, maybe a century or more before his own time. However precarious his situation, whatever plans his abductor had for him, it was impossible not to feel the thrill of knowing that again he had traveled through time. He found himself wondering what Xanthe would do in his position.

"Well, she wouldn't stand here gazing out the window like a tourist," he muttered, brushing the dust from his clothes, straightening his jacket, and heading for the door. He tried the handle. That it was unlocked surprised him. He opened it slowly, wincing at the loud creaking its hinges made. The narrow landing was empty. Unsure what to make of the fact that he was unguarded, he made his way to the stairs and descended them cautiously, every tread seeming to complain noisily at his stepping on it. The next floor was hardly less grimy and basic than the one he had just left. The doors off the stairwell were closed, but even the landings had about them a worn and comfortless feel. It was as if the house was little used or loved, and barely inhabited at all. There were no lamps lit, but the light falling through the tall windows was strengthening, telling him the day was beginning. He thought it might be harder to escape his captors in the daylight, but perhaps a safer time to try to navigate the unfamiliar city. It was only as he reached the ground floor that he found some signs of life. There was a worn rug on the floor, a mahogany hat stand and mirror, and a swayback sideboard. He paused to listen. Voices came from the room to his left, their volume too low and words too muffled for him to make out. He would have to cross the hallway and pass close to the entrance of the inhabited room to reach the front door. He started to walk forward, attempting to focus on what it would take to draw back the bolts on the door while at the same time listening hard to the murmured conversation, alert to any pause or change of tone that might suggest he had been heard.

He had reached the midpoint of the faded Turkish carpet when, without warning, a figure stepped out of the adjoining room. He froze, staring openly at the woman who came to stand before him. Even in her new outfit of somewhat drab clothing, there remained an elegance and poise about Mistress Flyte. He should not have been surprised. The sight of her stirred something in his recent memory. Some flicker of recognition regarding who it was who had wrenched him from Xanthe's side without so much as touching him. He tried to put together the pieces of the puzzle. He and Xanthe had been outside Mistress Flyte's tea shop when they tried to travel to their own time together. The woman had known what they were about to do. She had once been a skilled Spinner herself. It was quite possible she had the expertise to snatch him away, to divert him onto a different journey, before Xanthe could realize the danger and do anything to stop her. So, he more or less understood the *how*. But not the *why*.

"Mister Adams," she said calmly. "I am pleased to see you are recovered from your journey."

Liam glanced past her, checking for a henchman or two who might leap out and take hold of him. He had no wish to be dragged back up to the room at the top of the house and left there. He was so tantalizingly close to the door and to freedom.

"Where are we?" he asked. "And maybe more to the point, what year is this?"

"We are in London. It is not, I confess, a city that delights me. Alas, needs must. As for the year, it is 1878. Queen Victoria continues to rule in her inimitable if rather bombastic manner, aided by Mister Disraeli, and we are no longer at war with the Russians. Will that suffice as regards instruction in history? Would you not rather take some refreshment? For myself, spinning time leaves me thirsty and more than a little hungry." She stepped to one side, indicating that he should join her in the room from which she had just emerged.

"You can't keep me here," he told her. "I don't know why you stopped me from going back to my own time, but you had no right to do it."

"It was, I will allow, an imposition."

"Yeah, that's a fancy word for kidnapping right now, so I think I'll just be going." He strode over to the door. He was on the point of opening it when she spoke again, without a hint of alarm or concern in her voice.

"You will find the door unlocked. You are free to go. I will not have it said I made a prisoner of you."

Confused, he tried the door. The handle turned. He pulled it open, letting in the sounds of the street. Only paces away, people went about their everyday business, carting their wares, hurrying to appointments or work, leading a small child by the hand, strolling on the arm of a lover, haggling the terms of a deal. In general, living their lives in their own time and place, unaware that they had time travelers in their midst. He hesitated, fearing some sort of trick, wondering what would happen to him if he were to run from the house.

"Why did you bring me here?" he asked. "What do you want from me?"

She tugged at the lace on her cuff, minutely adjusting her sleeve until she was satisfied with it. Without looking at Liam she said, "You are at liberty, Mister Adams. Poor as it regrettably may be, this house is, for the present, your home. You may come and go as you please."

"And if I choose to go and not come back?"

"Flee if you wish, but consider carefully how difficult it will be for Xanthe to find you if you first allow yourself to be swallowed up by this hungry city." So saying, she turned and walked from the hall into the sitting room, leaving him to ponder the significance of her words.

—

The ormolu clock in the shop struck midnight. Xanthe knew she should get to her bed, try to sleep, recharge her mental batteries to be in better shape tomorrow. But it was hard to admit defeat and give up on yet another day. She had been so full of hope when she and Harley had set off for Old Sarum. Having accepted the place held no answers for her, she had decided to redouble her efforts with the *Spinners* book. It was such a plain little volume, with a worn leather cover bearing the single word "Spinners." There was nothing about its appearance to suggest the secrets and magic it held within its covers. She leaned back in the captain's chair that she knew she would never sell. It had become part of the shop, and she and Flora used it, as old Mr. Morris had, every day, positioned behind the broad Victorian desk that served as a counter. She opened the book, leafing gently through the pages, listening for whispers, searching without looking, asking without demanding, opening her mind to anything the book might choose to show her. Many of the pages remained blank, while others showed her things she had read or heard before. She needed something new. Ideally, another indication of how she might spin through time without the use of a found thing calling her to action. She could not simply wait for an antique to fall into her hands. The thought that Liam was suffering somewhere, trapped and alone, tormented her. She tucked her legs up under her on the chair, tugging her long nightdress and oversize fluffy jumper down to keep her knees warm, grateful for the thick socks she was wearing. The heating was not on, and any lingering warmth from the day had faded, so that the shop was quite cool. After another half hour passed with nothing to show for it she closed the book again and gazed around the room. Why was she being so unsuccessful in using her gifts? Why did it feel like the other Spinners had deserted her, just when she needed them most? She had managed to travel time-within-time on her trips to the past. She had been able to step back a little further and return to the point of her main journey accurately and safely. She had succeeded in taking Flora back to the early 1800s to show her how she traveled, just for a few moments. The key point was that even when she was doing these extra journeys, she had an object that sang to her, anchoring her to where she needed to be. Pinpointing the time and place for her. It seemed to be the case that, no matter how proficient she became at using what information she gleaned from the book, no matter how practiced she was at stepping through the years, back and fore, she could not do so without a triggering object.

"OK," she said aloud, addressing the collection of glass, china, kilims, lace, silver, and assorted curiosities, "if that's the case, I am just going to have to keep looking until I find what I need. Or until it finds me." Mustering determination, she tucked the book under her arm, switched off the table lamp on the desk, and headed upstairs.

2

AT THE BREAKFAST TABLE THE NEXT MORNING, FLORA PICKED UP ON XANTHE'S UPBEAT mood.

"Did you finally manage to get a good night's sleep?" she asked, slipping Pie a crust of toast. The little dog snaffled it eagerly.

"Not really, but at least when I was awake I came up with a plan."

"Oh?"

Xanthe set the coffeepot down and took the seat opposite her mother, reaching out to make a fuss of Pie while she spoke, enjoying the soothing feel of her short, silky fur. "I'm going to ring the number you gave me yesterday, Mr. . . . Did he leave a name?"

"No, I forgot to ask, just the number and the address."

"I'll go and see what he's got after closing today. If nothing sings to me there, I'm going to go to the antiques fair in Salisbury tomorrow. Nothing there, I'm going back into Liam's flat, see if I can connect with something. Meanwhile, I will also be working with the *Spinners* book pretty much constantly." She nodded in the direction of the dresser, where the book sat waiting for her to take it down with her for her shift in the shop. "And," she said, pouring coffee into two Clarice Cliff cups as she spoke, "I'm going to take the book and something of Liam's, something personal, out to the blind house, see where that gets me."

"Are you sure that's wise? I mean, you don't want to travel anywhere before you're ready."

"Mum, I've got to find him."

"I know. . . ."

She reached across the table and gave her mother's hand a squeeze. "I'll be OK. I know what I'm doing."

A knocking on the shop door interrupted their conversation. Xanthe left her breakfast and went to see who it was, the dog running beside her as she went. Through the glass she could see Gerri, a large box in her arms. She unlocked the door and let her in.

"That looks heavy," she said, as her friend staggered through the entrance and set the box down on the nearest bit of clear space.

"Just a bit! Worth the struggle, though. Wait till you see what I've got for our vintage clothes room. A friend of my cousin's has just closed down her shop in Chelsea. I got her to sell me a box of assorted garments, sight unseen, but guaranteed in good condition. I hardly paid anything. Friend of mine was driving down last night and dropped it off."

Pie jumped up, begging for a fuss.

"Good stuff?"

"Really good! I would have paid double for what she's sent. Shall I take it through to the other room?"

Xanthe was pleased to be able to participate in their joint venture again. Since Gerri had agreed to lend her expertise and keen eye to their vintage clothes room, sales had increased markedly. Not just where the clothes were concerned, but throughout the shop. It seemed she had been right about attracting new customers, about tempting a broader range of shoppers through the doors. Gerri had, however, noticed Xanthe's distracted mood during the past week. When she had explained that Liam's father was ill and he'd had to go to stay in Salisbury to support his mother for a bit, her friend had accepted the reason for her state of mind. But Xanthe knew she was perceptive. And caring. And that she might just read all sorts of incorrect possibilities into his sudden absence. It had been such a relief not to have to lie to her mother, or Liam, anymore, about where she disappeared to and what it was she did. It seemed, though, that now that she was a Spinner she would always be keeping secrets from someone she cared about. Always be forced to make up stories to people who cared about her. And it never got any easier.

She followed Gerri into the vintage clothes room and together they unpacked the box of clothes. The silk scarves, liberty blouses, leather mini-skirts, and tweed jackets were not old enough to be classed as antiques, but many of them were forty or fifty years old, so properly vintage and retro. Xanthe held up a cotton shirt with a broad collar, the purple and yellow swirling print shouting out sixties loud and clear.

"You're right. There are some lovely pieces here."

Gerri smiled, draping a chiffon square over her head and pulling a face. "Not old enough for you though? I know you prefer things that have been around even longer than these."

"Oh, I don't know. How could I not love this?" she asked, picking out a lime-green kipper tie.

"Here"—Gerri tugged at an ink-blue woolen coat at the bottom of the box—"this is more up your street." She handed the treasure to Xanthe, who stood up to let it unfold properly.

She felt a small tremor run through her as the navy greatcoat revealed its brass buttons on the front, cuffs, and epaulettes. For a moment hope stirred inside her. The military coat could be from the First World War, or even a little earlier. There were cut stitches on the breast of it suggesting medal ribbons had been removed. The coat clearly had history in spades. She closed her eyes, holding it close, breathing in the smell of old wool and mothballs, feeling the rough fabric between her fingers. Her eye as an antiques dealer and her sensitivity as a psychometric were both affected by the coat, but it didn't sing to her. Special as it was, it couldn't help her now. In that moment she let her guard down and Gerri was quick to spot it.

"You know, you can tell me stuff if you want to," she said gently. "I hope by now we're more than just business partners."

"I know, and yes, I'm lucky to have you as a friend. But really, there's nothing . . ."

"Are you and Liam OK?"

"We're fine," she said, a little too brightly.

"Fine? Last time I saw the two of you together you were hiring fancy dress costumes and going away somewhere. 'Fine' sounds like a downgrade."

"He's . . . busy with his parents right now."

"Any improvement in his dad?"

"I don't think so."

Gerri brightened suddenly. "You're pining for him! Aw, that's so sweet. I knew you two would be great together. I mean, you've got the band in common, and you just get along so well. And now it's something a bit more than just friends, right?"

Xanthe found herself blushing. By way of an answer she threw a felt hat at Gerri, allowing her to tease her some more, relieved at least that her friend was now satisfied with an explanation for the chink in her mood. Better that she think her merely lovesick and moping around because she missed Liam than that she imagine all sorts of complicated relationship issues that would no doubt require more half-truths and outright lies. And the truth was, she *was* missing him. Beyond being worried, she missed having him close by, missed his laugh, and the sound of his voice. Missed his strong arms around her.

"OK," she said, shaking off thoughts that were at best unhelpful, "this sort of treasure deserves a new window display, don't you think?"

Flora appeared in the doorway brandishing a letter. "Postman's been."

Xanthe noticed the franking stamp on the envelope. "Your solicitor? Mum, are those the final divorce papers?"

"Looks like I'm a free woman."

"Um . . . congratulations?" Gerri said with an uncertain smile.

Xanthe studied her mother's face for any sign of sadness but found none. The end of her parents' marriage had been shocking and hurtful, but time had passed and Flora had taken to her new life with gusto.

Aware of her daughter's scrutiny, Flora smiled. "A loose end tied up. That's all. Actually, I might even celebrate my new status a little. A drink after bell-ringing practice tonight. Anyone care to join me?"

"Love to, but I won't get a babysitter at such short notice," said Gerri.

"How about you, Xanthe? Stuart would very much like to meet you. So would the rest of the group."

Gerri and Xanthe exchanged glances. This was not the first time Flora had specifically mentioned one bell ringer over the others. "I'd love to meet them too, Mum, especially Stuart, but I'm going to the house out near Devizes, remember? Another time . . ."

"Oh, yes, of course. Another time," she nodded.

She was happy her mother had a social life of her own, and knew she would understand that with Liam so much on her mind she wouldn't have been much company for a fun evening.

After a busy day in the shop, Xanthe sped south in her black cab, relieved to be renewing her efforts to find her way to Liam. She and Flora still had a business to run, but there was something surreal and slightly panic-inducing about continuing normal life while Liam was lost in time somewhere. At least a trip to buy new stock and search for something that would sing to her was covering both aspects of her life in one outing. She had no way of knowing that there would be a special treasure waiting for her, but she believed she was beginning to see a pattern. She felt that just maybe the things she needed to find, the ones that would take her where she needed to go, reached out to her sooner than she had first realized. Could it be that they were calling to her silently in some way, drawing her to them, even *before* she heard them singing? She did not yet understand the idea fully, but it made sense to her. If she hadn't gone to the auction at Great Chalfield she wouldn't have been able to buy the chatelaine. If she hadn't gone to the house clearance in Laybrook she wouldn't have found the chocolate pot. If she hadn't gone to the estate sale at Corsham Hall she wouldn't have heard the wedding dress. If opportunities to find new treasures presented themselves, she wanted to believe it was for a reason.

She found the house easily enough. It was an unremarkable bungalow sitting in the cul-de-sac of a small development, apparently inhabited mostly by retired and elderly people. Xanthe parked outside number fifteen and made her way up the neatly weeded path across the restrained and tidy front garden. She rang the bell and waited. She could hear soft footsteps inside before the door was opened by a short gentleman dressed in smart but casual clothes with thick spectacles and a carefully combed head of purest white hair.

"Miss Westlake? How good of you to come." He shook her hand and then stood back to allow her to step into the little house.

"Please, call me Xanthe. I'm afraid Mum didn't take your name. . . ."

"Oh, William," he said, smiling, "seeing as we are already on first name terms. Please follow me into the sitting room. I have most of the best pieces for you to look at in here."

The interior of the bungalow was as understated and well-ordered as the garden it sat in. A glance as she walked along the short hallway told her that the old man did not surround himself with antiques. In fact, there were hardly any paintings or pieces of china or collectibles to be seen. The room he took her to was equally devoid of antiques, the furniture looking quite modern and nondescript. What was interesting, however, was the carefully laid out assortment of objects on the coffee table in the center of the room. The sight of the interesting pieces awaiting her inspection caused her heart to jump with hope, but what caused her real excitement were the sudden sounds that all but assaulted her. So strong was the buzzing, the high soaring notes of something singing, accompanied by a vibration of the air around her, that her hands went instinctively to cover her ears. If her host noticed her odd reaction, he was too polite to show it.

"I moved house, you see, and I don't really have room to store my collection any longer. This house is more . . . functional. It suits my current needs but, well, as you can see, there are things here that belong somewhere else now."

He stood back, indicating that she was free to examine the collection as she liked.

Xanthe stepped forward, her heart racing, desperate to discover what it was that was calling to her so strongly. There was no guarantee that it would be connected to Mistress Flyte or to Liam, but it was certainly making an instant and powerful impact upon her. The closer she got to the table, the more multilayered and disturbing the singing became. Instead of a clear sound with perhaps some snatches of speech or even a visual flash, there was a muddle of noise. It quickly became obvious that more than one object was singing to her. The first thing that drew her toward it was a writing box, or slope, as it was sometimes called. She lifted the lid and opened it up fully, so that the green leather inside presented a flat surface upon which to write. She decided the smooth wood, which had fine striations giving it an elegant, subtle pattern, was probably mahogany. There was a line of gilding around the edge of the slightly tatty leather. At the bottom of the writing surface there was a narrow compartment for holding pens, and two smaller trays for ink bottles or nibs.

The owner leaned forward. "You can lift the flat pieces," he explained, "to get at the storage space beneath it."

Xanthe did as he suggested. There was plenty of space for paper in the bottom of the box, which was still clean and dry despite its age. She put the writing surface in place again, running her hand over the leather, wondering how many letters had been written upon it. As the box sang to her, the leather growing warm under her palm, she imagined love letters, secret missives, wills, and perhaps bills of sale for a great house, all being penned in flowing copperplate and India ink, signed with a flourish, and no doubt sealed with wax and a family crest.

"It's a lovely piece, isn't it?" William smiled proudly. He did not seem, to Xanthe, to be someone who was simply out to make money. It felt as if he appreciated fine antiques, knew what he was talking about, and enjoyed sharing them with people. She had often found sellers finally deciding to part with a treasured item precisely because they wanted more people to be able to enjoy it. It was like finding an audience for a play or readers for a book: a treasure needed to be appreciated and adored.

She listened with great care, paying attention to anything that might indicate a connection with Liam. There was nothing in particular, and after all, why would there be? To her knowledge he had never owned a writing box, and it wasn't really his style. As she scanned the other objects, holding her hand a little above them, seeking out a vibration, a warmth, or even a jolt of energy, she had to admit to herself that there was nothing that in any way seemed relevant to him. Perhaps it would be Mistress Flyte that called her? After all, she was the one who had forced the situation by taking Liam. It was, in some ways, more her mission, her quest, her calling, that might summon Xanthe. The second thing that cried out to be noticed was an oval brooch. It was unusual. At first she thought it was a cameo, but on looking closer she saw the surface was not stone or shell but glass, and that it housed something that showed through it. When she picked it up it trembled, so that she had to refocus to make out what it was she was looking at. The moment she knew it was a lock of hair she experienced a shiver down the length of her spine.

The old man chuckled, noticing her reaction. "Not to everyone's taste, a mourning brooch. There is some sadness, of course, but also respect and remembrance. We can't know who died, but it's likely to have been a young child."

She held the brooch up to the light and found a hallmark on the gold. It was an expensive piece of jewelry, fashioned with skill, custom-made for a grieving parent or grandparent. The edges of the gold setting were worn smooth, having lost their pattern over the years and suggesting the piece had been treasured by its owner for a long time. Mourning jewelry—rings and lockets as well as brooches—had reached the height of its popularity in the Victorian era, but had been around for many centuries before that. It was a hard piece to date.

"It is beautiful," she murmured at last. Then, knowing the weight of gold alone would make it quite valuable, her business sense kicked in and she added, "Not easily saleable, though. Some people find mourning jewelry a bit creepy." Even as she tried to imagine what her mother would say and how she would negotiate a good price on the piece, Xanthe knew that, like the writing slope, she would have to have it, whatever the cost. It spoke to her so strongly she was reluctant to let it go, but knew that she must at least pretend to be interested in the other items that were being offered to her. And besides, Flora would not be impressed if she only came home with objects that sang to her and no new stock for the shop. And there were some lovely things. Two silver candlesticks, probably Georgian, which were in good condition, and were always quick sellers. There was a Minton soup tureen with an attractive green-leaf pattern on it; a powder-blue Wedgwood plate; three silver bracelets, probably Indian; two tall glass vases; a rather gaudy piece of majolica ware; and a proud pair of china poodles.

"These are sweet," she said, picking up one of the little dogs, trying to remain calm, detached, and businesslike while all the time she was being bombarded by the wild notes and chiming from the found things. "Staffordshire, aren't they?" she asked, blinking away a headache that was taking up residence behind her eyes.

"Yes," he confirmed. "Rather fine examples, and no chips or crackling on the glaze."

She reluctantly put the brooch back down on the table so that she could take a closer look at the poodles. The noise was a real distraction, so she stepped a little farther away, moving along the length of the table. She was astonished to find that instead of growing fainter, the clamor increased. It was only then she realized that there was a third treasure singing to her. It was a lot to take in, but the more she considered the idea, the more certain she became. She studied the remaining pieces in front of her, quickly setting down the china dogs. There was a pile of sheet music, a brass door knocker and, hardly visible beneath a fringed Spanish shawl, there was a hatpin. It was a beautiful example, silver, with a blue stone worked into one end, set into curls of filigree. She had to resist a little cry of delight at how lovely it was. When she held it, the sound it made to her was also sweet and pretty, unlike the more discordant and urgent noises of the writing slope and the mourning brooch. However different the sound was, it was singing nonetheless, loud and clear and demanding her attention. Three found things! She had never had this happen before.

"The stone is lapis lazuli," the owner told her, peering over her shoulder. "Early Victorian, I believe. And quite collectible."

He was right about that. Xanthe recalled many eager bidders at her father's auction house fighting over just such a pin to add to their own private hoard. At least it would be a very saleable item, eventually. Once she had learned its story and answered its call. She felt her whole being tune in to the sounds the treasures were making now, so that it was no longer the cacophony she had experienced when first she'd entered the room. Now it was a harmonious symphony. And then she saw it clear, a flash, like a freeze-frame from a movie of her recent past—a vision of Liam's face. He looked confused, startled maybe. It was as if she was being shown a tantalizing glimpse of him at the moment they were separated. However unlikely it was that any of her new treasures had ever belonged to him, there was a connection at the very least to what had happened to him. For a moment she questioned the coincidence of the events. Why had the old man chosen this moment to contact the shop and sell some of his collection? If he had not done so, would she have been unable to go back to the right point in time? It seemed that as quickly as she came close to answers, what was required of her threw up further questions. Whatever the truth that remained to be revealed, the fleeting vision of Liam was sufficient to convince her that she was on the right path.

She turned and smiled at the seller, determined to be professional and fair but also do her best to strike a good bargain for the pieces she wanted.

"I'm interested in the hatpin, the slope, the brooch, the Georgian candlesticks, the poodles, and the tureen. What's your very best price?"

William's eyes widened and his pale face lit up with genuine delight. "You have a very good eye, Miss Westlake! Such fine pieces. Let me see . . . I have to remember what I paid for them, of course . . . a piece of paper would help, so that I could write it all down. Where did I put my notepad?" He began to search the room, opening drawers in the occasional table beside his winged chair. Xanthe felt a stab of remorse that she had been quite so hasty. It was entirely possible the old man spent many hours or days alone. He might have been looking forward to this encounter with a fellow antiques enthusiast for a long time and here she was rushing to offer him money within minutes of entering his house.

"Actually," she said brightly, "I'd love a cup of tea."

William stopped searching for the notebook and turned to look at her again.

"You would?"

"Treasure hunts always make me thirsty. I expect you find the same. So if it's not too much trouble . . . then we could look at each piece together, and agree on prices. Would that be OK?"

He nodded slowly, a smile growing as he did so. "I think that a splendid idea," he replied. "Now, you browse through the pieces again, while I go and put the kettle on. Would Darjeeling suit you? And I opened a packet of shortbread biscuits yesterday . . . yes, a splendid idea," he repeated as he went through the door to the kitchen.

Xanthe took the hatpin over to the window, the better to examine it in the light. It certainly was a lovely one, quite large, designed to secure a fairly sizeable hat onto a good head of hair. The lapis was a rich, dark blue shot through with threads of gold. The actual pin was sharp too, and it crossed her mind it would have made an effective weapon of self-defense for a lady who found herself in a tight spot. The sweet notes coming from it made her own heart sing. She hurried back to the table and moved things around so that the items she wanted were grouped together. The writing slope seemed to be making the most noise, its notes stranger, stronger, and more insistent.

"Are you the one?" she asked it softly. "Can you help me find Liam?" She waited, but no more clues came to her. She returned her attention to the mourning brooch. When she picked it up it felt unnaturally heavy, as if weighed down by the grief of its original owner. Although her first guess at its age had been nineteenth century, now she was not so certain. The setting looked wrong somehow. Earlier. And the color of the gold was soft and rich. She would need to do some research to find out as much as she could. The thought occurred to her that she ought not to take all three pieces into the blind house at the same time. She could, after all, only travel to one place at a time. To one *time* at a time. How would she know which piece would take her to Liam, though? If she chose the wrong one she might head off on a quest completely unrelated to finding him. However important that might be, the thought of him spending even more time lost and going through who knew what because of something she did tormented her. She would have to be certain, before she ever set foot in that humble little building at the end of her garden, that she was taking the right found thing into it. While she might be capable of quickly returning to her own time if she found herself somewhere other than where he was, there was more to consider than the mechanics of time travel. What if she landed somewhere dangerous, in a set of circumstances that prevented her immediate return? Or what if she was in fact answering the call of someone desperately in need of her help? Could she turn her back on, say, a child in peril, a child who had no one else to help, and simply abandon them? She knew she could not. With a jolt of longing for him, she knew Liam would not want her to. No, she had to be more than careful, she had to be as certain as possible that she was choosing the right treasure with which to spin.

"Here we are!" The old man returned bearing a tea tray in shaky hands.

She helped him set it down on a free table and there followed the timeless ritual of tea pouring. She noticed he had a good quality set of china but nothing fancy or expensive or even antique. The cups were plain white with a narrow gold band at the rim. From habit, she turned the saucer over to read the maker's name underneath.

Her host gave a hoarse chuckle. "The set is from Germany. Thomas. Not so well known as it should be, in my opinion."

She frowned. "That's a modern company, isn't it?"

He poured milk into the cups. "The antiques and collectibles of tomorrow," he said simply.

His comment made her think about how all the things she and her mother loved and revered had once been the height of modernity, the current, the everyday. How could the people who made them, commissioned them, bought them, and used them, ever have imagined that centuries later their workaday pieces would be treasures?

"I was wondering," she asked as she accepted a piece of shortbread, "how you come to have these wonderful things. I mean, you don't choose to display them in your house, but you have kept them very carefully. Did you inherit the antiques, perhaps?"

He shook his head. "I used to be in the trade, though I have always disliked that expression. When I retired a while ago I sold my business and most of the stock with it. Aside from a few treasured items. I have an . . . attachment to some of the things you see here. Which is why I have held on to them for so long, I suppose. Some pieces are harder to part with than others, don't you find?"

"That's very true. Well, I promise you, they will be looked after, cleaned, and restored by my mum, who's a stickler for getting things in the best shape, and then properly displayed in our shop. Our customers are enthusiasts, for the most part. They only buy something if they love it, so the treasures will all find good homes. In the end." She sipped her tea, aware he had noticed her somewhat odd remark.

He studied her face as he spoke. "Are there, perhaps, some things here that you would wish to keep for yourself?" When she hesitated he went on, "I would often find that myself; that some object, often one of the unexpected, less valuable ones, would simply shout out to me to be taken home. And then I would find I was reluctant to sell it on. At least for a while, until I understood it better."

Xanthe met his gaze. His glasses were thick, making his gentle eyes large and owl-like. She sensed, just for a moment, that he had picked up on something unusual in what she was doing, or in the way she had reacted to some of the collectibles. It was surely just coincidence that he spoke of the things "shouting" to him. It was, after all, a common enough expression, particularly when a person was justifying an expensive purchase or impulse buy of some sort. The idea that he had to keep something until he understood it was harder to explain to herself, however. She experienced a moment of disquiet and was certain then that the old man was not telling her everything about himself or his collection. He was deliberately holding something back. She tried to shake away the feeling, telling herself once a dealer, always a dealer. He was, in all probability, talking up the pieces so he could get a better price for them, that was all. He certainly knew a great deal about the things he had kept and delighted in telling her about them. He was so enthusiastic and persuasive that she soon found she had added another six items to her pile and was beginning to think he was a pretty sharp salesman after all. They turned to the thorny matter of price, discussing each item, considering how much she was willing to pay against how much he felt it was worth. As he must have anticipated, she put forward the argument that the purchase price had to allow her to make a profit. There were costly overheads involved in running a shop, and that had to be taken into consideration with everything they committed to for stock. They both knew he might do better at a good auction, but he did not seem interested in that idea. At last they agreed on prices for most things, rounding down the figure as if she were buying a job lot rather than just a couple of pieces. She picked up the mourning brooch last of all.

"This is very special," she said carefully, "but I'm afraid it might be outside my budget." She was doing her utmost not to show how important it was to her. She knew she would pay just about any price, but she couldn't let him see that. She waited, continuing to inspect the brooch, hoping he would be so pleased with what they had already agreed on that he might let it go for a low price.

Slowly, he reached over and closed her hand around the brooch.

"There's no charge for that one," he told her.

"Oh but . . ."

He put his finger to his lips to silence her. "I want you to have it, and that's that." He held out his hand. "A bit of luck to seal the deal."

She was about to protest, but his expression showed he would not be talked out of it. Xanthe felt a surge of affection for the old man, not simply because of the kind gesture, but because he seemed to understand her so well. And it mattered to him that she have the piece that was important to her. The practice of the seller giving back some of the agreed cash "for luck" was an ancient one, but this was a generous amount of good fortune indeed.

She took his hand and shook it. "A pleasure doing business with you," she said, and meant it sincerely.

They packed up the purchases, with William taking his time to wrap them individually in old copies of the Wiltshire *Gazette and Herald*. It was as if he were saying farewell to every piece, and as if parting with them was significant in ways Xanthe could not quite make sense of. She paid him in cash, wondering what the old man would choose to spend it on. His lifestyle looked modest, and he did not appear to her to be someone who went in for extravagances. Perhaps it would be a nest egg sitting ready to top up his pension in the coming years.

Outside was sunny, the air warm as they loaded the treasures into her taxi. Resting her receipt book on the bonnet, she took out her pen and itemized the sale. "What name shall I put on this?" she asked him as she wrote.

"Oh, a bill of sale won't be necessary. . . ."

"It's no trouble. I've got to process it all on our end, so it makes everything tally up."

"Morris," he said. "William J. Morris."

Xanthe filled in the final details, tore off the top copy, and handed it to him.

"Thank you," she said again. "For such lovely pieces, but especially for the brooch. That was very generous of you. It is . . . special."

He batted away the thanks, slightly embarrassed. "It has found the right home. That's what matters."

As she drove away, waving from the window, she thought how small and how alone the old man looked and promised herself she would call him up one day soon in the not too distant future, just for a chat. She turned out of the little housing development and headed back toward Marlborough, serenaded by the music of her singing treasures.

3

WHEN XANTHE ARRIVED HOME IT WAS TO FIND THE HOUSE EMPTY SAVE FOR PIE. WHILE the dog was pleased to see her and greeted her effusively, she was no substitute for Flora. Xanthe badly needed to share her wonderful finds with her mother, as she did after any treasure hunt, but more than that, she needed to talk about the three things that were special to her. It was only seven thirty. With a sinking heart she realized her mother would be out celebrating with her friends after bell-ringing practice and might not be home for some time. Breaking her own rule about avoiding discussing Spinner business over the phone, she called Harley.

"Can you talk?" she asked.

"Give us a minute, hen," he said.

She could hear the lively chatter of the pub in the background grow fainter as he found a quieter spot.

"OK, I'm in the backyard. Annie's busy serving in the bar. Have you heard from Liam?"

"Not quite. I've found something that might take me to him, though."

"You have? That's bloody fantastic! What is it?"

"I'm not entirely certain."

"You mean . . . you've found something that's singing to you, but you don't know what it is? Correct me if I'm wrong, lassie, but are you not the expert in all things antique?"

"Harley . . . I've found three things. Three things that are singing to me, each one as strong as the other!"

There was a brief, stunned pause, followed by a low whistle, before Harley said quickly, "You're not thinking of going in that wee building of yours with all three, now, are you?"

"No. That's the problem. I don't know which of them to use. I did have the briefest vision of Liam. . . ."

"Could you see where he was?"

"No, I just saw his face for a fraction of a second. And I couldn't be certain which object sparked the vision. This has never happened before. And I haven't come across anything like this in the *Spinners* book. . . . Maybe I should just take them out and stand close to the blind house, see if I get any more flashes of anything."

"I'm coming over. Promise me you'll not set foot in the garden before I get there?"

"OK. I promise." She clicked off the phone and looked at the three objects now sitting unwrapped on the old desk in the shop. Pie sniffed them, decided they were of no interest, and jumped up onto the cushion of the captain's chair for a nap.

Harley arrived at the shop door ten minutes later, a little breathless and clutching a net of limes. "I told Annie we were running short and I'd pop out to the supermarket and get some," he explained, holding them up and following her inside. He spied the collection of finds on the desk. "Ah, so these are the magical objects, then?"

"The old man had some quality stock, so Mum will be pleased about that, but these three things are the ones that are singing to me."

"All three of them?"

"Loud and clear."

He studied the little group. "D'you perhaps notice a difference in the sounds? Any one of them louder . . . I don't know what I'm asking here, hen, to be honest."

"Well, yes, as a matter of fact, the hatpin has quite a sweet song, and feels less demanding than the other two. Does that make sense?"

"Who the hell am I to tell you? But it's something to go on, isn't it? I mean to say, if Liam was calling you, I'd reckon he'd be pretty bold about it, don't you think?"

She nodded. "Liam or Mistress Flyte."

"What's that?"

"I've thought about it . . . she's the one leading this dance. It's because of her Liam is . . . wherever he is. Maybe something connected to her will call me."

"Hell's teeth, lassie, you might be onto something there."

"In which case, given the drastic measures she's gone to, a sweet song wouldn't be a good fit. OK, so maybe we can set the hatpin to one side. That still leaves the writing slope and the mourning brooch, and they are both vibrating, buzzing, singing, and generally demanding my attention pretty damn strongly."

"What about the dates? Do you know when they originate from?"

"The writing box is almost definitely mid-1800s. Everything about it, from construction, size, shape, to what it's made of, and the style of the thing . . . all solidly Victorian."

"And the wee pin?"

"Harder to pin down."

"Hen, I'm on a run for limes; we don't have time for jokes here."

"Sorry, I'm just excited," she said, grinning.

"You've been fretting about Liam, this is a major breakthrough; it's understandable," he said.

"Mourning jewelry was very popular in the nineteenth century," she said, "but was around for centuries before that, of course." She picked up the brooch, turning it over in her hands, examining it closely again. She took a magnifying loupe from the desk and put it to her eye.

"The maker's mark is too worn to read . . . it could be Victorian, but I'm not sure."

"So, it might be the same date as the writing box?"

"It's possible."

"So, both these pieces might take you back to the same time?"

She shook her head. "I'm just not certain enough to take that risk. . . ." They stood in silence for a moment before she made a decision. "The only way I'm going to find out is to take them to the blind house."

"What if you start to travel and . . . I don't know . . . you get pulled in two different directions?" He made a theatrical but highly descriptive gesture with his hands.

"OK, I won't take them both in. One at a time," she said, tucking the slope under her arm, holding the brooch in her hand, and heading for the back door. Harley hurried along behind her. As they went into the garden Xanthe firmly shut the door before Pie had a chance to join them, not wishing to inadvertently take the dog with her a second time. It was a pleasant spring evening. As dusk fell, a wood pigeon cooed softly from somewhere among the branches of the silver birch tree next door. The nearer she got to the little stone building, the louder the treasures sang, so that soon, for Xanthe, the pigeon was just a background accompaniment. She carefully set both pieces down near the old wooden door, which stood ajar as always, inviting her to enter.

"So, what's the plan, exactly?" Harley wanted to know.

"I'll try the writing slope first. Take it inside. Listen. Wait. See what happens."

"Not impressively scientific, if you don't mind my saying so."

Xanthe shrugged. "It's worked for me so far."

"But, wait, how long will you be gone? If you go . . . and what do I do if you don't come back?"

She stepped over to her friend and gave him a hug. "It's OK. I understand it's a bit scary for you. I know how to do this bit. I'll be safe."

He shuffled from one foot to the other, embarrassed to be thought flimsy. "Hearing about it is one thing, and I've seen you come home before, but watching you disappear, and we don't know where or when you're going to . . ."

She stepped back, her face serious now. "I'm a Spinner, Harley. It's what I do."

He nodded, clearly torn between wanting to protect her and wanting to be a part of the whole adventure without holding her back.

She knelt down beside the smooth wooden box, which was gleaming beneath the soft light of the fading day. Taking a deep breath, she placed her hands upon it, about to pick it up, when a snap of light, bright as a thunderbolt, blotted out the garden, just for a fraction of a second. As her eyes adjusted she saw an attic room, bare and dusty, and on the floor a cravat, brightly colored and spotted. And then it was gone. The glimpse of a vision vanished as quickly as it had arrived. She blinked, refocusing on Harley. Relief and elation flooded through her. There was no mistaking the cheap, flashy neckwear: it was the one Liam had hired from the costume shop in Devizes. It was the one he had been wearing when they started their journey home.

"What is it, hen? Something wrong?"

"You didn't see that? No, of course you didn't." She stood up slowly, still a little disorientated by the intensity of the light that the box had shown her. "You can relax. I don't need to go inside the blind house."

"You don't? No time traveling?"

"Not today. The writing slope showed me something. Something of Liam's. This is it, Harley. This is the thing that will take me back to him."

When at last she had convinced her friend that she was not about to change her mind and travel back then and there, Harley picked up the limes and returned to the pub. Xanthe took the found things, retrieved Pie from the shop, and went upstairs. She made herself a sandwich and nibbled at it while she examined the slope again, her stomach knotting in excitement. She knew she should eat if she was going to travel. She needed to be rested and ready. In the sharp light of the kitchen the imperfections of the writing box were more noticeable, but it was still a beautiful piece. It had acquired a few knocks and nicks over the years, but the key still turned in the lock, the hinges still worked smoothly, and even though the leather was tatty, it was in place and not beyond being restored. She felt a new attachment to the thing, now that she knew it would send her where she needed to go. Could it be that the box had once belonged to Lydia Flyte? Or that she had it with her in the time and place where she was now? Where they now were? Was that enough? It somehow didn't seem sufficiently personal for such a powerful connection.

An hour later Flora returned and found Xanthe still in the kitchen.

"Oh, a successful trip then?" she asked, looking at the treasures.

"Mum, you don't know the half of it."

She sat her mother down and fetched cold white wine from the fridge, pouring generous glasses. Over the next half hour she filled Flora in on her trip to the old man's bungalow, the lovely things she had bought for the shop, and, with mounting excitement, the three found things. She told her about having called Harley over, and how she now knew which piece she was going to use to travel.

"When will you go?" was her mother's first question.

If her mother was worried, she would never let it show. Nor would she want Xanthe to be concerned about leaving her alone. Increasingly, Xanthe realized, she was able to leave her to manage both her disability and the shop on her own without fretting. Flora was a determined woman who had embraced her new single status and independent life with gusto. Looking at her now, Xanthe also detected a new glow. A slight sparkle that had not been there before. It warmed her heart to think that her mother was at last making new friends, and perhaps even contemplating dating again.

"I need to put an outfit together and pack a bag."

"You must be getting quite good at both those things by now."

"Every time there is something I wish I'd thought to take. At least the clothes shouldn't be too difficult. My own vintage stuff has quite a lot of flouncy skirts and pinafores I can adapt. And I'll need to go through our collection of coins again, maybe some silver jewelry I can trade in when I get there."

"What you saw, you said it was something like an attic room. I don't suppose there were any clues about where it might be?"

"Nothing. It was just a fragment of a vision, really. But it was enough. I know I will find him. And this time, I'll bring him home."

Flora reached across the table and squeezed her hand. "I know you will. Have you had any more thoughts about why he was taken there? Might help you figure out what to expect. I mean, the old woman must have had her reasons."

"It's baffling. Everything I know about her past points to conflict among the Spinners and a broken love affair, but why she would want Liam for any of that . . . it doesn't make any sense."

"Yet."

"Yet," she agreed, nodding.

"Right." Flora got to her feet, picking up her crutches and striding purposefully toward the door. "We'd better get you packed then," she called back over her shoulder.

Again, Xanthe was grateful for her mother's help. Sharing the preparations for time travel with her was so much more enjoyable and reassuring than doing it all on her own. She raided the vintage clothing room for extra garments while Flora sifted through the box of old coins they kept in the glass cabinet in the shop. They had to be dated before the exact date of travel, or they would not make the journey, but if they were too early they would not be legal tender and thus be useless. As Xanthe did not know the precise date she would arrive, they could do no more than fill a purse with as many coins as might possibly work.

To guard against ending up penniless, she would also take three silver chains, a pair of silver sugar tongs, and a silver serving spoon. All could be easily turned into money at the nearest silversmith with no awkward questions asked. Back up in her bedroom, she pulled her trusty leather satchel out from under her bed. It served very well as a timeless piece of luggage, and it was fast becoming an essential part of her travel kit. Into it she put painkillers, plastic sutures, a bottle of strong antibiotics, a Swiss army penknife, matches, a tiny flashlight, two pencils, and a small notepad. She added moisturizer and a handkerchief, a packet of mints, a toothbrush, a comb, lip salve, a bar of chocolate, and the bag of barley sugars she had been saving for a hike. The bag felt heavy already, but there was room for the *Spinners* book, carefully wrapped in a long T-shirt that would serve as a nightie.

By the time everything was ready it was properly dark and a light drizzle had settled in, reminding her that she had no way of knowing what time of year she would arrive in. She fetched her khaki army greatcoat from her wardrobe and shrugged it on over the Laura Ashley dress she had found to wear. On impulse, she pinned on her gold and pearl horseshoe brooch, pausing to fondly remember the moment Liam had given it to her. This time she was going in her precious Doc Martens, as they would pass as working boots even for a woman, and for the most part would be hidden by the long skirts of her dress and the flounced petticoat she had found to go beneath it. She twisted her long blond curls up into a tight bun, securing it with lots of pins. As always, the issue of a hat was a challenge. To go bareheaded was to mark her out as somehow chaotic or possibly a person of no means or family, but anything she tried to fashion into a passable Victorian bonnet looked laughably bad. She decided she would buy something inexpensive when she got there. She had already become accustomed to repeating the tale that her luggage had been lost in transit somewhere to explain her limited wardrobe.

She texted Harley with a short message simply saying she was leaving for a trip tonight. If anyone were to read the text over his shoulder it would not sound crazy. He had messaged back straightaway, saying he would come around again and not to leave before he turned up. When he arrived, Flora let him in, and the three of them gathered in the garden. Flora had pulled on an anorak, but Harley had come straight from serving behind the bar. His tattooed arms, bare beyond his T-shirt sleeves, began to color up under the light fall of rain, droplets of which glistened in his beard and bushy eyebrows.

"Are you sure you have everything you need, lassie?" he asked. "*Spinners* book? Knife? Did you pack a knife this time? And what about money? Flora, did you manage to find the girl some decent silver?"

Flora rolled her eyes at him. "Harley, I'm her mother. If anyone's allowed to fuss like an old chicken it's me. And I'm not, so please calm down. Xanthe knows what she's doing."

"Aye, fair enough."

Xanthe pulled the gold locket from under her collar. "And my ticket home, see? I've double-checked my list, Harley. I'm as prepared as I can be."

There was a moment's quiet as the trio stood on the verge of separating, none of them quite knowing how best to do so without getting emotional. At last, Xanthe spoke up.

"Well, I'll be off then."

She slung her satchel over her shoulder and picked up the slope. When she reached the door of the blind house her mother called out to her.

"Love, hold on! I've thought of something."

"What is it?"

"Writing slopes, they nearly always had a secret compartment. Have you checked?"

"No, I haven't." She set the box down on the wet grass. The others hurried over to help her search it. She checked all the compartments carefully, pulling and pushing at parts of the box wall gently to see if anything would give.

Harley tapped the sides.

"Here," he said. "It sounds different here. Like there's another hollow place inside."

"But how do you get to it?" Flora asked.

Xanthe paused in her frantic examination of the piece and instead listened carefully to it. "What are you hiding?" she asked it gently. "What secrets have you got to show me?" Then, as if a distant memory was stirred, she thought to take hold of one of the slim dividing sections between the compartments for nibs and stamps. Instead of pushing or tapping the thing she grasped the top of it between finger and thumb and gave it a sharp upward tug. It instantly released a tiny spring so that a piece of the lining sprang open to reveal an extra compartment.

"You did it!" Flora leaned in for a better look.

"Anything in here, hen?"

There was an expectant pause while Xanthe shone her torch into the little space.

"Empty," she declared at last. Seeing how deflated everyone was she added, "but it's a good thing I checked. Could have missed a vital clue, and now I know there's nothing I'm missing. So, well done, Mum." She got to her feet again, having reassembled and shut the box. "Look, lovely as it is to have you both here, I can't cope with these fond farewells, so you two go back into the house, I'm going into the old jail, OK?"

Flora gave her a quick peck on the cheek and whispered, "I'll be waiting, love, and I'll look after the blind house and your other treasures for you," before turning on her sticks and walking briskly back across the scruffy lawn.

Harley put a huge hand briefly on her shoulder. "You know how much I wish I could go with you," he said. "You tell young Liam from me he's a lucky beggar and to get his arse back here this time or he'll have me to answer to."

She smiled, waiting for him to follow Flora into the house, then she straightened her shoulders, clutched the writing box tightly, and stepped through the low door and into the ancient stone building.

—

After a moment's hesitation, Liam followed Mistress Flyte. He needed to find out more. And besides, he needed to eat. Whatever challenges lay ahead he would be better prepared for them fed and watered. The sitting room was as unimpressive as the rest of the house, but it was adequately furnished with two small sofas, a table and chairs, a black range in the fireplace, candlesticks on the mantelpiece, and a slightly more youthful rug than the one in the hall. Mistress Flyte sat at the table and poured tea.

"Will you take milk?" she asked, setting a cup down in the place opposite.

He took the empty chair, waiting for her to add milk to his tea. Now that he looked at the cold meat, fresh loaves, and truckle of cheese set out upon the lace cloth he realized how fiercely hungry he was.

"Please, help yourself," said the old woman.

He needed no further invitation but loaded his plate, using the wafer-thin but razor-sharp carving knife to slice ham before cutting off a thick chunk of bread. The cheese was salty and strong, and went very well with the pickled eggs and onions.

"So," he said, after a few minutes devoted to the serious business of eating, "why don't you just tell me why I'm here? Xanthe's the one who works out mysteries; I just like to call a spade a spade. Keep things straightforward."

"An admirable way to live your life, no doubt. Alas, my own existence is perhaps more complex and peripatetic than that of a footloose young man. There are elements I am compelled to hold close. There are matters I am not at liberty to discuss freely."

"You are really very good at avoiding answering questions. Ever thought of becoming a politician?" he asked as he spread more thick yellow butter onto bread.

Mistress Flyte chose her words with care. "It is essential that Xanthe be persuaded to come here, to this place and this time."

"Spinners' business?"

"Indeed, Spinners' business."

"And you didn't think to just ask her? I mean, she's pretty committed to what she is. I'd have thought she'd proved that already."

"She has."

"Then why not just tell her you need her help and ask her to come here?"

"She might have refused. I had to be certain. Having you here, I believe, gives me that certainty."

"OK, so say she comes. She gets whatever it is she needs to find her way here to you, to me. What then? You are not going to be her favorite person. She might decide, after you've tricked her, that she doesn't want to help you."

"I wish Miss Westlake no harm, I assure you of that. I have her welfare uppermost in my mind. However, dangerous times call for desperate measures. I have done only what I consider reasonable and necessary in the circumstances in which I find myself. She is loyal and brave. She will come looking for you. And then, when she is here, she will see the . . . situation for herself. She will make her own judgment. I trust it will be the right one."

Liam sat back in his chair, frowning at his host. "Mistress Flyte, I don't think you are in any position to talk about trust," he said levelly. It was clear to him she was not going to give away any more information than she absolutely had to in order to keep him cooperative. He would, he reasoned, have more freedom and be better placed to help

Xanthe, if he at least appeared to go along with what the old woman wanted. However much his captor insisted she cared for Xanthe's safety, he was wary of her. Someone who would consider it reasonable to kidnap a person in order to gain the help of another was someone capable of extreme measures. Someone, in his opinion, who needed close watching.

THE OVERRIDING FEELING XANTHE HAD AS SHE TRAVELED BACK THROUGH TIME WAS ONE of excitement. Gone was the fear and anxiety of her earlier journeys. While she was worried about Liam, she did not believe Mistress Flyte would do him real harm. It had already occurred to her that he might be bait, luring her to a time and place that suited the old woman. Beyond that she could only guess, and she had learned that guessing was a waste of time. Lydia Flyte's past was as obscure as it was long. She would go where she was led, find the strange Spinner, find Liam, and find her answers then and there.

She emerged onto the worn cobbles of a narrow alley. It was evening. The alleyway was dark and empty but where it met a wider street she could see the lamplighter setting a spill to one of the lamps. She took a moment to steady herself, waiting, listening, looking carefully at where she had arrived. The found things always took her to a place of significance, if not on the exact spot where she emerged, at least close by. Something should be visible or easily discoverable. The passageway offered very little. Indeed, it was so dark she might have missed anything there. It was too risky to start using her torch or even striking a match. As important as gathering information was, remaining as unseen as possible was also crucial, at least until she knew more about her environment. Aside from the gloom, the most noticeable thing about where she stood was the smell. It was evident the alley provided a handy facility for those in need of a toilet. The stink of urine was strong enough to make her eyes water and make her especially glad of her robust boots. Lifting her skirts clear of the filth, she walked toward the light. She was on the point of stepping out onto the street when a large man blocked her exit.

"Hello, my beauty," he slurred, the alcohol carried on his breath for an instant blocking out the earlier stink. He moved unsteadily toward her. "You're new here, ain't ya? I'd never forget such a pretty face, or that golden hair. How much to make a fella happy on this damp evening, then?"

Quelling her indignation at being taken for a prostitute—so much for deciding against a bonnet—Xanthe kept her voice calm and level. She sensed that any sign of fear might trigger further unwanted behavior from the drunkard.

"I'm too rich for your blood, sir. Find another," she told him.

"What? D'you think me a pauper?"

"I think you might have spent tonight's money on gin. Go home. Come and find me when you've more money in your pocket." She gave him what she hoped was a bold but firm smile and went to step past him. The man barred her way.

"No need for such a hurry," he cooed. "Why not stay awhile. Might be I could persuade you to drop your fees, just this once. Next time I'll reward you better, that's a promise."

"Promises don't pay the rent," she said. She placed both hands firmly against his chest, feeling the grime of his coat under her palms as she shoved hard. This had the effect of putting him even more off balance, so that she was able to push past as he stumbled against the rough brick of the wall. She heard him curse as she slipped out into the main street, but he was more in control of his actions than she had given him credit for. She felt his calloused hand grasp her wrist. She cried out as he yanked her back into the shadows.

"Not so fast, missy. Who are you to think yourself better than the next? Better than me? A whore's a whore, no matter the price she puts on herself. And you look too skinny to afford pride, woman. Stand still now!"

He turned, spinning her around so that he could trap her against the wall. With her satchel over her greatcoat, she was less nimble than she would ordinarily have been. She briefly noticed that she was more angry than scared. She had important work to do, and this drunken lout was not going to stop her doing it.

"Let go of me, you stinking oaf!" she yelled at him as loudly as she could, hoping she might startle some sense into him or possibly make him wary of being discovered by passersby. When he paused in pulling at her clothes she thought she had succeeded, but she was wrong. With another surprising show of speed, her assailant drew back his hand and slapped her face hard. She gasped, as much from shock as pain.

"I told you to hold still. Now hold your tongue also!"

She turned her head away as he attempted to kiss her, aware that he was succeeding in fighting his way through her many layers of clothing. Now fear began to take hold. This could not be happening. She would not let this happen. She thought about trying to use her golden locket to travel back to her own time. What better escape than to vanish? The man might never drink again! But he had her arms pinned, one being held at the wrist, the other wedged between his own bulky form and the wall. However much she squirmed, she could not free herself enough to raise a hand to her throat. All she could manage was a scream of rage and desperation as the man used his body weight to pivot and throw her to the ground. He loomed above her as she lay winded by the force with which she hit the cobbles.

The next moment everything changed. There was a shout from the street. The light from the lamp was partially blocked, throwing another shadow into the half-light of the alleyway. While her assailant hesitated, Xanthe seized the moment and scrambled to her feet. The newcomer was nowhere near as heavy and powerful as the man who had, until that moment, been attacking her, but he was clearly younger, and possessed of an obvious bravery. He cursed the man for a blaggard and a swine, sidestepping quickly to avoid the lumbering blow thrown his way.

"Leave her be!" he shouted.

"Find your own wench, can't you? There's plenty more. This one's taken my fancy and I mean to have her. What's it to you?"

"Step away while you still can." The younger man stood his ground.

"Threaten me, would you? Young—"

He did not finish the insult. The second man caught him off guard, kicking his ankle from under him, tipping him forward, sending him toppling with a swift blow to the back of the neck. The older man yelled more abuse as he crashed to the ground, but now his drunkenness slowed his heavy limbs and made his movements ever more awkward and clumsy. He flailed about, trying to right himself, all the while uttering oaths and curses. The young man stepped over him and offered Xanthe his hand.

"Come, miss. Let me assist you."

She allowed him to help her past her attacker, to lead her out into the street and quickly away from the would-be rapist. Once in the light her rescuer looked at her more closely.

"You are hurt! I must summon a constable. He should be held to account. . . ."

"No, please. Don't concern yourself." She was keen to avoid having to answer questions; the last thing she needed was to involve the police. "There is nothing to be gained by it," she went on. "I thank you for your timely assistance and bid you good night, sir." She began to walk away but he stepped after her.

"I cannot let you go in such a state," he said, taking a handkerchief from his pocket and handing it to her. "You are bleeding. He struck you, I think."

She pressed the cotton square to her nose and it came away crimson.

"Please, allow me to take you to my home. My mother is a physician and will treat your injuries. I assure you, you will be safe. And it is but a few paces, see?" he asked, pointing up the street.

She was about to protest further but then she saw which building he had singled out. At the top of the hill, on the left-hand side of the broad road, there stood a tall building set into a terrace of many. It was neither remarkable nor grand, and had a modest shopfront to it, which included a wide window and glazed door. It was the words inscribed over that door, and the name in particular, that made Xanthe smile. In smart but businesslike lettering the sign declared the premises to be those of ERASMUS BALMORAL ESQUIRE, BOOKBINDER.

"Yes!" she said to herself rather than her new acquaintance, the barely suppressed whoop of joy in the single word clearly surprising him. She was scarcely aware of how strange her reaction to the sight of the shop might seem to him, so delighted was she to realize that the found thing had brought her within sight of such an important person in Lydia Flyte's past. She recalled the story the *Spinners* book had revealed to her, of how the old woman, when young and beautiful, had a lover who was also a Spinner. A charismatic and good-looking man who had loved her and yet left her, all because of some conflict within the group of Spinners to which they both then belonged. She recalled how when she had succeeded in traveling time-within-time, stepping back further from her mission briefly, she had seen them, in the garden of the great house, parting for the last time, their hearts breaking. Here was, surely, a man who would lead her to Lydia. Who would lead her to Liam.

The CLOSED notice was displayed through the shop window, and the young man used his key to open the door. It was a lovely space, with a high wooden counter running along one side, raised up slightly to give it an almost stagelike appearance. The shelves behind it displayed beautifully bound books in many sizes, all samples of the bookbinder's work. Some were laid open to reveal creamy pages awaiting notes or journal entries or accounts. Others were set up to show the loveliness of their leather covers, gold-tooled lettering, and finely crafted binding. The room smelled of beeswax polish and leather, transporting Xanthe back to both her own current home and that of her childhood. She watched the young man as he relocked the door not only with a heavy key but with sturdy bolts. He was not tall but had a strength about him, closely cropped brown hair beneath his cap, and a pleasant if guarded expression.

"My father will be in his workshop," he explained. "Mother!" He strode over to a door in the corner of the room and opened it to call up the stairs. "Mother, come quick. You are needed!" Turning back to Xanthe, he indicated a second doorway. "Please, follow me to the kitchen where my mother can tend to your face."

She did as she was asked. The second room was such a fine example of a Victorian parlor she felt she had stepped onto a film set. There was a splendid range in the hearth, lovingly blacked and maintained, with a low coal fire burning in it. A kettle hung to one side on a swiveled arm, waiting to be set above the heat. Pipes leading off the back of the stove suggested a system that would provide hot water inside the house, a highly modern innovation for its time. The most notable feature of the room, however, was one that was, on reflection, slightly out of place. Against one wall stood a handsome oak dresser of the type usually found in farmhouses or some of the bigger country cottages. It was rustic and simple, its purpose function rather than decoration. There were shelves above and cupboards below. What was housed behind the small wooden doors Xanthe could only guess at; the shelves, on the other hand, displayed their contents for all to see. There were rows and rows of jars, large and small, clear or blue glass, some with waxed cotton tops, some with glass lids or cork stoppers. She stepped forward, drawn to these gleaming containers, curious to identify their contents. These were not stores for winter. There were no pickles or jams, no onions or eggs in vinegar nor syrupy fruit in bottles. These held altogether more unusual contents. As far as she could make out, the smaller ones contained treatments of some sort, and were labeled "oil" or "tincture" for the most part. The larger jars housed dried herbs, flower petals, seeds, and nut husks, again all meticulously labeled. There was something about this rare and impressive collection that did not fit in a kitchen at all, but would have been better suited to an apothecary. The young man noticed how her attention was taken by the dresser.

"That is my mother's pharmacopeia," he said casually, as if it was the most normal thing in the world to have instead of food and provisions in a kitchen. "There is nothing for which she does not have a remedy at hand. You'll see. Here, sit by the fire. The night air is damp and you might take a chill." He moved a small wooden chair closer to the range.

Xanthe gratefully sank into it, suddenly feeling the effects of the brutal encounter she had just experienced, coupled with her clothes being wet and her legs grazed from where she had been thrown to the filthy cobbles.

"Thank you . . . oh, I don't know your name."

He blushed a little, flustered at not having observed the formality sooner. "Thomas Balmoral," he said quickly.

"Xanthe Westlake."

"I am pleased to make your acquaintance, Miss Westlake," he told her.

She smiled. "Not as pleased as I am to make yours. I am grateful for your help. It was brave of you to come to the aid of a person you do not know, in such a place."

"I did only what any man of good character would do, when hearing a woman in peril. But you are right in what you say, that alleyway is not—"

"Not a place for a sensible woman to find herself in. Don't worry, I won't make the same mistake twice."

"You are recently come to London, then?"

Xanthe absorbed the useful information and steeled herself against more difficult questions. She needed to take care to give the answers she had prepared so that people might not think her suspicious.

"I arrived this afternoon. My luggage was lost on the stagecoach. I was in search of lodgings and became disorientated."

"Are you perhaps visiting a relative?"

She was saved the trouble of responding by the arrival of a tall, middle-aged woman with fine features, soulful eyes, and glorious auburn hair made all the more striking by the broad streak of white that ran through it from her left temple. She looked to be perhaps fifty years old, but moved with the grace and ease of a younger woman. On seeing Xanthe's injury she hurried to her, taking her face in her hands and tilting it gently upward.

"My dear girl, what has befallen you?" she asked.

Xanthe was touched by her concern for a stranger. She was not bothered by the formalities of introductions, nor did she for a moment question the character or trustworthiness of the wounded girl brought into her house unannounced as night fell. She simply saw a need for care and rose to it.

"She was attacked by a ruffian," Thomas explained.

"Really, it is not serious," said Xanthe. "I was fortunate your son heard my shouts, though. I am grateful to him. He saw the man off."

"I should have taken him by the scruff and dragged him to the constable!" Thomas said, shaking his head, hindsight lending him a new anger.

"We need no constable here," his mother said, continuing to minutely study her patient's wounds. "Nipper, fetch me water and clean cloths from the linen press. Jump to it, now."

Xanthe smiled at the use of what she assumed was a family name for the young man, the action causing her to wince as the swelling of her lip and nose were increasing. She was aware of a soothing quality to the woman's touch.

"You were fortunate, in fact," she told Xanthe, "that the wounds are not deep. The skin is broken, yes, and there is a degree of abrasion, but the injuries are superficial. What we must manage is the swelling, which is what currently causes your discomfort. And the possibility of infection. I will clean the site of the injury and apply an ointment to keep it protected and reduce the inflammation." She moved to the dresser and searched along the shelves until she found what she needed, selecting two small bottles. Xanthe watched her closely. If this was Erasmus Balmoral's wife, did she know about him being a Spinner? Did she know he once had a lover, in another century, who now inhabited the same time and place as him again? There was something about her that gave the impression of wisdom. Of a quiet strength. It crossed Xanthe's mind that this was not the sort of woman who would be unsure of her own place in the world or in the affections of her husband. When Thomas returned with the cloths she gently and efficiently set about her task. As she worked she spoke to her son.

"Now, Nipper, you may tell me who your young friend is, for I am certain you have manners enough to have introduced yourself before bringing her into our home," she said, not for a moment taking her eyes off Xanthe's face.

"This is Miss Xanthe Westlake," he said, "who is but recently arrived in the city and unfamiliar with its streets and dark ways."

"Evidently."

"She has had the misfortune of losing her luggage from the stagecoach, and became confused in the area unknown to her while searching for lodgings."

"One misfortune upon another," the woman murmured. At last, satisfied with her work, she stepped back from her patient. "You will do, Miss Westlake. I advise you to refrain from touching your face, and I will give you an unguent to apply to the wounds for the next day or so. I am confident all will heal well."

"Thank you. You've been very kind," Xanthe said. "My fortune changed when I landed at your door, I think, for I could not have hoped for better treatment."

"I have worked as a medical practitioner for many years, though I rarely practice now. The skills of a healer never leave one, and for that I am often grateful. Well, as my son is being slow in the extreme at completing the introductions, I will tell you myself that my name is Elizabeth Balmoral. I expect Thomas has told you that his father is the bookbinder named above our door."

"He did. Such an interesting profession . . . to be able to make such lovely books as the ones I noticed in your shop."

Elizabeth considered this remark carefully. "You have an interest in books?"

"Well, some books."

"And is that what brings you to London? I cannot imagine a young woman of good sense would brave the dangers of an unfamiliar city unaccompanied merely in search of something instructional to read."

"I came in search of work," she replied. "I am a singer. I was hoping to find employment in one of the music halls." She waited to see how the woman would react to this news. A music hall singer, a woman who disported herself upon the stage for the entertainment of others, could often be viewed as little more respectable than a prostitute. She was pleased to see no sign of judgment in her expression.

"I believe there is a high demand for talented singers in Drury Lane, though it is not a place I know well myself."

Thomas spoke up. "The Strand Musick Hall does a highly popular show on a Saturday night. Fine performances and completely respectable."

"Nipper? I did not know you were a patron of musical theater," his mother commented with a small smile, enjoying teasing her son.

"I have visited that particular establishment," he confessed. "On occasion. If it would suit you, Miss Westlake, I could take you there. To avoid you getting lost in the city again."

"That's very kind of you, but I don't think I'm looking my best at the moment. Perhaps in a few days' time?"

Elizabeth set a bottle of ointment on the table. "This is for you. Apply twice a day for three days, no more." She turned to Thomas. "At this moment, I should imagine Miss Westlake is more concerned with the matter of securing lodgings than employment."

Thomas looked embarrassed at not having thought of this. Before he could think of a response his mother went on.

"It is getting late, the night is damp, I would be remiss as a physician if I were to send my patient out in such conditions. Miss Westlake, you may have a room here for tonight. Rest, and then Thomas can assist you in finding suitable accommodations in the morning."

It was an offer simply made and sincerely meant, without preamble or fuss. Xanthe found herself liking her new acquaintance more and more. A safe place to stay, friendly company, and the house of the very person the writing box might have been directing her to. It was so much more than she could have hoped for in such a short time. Already her face was starting to feel better and the memory of the assault fading.

"If it's not too much trouble," she replied, "I would be very grateful."

"Then it is decided. Now, come upstairs and meet my husband. He is a little unconventional in his ways but a kinder man you will not find. He will be happy to hear we have a guest, for we rarely mix in society, a habit which is more mine than his, I confess."

Elizabeth led the way up the old wooden staircase, the bannisters and handrail of which were worn with age and use but burnished with polish and care to a deep gleam. There was a red Turkish runner up the center of the stairs, an impressive collection of oils and watercolors on the walls, and the sonorous ticking of a grandfather clock to mark their progress. On the first floor a door on the landing opened into the living room, which ran the width of the front of the town house with two tall windows giving onto the street below. As she entered the room, Xanthe could clearly hear something singing to her. She searched for the source of the musical sounds and quickly spied the writing box sitting on a small desk in the far corner of the room. Her pulse raced. This was indeed where she was meant to be, there was no doubt about it. How close she was to Liam she was yet to discover.

Elizabeth set about closing the wooden shutters.

"Take a seat by the fire, Miss Westlake. You must guard against shock after your experience. Nipper, fetch your father, dear, he should finish his work for the day. He will protest, but the light is too poor for him to work longer. Tell him we have a guest and he will come willingly."

Xanthe chose a red velvet sofa to the left of the hearth. It was seductively soft and as she sank into its cushions she wondered at how quickly she had been made to feel at ease with these people she had only just met. Their home was so welcoming and their willingness to assist a stranger so heartwarming, she felt deeply grateful.

The man of the house could be heard before he even reached the living room. His cheerful, slightly hectic voice preceded him through the house until at last he all but bounded through the doorway, hand outstretched, a ready smile directed at Xanthe.

"Aha! Our unexpected visitor. But nonetheless welcome for that. Delighted to make your acquaintance, Miss Westlake." He grabbed her hand as she tried to raise herself from the unhelpfully soft sofa. "No! Do not disturb yourself. Not on my account. I hear you have been in the wars? Yes, yes, I see it now. But my wife has tended to your wounds and she really is the most excellent nurse any person could wish for." When he finally drew breath, Elizabeth came to stand next to him, taking his arm affectionately.

"My husband, Erasmus Balmoral," she said.

Xanthe looked up at the attractive man. His collar-length salt-and-pepper hair was swept back from his brow in a somewhat untidy manner. His navy velvet jacket and sunset silk waistcoat gave him the air of someone comfortable in his own skin, at ease with himself, and ready to take on the world. About his eyes there was a darkness, though, a flash of something that suggested it would be dangerous to cross him. In that moment of meeting him, she knew for certain that this was the same man she had seen in her time-within-time travel. This was the man who had kissed Lydia Flyte but told her he must leave her. This was the man whose found treasure had called to her. This was an ancient, successful, and highly skilled fellow Spinner.

AFTER HIS CONVERSATION WITH MISTRESS FLYTE, LIAM ACCEPTED THAT SHE WOULD tell him only so much about her plans and would not be persuaded to reveal everything. Her precise reasons for wanting Xanthe in this time, and her reluctance to simply ask for her help, made him weigh all her words carefully. Without knowing her full intentions, he could not be certain of Xanthe's safety. Having eaten well he had thought of catching up on some sleep, but his bare room was dreary, and he was too restless to simply go to bed. Testing his hostess's claim that he was at liberty to come and go as he pleased, he announced he would take an evening walk. Mistress Flyte not only accepted this without objection, she had her maid find him a change of clothes. This consisted of a crisp white shirt with a winged collar and navy-blue necktie, a pair of quite ordinary-looking corduroy trousers, brown leather shoes, a blue plaid waistcoat, a dark tweed jacket, and a hat. He spent some time at the mirror in the hall adjusting the brown bowler until he felt he'd got it right. It occurred to him that although he would never get used to wearing hats all the time, they did lend a certain panache to a workaday outfit.

As he was about to leave, Mistress Flyte called from the sitting room. "Have a care, Mister Adams. The city now is not the one you are familiar with. Hunger and poverty make brutes of men, harlots of women, and thieves of small children. Guard against your trusting nature."

"I think I've learned that lesson already," he replied, as much to himself as to her.

Outside, night had enveloped the streets, and with it a heavy fog. These combined with the miasma spat up by the rolling river resulted in a wet gloom. Any lingering heat of the day had gone, to be replaced with a chill that infused the dampness. It was as if the city hoped to dissolve the grime and so wash itself of its filth under cover of darkness, but the dirt of the humanity of such a place could not be so easily dispelled. It took Liam several minutes to adjust to the all-pervading smell that rose up from the muddy shore, from the mired gutters, from the boats and ships at the dockside, from their fetid cargos, and from the inhabitants of the docklands themselves. He saw then that the house he had just stepped from was set into a long row, but not all were residences. Homes of the more basic sort were squashed in between warehouses, chandleries, offices, and sundry shops, along with the ever-present alehouses.

He strode forth, heading he knew not where but knowing hesitancy would mark him out as a newcomer. Even without Mistress Flyte's words of warning, he knew enough about cities to know that opportunists preyed on the weak. He would give the appearance of someone who knew where they were going, when in truth he did not even know where he was. He glanced about to take in landmarks that would enable him to find his way home. An inn called The Sailor's Return. A slipway to the water with an upturned blue rowing boat. A streetlamp that listed slightly. These would be his markers so that he could return to the drab house with the dark brown door. However much he disliked the fact, his captor was right: his best chance of helping Xanthe to find her way to him was to stay close to Mistress Flyte. He wondered, as he walked, whether or not she would have found something to sing to her. He was still unclear on the finer details of how a Spinner did their work. Would she need something of his? Something belonging to the old woman? Something from this exact date? He had to trust her to do her job. He did trust her. He only hoped he wasn't being made to be part of something that would draw her into danger.

He headed up a road that turned left from the water. It seemed to lead toward better houses, grander buildings, cleaner streets, and away from the grime and hard work of the docks. The farther he went, the more shops began to appear: haberdashers, milliners, tailors, bakers, jewelers. About him walked ladies in dresses full and long that they held up with clever devices to avoid sweeping through the muck on the ground. None walked alone, but each was on the arm of a gentleman, mostly dressed in what looked to Liam to be tails, like the morning suits men wore to weddings in his own time. Everyone, but everyone, wore a hat. Some of the women had elaborate bonnets, others something simpler, most secured with bejeweled pins or tied beneath the chin with broad silk ribbons. The better dressed men wore tall top hats, brushed to a gleam, and these they raised to greet people as they passed. Lesser mortals, who evidently inhabited a more lowly station on the social scale, wore bowlers such as his own, or cloth caps of varying degrees of floppiness. Despite the dampness of the night, it wasn't in fact cold, so that Liam soon found himself warm in his unfamiliar clothes. He would dearly have loved to wrench off his tie and take his jacket off, but he could see that would mark him out as strange, or possibly drunk. At one point, checking behind him to make sure he did not lose his way, he became aware of two men who were very clearly following him. He wondered briefly if he had behaved in a way that somehow marked him out as vulnerable. Had he revealed himself to be a stranger, to be uncertain of where he was going or what he might find? He strode forward with more confidence, and then a thought occurred to him. What if Mistress Flyte, for all her insistence that he was a free man, had arranged to have him followed? He dismissed this idea. The old woman knew that he must have figured out his best chance of going home was to remain where Xanthe was most likely to find him. And as far as he could work out, that meant staying close to the person who had brought him here in the first place. So, if the two men sliding along the shadows behind him were not sent by her, then who? Perhaps they were, after all, random thugs intent on mugging him for whatever money he might be carrying.

In an attempt to shake off his stalkers, Liam ducked down a side alley, resisting the urge to run, before quickly taking another right turn. He stepped back into a shadowy doorway and waited, watching the illuminated end of the street. Sure enough, after a few moments the two burly men appeared, obviously searching, looking this way and that, picking up their pace in an effort to catch him up. He waited a little longer and then emerged from the gloom, turned left, and walked briskly to the far end of the alley. He was brought up short at the end of it, however, when the same two men stepped out of the adjoining passageway and directly in front of him. It seemed their knowledge of the area had paid dividends. Up close, Liam was able to see them properly for the first time. They were not, as he had first thought, merely hired muscle. There was about them both an air of sharp intelligence, canniness, and ruthlessness. Something in the angle of their bowler hats, tipped low over their eyes, the breadth of their shoulders tight beneath their well-cut jackets, and the stern expressions with which they now studied him, suggested a confidence and a standing that would not easily be shaken.

"Gentlemen," he said calmly. "Something I can help you with?" He was not sure his voice had quite the casual tone he had hoped for.

The heavier of the two men spoke first. "You are to come with us," he said simply.

"Look, I'm sure you have a job to do, I appreciate that, but Mistress Flyte has explained the way things are to me. I'm just having a walk, OK? I'll be back home tucked up in bed like a good boy before midnight. No need to worry." Even as he gave his answer he knew these men had nothing to do with the old woman. A point confirmed by their response.

"You won't be going back there," the second man told him. "We've a carriage waiting. This way," he motioned, indicating that Liam should walk with him.

He was confused. Why would muggers take him anywhere? Why the carriage?

"Well, it's good of you to invite me, but, sadly, I have a prior engagement and am expected, so if you'll excuse me . . ." He turned on his heel and broke into a run but not before both men had leaped into action. One sprinted past him with an impressive show of speed, skidding to a halt in front of him, holding his arms akimbo to block the way. The second man caught hold of Liam's arms from behind and pinned them to his sides. Everything happened with bewildering speed. He felt himself being manhandled and turned. It was clear they intended dragging him to their waiting carriage and taking him somewhere he was fairly certain he did not want to go. Whoever they were, they would take him against his will if they could, and to be removed from Mistress Flyte was, as things stood, to be removed from his best chance of being reunited with Xanthe. On top of which, it was to be removed further from the possibility of ever returning home to his own time.

He had no choice but to put up a fight. A sharp backward jab with his elbow found its mark in the solar plexus of the man behind him, causing him to gasp and fold forward, momentarily loosening his grip on his victim. Liam sprang to the side but there was not room to pass the heavier man who stood menacingly before him. The two sized each other up and then, suddenly, the stranger made his move, lunging forward. Liam ducked, diving beneath the man's outstretched arms. He lost his hat in his haste, but was not quick enough to gain his freedom. The man grabbed him as he moved forward, taking hold of his jacket and yanking him back toward him. Now he swung a punch. Again Liam ducked, feeling the air disturbed by the man's fist as it whistled past his left ear. He straightened up and saw his chance. His assailant was briefly off guard and off balance. Liam drew back his arm and put all his strength into the first proper punch he had ever thrown in his life. It was a lucky blow, catching the man on his jaw at such an angle that it not only sent him sprawling but knocked him out cold. Liam stared at the inert figure on the cobbles, stunned at what he had just done, horrified that he might actually have killed the man. The second stranger made as if to grab Liam, confirming the importance somebody had placed on him being taken, as the second thug was apparently prepared to leave his friend unconscious and wounded on the ground to do so. He had just taken hold of Liam again when there came a shout from behind them.

"Hey there! What are you about, ruffian! Be gone, I tell you. Leave him be!"

A stout figure had stepped out of a doorway. He was backlit by the lamplight from within, his rotund silhouette topped off by a particularly tall top hat, worn at a slight angle. Though short, he had a bearing, and when he raised his cane and spoke again his words carried a certain weight.

"Must I tell you again? I will not take kindly to repeating myself, damn your eyes! Nor will you relish the results of my bad humor, I give you fair warning, fair warning, I say. Now, begone!"

Much to Liam's surprise, his assailant released him. Without hesitation he instead took hold of his friend, who was now groaning and stirring into consciousness, and helped him to his feet. The pair threw anxious glances at the new arrival to the party before turning wordlessly and disappearing down the street and away.

Liam caught his breath and picked up his hat, dusting it off on his trouser leg and replacing it on his head.

"Thank you, sir," he called to the man in the doorway. "I am grateful for your timely assistance, and I bid you good night." He touched the brim of his hat courteously and then made to leave.

"Hold! Hold, young man. Why the rush? Why the hurry? Do not

be so quick to turn your back on poor old Albert Taverstock. Let us meet proper and shake hands, for God's sake," he said, moving across the cobbles on slightly bandy legs, his hand outstretched. Now that he was revealed in the borrowed lamplight of the narrow street, his personal style was unmistakable. Here was a man, however diminutive his stature, for whom the word "flamboyant" might have been invented. His collar was entirely obscured by the frothy silk confection of his turquoise neckwear. His cummerbund, also silk, was an equally bright blue. His jacket was deepest plumb and cutaway, with brass buttons, almost in the fashion of a big top ringmaster. His silver-topped cane was twisted like a barley sugar, and there was a kingfisher feather in the band of his hat. All would have been impressive, had they not a threadbare, worn, and weary look to them upon closer inspection.

Liam would far rather have simply left, but he felt obliged to thank the man properly. He liked to think he would have got rid of his attackers on his own, but he was not sure it was the truth. The new stranger's intervention had seen them off, though, and that in itself was strange. They did not seem the types to scare easily, and this newcomer was short, stout, unarmed, and alone. What had made them back off so quickly, he wondered? Why had they wordlessly retreated at the sight of him? He shook the offered hand.

"Liam," he said, adding, "from the north," in an attempt to head off questions and yet not seem suspiciously unfriendly.

"Oh, the north, very fine. Fine indeed! I have been there myself on more than one occasion. Capital schools up there, as I recall. Are you, perhaps, a master? Is it from an academic establishment you gained your sporting prowess?"

"My . . . ?" For a moment Liam was at a loss and then he remembered the single lucky punch that had floored his attacker. "It's not really what I'd call prowess."

"Come, come, false modesty is unflattering. I know skill when I see it. I know talent. Yes. You have the physique under those . . . garments."

Here he paused to indicate Liam's drab outfit, which was in every way the opposite to his own.

"Well, again, thank you, Mr. Taverstock. Now, if you'll forgive me, I am expected home." He continued to do his best to speak in a way he hoped did not sound jarringly modern.

As if the thought of losing his new acquaintance caused the man physical pain he clutched at his heart. "But you will not go now that we are friends! No, no. Say you will at least take a cup of ale with me. Here—" he gestured at the building he had stepped from. "It is a lowly establishment, but the beer is above tolerable, I will vouch for it. And besides, Mister . . . Mister Liam"—here he lowered his voice and tapped the side of his short, broad nose—"there is something inside I guarantee will be of interest to a fellow such as yourself. I guarantee it! Now, I will not be gainsaid. Come, come, this way." He turned and waddled back to the doorway in full expectation that he would be followed.

Liam considered simply heading off in the opposite direction, but the man had helped him, and a beer was tempting. And, after all, had he not wanted to see something of this time and this place while he had the chance? On top of which, his would-be abductors could very well be lying in wait for him around the corner. It seemed sensible to delay heading down any more dark streets on his own for a while.

He had expected to be led into some sort of tavern, but instead found himself in a small room, empty save for two large men who appeared to be there to guard the inner door. Having just been assaulted by a pair of strangers out to do him harm, he balked, stopping at the entrance. Mr. Taverstock sought to reassure him.

"No need for alarm, my young friend. No need, no need. You are safe here. My lads are to protect us, indeed, and our enterprises, as you will see. Come, come."

Again he beckoned. The two men stepped aside, one pushing open the second door. Cautiously, Liam stepped through it. He followed

Taverstock along a passageway so narrow that the portly man almost stoppered it like a cork. There were gas lamps upon the walls, so that the way was well lit, revealing no decoration or furnishings. As they neared the end of the corridor, there came strange sounds from up ahead. Sounds of shouting and cheering. The other thing that reached him was a stink, easily recognizable as a pungent blend of sweat and alcohol, with high notes of urine. When the final door was opened a great roar of the assembled crowd prevented him asking any questions. Before he had time to try to make sense of it, they emerged into a large space, as huge as it was unexpected. This was no inn, nor a domestic residence. The building might once have been a warehouse for goods traveling through the dock. Now, it was something else entirely. Interior walls had been removed to create a large space, which was, at that moment, almost filled to capacity with men. They stood facing the center, in which was placed a roughly shaped ring with straw bales as its boundary. This was not raised in any way, but had a layer of scuffed sawdust in it, which Liam realized, with a lurching stomach, was there to soak up the blood. Two men in white knee breeches, bare-chested and bare-fisted, slugged it out. By the way they were staggering and flinging wild, largely unsuccessful blows at each other, he decided the boxing match must have been going on for some time already. They were ill-matched. One fighter was tall and his reach long, but he did not look strong, and was clearly in a weakened state. His face bore evidence that his opponent had landed several effective blows, his lip being split and blood flowing freely from his nose. The other man, though shorter, was muscular, fierce, and dangerous. It struck Liam as odd that he had not yet flattened his skinny adversary. The two danced around each other, feet dragging slightly through the sullied sawdust, fists held in front of their faces, eyes not for a moment leaving those of the other. Through it all a loud bearded man, more master of ceremonies than referee, or perhaps more choreographer of a macabre and violent dance, exhorted the men to fight on, and challenged the rabble to up their wagers. Among the crowd notes were thrust into outstretched hands, palms were spat upon, dubious words given, and bets placed, all fortunes standing or falling on the pain of the pugilists.

Liam felt a tapping on his arm. Mister Taverstock sought to gain his attention by use of his silver-topped cane, as conversation was not possible. He indicated the makeshift bar at the far end of the room and led the way through the excitable melee, which parted as the Red Sea before Moses at the sight of him. When they reached the boards and crates the man was given two bottles of ale without having to request or pay for them. Liam was beginning to understand that he was in the company of someone important in these particular circles. He sniffed at the contents of the bottle, registered surprise at the sweetness of the beer, and drank. It was good, and washed away some of the dust and dirt of the place.

Mister Taverstock smiled, his cheeks reddened now by the heat of the room. He raised his voice to make himself heard, rendering it strangely high with a tendency to squeak on some vowels. "Did I not promise you quality ale? Quality, in all things, is my watchword. As you shall see. As you shall see."

Liam found himself unable to take his eyes from the spectacle inside the ring. He had never thought watching two men beat each other made for entertainment, and nothing he could see now changed his mind. The tired fighters battled on, weary and bruised, driven by who knew what motivations to keep slinging blows beyond a sensible point of doing so. If one was knocked down he was exhorted with shouts and curses by the crowd to drag himself to his feet and back into the fight again. The combination of such male aggression and fortunes to be won or lost on the outcome of their combat charged the air so that he could almost taste the violence. At last, the lighter of the two men sustained a punch to the head that left him unable to continue. Amid tumultuous noise, the hand of the winner was raised by the referee. The favorite had prevailed. A popular win. The loser was carried from the room.

"Capital! Capital." Mister Taverstock was delighted. "A reliable fighter, a crowd-pleaser. Money to be made here for the right man." He turned and faced Liam. "How about you, my friend? Do you fancy your chances?"

"Me?"

"You are not large, 'tis true, but size is not always the main factor, no indeed not. And I witnessed your talent for myself. I know what I know, and I know what I saw." He tapped the side of his nose again.

Liam thought of the way he had dropped the first of his assailants outside and how Mister Taverstock must have seen him do it. "A lucky punch, that's all."

"Come, come, a man's talent may be his fortune, has he courage to use it."

"I promise you, I am no boxer."

"Money to be made, I said, and you would know the truth of it. Fellow such as yourself, unknown, a dark horse, not heavy-looking, no form. You have no reputation and that can work in your favor, do you see? Allow me to put you on the card is all you have to do. One good fight and your fortune made, with a talent such as yours, yes, such as yours." The little man licked his lips, the thought of possible winnings on wagers clearly driving him on.

Liam finished his ale and placed the bottle back on the board. "I say again, I'm no fighter. Now, thank you for the ale, for your help, but I am expected, so I'll say good night to you." He touched the brim of his bowler once more, nodded at the man, and stepped away, relieved that he was allowed to do so and suddenly eager to be gone from the place. As he left the room he heard Mister Taverstock's reedy voice.

"If you change your mind you come tell Albert Taverstock!" he called after him.

Outside a light but steady rain had set in. Liam checked the street to reassure himself that the kidnappers were not lying in wait, turned up his collar, stuffed his hands in his pockets, and walked briskly in the direction of Mistress Flyte's house.

—

Xanthe had spent a pleasant hour in the company of the Balmoral family in their warm and welcoming home. Thomas was quieter in the presence of his father, but only because Erasmus had about him such a restless energy that he tended to speak before anyone else could do so. Elizabeth was the calmer of the couple, her voice softer, her words more thoughtfully chosen, and yet her husband deferred to her at once if she cut in to his chatter. Xanthe knew that because he was a Spinner he would be able to detect the presence of another. She was aware at moments of him watching her, studying her, almost, and yet he did not ask questions that might have told him anything beyond her cover story. They all accepted that she had come to London in search of work in the music halls, there being little employment in the small theater in the provincial town in the west country she claimed to have hailed from. She wondered how and when she would be able to talk to him on his own. It was important to tread carefully. After all, his wife might not know of his past, or the fact that he traveled through time. If she was to gain his trust and get him to help her find Lydia Flyte and Liam, she could not afford to cause trouble in his household or turn Elizabeth against her. Eventually, Thomas took himself off to bed and Erasmus took his cue from his wife, who suggested he do the same. It was clear to Xanthe that she wanted to speak to their visitor alone. When the men had gone, Elizabeth lit a candle on the mantelpiece, even though the house was fitted with gas lights. She dropped some dried petals into the wax, which spat briefly before settling to a pleasantly perfumed flame. She turned and smiled at Xanthe.

"I rarely have the company of another woman in the house," she said. "It is an agreeable novelty. You are not too tired to sit awhile longer?"

"Not at all." She watched Elizabeth as she seated herself on the sofa opposite. There was something singular about her beyond her striking appearance. She felt an attraction to her she did not fully understand. It was nothing sexual; it was something altogether less easily explained. All she knew was that she liked being near her, liked listening to her speak, liked the way her wise eyes regarded her when she, in turn, listened. Her thoughts about this unusual woman were interrupted by the singing of the writing box, which had suddenly grown louder. In an unguarded moment, Xanthe turned to look at it, an action that did not go unnoticed by Elizabeth.

"You like the writing slope?

"I couldn't help noticing it when I first came into the room. It's very fine."

"Please, take a closer look if it interests you."

In truth, Xanthe neither wanted nor needed to get closer to the box. It had brought her to Erasmus; that was all it could do to help at the moment. In addition, its insistent song had become quite uncomfortable, shifting to a vibrating buzz, and stepping closer to it only made the noise louder. Not wanting to offend her host, however, and unable to think of a sensible reason for not accepting the offer, she went to the corner of the room and sat on the chair at the desk. The box looked less worn than in her own day, its brass inlay free from scratches and its walnut frame devoid of nicks or dents.

"Open it, if you like," said Elizabeth.

She did so, lifting the lid and opening it fully so that the inside formed a leather-covered flat surface on which to write, which was set at a perfect angle to anyone sitting in front of it. Much to her surprise, as soon as it was open the box released the smell of lavender. The scent was so strong and so unexpected she giggled.

"Something amuses you?"

"Oh . . . I can smell lavender," she said. "I suppose I wasn't expecting such a feminine fragrance inside something belonging to a gentleman."

"But this is my writing box," Elizabeth told her.

"Yours?"

"Yes." She got up and came to stand on the other side of the little desk. "Erasmus gave it to me. After he made me my . . . journal. He knows I love to record things in it every day and could see I would do so with more comfort had I a proper slope. You see?" She reached forward and picked up a beautiful book bound in green leather with gold lettering tooled on it. Before Xanthe could read the inscription, Elizabeth opened the journal and set it, with two blank pages facing upward, onto the leather of the box. "Just so. Very pleasant to work on."

Xanthe was still trying to process this new information. The found thing did not belong to Erasmus. It had, nonetheless, brought her to him, but there was something odd about the fact that it wasn't his. Why hadn't she been called by something that was personal to him? It wasn't as if this was some random piece of furniture or painting or curio that was simply in his house to attract her to the right place. The writing slope was a hugely personal item belonging to someone else. True, Erasmus had given it to his wife, but still that put it at a remove from him. The more she thought about it, and the more she looked at the tall, charismatic woman standing in front of her, the more certain she became that the treasure had been specifically drawing her to Elizabeth, not Erasmus. But why?

6

A LITTLE LATER, ELIZABETH SHOWED XANTHE TO A SMALL GUEST ROOM AT THE BACK of the house. It was comfortably and prettily furnished. There was a brass bed with patchwork covers, warm, heavy curtains at the window, two thick rugs, a wardrobe, a washstand with bowl and water jug, and a small chair. A fire had been lit in the modest hearth and fresh flowers set on the bedside table. Gas lamps gave a warm glow. The whole effect was charming. After her host left her, she did not undress, however, but sat on the bed, attempting to make sense of what she had learned and plan her next move. She had got no further than repeating to herself that she had been called to Elizabeth and not Erasmus when there came a light knock on the door. Opening it, she found the man himself, his face serious.

"Miss Westlake, forgive me for disturbing your rest, but it is important you and I speak with each other, do you not agree?"

"I certainly do. Please, come in."

Erasmus looked uncomfortable. "I would not intrude . . . perhaps your bedchamber is not an appropriate venue for our discussion. Allow me instead to invite you to my workshop. It is on another floor and we will not be interrupted in our conversation there."

He stepped back with a small bow, indicating that she should follow him. Xanthe picked up her satchel and then walked quickly after Erasmus, almost having to trot to keep up. She was beginning to understand that the man did everything energetically and at speed. He led her up the stairs and into a room that occupied almost the entire floor. It was a workshop her mother would have been very happy in indeed. The center held a long, low workbench, strewn with the tools and materials needed for the binding of books. Drawers, shelves, and cabinets lined the walls, each filled with bolts of fine leather, boxes of paper, implements, or beautifully finished books. To the aromas of leather and linseed oil were added those of ink and sawdust.

"Please, be seated," he said, pulling a stool out from the workbench.

Xanthe sat down, setting her bag at her feet. Erasmus, naturally, did not settle, but instead strode about the space as he spoke, returning to study her expression when he waited for a response to anything, only perching for the briefest moment on the stool beside hers before setting off pacing once more.

"You will know, of course," he said, "that one Spinner is able to detect the presence of another."

"Yes. I was hoping you would know who . . . what I was. Makes it so much easier to broach the subject. I couldn't be certain, when we were in company. And I didn't want to say anything that would be . . . difficult. For you. And your family."

At this Erasmus paused in his marching. "You need have no concerns on that account. Both my wife and my son are aware of my identity. In point of fact," he said, a warm smile spreading across his handsome face, "it was because of my work that I met Elizabeth. I will be forever grateful for that. And we have no secrets from Nipper."

It was her turn to smile. "That's such a sweet nickname for him. But he introduced himself as Thomas, is that right?"

"It is. He was named after my wife's much loved brother. Who died in somewhat tragic circumstances."

"Oh, I am sorry to hear that."

"It was a very long time ago. It brings her comfort to have given his name to our boy. She says there is much about him that reminds her of her brother."

"So, they both know what you are. And do you still travel through time?" However often she herself moved through the centuries, however much she now considered herself a true Spinner, she doubted she would ever get used to hearing herself say those words aloud to someone else.

"On occasion, though Elizabeth and I have made our life here for a number of years now. Having a son to raise required alterations to our positions in the world, and we were happy to do it. I should perhaps explain that he is our adopted boy, though none the less precious for that. He came to us when he was only five years old. Or thereabouts. His history was a sad and lonely one, so that none of us ever knew the exact date of his birth. But there!" He clapped his hands, dispelling any gloominess. "Our paths crossed, time permitted our meeting at the opportune moment in many ways, and we were blessed with a family we might not otherwise have had. But it is not Nipper who is important in this discussion. It is you, Miss Westlake, who has my undivided and, I confess, eager attention. You are most definitely a Spinner, and if I am any judge, one of the highest order."

"That's kind of you to say, but—"

"Not kind, accurate."

"I'm sorry, but how can you tell? I mean, beyond arriving at this point in time, I've done nothing to show how I can use my gift."

"That you call it a gift is evidence of your character. Some call it a burden. Some consider it a birthright. It is true, I have not yet had the opportunity to confirm my assessment of your skills. But I have your signal."

"My . . . ? You mean, the thing that makes me detectable to another Spinner?"

"Yes. I find it particularly strong."

"Does that mean other Spinners will too?" she asked, thinking immediately of Mistress Flyte.

"Unless you mask it in some way, that is likely, yes. Though some are less sensitive to the presence of others. It is a skill of listening, akin to hearing the calls that we are alert for from those who need us. If a Spinner has turned away from answering those calls, their ability to detect the presence of another of their kind can be diminished. But tell me, what is it that brings you here? To me? To now?"

"It's hard to know where to start . . . you are right about me being a Spinner, though I don't think I can claim to be the expert you think me to be. The fact is, the last time I traveled I was not alone."

"Ah, you assisted another to make a journey?"

"It's more accurate to say he was assisting me, though he is not a Spinner."

"And your mission, was it a success?"

She thought of Petronella and her new life, safe, free from the threat of Fairfax, as she herself was now too. "Yes," she said, "it was a success. Up to the point where we attempted the journey home to our own time."

"'Attempted' suggests something went awry."

"That's one way of putting it." She hesitated, surprised at how emotional she felt when talking about what had happened. She looked away from Erasmus, struggling to meet his intense gaze. "I must have done something wrong. I've been over and over it in my mind, and I can't see what it was, but it was my fault. I should have been able to keep him with me and keep him safe but I didn't."

"You think him lost in time?"

"Oh no," she said, understanding at once what he meant, that he was referring to the terrifying limbo awaiting unsuccessful time travelers, "not that. Someone . . . took him. As we were about to travel, they took him. To a different time and place."

"Another Spinner did such a thing!" Erasmus was appalled.

"I was tricked."

"And do you know why this person committed an act so completely against all that a Spinner might stand for?"

"I don't. But I believe the treasure that sang to me brought me here to you, because you and she are connected. And that she is, for some reason I have not yet been able to work out, here too. Here and now."

"She?" A shadow passed over his face and for once he stood completely still.

"Her name is Lydia Flyte."

As if he might have been half expecting this answer, Erasmus nodded. "Lydia. After all this time."

"Can you sense her presence? I mean, she is a Spinner, like us . . . can you detect her here, in the city somewhere?"

"Firstly, though you and I are newly acquainted, I think I may say with confidence that you are not like her, Spinner or no. Nor, it must be said, am I. But no, to answer your question fully, I cannot detect her. Which is, I'll allow, a little surprising."

"Could she be cloaking her whereabouts, do you think?"

"Yes, she must be actively doing so. Which means she does not wish to be discovered. At least, not by me."

Xanthe felt suddenly weary. It had been a long day. Time travel, being assaulted, the lateness of the hour, and now the news that Erasmus had no more idea than she did of where Mistress Flyte might be found, all combined to drain her of her last ounce of energy. "It doesn't make any sense," she said quietly. "If she's taken him somewhere in the hope I will come looking for her, why would she hide from me?"

"Lydia Flyte does nothing without careful thought. It may be she is awaiting the right moment to reveal herself to you."

"Or to you."

"I think not. Our . . . association ended many years ago."

"But the found thing, the treasure that sang to me and enabled me to travel through time, it brought me to you."

"What was it?"

"That's something else I don't yet understand: it is the writing box."

"Elizabeth's writing box?"

"Yes. And yet it is *you* I needed to reach. Because of your connection with Mistress Flyte."

Erasmus thought for a moment and then said, "That may or may not be the case. We might return to Elizabeth's part in this later. For now, what interests me in particular is this: we have never met before, you and I. Indeed, to my knowledge we have not even inhabited the same time. How is it, then, that you know of me, and that you know I was once acquainted with Lydia Flyte?"

"I saw you together," she told him. When he looked puzzled she reached down to her satchel and took out the *Spinners* book. "This showed me," she said, carefully placing it on the workbench in front of him.

She could never have anticipated the strength of his reaction to the sight of the book.

Erasmus gasped, stepping forward as if to take hold of it, but stopping short of doing so. He sank onto the stool beside the workbench and stared at it. At last he reached out and laid a hand upon the worn leather cover and closed his eyes, letting out a deep sigh. When he opened his eyes and turned to Xanthe she saw that there were tears in them.

"I had thought never to see it again," he said softly.

"Was it yours once?"

He smiled then, blinking away the tears, a little embarrassed, she thought, by this show of emotion. "I doubt such a book can ever belong to one person, man or woman. No, my connection with *Spinners* is not one of ownership, rather of parenthood." Here he stopped talking and slowly moved his hand in a gesture that encompassed the many newly made books upon the workshop shelves.

Now it was her turn to gasp.

"You made it!"

He nodded. "Many years ago. In point of fact, many centuries ago. Both the book and myself have our origins in the late 1500s."

He waited for her to digest this fact. Had this been her first experience of traveling through time she might have been unable to take it in at all. Now, though, after everything she had done, after what she had seen, crucially, after all the people she had met, it seemed wondrous but not unbelievable. For a moment she thought of Samuel, living his life through the seventeenth century. A life that was forever changed for meeting her but could not, in the end, continue with her. She brought her mind back to Erasmus and the book.

"But, you didn't write it. I mean, you didn't put in all the stories, all the maps, the illustrations, the incantations . . . that could not have been the work of one person."

"Most certainly not! I am a bookbinder, not an author. While my own story may be held within its pages, I did not inscribe them. That's not how the stories find their place there, after all. No, I was commissioned to construct the book. It was not mine to keep."

"Commissioned by whom?"

"Why, by the Spinners themselves. The company predates the book, naturally. It was as their work became more and more diverse, and grew in importance, that it was decided their stories, and their wisdom, should be collected."

Something struck Xanthe as strange. "Mister Balmoral—"

"Please, I would so much prefer you to call me Erasmus."

She smiled. "If you will call me Xanthe."

"Such an unusual name," he commented. "And one that suits you very well, I must say. It translates as 'the shining one,' does it not?"

"My mother had embarrassingly high expectations of me," she joked.

"Which, it seems to me, are to be fulfilled. But I interrupted you, forgive me. Pray continue."

"It's just that, well, you are a Spinner, and yet you talk of 'their work.' As if you don't see yourself as one of us anymore."

"You see, your mother's intuition was correct: you are bright indeed! I was a Spinner, and considered myself blessed and privileged to be so. Alas, there came a time when I found myself unable to tread the same path as others who carried that name."

She cast her mind back and recalled what the book had shown her about Erasmus. Both times it had revealed him unhappy with his connection to the Spinners, turning away from their work, it seemed to her. Turning away from Mistress Flyte. She waited, wanting him to continue, not wishing to somehow prevent him revealing what she needed to know. It seemed to her that his connection to and dispute with his ex-lover was key to working out what the old woman wanted from either of them.

He straightened up a little, drawing back from the book, prepared to wait a short while longer before holding it again. "Spinners had always followed the call to help those in distress, those who faced an injustice. Where our help was needed we would go. Our gifts were given to us for this purpose. However, with such talents come responsibility, and part of that responsibility was to resist the abuse of our power. Some found themselves unable, or unwilling, to resist."

"Some like Benedict Fairfax."

"He was such a man."

"Surely Lydia Flyte has more integrity? I mean, I still don't want to believe her capable of abusing her skills, even now, even after what she has done. It just doesn't fit with the person I believed her to be. Maybe I'm just reluctant to accept the truth about her but—" she paused, shaking her head "—her doing something so awful, so drastic, as taking my friend, it's not the action of the person who risked so much to help me."

"Lydia's own situation, her part in the history of the Spinners, is one of great complexity and I fear that story is not for this moment. What

I will tell you is that there occurred a shift in the way some Spinners worked. To further their own ends, or those of some who would pay handsomely, they did not spin through time, they rather sought to *spin time itself.* Imagine, if you will, a spinning top: it rotates at tremendous speed and can move from one point to another. It does not, however, affect things around it. Thus, a Spinner should travel. Now picture a whirlpool, a vortex in perhaps an otherwise tranquil watercourse. As the whirlpool spins it pulls at the water around it, snatching anything it touches, drawing it irresistibly into its own movement, altering everything in its path. This is precisely how a Spinner should *not* travel. And yet, if an unscrupulous Spinner changes things against the way they should be . . ."

"The proper order, you mean? Which is what I always thought we were supposed to help maintain?"

"Precisely that! If a Spinner chooses not to help keep that balance, restore that order, but instead makes changes to suit himself, to further his own endeavors, even knowing they are counter to what he should do . . ."

"Can he, or she, always know?"

"Have you not always known?"

Xanthe thought about this. Thought about saving Alice from the gallows. Thought about protecting Petronella from Fairfax. "Yes," she said. "Yes, I have."

"And so has every other Spinner. Mark my words: if anyone with our gift uses it against the tenets and good purposes for which it exists, they do so knowingly."

"If we bend things against what they were supposed to be. Change the way things should pan out, there could be awful consequences, couldn't there?"

"Indeed it could."

Xanthe shook her head. "It was the thing that worried me most when

I began to time travel: that I would somehow influence the future . . . my present even . . . in ways that would have terrible results. Like, I don't know . . . perhaps someone might not have been born. Or someone else might have missed meeting a person vital to their lives, or gone in a different direction . . ."

"A Spinner who follows our original rules need have no fear of such destructive outcomes."

"So, these Spinners who wanted to change things against the real order . . . these are the ones you tried to stop?"

"I try still," he said. It was such a simple statement, and yet carried such weight. Xanthe was still considering it as Erasmus continued his explanation. "In order to continue my work I, and several other Spinners, broke away from the original group and formed our own community. We became Time Steppers, so called because that is what we do. We carefully step through time to when and where we need to be. We have no desire to spin time to suit our needs. As you point out, that would be the very opposite of what we do."

"But," she felt she had to say what was in her mind, "what about the *good* Spinners? I mean, not every Spinner would have abused their gifts. I don't, for a start. There must be plenty who are not just in it for their own gains. Couldn't you have stayed with them and dealt with the rotten apples?"

"I tried, as did others. And yes, of course, there have been, and continue to be, many wonderful Spinners of the utmost integrity. You have to understand that we are going back in time several hundred years. We were a young community then. There was, shall we say, jostling for position. And argument about our purpose and how best to serve it. In the end, the split was inevitable. That is not to say the two groups are at odds. Far from it. Spinners and Steppers have worked alongside each other happily for generations now. Perhaps because of what prompted the schism, the Steppers have often taken the position of policing the actions of those who have misused their gifts, but we do not do this exclusively. There have been Spinners who have made it their life's work to maintain the integrity and good work of their fellows, with or without our help."

Xanthe rubbed her temples, trying to stave off a burgeoning headache. Erasmus noticed the small but significant action.

"I am tiring you, forgive me. I am apt to forget how wearying spinning can be, particularly to those newly come to it. I must let you get your rest and we will continue our talk in the morning."

"There is so much I need to speak to you about, but the main thing I need your help with is finding my friend."

"The one who traveled with you and was lost?"

"Yes. Mistress Flyte has him, I'm certain of it. If we find her then I find him."

"Alas, I have not seen her for a great number of years. I have no knowledge of where she might reside, and if she is cloaking her whereabouts we will neither of us be able to detect her."

"But I have to look for Liam."

"My advice to you is to bide your time. You are safe here, and if the treasure has brought you to us this is the place you need to be. Lydia will, I suspect, make herself known to you, or to us, indeed, but she will do so only when it suits her."

"I can't just sit and wait."

He smiled. "A sentiment my wife will tell you I share completely. However, in this case, I fear we have no option."

Although it clearly pained him to tear himself away from the *Spinners* book, Erasmus insisted they retire. They exchanged promises; that he would answer further questions the next day in order to help her find Liam, and that she would permit him time with the book. Once back in her room, Xanthe could not resist sitting up in bed, placing the candle as near as she could, and opening the book again to see what it might reveal. She had scarcely begun to focus on the pages when she heard a voice. A voice that startled her because she recognized the speaker.

"Elizabeth!" she whispered, attempting to speed-read the words as they formed while the words were spoken directly into her mind.

—

I turned to find the miller standing behind me. He had washed the flour from his face, though his unkempt, shoulder-length hair was still dusty with it, and he now wore a jacket of dark tweed with a scarlet, spotted kerchief knotted at his neck. So revealed, he was younger than I had first thought, with pale gray eyes that crinkled when he smiled, which he did frequently.

He dipped a swift bow, then stuck out his hand. "Erasmus Balmoral. Exceptionally pleased to make your acquaintance," he said. "Though of course, we have already met, albeit without introduction. I apologize for the somewhat intimate nature of our interactions so far. I often feel it is a poor way to encounter someone for the first time, something of a leap over the usual order of things, but there we are. Time stepping is an inexact science. More an art, in truth. And as such, I suppose, we must forgive it the occasional impropriety."

*I stared at him. "*You *are the Time Stepper?"*

"For my sins. I trust you have not suffered any ill effects? Some find a ringing in the ears persists, or a giddiness. Headaches, perhaps?"

"I am quite well, thank you. But I confess, I wasn't expecting . . ." I hesitated. This was not how I had pictured a Time Stepper. They were bookish people, exceedingly clever, committed to their calling, having spent years studying their singular craft. This man was roughly hewn, shabby-looking, disheveled, and engaged in manual labor.

". . . a miller? No, I don't suppose you were." He grinned, waving his arm at the windmill behind him. "It is rather splendid, though, don't you agree? True, the living quarters are a little basic, but I believe I have made them acceptably comfortable. Why don't we go in, and I'll prepare a light luncheon? You must be hungry, after all, you haven't eaten in centuries!" He laughed loudly at his own joke and offered me his arm. I took it and allowed him to lead me briskly back into the windmill. It seemed he did everything at some speed. He released my arm to bound up the stairs ahead of me to the

chamber in which I had awoken. He hastened to throw open all the shutters, clearly a man given to energetic movements, and I saw that there was a simple stove on the far side of the room, with a water bowl and jug. There were shelves with cooking utensils and platters. I sat at the small table and watched as he took bread and cheese from a slatted cupboard and placed them before me, snatching up a jar of pickles and a pat of butter too.

"Please, help yourself," he said, taking a stone jar of ale from the highest shelf and using his sleeve to wipe dust off two earthenware beakers. "The cheese is unremarkable, but the bread is delicious, if I say so myself. I baked it yesterday. One of the advantages of my newfound trade; a miller is never short of flour. 'Tis only cheat bread, but fortunately I am a more accomplished baker than I am miller. Come along, tuck in. I'll have no guest of mine die starving because of manners."

He sat opposite me and began carving generous chunks from the loaf with the same bone-handled knife I had seen him use on the sacks earlier. Even slicing the bread was a task he tackled with alarming speed, the blade glinting in the summer sunshine, yet more flour rising up from the crust of the loaf.

"I am a little confused," I told him.

"No doubt. Everyone always is. Lots of questions, naturally. Ask away!"

"I had anticipated some manner of communication between us before . . . before we were to travel."

"I heard your call, loud and clear. Very good it was, very—" he paused, motionless for the briefest of moments, eyes raised to the high ceiling as he searched for the appropriate word. "Forceful," he said at last, before resuming piling food onto his wooden platter.

"But how did you know where . . . when *I wanted to go? I had given you but the scantest details."*

"English Civil War," he spoke as he chewed. "Batchcombe Hall." He used his knife to point over his left shoulder, evidently indicating the location of the great house. "Plenty to be going on with."

"As I recall, this country was engaged in sporadic war for over fifteen years. I only mentioned summer, and some details regarding the uniforms. You may have brought me to the right place, but what of the time? We could be years adrift from the date Gideon disappeared to."

"Possible," he conceded, washing down his bread and cheese with a long gulp of ale, "but unlikely."

His relaxed attitude began to grate upon me. "Mr. Balmoral—"

"Oh, call me Erasmus, I implore you!"

"I do not think you are fully aware of the gravity of the situation."

"Am I not?"

"I am not here on some flight of fancy. I did not undertake time stepping lightly. I understand it is not without risk. I have come here because I must, because someone dear to me, someone who depends upon my help, is in great danger. I must find her, and I must find her quickly. To be successful it is imperative I have arrived at the right time; I cannot afford to let the trail go cold. Tegan's very life depends on my finding her before . . . well, the point is, there is no time to be wasted. I have neither the patience nor the wish to observe the niceties of being a guest, or to take in the view, or to sit here while a violent, evil man holds an innocent young woman captive."

Erasmus finished his mouthful and dabbed at his lips with a floury kerchief, which he then dropped onto his plate, before leaning back in his chair. He studied me, his head tilted, and when he spoke his voice was, for the first time, level and serious.

"Madam, trust me when I tell you no one engages in the potentially perilous business of time stepping without a compelling reason to do so. Aside from the individual's own wishes, no Time Stepper would agree to be of service to or for, as you so quaintly put it, a 'flight of fancy.' What is more, while you yourself are by all accounts, a highly . . .

Xanthe squinted at the page as the flame of the candle guttered, the writing becoming blurred. At the same time, Elizabeth's voice faded. She concentrated on the words as they continued to be formed and strained to listen to the story she was being told, but she had the sense she had missed a slice of the tale. She did not have time to wonder how significant that gap might be as the writing became clear again and Elizabeth's rich tones took up the story once more.

". . . and prepared to kill anyone in order to do so," I added.

"So it would seem," he agreed. "A warlock, you said in your summoning, given to using aliases, then?"

"Indeed he has used many variations on his name . . ." I stopped speaking as, at

that moment, a movement caught my eye. Aloysius had been tempted from his hiding place by the smell of fresh bread and pungent cheese. He scampered across the table. With startling speed my host drew back his knife and threw it. I had not time to shout, but instinctively released a protective pulse of magic that reached the mouse a fraction of a second before the blade, deflecting the knife and sending it crashing to the floor. It was not a spell as such, not a considered act. It was a natural response for me when someone close was threatened.

"Good Lord!" Erasmus exclaimed.

"This is Aloysius. He is accompanying me on my quest," I explained, breaking off a morsel of cheese and feeding it to the mouse, who was utterly unperturbed.

"I don't know which surprises me more," Erasmus said, retrieving his knife, "that your skill is so impressive, or that you choose to bring a rodent with you."

"He belongs to Tegan. He may be of assistance." When this remark was met with raised eyebrows, I went on, "He is no ordinary mouse."

Erasmus laughed loudly at this. "I fear his singularity may be lost on the family of cats that patrol the mill!"

"We will be on our guard for predators," I assured him. "And we would appreciate you not using him for target practice."

"Forgive me . . . Aloysius, was it?" He made a solemn bow to the mouse. "I rarely fling knives at my guests. I promise not to do it again. You are most welcome here." He poured us both a little more ale.

The voice fell silent. The words stopped their flow. Xanthe waited, breath held, hoping for more. Nothing. Whatever message, whatever wisdom or information the book had wanted to share with her was at an end for the moment. She let out the held breath, letting it turn into a long, heartfelt sigh. Somewhere in what she had been shown—which was clearly the first meeting of Erasmus and Elizabeth—lay a gem of illumination. She could not be certain, but she was fairly sure that it was more than likely centered around what Elizabeth had quite plainly described as magic.

She closed the book, pulling it into a close embrace under the warm covers, blew out the candle, and closed her eyes. Unable to fight fatigue anymore, she hoped fervently that in her dreams, her mind might make sense of what she had been shown.

The next day she was woken up somewhat earlier than she would have preferred by Elizabeth walking into her room carrying an armful of clothing, which she dropped onto the bed before stepping to the window to open the curtains.

"Good morning, Xanthe," she said cheerily. "I may call you by your first name, I hope? Erasmus told me of your conversation last night and how happy he is to have you here."

Xanthe yawned, blinking away sleep, trying to shake slumber from her mind and focus on what Elizabeth was saying. "Morning. Goodness, it's bright out there," she added, shielding her eyes from the sunshine streaming into the room. She adjusted her mindset to accommodate the fact that her hostess would now know all about her being a Spinner and the purpose of her being in London at that particular time. It was a relief to be able to drop any pretense, and reassuring to think she now had the assistance of both Balmorals. What Elizabeth could not know was what the *Spinners* book had shown her the night before. The intriguing glimpse into her hostess's character and capabilities made her look at the tall, poised woman in a fresh light.

Elizabeth turned to her, hands on hips. "A fine morning for a walk," she said.

"A walk?"

"It will enable you to find your bearings. To comprehend where, and indeed when, you are. Your mission is not an easy one. The better you understand your surroundings, the better prepared you will be to survive them."

"Survive them! That sounds as if you think this is a dangerous place to be," she said, sitting up and pushing her unruly curls off her face.

"That bruise on your cheek and the cut on your lip should remind you of precisely that. Though it is not the city's more ordinary inhabitants you need fear. You tread a singular path, my dear. You may venture into places where you are not welcome by all, in order to achieve your goal."

"Which is to find Liam. Which is why I'm not sure I have time to go for a walk."

"Indeed? And what else would you be doing?"

"Well, there are things Erasmus and I need to talk about—"

"Which you can do well enough later in the day. I believe he counseled patience. The waiting will be more tolerable if you are occupied."

"But, he wanted to talk to me. I still have so many questions."

"And you will form them all the better after some air and exertion."

"And the *Spinners* book—"

"Can there be anywhere safer for it than with he who bound its pages and worked the very leather of its cover? And besides, while we are walking we can both of us be alert for any sign of your friend, or his abductor. If we encounter people I know who might assist us in our search, so much the better."

"Fair point," she conceded, swinging her legs over the side of the bed. She was aware at once how peculiar her long T-shirt must look to a woman from the Victorian era. Elizabeth, however, made no comment about it. Instead she sorted through the clothes that she had brought with her.

"We will pass more easily in all quarters if you are more . . . suitably attired. To this end I have found you an ensemble. It belonged to a young friend of mine. She keeps it here for visits. I believe you are almost the same size, though you are a little taller. Come, come, let us steal a march on the day." She held up a fine cotton camisole, giving it a little shake as if to encourage Xanthe to make haste.

The outfit was far more complicated than anything she had worn on her most recent bit of time travel. Mercifully, the fashion for enormous hooped crinolines had passed, so that she was spared having to wear anything so vast and cumbersome. There was a tight corset, which fitted over the camisole, but was surprisingly comfortable. This was partly due to it being cut at the front in a shape that allowed for a person actually having a stomach and curves. It also helped that she was naturally slim, but even so she felt a tiny bit claustrophobic as Elizabeth laced up the stays for her.

"You will become accustomed to it in time," she told her, tying off the laces. She held up a pair of bloomers, took in the sight of Xanthe's modern underwear with a raised eyebrow and changed her mind. "Perhaps not," she said, putting them to one side. "Now, petticoat next."

Xanthe stepped into the full white cotton underskirt which was then tied at her waist. On top of this was secured a small bustle. She could not help giggling at the use of such a thing to exaggerate her rear end in a way that would horrify a modern woman. It wasn't heavy, however, and did have the effect of making her already slender waist look even smaller. A lightweight sleeveless vest went over the corset to hide the lines and fastenings. Elizabeth handed her fine silk stockings, which she sat down to roll up over her feet. Two lacy garters held them in place. While she was seated, Elizabeth passed her a pair of brown leather lace-up boots and a buttonhook. After watching Xanthe fumble for a moment she took the hook from her and finished the lacing.

"Stand up," she said, lifting the skirt from the bed. "This you can step into, yes, that's right. And fasten it yourself, as the buttons are at the side, do you see?"

Xanthe did as she was instructed. Finally she was handed the matching jacket, which she shrugged on. It was a good fit, the shape flattering as she did up the row of tiny covered buttons down the front. She ran her hands down the pretty cotton. The fabric was pale blue with tiny white flowers and sprigs of green leaves, giving the whole outfit a cheerful, summery feel. The long jacket nipped in at the waist and flared over her hips, cut away at the front to reveal the skirt beneath, the waistband of which was a contrasting navy, as were the cuffs and hem. She stepped in front of the looking glass in the corner of the room and turned around slowly, feeling really quite pleased with how she looked until she saw Elizabeth's frown.

"Isn't it quite right?" she asked.

"Not yet. One or two things are missing." So saying, she pulled open the doors of the wardrobe and after a moment's rummaging emerged with a pair of navy gloves, buttoned at the wrists, and a small blue and green straw hat. Xanthe was relieved not to be forced into a floppy bonnet that would make her feel blinkered. This headgear was more like a fascinator, to be worn at an angle and finished with a perky plume of matching feathers. She lifted her heavy hair and twisted it into as tight a bun as she could manage, taking the proffered hairpins to secure it in place. Elizabeth found a fearsome hatpin with which to secure the hat.

For an instant Xanthe thought of the hatpin that had sung to her. Should she have followed that first? Might it have taken her directly to Lydia Flyte? No, she had convinced herself, this was where she was meant to be. For now, at least.

"Let us have another look at you." Elizabeth held her gently by the arms and turned her toward the window and the light. At last she smiled, a beautiful, warm smile, her eyes a little wistful, as if she were remembering someone else dear to her.

"Will I do?" Xanthe asked.

"Yes, my dear, you will do very well indeed."

7

THE MORNING CONTINUED BRIGHT, IF COOL. AS SHE STEPPED OUT OF THE FRONT DOOR onto the busy street, Xanthe experienced once more the thrill of being among people from the past, stepping into their lives, moving through the crowds for all the world as if this was her place and her time. A handsome couple, dressed for a morning ambulation, brushed past her so close she could smell the rose water on the young woman's clothes and feel the swish of her skirt, which had a fish tail, hitched up by a clip so that it did not drag in the dirt. Horse-drawn cabs moved swiftly up and down the street, and pedestrians trod warily if they needed to cross, having to navigate both vehicles and dung. A newspaper seller called out headlines from his corner pitch. A barrow boy wheeled a cart laden with fruit slowly along the length of the street. In an alleyway off the main route three dogs fought over a bone. Smartly dressed men of business strode by with purpose, many sporting gleaming top hats. Two shoeless children, no more than five or six years old, sat on the cobbles, hands out, palms up, begging for coins. It struck Xanthe that this was a part of the city where poverty and privilege lived cheek by jowl.

As they weaved their way through the melee, Elizabeth pointed out places of interest. They were in Holborn, she explained, between the financial part of the city which housed the Bank of England, and Drury Lane, leading to Shaftesbury Avenue, where most of the famous music halls and theaters were situated. As they made their way west, Xanthe found herself examining the faces of the people she passed, searching for Lydia Flyte among the women, and for Liam among the men. However unlikely it was that she should spot either of them, it was impossible not to try, not to hope. Impossible, indeed, to fully concentrate on what she was being shown, when all the time finding Liam was uppermost in her mind. Whatever her hosts thought about biding her time, waiting for Mistress Flyte to make her move, it was torture to be so passive in the whole situation. She was in the right place—the city at least—and the right time, that much she was certain of. And Erasmus agreed. How could she just twiddle her thumbs until the moment suited the woman who had, after all, kidnapped her friend?

As if reading her mind, Elizabeth stopped walking for a moment and turned to her. "You will tire yourself, worrying so," she said.

"I can't help it. I shouldn't be sightseeing. I should be searching for Liam."

"Don't you know that is precisely what you are doing?" When Xanthe looked puzzled, she continued. "As you are aware, a Spinner can detect the presence of another. As can a Stepper, of course. Rather than have you sit and wait in one place, Erasmus decided it would be more effective if you were to circulate among the population. To move slowly about the area."

Understanding dawned. "You are using me as bait?"

"No. You are using yourself as bait." With that she resumed walking, her stride long and elegant, her back straight, but a noticeable upward curve to her lips.

Xanthe scurried after her, unaccustomed to the weight of her skirt and the curious way the bustle unbalanced her. She found she could only move more swiftly if she too maintained a ramrod spine and upright deportment. "Wait a minute . . . all that nonsense about fresh air and keeping busy . . . you and Erasmus just wanted me out here to, what, draw the attention of another Spinner?"

"My husband is experienced in the business of finding people. His ways are, for the most part, successful." Elizabeth stopped walking. After a moment's thought she put a hand on Xanthe's arm and said simply, "Trust him. Like you, I had to, when I had only just met him. That trust was a leap of faith. He has never given me reason to regret it." She slipped her hand under Xanthe's arm then, patting her hand affectionately. "Come along. We require the attention of a Spinner, not the curious stares of passersby who are of no use to us whatsoever."

They walked on along High Holborn, turning down Drury Lane, and toward the mayhem and bustle of Leicester Square, the very center of theater land. The people altered subtly as they moved away from the businesslike area toward one of entertainment and gaiety. Even though it was morning, there was a sense of the theatrical about the place. Performers were arriving for rehearsals. Sets were being constructed. Musicians practiced in rooms off the main street, doors flung wide to let the air in and the notes out. Through open windows came the sounds of dance masters drilling the corps. Singers trilled scales. Dray horses, huge, with great hairy legs and hooves the size of dinner plates, clopped by bearing wagons loaded with barrels of ale to replenish stocks in taverns and inns and playhouses. Everywhere was activity and purpose, and that purpose was to put on a show and make money by the doing of it.

Xanthe felt drawn to the creative energy of the place. She almost wished that she had to use her cover of being a singer and actually find work in a music hall. To stand on a Victorian stage and sing to a full auditorium would be quite something. At last they reached Leicester Square.

There was a stall selling fat quartered oranges and Elizabeth purchased two, handing one of the squares of waxed paper to Xanthe.

"Here," she said, "I challenge you to eat these without getting juice on those fine gloves."

"That's impossible!"

"Like so much else, it is merely a matter of practice and determination. See?" She picked up a piece between finger and thumb, tipped back her head slightly, and expertly bit the flesh of the orange from its peel without a drop of juice escaping. The skin was completely clean.

Xanthe tried to copy her technique but failed messily, juice running beyond the glove and down the sleeve of her dress. Over Elizabeth's gentle laughter she asked, "How did you do that?"

Her host took another slice and repeated the trick. Once again, she ate every scrap of orange flesh without the merest hint of juice reaching her glove.

Xanthe tried again. This time juice dribbled down her chin and onto her jacket. "It's impossible," she said, taking the handkerchief she was being offered. "I have no idea how you manage it."

"Oh, just a little magic," Elizabeth replied, smiling.

She was just about to have a third attempt when she felt the tiny hairs on her arms prickle and rise. She was being observed. She was being scrutinized, and not by a man appreciative of her looks, or a thief checking the opportunity to pick a pocket. No, in that instant, she knew she was in the presence of another Spinner. She pivoted on her kitten heel, scanning the crowd, searching for Mistress Flyte.

Elizabeth noticed the change in her demeanor at once. "What is it?" she asked. "Have you seen someone you know? Have you heard something?"

"Not heard . . . but sensed. There is a Spinner nearby."

"Is it Lydia Flyte?"

"I can't be certain. Whoever it is, they're close." She wheeled round again, continuing to scour the throng of people in the square, but she saw no one she recognized. Her attention was snagged by a burly man, smartly turned out with cane, cravat, and topper. He was standing motionless as pedestrians surged around him, a river of humanity swirling around a rock in their midst. He paid them no heed. His focus was entirely on Xanthe. She met his stare with a steady gaze.

"Here I am, then," she said beneath her breath. "Come and get me."

—

As Liam was getting dressed there came a knock on his bedroom door. Opening it, he found the somewhat flustered kitchen maid holding a freshly laundered shirt and necktie and a long black jacket. She bobbed a curtsey.

"If you please, sir, ma'am says you are to wear these. She asks that you come down directly, as a carriage has been booked for ten o'clock."

He took the clothes. "Thank you . . . I'm sorry, I don't know your name."

"Millie, sir," she replied in a tiny voice.

"Millie, thank you for coming up all those stairs to bring me these. I know how busy you are. I appreciate it."

Millie turned pink to her ears and bobbed another curtsey. Liam wanted to put the girl at her ease but feared he was doing the opposite. He knew it could be helpful to have an ally in the house, but he wouldn't do anything that might get her into trouble with her mistress.

"Will that be all, sir?" she asked.

"Yes, Millie. Thank you," he said again. As he watched her go he thought about how hard and how cheerless her life must be, working in such a drab house with an employer who came and went mysteriously, and precious little money for anyone, by the look of it. This was something that had already struck him as odd. Lydia Flyte was evidently adept at spinning through time when it suited her. According to Xanthe, she'd been a successful businesswoman in several centuries. Why, then, with all the advantages time travel could give her, was she living in comparative hardship?

He dressed quickly, struggling a little with the unfamiliar neckwear, and went downstairs. He found his captor taking tea at the table in the small living room. He noticed she was wearing a more expensive-looking gown than the day before, in a dark green with cream lace, and had found a few pearls to dress it up.

"Will you have something to eat before we leave?" she asked, offering him a seat.

He sat opposite the old woman, helping himself to scones and jam as she poured strong black tea from an elegant but chipped china pot.

"Are you going to tell me where we are going? Or why we are going there?" he asked.

"There is no necessity for you to have that information at this point."

"I'll take that as a no."

"Suffice to say, I require your presence at a meeting. You will not be called upon to do or say anything in particular, merely to attest to your origins. That will be enough."

Liam finished a mouthful of scone. The jam was watery, as if made cheaply, and there was no butter at all. "So, I take it the people we are going to see, they know what you are. They know that you've brought me here. Do they know you took me against my will?"

"That is a detail in which they would have little or no interest."

"In that case, I can't wait to meet them." He thought about the two men who had tried to abduct him from the alley the night before. He knew they were not out to mug him. They had made no attempt to rob him. They had wanted to take him somewhere. He couldn't remember being so in demand. It was a joke he would have enjoyed sharing with Xanthe. He felt a stab of longing for her, tinged with worry. He needed her to come after him, but what would she be stepping into? How much danger was she risking for him? He was far from comfortable with the thought that he was a helpless pawn in some elaborate game. Whoever Mistress Flyte wanted to parade him in front of, they evidently would not care at all for his welfare. He thought fleetingly of telling her about the would-be kidnappers but decided against it. She was not his friend. That much he knew.

Across the table, the old woman appeared to be contemplating her next words carefully too. She finished her tea, setting the little cup down in its saucer and staring into it as if seeking answers there. At last she looked up at him, her sharp blue eyes regarding him levelly.

"You may not approve of my methods, Mister Adams. You do not, I accept, understand either my motives or my goal. I would ask you to trust me but I am aware I have forfeited that trust by my actions. All I can reasonably hope for, I believe, is your cooperation in the small things I will ask you to do while we wait for Xanthe to find us."

"You think it's reasonable for a kidnapper to ask for cooperation from her victim? Really?"

"If not reasonable, let us say instead . . . advisable."

"Why is it that you turn asking for my help into making a threat?"

"I have no wish to see harm befall you."

"But you're willing for that to happen if it suits what you want. Look, I'm not going to make deals with someone who has abducted me. Whatever you were to Xanthe, you've thrown that away. Like I said, if you needed her help, you should have asked her."

"And as I believe I told you, I could not risk her refusing me." She stood up. "Come. The carriage will be outside, and we are expected elsewhere. It does not do to keep such people waiting."

The rented gig was pulled by a single, unremarkable horse, and consisted of a small covered conveyance with the driver sitting outside and up front, room for only two people in the boxlike arrangement behind. There was no footman from the house, and the driver clearly did not think it his job to move from his seat. Despite his views on what she had done, Liam found himself instinctively helping Mistress Flyte up the step and into her seat. She was, after all, elderly, and had not in fact done him any harm. So far. With the door shut, the driver issued a "Hup" and the carriage moved off, lurching forward, quickly giving away the fact that it had poor suspension and hard wheels. They rattled through the streets, being steered deftly if a little wildly away from the docks and through the increasingly busy streets. They skimmed the sides of the staggeringly high omnibuses crammed with people, and veered away from dray carts and wagons carrying goods to and from the waiting ships at the quay behind them.

As they moved north they encountered smarter outfits, more of them private conveyances, the horses and carriages improving in quality even to Liam's untrained eye. The men and women looked smarter too. Flat caps were replaced with bowlers or top hats. The dresses of the ladies became more elaborate and suggested more and more lives of leisure rather than work. There were fewer hawkers or beggars too. Their cab turned sharply right and had to slow to join the melee of traffic that was moving toward the east of the city. Liam took in the strange shops and businesses that lined the route: a haberdasher's that reminded him of the one in Bradford-upon-Avon; a pawnbroker's with bars on the windows; a pie shop with a small gathering of dogs waiting hopefully outside it; a gentlemen's outfitters; a sweet shop; and there, suddenly, a bookbinder's establishment. At that moment, the congestion on the street caused their driver to rein in his horse, so that they came to a halt outside the window of the business that declared itself to be that of ERASMUS BALMORAL ESQUIRE, BOOKBINDER. A distant memory stirred in Liam's mind. Something Xanthe had spoken of. Something he could not quite recollect properly. He noticed too a minute alteration in Mistress Flyte. Her whole body seemed to stiffen, and she turned slightly, not to look at the shopfront, but to look pointedly out of the window on the other side of the carriage. She called to the driver, urging him to move on and be quick about it. There came a gruff, unintelligible reply and the horse leaned into its collar once more, picking up the pace and bearing them on and away.

After a further ten minutes' driving they had left the hectic center of the city. They had moved too from the salty, dank smell of the dockside, through the grimy, dung-filled aroma of the busiest streets, to a place that smelled of sweet chestnut trees, macrocarpa hedges, and roses. Liam saw now that the roads were wider, avenues, in fact, with more trees shading and sheltering the pavements. Most of the buildings were not businesses but residences. There were some modest houses, but the majority were quite grand, white stucco, some with Grecian porticos in the Georgian style, set back from the road. They had gardens and room for a carriage or two. Some had stables attached. There was an expensive, prosperous, lavish feel to the area, making him wonder at the fact that Mistress Flyte moved in such circles.

The cab took them to one of the largest houses in the avenue. It swung onto the private drive and pulled up outside the smart entrance. Mistress Flyte turned to Liam.

"I may not have taken you into my confidence regarding the purpose of my visit, but know this," she said. "It is work of the upmost importance we undertake here, whether willingly or not. I make no threat when I say it will be better for all of us that I have your cooperation."

"And what would that cooperation look like, exactly? If I don't know what we're here for . . ."

"Follow my lead. Do not volunteer information. Answer direct questions truthfully but with reserve."

"I have a question for you first," he said, his hand on the door handle to prevent her opening it. "Will my helping you make things safer for Xanthe?"

She looked him in the eye. "As I have said, Mister Adams, it will be the better for all of us."

When he could see she wasn't going to elaborate he turned the handle and pushed open the door. A footman had dashed out from the house in time to offer his hand to Mistress Flyte and assist her down the step. Once they were both outside Liam paused beside her. He knew she could not be entirely trusted and yet there was something about the way she spoke to him, something in the seriousness with which she approached what they were doing, that made him believe what she told him now. He needed to go along with her plan, even though he didn't know what it involved or where it might lead. He held out his arm for her.

"Shall we?" he asked.

Clearly relieved at this indication that he would do as she wished, she nodded, put her gloved hand on his arm, and together they went inside.

The hallway was both broad and tall and designed to impress. There were two marble pillars at the start of the grand sweep of stairs. The floor was also marble, and the walls painted white, giving the whole place a crisp, classical, and sophisticated feel. Maids and footmen appeared on swift and silent feet to take hats and gloves from the guests. Liam noticed another carriage drawing up behind them. From upstairs came sounds of chatter and activity. They were not to be the only visitors to the elegant and imposing house, it seemed. Despite the early hour, they appeared to be about to attend a party of sorts.

They were invited to follow a footman to the first floor. He took Lydia's arm again as they mounted the staircase. They were led to a room that ran the width of the house, with six floor-to-ceiling windows facing out onto the avenue, letting the morning sunshine flood inside. The room was dressed with restraint and taste, rather than the overfilled and eclectic Victorian fashion he had half expected. There were slender-legged sofas and chaises placed in small groups to encourage sociability; card tables set in one corner, already busy with keen players; a grand piano at the far end, being played well by one of the guests while another sang; and areas where yet more visitors stood and mingled, chatting brightly while servants flitted among them replenishing glasses of champagne or offering strong Turkish coffee from tall pots. Trays of canapés were distributed with equal skill so that nobody should ever go hungry or thirsty. It did not escape Liam's notice that the men were expensively turned out and the women wore a striking amount of jewels.

He accepted a flute of champagne, though Mistress Flyte declined one. He could see she was, if not actually nervous, then definitely on her guard. He scanned the crowd to try to work out who the hosts of the event were. Everyone looked so well dressed and upper class it was hard to single out one person or couple who might own such a fine house. Not one to usually bother much about his clothes, even he began to feel underdressed.

He leaned close to Mistress Flyte.

"So whom are we here to see?" he asked quietly. "Which one is our host?"

"I am here on the invitation of Mister James Dawlish. You are here because of me. Everyone else is here to further their own interests."

"Which one's Dawlish? He must be pretty wealthy to own this place."

"He and his associates are indeed in possession of a great deal of wealth. Not all of it in truth their own and little of it legitimately come by. There, the gentleman with the trimmed whiskers and monocle."

Liam followed the direction of her gaze. He was surprised to see a red-faced, jovial man with a broad smile evidently sharing a successful joke with his guests. If it was serious business they were engaged in, James Dawlish was doing a great job of hiding that seriousness.

"The man beside him," Lydia went on, "the one with fair hair and the scarlet waistcoat, that is his associate, Sir Harold Brook-Morton. This is an enterprise in which they are equally complicit."

He tried and failed to work out whether or not this meant they were more than business partners. The blond man appeared as relaxed and easygoing as his partner, happily engaged in conversation with his guests, hailing a footman for more champagne with a click of the fingers and a smile, for all the world as if the two were celebrating a birthday or a win on the horses.

Lydia Flyte whispered urgently, "I must talk with them, and it is better I do so in public. Come." She set off in the direction of the two men. Liam followed.

On seeing her, James Dawlish beamed and his associate quickly brought his own conversation to an end. Both hosts turned their full attention not to Lydia but, much to his surprise, to Liam himself.

"Ah, a new member for our little society! And our thanks to you, Miss Flyte, for bringing him here," said Dawlish, adjusting his monocle for a better view.

Brook-Morton offered his hand and Liam found himself shaking it without having much choice in the matter.

"Delighted to make your acquaintance, young man. Delighted indeed," he said enthusiastically, though he did not ask for his name. "Miss Flyte, he is . . . as you assured us?"

The question was annoyingly vague. Liam studied Lydia Flyte's face as she answered. "He is. And I have brought him to you as I promised I would." She made a point of taking in the people standing nearest to them as she spoke, deliberately including them in what seemed to Liam to be a rather private conversation. If he knew anything about her, he knew she would have carefully thought out reasons for such an action. "I have fulfilled my part of the bargain," she stated.

Dawlish widened his eye so that the monocle fell to dangle on its string. "Time will tell, madam," he insisted with a broad grin, which displayed the gap between his two front teeth. "Time will reveal all."

Brook-Morton had at last released Liam's hand but was now scrutinizing him in the manner of somebody assessing a horse for possible purchase. "He is well? He has suffered no ill effects?" he asked.

"None at all," Mistress Flyte confirmed.

Liam became uneasy. Was he being sold? His presence at the event was evidently part of a bargain struck by his abductor and these strange men. What was even more curious was that she wanted as many people in the room as possible to know of the transaction. To witness it, and somehow to then make sure that the men upheld their part of the deal. But what was she expecting from them? And did she really mean to give him over to these strangers? He felt a surge of panic and anger. She was betraying the small trust he had only just decided to place in her. And if she sent him away with these men, surely it would be harder for Xanthe to find him. After all, she must be able to find another Spinner more easily than a non-Spinner. He needed to stay with the old woman, and he needed more answers.

"My name is Liam Adams," he said as naturally as he could. "Pleased to meet you. Thank you for inviting me to your beautiful home." Out of the corner of his eye he saw Lydia shoot him a stern glance. This was not the behavior she had asked of him. He ignored her. He was not going to stand by and be part of a deal he had no say in.

Now it was Dawlish's turn to shake his hand. "Your arrival has been most keenly anticipated," he assured him. "Will you take more champagne?" He hailed another footman and pressed a fresh glass into Liam's hand, relieving him of the one he had only just finished. "You will, I have no doubt, be a valuable and successful member of our little club. Don't you think so, Harry?"

Brook-Morton nodded, his blond hair flopping into his eyes as he did so. "Hear him speak, James! See the way he stands. He is exactly what we have been waiting for."

Liam's stomach lurched. He now felt deeply uncomfortable. What the hell, he wondered, was Lydia Flyte playing at? He threw her a look, trying to read her reaction to what the men were saying and the way they were saying it. Her face was impassive. Dawlish was waffling on about the house.

"We are but recently settled here. It gladdens me to know it is to your liking. You will be happy here, I believe."

"Happy and successful!" put in Brook-Morton.

Liam opened his mouth to protest. He wanted to make it pretty clear pretty quickly that there was no way he was going to be staying in the house. He felt the touch of soft glove leather as Lydia took his hand. She smiled up at him and then at her hosts.

"So eager, gentlemen. I understand your fervor, believe me. Alas, such complex and important arrangements as ours require time in the planning and the unfolding. As we agreed, if you recall? I cannot possibly give up Mister Adams's company so soon."

Both men took in her words with reluctant good humor, that much was obvious. They mastered their impatience, however, and were soon all solicitous smiles once more.

"Your diligence does you credit, Lydia," Brook-Morton told her, the use of her first name drawing interest from those listening. Whatever was taking place, the old woman had now secured a position in the inner circle of the club Dawlish had mentioned. Liam still didn't know what the purpose of the group could be, or why she was so determined to be a part of it. What was becoming increasingly clear to him, however, was that, somehow, he himself played a vital part in her getting what she wanted. The stakes were as high as they could possibly be.

One of the other partygoers—a middle-aged woman in a black silk dress—stepped in.

"Perhaps our new friend would like to play a hand of cards. I find myself in need of a partner."

For the second time in as many minutes, Liam found himself being assessed as if he were goods for sale. It was not a feeling he was eager to repeat.

"I am sorry, madam, I have no talent for card games."

"Oh? Such a shame," she said, disappointed.

Lydia still had hold of his hand. He was surprised when she began to lead him in the direction of the piano.

"Mister Adams," she revealed to anyone who wanted to hear, "is, in point of fact, accomplished at the piano. Would you play for us, Liam?" she asked.

He knew a diversion when he saw one and was grateful, at least, for the way she was putting him beyond the reach of anyone who seemed to want to monopolize him. He nodded, as there was a clamor for him to play. As he took his place at the keys he experienced a moment of blankness when he tried desperately to bring to mind a piece of music that would fit the period. He could hardly bash out one of the indie rock tunes he and Xanthe and Tin Lid performed at The Feathers. He was fairly certain Beethoven predated the era. Offering a tiny prayer of thanks to his mother for forcing him to attend traditional piano lessons for years after school, he picked his way cautiously but successfully through *Moonlight Sonata,* his fingers working through distant memory, while his mind raced to find a way out of the increasingly worrying situation in which he now found himself.

8

BY THE TIME LIAM HAD PLAYED BEETHOVEN'S WORK FOR A SECOND TIME AND THEN treated the room to an improvised piece made up of snatches of remembered classics and riffs of his own imagining, he had garnered rather more attention than he wanted. As he played he was both surprised and interested to see the woman in black silk engaged in a highly flirtatious exchange with Brook-Morton. He took this as a hopeful sign that he had not been procured for some sort of tryst with the men at least. As he stood up, took a little bow, and moved away from the piano he saw that James Dawlish also had a pretty girl on his arm. Lydia Flyte congratulated him on his recital.

"You play better than I expected," she said.

"Then you must have had fairly low expectations," he replied quietly. "Now, are you going to tell me what those two men want from me or not? Because I give you fair warning, I am not being left here with them, no matter what deal you think you've struck using me as a bargaining chip."

She took his arm again, smiling to put onlookers off the scent of the seriousness of their exchange. "You are far too valuable an asset to me to be handed over on first meeting. No, we will leave here together but not for some time. When the other guests have left we will talk with the pair and you will understand what is afoot. For now, I suggest you enjoy your newfound popularity. Be pleasant. Be evasive.

Make the most of the refreshments on offer. Tonight, you shall have your answers."

A glance around the assembled company revealed a number of women watching him keenly. Liam gave a shrug. "Once a pop star . . ." he said, helping himself to a smoked salmon canapé from a nearby silver platter. The following hours passed with him taking part in a social dance of engagement and avoidance. He joined in light chatter, giving away so little about himself that he merely succeeded in adding to his appeal with mystique. Fueled with good champagne and delicious food he found it easy enough to flatter the women or listen with feigned interest to the tales the men spun of their wild boar hunting in France, or fishing on their Scottish estates, or sharing risqué jokes with minor royals. He made sure not to get drunk, and always to keep Mistress Flyte in sight. Despite her assurance that they would leave together, he was determined not to give her the opportunity to slip away unnoticed. The gathering was good-natured and pleasant, the guests evidently accustomed to luxury and not given to excesses, at least when attending a daytime function. Liam did his best to work out what it was, beyond their obvious wealth, that connected them. He wasn't familiar with Victorian social habits but even he could tell there was something unusual about this gathering. Dawlish and Brook-Morton had both mentioned a club or society, but no one had named it, and he had no idea what it was for. Whatever it was, a common factor was most definitely money, a point that was confirmed by the high stakes at the card table where people risked, lost, or won with equanimity. It was nearly six o'clock when the footmen showed the last of the other guests out of the house. Liam and Lydia were invited to move to the small study off the grand reception area. This was a room beautifully paneled with oak, with tall bookshelves and red leather Chesterfield sofas. They took their seats on one side of the fireplace, with their hosts sitting opposite. A butler served strong Turkish coffee in tiny china cups, into which were plopped golden nuggets of sugar. Liam stirred his thoughtfully, glad of the coffee to sharpen his mind after all the champagne. It was Mistress Flyte who spoke up first.

"Gentlemen, I believe the time has come for Mister Adams to be fully appraised of your work here, and, of course, of his possible role. Should he undertake to accept it."

He was surprised to hear he was to be allowed a choice.

It was Dawlish who took it upon himself to explain. He removed his monocle and leaned back in his seat, his ruddy cheeks all the redder for an afternoon of drinking, setting his coffee cup on his knee, smiling. He was a man who exuded confidence in himself, his place in society, and the details of that rare existence that he was about to present to his new acquaintance.

"Many years ago, I met my good friend Harry—" here he paused to nod to Brook-Morton "—in strange circumstances. We were both engaged in missions, let us call them, for the furtherance of our own fortunes, in a way that many young men are. What was curious, in our cases, was not the purpose of the endeavor, rather it was the methods we employed to enrich our finances, our experiences, and our standing in this harsh and unforgiving world. For though our paths had not previously crossed, we shared a singularity that set us apart from others and placed us within a community that is at once rare and privileged. On meeting we quickly learned that we were both Spinners of time." He delivered this last line with a theatrical flourish before resting, letting the words settle on the listener's ears before continuing. "Of course, Mistress Flyte, being one of our own, is fully aware of what we are and what it is we do. I understand, from what she tells me, that although you have succeeded in traveling through the centuries you are not, in point of fact, a Spinner yourself. Have I that aright, Mister Adams?"

"Exactly right," he replied cautiously. He had not expected this revelation and felt a little stupid for not seeing that the connection Mistress Flyte had with these men was that of time travel. Xanthe would have detected their presence straightaway, but he could not do that. He had the uncomfortable sense that he was in a weak position, always a step behind, forever in the dark until or unless these incredibly gifted people felt like enlightening him.

"Ah," Dawlish went on, "then you will have experienced the thrill and delight of that adventure, while not, alas, being in possession of the power and freedom it bestows upon you. It is a privilege, there is none can deny that. It is also a gift, and as such, we believe, permits us to use it to our best advantage, to fulfill our potential, and to pass on that advantage to others."

Liam raised his eyebrows. "You see yourself as philanthropists?" he asked, failing to keep a loud note of skepticism from sounding in his question.

At this, Brook-Morton gave a sharp bark of laughter. "Ha! Much as James professes to see nothing but value in what we do, I doubt even he could lay claim to altruism."

Dawlish's ever-present smile faltered a little but did not entirely disappear. "We do well by our fellows and they by us. Less philanthropy, more symbiosis."

"I'll scratch your back if you scratch mine?" Liam suggested.

Lydia Flyte frowned but Dawlish found the idea highly amusing.

"A fair analogy!" he decided.

"What James is taking an age to tell you," put in Brook-Morton, "is that we established an organization. We named ourselves the Visionary Society, and it is this club, if you will, that offers all manner of unique services, all of which, on payment of a membership fee, guarantee an increase of wealth and a sound return on that investment."

"The Visionary Society?" Liam was surprised. "That sounds more spiritual than financial."

"We feel," Dawlish explained, "that it neatly encompasses what we are able to do with what it is our members require of us, and indeed, how they assume we go about gaining them their advantageous information. You see, you yourself are highly unusual, in that you not only know a Spinner, but you have moved through the eras yourself. No other members have your experiences or insight. And it is best they remain ignorant of our . . . methodology."

"After all"—Brook-Morton took a large cigar from a humidor on the table next to him and trimmed it—"we are not obliged to divulge our methods. Members pay their subscription so that we can furnish them with information that will give them enormous, almost priceless advantages in, say, the stock market, or at the races, or in matters of innovation or industrial design. They do not, nor must they, ask the how and the wherefores."

Dawlish nodded emphatically. "It is a condition of acceptance into our society that they do not probe deeply regarding our operations. They are permitted to set before us their requests, and to make them specific. Once we are satisfied they are not unreasonable, or impossible, we undertake to provide them with knowledge that will serve them well."

"So, let me get this straight," said Liam, quickly draining his coffee and holding out his cup for more with a quick smile of thanks to the butler. "You run a club where rich people pay you money to find out stuff that gives them the edge in business and so on to make them richer. How do they think you do it?"

"We don't let them question us on our methods."

"Yes, you've said that, but these are not shrinking violets. I mean, at least some of them must get eaten up with curiosity and want to know how you know what you do. What do you tell them?"

"You are correct," said Brook-Morton, "and initially it was something we were unprepared for. We quickly realized people need an explanation they can satisfy themselves with, even without proof. So we fabricated one that was not so very far from the truth—"

Dawlish could not stop himself interrupting. "Clairvoyance! You will have heard about the fashion for attending séances, I'm certain, for it is the very thing to be doing. Society ladies, their husbands, everyone loves to talk of the wickedly spooky and supernatural table at which they once sat to speak with the departed!"

"They think you get your information from dead people? They swallow that?"

Brook-Morton was affronted. "Truly, is it any more implausible than the reality of what we do, sir?" he asked, lighting his cigar at last and puffing crossly on it.

"Well," Liam chose not to notice the man's irritation, "it seems to me you gentlemen have got a pretty good racket going on. Plenty of well-heeled members, by the look of those partygoers. But I have no money. And I'm not a Spinner. What could you possibly want from me?"

Here Lydia Flyte sat a little straighter in her seat, setting her coffee cup on its saucer with the tiniest rattle of china upon china and betraying the fact that her delicate hand trembled as she spoke.

"It will not have escaped your notice, young man, that I am not a woman of means. I wish to become a member of the Visionary Society in order to improve my circumstances. Alas, I lack the funds required for the membership—"

"But," Liam could not help interrupting, "you're a Spinner yourself. Why do you need these people? Why don't you just do what they do, gain valuable information and use it to make money one way or another?"

"The plain fact is, I am old. A Spinner may delay their own aging to an extent by inhabiting different eras, but the years will ultimately take their toll. Now I am only able to spin through time at great personal cost. Indeed, it is something I may not do again. Inclusion in the Visionary Society is, I have come to believe, the only way for me to secure a comfortable retirement and shield me from poverty as my health declines."

He looked at her anew. She had been able to abduct him, showing great skill as a Spinner, whisking him away from Xanthe in a maneuver that was highly challenging and dangerous. She had succeeded in transporting him back in time to a precise place and moment. It was quite a leap to now see her as a frail old woman fretting about her pension. There was something more to it, he knew it. Something she was hiding not just from him, but from the men she now sought to impress. He turned to Dawlish, having decided that for all his bonhomie, he was in fact the senior of the two. He was the one who had to be watched the closest.

"So"—he put down his coffee cup and leaned forward—"Mistress Flyte needs a ticket into your little club, and if I've followed the way this is going, I am that ticket?"

Dawlish beamed. "Such a bright boy!"

Brook-Morton left off puffing his Havana for a moment. "I feel I should explain before James gives you entirely the wrong impression, however unintentionally. Our interest in you, Mister Adams, is one of a business nature. It is, as is so much of life, all about money. And, you will be pleased to hear, as men of business we understand that a transaction has the greatest chance of success if it is beneficial to all parties."

"You mean I could make money out of this too?" he asked.

"If you were prepared to assist us in our endeavors, a great deal of money," the blond man confirmed.

"And I would have to do what, exactly? I can't trot backward and forward in time like you can."

Dawlish shook his head, "On your own, no. But you have traveled as, shall we say, a *passenger,* several times."

"And suffered no ill effects," Lydia Flyte reminded them.

"While we still have many years spinning in us, being relatively youthful," Dawlish continued, "there is another limitation to our journeys, and it pertains in particular to traveling forward in time. Which is, after all, where we must go in order to gain information most of value to our members. You will appreciate, having spent time in an era other than that which you were born to, that it places certain demands and challenges upon a person, and puts them in quite a broad range of perils. These dangers, I am sad to say, increase exponentially the farther we travel into the future. It is a matter of incompatibility, you could say. Of our not fitting into a more modern time. Of our being, as it were, all at sea, with technology and so forth. Can you imagine?"

Liam thought about it and could imagine very well. Whereas traveling back in time had its own difficulties, a person from the modern world was, if anything, at an advantage. Someone going in the other direction, however, would be lost amid fast cars, digital devices, modern weapons, computers . . . they would be catastrophically vulnerable and unable to make sense of most of the information they found.

Dawlish raised and dropped his arms in a gesture of exasperation. "We attempted a journey to the late twentieth century and we were innocent babes among ravenous beasts in a jungle beyond our comprehension," he said.

Now Liam understood. "You need a guide. An interpreter. Someone who can protect you in the modern day and decipher stuff for you, help you find what might be saleable back here. Back now."

Brook-Morton nodded slowly. "There you have it," he agreed.

Dawlish sat back in his seat now, slapping his thighs. "He has it, yes! Capital! Here is a young man destined to make all our fortunes, I'd stake my house on it!"

To Liam's surprise, Mistress Flyte got to her feet.

"And now, gentlemen, we will take our leave. There is much for us all to consider. I have, I believe, kept my promise in bringing you someone from the future, as you requested. I trust this will facilitate my acceptance into the society, but I am aware Mister Adams will need time to decide for himself whether he wishes to be a part of what you do."

The men rose from their seats. They did not press the point by asking Liam directly if he would agree to work with them. He was uncertain whether this meant they were more or less reasonable. It could signify that they would wait patiently in the hope and expectation that he would see the wonderful opportunity they were setting before him and decide to join them. It could, on the other hand, indicate they would have his cooperation whatever it took and were merely allowing him the chance to comply and work for them willingly. If he decided to refuse, well, then he felt he might see another side to them. A more ruthless side. One that did not involve champagne and canapés.

In the hallway he was handed his hat. As Lydia Flyte was putting on her gloves and exchanging polite farewells he caught sight, through the window, of a man walking briskly toward the side entrance of the house. It was only a glimpse, but the burly shape, the broad shoulders, the stomping gait, and the set of the man's jaw were unmistakable. They were, after all, fresh in his mind, for it was only the previous evening that the very same man had attempted to abduct him in an alleyway and drag him into a carriage.

—

To Xanthe's surprise, the Spinner who had been watching her had not approached her. Instead, he had turned and melted away into the Leicester Square crowds. Anxious not to lose any possible connection to Mistress Flyte and Liam she had given chase, with Elizabeth at her side. They had weaved through the throng, both using their comparative tallness to scour the faces and shapes of the people ahead of him, but it was no use. Within moments the man had vanished, the trail gone cold. Xanthe had felt the weight of disappointment as they walked home. The city was noisy, smelly, dusty, and overcrowded. Her outfit, however lovely, was hot and heavy and restricted her movement. The streets themselves were full of fast-moving carriages, omnibuses, and wagons, none of which appeared to follow any sort of highway code or rules, so that crossing was an action fraught with hazard.

On their return, Elizabeth had insisted on a rest for her guest, citing her injuries of the previous evening, her time stepping, and her anxiety all as causes for fatigue. She had protested, but was eventually persuaded by the promise that she and Erasmus would spend the evening studying the *Spinners* book together and searching for clues as to Liam's whereabouts. A young housemaid, who worked only days, appeared in her room to help her undress. She left a china jug and a bowl of fresh water on the washstand. The damp weather of the previous day had been replaced by a warmer, heavier air that suggested thunder might not be far off. Xanthe was glad of the chance for a cool wash. She lay on the bed in her cotton slip and, despite still fretting about the slowness of her hunt for Liam, was soon asleep.

That evening, after a supper of cold meats, pickles, and a light soup, she and Erasmus went to his workshop together. For two hours they dived deep into the pages. It was a rare treat for Xanthe to be able to properly share the contents of the book, which were revealed to her host exactly as they were to her. Some of the stories that appeared were ones she had read before, including one of those that involved Erasmus and Lydia Flyte. She watched him carefully as he read about their love affair and thought how strange it must be to revisit it in such a way, centuries after it all happened. She was moved by how much reconnecting with the book affected Erasmus. He was able to explain some of the maps to her, and even found one she had not seen before that showed the blind house in her garden positioned on an intersection of two ley lines. He delighted in finding old friends depicted in some of the illustrations. That all of it meant so much to him she found both endearing and reassuring. It was as they were about to retire for the night that they heard shouts from downstairs. In the time it took Xanthe to gather her wits and recognize Nipper's voice, Erasmus had sprinted from the room.

"Secure the book!" he yelled to her as he left. "Protect it at all costs and do not for one moment put it aside!"

She picked up *Spinners,* wrapped it in a cotton cloth, opened her jacket, and pushed the package down into the waistband of her skirt, re-buttoning her jacket more loosely so that the book was hidden. From downstairs came further shouts and curses and sounds of a scuffle. She could hear Nipper and Erasmus. When she heard a short scream from Elizabeth she started toward the door. How could she stay hiding when they were clearly under attack and needed her? She had to fight her instinct to run down the stairs, Erasmus's words ringing in her ears. *Protect it at all costs!*

After another tortuous moment of shouting she heard a door slam and then silence descended. She crept to the top of the staircase, straining to make out the quieter voices that now replaced the earlier cries and oaths. She called down gently.

"Erasmus? Elizabeth?"

It was Nipper who appeared at the foot of the stairs, a handkerchief held to his bleeding mouth. "You may come down now," he said. "It is safe."

In the kitchen she found Elizabeth preparing a wash for Nipper's split lip. Erasmus's hand and sleeve were covered in blood. Xanthe gasped at the sight of it.

"Be at ease," he told her. "It is not mine."

She watched him rinse the blood from himself and from the thin, sharp knife he held. He wiped the blade carefully on a clean cloth and returned the weapon to a hidden pocket in his jacket.

Elizabeth bathed Nipper's wounds. The boy was more agitated than hurt.

"They came through the door!" he said through gritted teeth. "Our very front door! The louts! Would that I had a gun."

"Which would have likely caused you more harm than anyone else," Elizabeth said, dabbing a balm on his bruised eye that was beginning to swell.

Nipper winced and then frowned, which made him wince again. "The ruffians had cudgels. They were about the work of scoundrels, after the takings from father's business, thinking it easy money, no doubt."

Erasmus shook his head. "That is what they wish you to suppose," he said. "Their mission was not to rob us of a few pounds and the family silver." He paused and turned to Xanthe. "They came for the book."

"What?" She was confused. "Why do you think that? How would they even know it was here?"

"First," he replied, taking a bottle of wine from the shelf and fetching glasses as he spoke, "because at least one of them was a Spinner. I had no difficulty detecting that, being at such close proximity, though it was, in point of fact, his fellow thug who acquainted himself with my blade." He pulled the cork from the bottle and poured four generous measures of claret into ornate red Venetian glasses. "And second, they knew it was here because they followed you to our house."

It was Elizabeth's turn to be shocked. "But we attempted to follow the Spinner we encountered in Leicester Square and were unable to find him. How could he have followed us without our knowing?"

"I suggest by losing himself in the crowd and allowing you to think he had gone elsewhere he was able to track you unnoticed all the more easily. It was ever his intention to have you reveal to him where you were staying, which is, in all likelihood, where he would find the book."

Xanthe felt her own fury growing. "Damn it, I led them straight here! To the book and to your home." She looked at the state of poor Nipper's face and thought of how fierce the fight must have been. If the men had brought knives it could have ended in tragedy. "I am so sorry," she said quietly.

"Do not reproach yourself," said Erasmus, handing her a glass of wine. "We wanted to flush out Spinners, did we not?"

"Yes, but not like this! Not bringing your family into danger."

Here Nipper gave a snort. "Ha! Think you I am afraid of such men? We have known worse, in the course of father's work. They caught me off guard, is all," he added somewhat sulkily, showing the greatest wound was perhaps to his youthful pride.

Xanthe took a sip of her wine. It was rich and dry and strong and she was grateful for it. "So, if I've got this right," she said, choosing her words carefully, "there are Spinners out there who were waiting for me, who detected me once I was out and about, and who followed me here. Which means they knew I was coming, and they knew I would have *Spinners* with me."

"Which tells us," said Erasmus, pausing to taste the claret himself, "somebody has to have told them of your imminent arrival."

She nodded, her feelings of guilt for what she had brought upon this family being replaced with fury at the person most to blame for it. "And that person can only have been Mistress Flyte!"

"Indeed," Erasmus agreed.

"Then we have learned something else," said Elizabeth, drying her hands after putting away her medical kit. "Until this moment, Lydia Flyte did not know where you, Xanthe, were to be found."

"Of course," said Xanthe, "she wasn't expecting me to come here! She must have hoped I'd find something to take me straight to her."

Erasmus laughed briefly. "But then Spinners who are called are not sent where we wish to go, which, naturally in your case, Xanthe, would be straight to your lost friend. No, they are sent where they need to go."

Elizabeth nodded. "And you needed to come here," she said. "To us."

Xanthe thought again how she had still not entirely made sense of the fact that the writing box belonged to Elizabeth. She remembered that Erasmus had said they would talk more of the part his wife might play in her rescuing Liam. She made a mental note to make sure they had that conversation, and had it soon. "So, they know where I am. Presumably she will too, if she doesn't already, but we still don't know where she is. We're no further forward, back to waiting for her to reveal herself when she wants to." She sat down heavily on one of the kitchen chairs, her hand instinctively going to the book still concealed beneath her clothes. "I can't wait any longer," she announced. "Not after this. Who knows what they'll try next. I've got to take control of this situation."

Nipper took the compress off his eye. "I'm all for action," he told her. "Tell me what you would have me do, so that these ruffians may be brought to account."

"Thank you, Nipper, but for now it's me who has to do something. I have to go back to my own time and use the other found things. This time, I have to find the one that will take me to Lydia Flyte. No more waiting. I'm going to her at the time of my choosing and on my terms."

AS XANTHE PREPARED FOR HER RETURN JOURNEY, ERASMUS PACED THE SITTING ROOM offering advice.

"Do not, under any circumstances, attempt to travel with more than one object which sings to you. Successful journeys, whether considered spinning or stepping, depend on focus. Focus is all. By having two objects pulling in different directions you undermine that crucial aspect of our work."

"I will choose one found thing only," she assured him, standing still to let Elizabeth pin her hat to her hair. They had decided she should wear her new outfit. That way, when she followed the singing treasure to what she hoped would be Mistress Flyte's home, she would be properly dressed. She had discovered, on previous journeys, that things taken forward from the past had only a short life in the modern day. She remembered how the precious letter Samuel had given her had faded and crumbled in a few brief weeks. As she only planned to stay in her own time a matter of hours, this should not present a problem.

Erasmus continued both pacing and instructing.

"As you will have learned, time shifts at its own pace, and not ever at the same rate in different eras."

She nodded. "Straight there, choose object, straight back."

"Though you must not act so fast as to hasten that choice!" The conflicting requirements of her mission disturbed him. "It may take you some time to be certain. There is no room for error. Better your young friend tarry awhile longer in his place of incarceration than you make a false move. To determine the correct treasure I recommend listening to each away from the other so as not to be influenced, unwittingly, by the stronger pull. Which may not be the one you need. It can happen that more than one call to arms occurs at the same moment. Particularly—" here he paused to look at her "—particularly when a singularly gifted Spinner is involved. Tell me again what the objects were."

"A hatpin with a lapis lazuli stone, and a mourning brooch, hair woven into a picture behind glass in a gold setting. The hatpin is definitely Victorian. I think the brooch may be earlier, and more valuable."

Erasmus frowned. "I do not recall Lydia owning any such things."

"She may have acquired them after you stepped out of her life," Elizabeth suggested, betraying no hint of jealousy or reproach.

"Alas, then I can be of no assistance as to which might lead you to her," he said to Xanthe. "Perhaps I should travel with you! Yes, that may well serve our purposes. I can examine the treasures with you, aid you in your selection, and then we might travel home together. You should not, after all, be left to face the woman and her associates alone. This way I can accompany you . . ." He was lit up by the idea.

"No," she said gently, "thank you but no. I am traveling to my own time, so that bit's safe enough."

"That may be, but the return journey—"

Elizabeth put a hand on her husband's arm. "Erasmus, let the girl be. She knows what she is about."

He opened his mouth as if to argue the case further but, seeing the look on his wife's face, changed his mind.

Xanthe sought to reassure him as she hitched her satchel over her shoulder, the *Spinners* book safely inside it. "I know where you are now," she reminded him. "I know where to come for help if I need it. That was surely the point of the writing box, wasn't it? To bring us all together." Here she deliberately included Elizabeth and Nipper. She noticed the young man react to this, standing a tiny bit straighter, even blushing a little beneath his bruises.

Erasmus reluctantly conceded the point. "Yes. Yes, of course. You are right. We shall remain vigilant, awaiting your summons. From where do you wish to step?"

She was touched by his sensitivity. There was something private about beginning a journey through time. At home she had the seclusion of the blind house, and ordinarily secrecy was an important part of her travel home. On this occasion, however, in the company of people who knew exactly what she was about to do, she would have felt awkward asking for privacy, yet be self-conscious spinning while they watched.

It was Elizabeth who came up with an idea. "Might I suggest the roof? Come, let me show you." She offered her hand and Xanthe took it, following her out of the room before there could be any further farewells or advice given. They made their way up to the top floor and to a small, unremarkable door at the end of the landing. There were two heavy bolts across it, but the ease with which Elizabeth drew them back suggested the door was in fact in frequent use. She followed the older woman out onto the leaded valley between the slopes of two roofs. They walked a dozen or so yards before coming to a more open area of the roof; a small flat space at the base of a broad chimney stack which served as a safe side wall in their high location. A lower parapet, not visible from the street because it was set back a little from the facade of the building, provided another modicum of safety. From where they now stood the nighttime view of the city was spectacular. The night, though cloudless, was heavy with the smell of chimney smoke. The streets were gas lit, the lamps a thousand points of pulsing warm light. To the west lay the busy center spreading into acres of houses. To the east, Xanthe could make out the dome of St. Paul's Cathedral. Looking south she could see the slope of the city leaning down toward the Thames, which wound its way through the docklands. The sounds of late-evening traffic and revelers drifted up to them but seemed somehow more distant than a few storeys. It was as if they were removed to the position of observers of city life, rather than participants. The stink of the gutters was lessened, but the smoke from the factories a mile or two away carried on a light breeze and left a bitter taste on the tongue.

"This is a wonderful spot," she said, allowing herself a moment to marvel at the magic of where and when she was and how she came to be there.

"It is my little place of solitude," Elizabeth said, moving to stand beside her. "I was accustomed, for many, many years, to living alone. And mostly in the countryside. Becoming a wife and mother and making my home in the metropolis required certain adjustments. When I miss that solitary aspect of my life I come up here."

"I like the way it puts things in perspective. It seems to say we are tiny pieces of a bigger whole, and at the same time, that we can stand back from it all when we need to. For a clearer view."

Elizabeth smiled, her face illuminated only by secondhand lamplight from the streets below and starlight filtered through the exhaled breath of the city. "You can be sure that Erasmus has faith in you."

"He has?"

"Indeed. As do I." She paused, gazing out at the cityscape for a moment, her expression suggesting she was remembering something both distant and important. When she spoke again her face was serious. "There are some who are chosen for a higher purpose because of their strengths and talents. Others fall into their place in the world through events and circumstances not of their own making. Yet others move from one way of being to another and in doing so fulfill a potential the like of which they could not have dreamed. It matters not how we come to be who we are. What matters is how we proceed from that point of awakening. What we do with the challenges set us. How we behave toward others while we follow our destiny." She reached out and touched Xanthe's cheek lightly. "You put me in mind of myself when young, and of . . . someone dear to me. She too had your spark, your brave soul, and your determination."

"What happened to her?"

"She follows her own path, which rarely crosses ours, sadly. But that is as it should be. She has no need of me, and others have need of her gifts. Just as now, others have need of yours. You will prevail, Xanthe, of that I have not the slightest doubt. But still"—she dropped her hand and smiled again—"before I leave you to step through time, let me say a few words to send you safely on your way. Good wishes are never unwanted, wouldn't you agree?"

Xanthe nodded. As she watched, Elizabeth closed her eyes, raised her hands toward the sky, and began reciting strange words. Her voice was low, and the language unfamiliar to Xanthe, so that she had no way of knowing what was being said. She was, however, acutely aware of how the words made her feel. A peacefulness descended upon her, and at the same time a light prickling of her scalp. She experienced the prayer, if such it was, as a soothing balm for her taut nerves, a gentle caress of her soul, a protective wave of goodwill and sincerity that washed away tiredness and anxiety in seconds.

When Elizabeth had finished the incantation she opened her eyes and dropped her arms by her sides, a little out of breath.

"Travel well, young Spinner," she said, and then turned and stepped through the low door back into the house.

Alone at last, Xanthe took a breath, though she did not need to gather her wits. She felt suddenly entirely focused, calm, and determined. She fished out the gold locket from beneath her collar and held it firmly, registering the familiar warmth and smoothness of the precious metal. It was only as she closed her eyes and began her journey home that it occurred to her that what her new friend had bestowed upon her was not in fact a prayer, but a spell.

—

When she emerged into her own time and her own garden it was into bright sunshine. For a moment she was dazzled and stood blinking, waiting for her eyes to adjust to the light. She jumped when she felt something brush against her leg and then remembered Pie. The little dog wound itself around her in a frenzy of excitement.

"Well, pooch, that's a nice welcome home." She stooped to stroke the whippet's shiny black-and-white coat. "Did you miss me?" Together they made their way to the house. As she opened the back door she heard voices and did not have time to react before her mother and a broad-shouldered man appeared in the hallway. Flora gasped before recovering herself, hastening to find an explanation for the way her daughter had suddenly appeared from the back garden, apparently wearing fancy dress.

"Xanthe, love! I didn't hear you come in. On your way back from rehearsals?" Without missing a beat, she turned to her friend. "You remember I told you my daughter sings in a band? They're doing a night of old English folk songs. Doesn't she look lovely? Xanthe, this is Stuart. A fellow bell ringer."

"Hi, nice to meet you," she said, shaking his hand a little too enthusiastically. "Just finished. On my way upstairs to change." She gestured vaguely in the direction of the upstairs apartment, already slipping past the slightly puzzled middle-aged man.

"I'm glad to finally get to meet you too." He smiled. "That is an impressive costume. What a lot of trouble you go to for your music."

Flora took his arm and began to walk him toward the garden. "Which is why the band is always booked up. Very popular. Go on out and put up the umbrella, Stuart. I'll be with you in a second," she added, all but shoving him toward the door. As soon as he was out of earshot she spoke to Xanthe in a stage whisper.

"What are you doing back so soon? Where's Liam?"

"I haven't found him yet."

"What? The writing box didn't take you to him?"

"It didn't. I'm sorry, Mum, I don't have time to go through it all. I need to try the other treasures."

"They're up in your room."

"OK, I'll need to use the blind house. Can you lure your friend away again?"

"What? Oh, yes, of course. Don't worry, leave it to me."

"Thanks, Mum."

"I'd love the chance to talk to you before you go back. And how are you going to choose which thing to follow this time? I've so many questions! No, never mind. You know what you're doing. We've got to get you back there as quickly as we can."

"Exactly. Time moves differently in different eras. It might be a few hours or days for us, it could be much longer for Liam. But I can't just rush straight back. I have to know I've chosen the right piece to follow. I've got to get this right."

"You need to talk to Harley about it before you go. He's got news of his own. It might make a difference."

There came a shout from the garden. "Flora, do you want me to move the chairs into the shade?"

She squeezed her daughter's hand. "Go to The Feathers. Speak to Harley." Seeing Xanthe hesitate, she added, "It'll give me time to convince Stuart we'd be better off going out for a drink. OK?"

"OK. But half an hour and I'll be back. I need to make a start on listening to the found things and I really need to do that as close to the blind house as possible."

"Half an hour." Flora nodded.

As she turned for the back door Xanthe leaned forward and gave her a quick peck on the cheek.

"Don't worry, Mum. I've found help, in the time where Liam is. It'll be all right."

Flora smiled. "I never doubted it for a minute," she said. "Now go!"

After five frantic minutes of undoing tiny buttons and wriggling out of layers of Victorian clothing, Xanthe threw on a favorite vintage tea-dress, pushed her feet into her Dr. Martens, left the shop, and hurried through town. When she arrived at The Feathers she was astonished to find it closed. A notice on the door apologized for the inconvenience to customers and said the pub would be shut for "necessary refurbishment" for at least two months. She hurried along the lane at the side of the old inn and across the yard to the door at the rear. As always, it was unlocked. She pushed it open and called in.

"Harley? You around?" Hearing muffled cursing from the direction of the cellar she went to the entrance and peered down. "Harley?"

A familiar whiskery face appeared at the bottom of the stairs.

"Xanthe, hen! Back already? Is young Liam with you?"

"I haven't found him yet. I need to follow one of the other two things that sang to me. Harley, what's going on? Why is the pub closed?"

He hauled himself up the stairs, wiping his brow with a bar cloth.

"Deathwatch bloody beetle," he announced on reaching the top.

"What!"

"Aye, an infestation of the little bastards. Attacking the timbers. Munching their way through the very bones of the old girl," he explained, reaching up to pat a beam affectionately. "Have to have the whole place fumigated, at no small expense, I can tell ye. We're off up to Scotland to stay with Annie's mother." He wore an expression that showed something between despair and resignation.

"Oh, that's awful. I'm really sorry, to have to close the pub . . ." She knew it would have been a tough decision with serious financial implications.

"Never mind our wee bug problem, did the writing box not take you to the right place?" He glanced over his shoulder. "Annie's upstairs packing. Shall I come to yours for a chat?"

"I don't have much time."

"Step into the bar, then. I can still find us a couple of beers, surely."

He dropped the hatch on the top of the cellar stairs and they moved to the empty main bar. Xanthe felt a pang of nostalgia for the usual buzz and chatter, and for the last time she and Liam played there with Tin Lid. She wriggled onto a stool while Harley fetched bottles of local ales and expertly removed the tops before handing her one.

"So, in a nutshell, hen, what the hell happened?"

As briefly as she could, she recounted the tale of her travel. When he tried to interrupt with questions she had to hold up her hand, knowing it would take far too long to give him all the details. At last, he drank deeply from his beer bottle, wiped foam from his moustache, and gave a sigh.

"So," he said carefully, "let me see if I've got this right. The box took you to a Spinner's house, or rather to his wife, only he's not a Spinner anymore he's a Stepper, and Spinners and Steppers are agin one another, and Mistress Flyte has Liam in the middle of it somehow, and you've been followed and the house broken into, but we still don't know where Liam is."

"Steppers only have a problem with the bad Spinners, not the good ones. Otherwise, that's pretty much it. I can't wait any longer for Lydia to show her hand. Not with the other Spinners prepared to resort to violence. I have to choose the found thing that will take me directly to her."

"And have you decided which one that is? Hatpin or brooch?"

Now it was Xanthe's turn to sigh. "I wish I knew. Erasmus told me to listen to each one separately, for a clearer signal, as it were. I'm going to try that and then go straight back. Hopefully, straight to her, if I choose the right one."

"And if you choose the wrong one?"

"It could take me anywhere, a completely different time."

"And if it does take you to your old woman, what then? I mean to say, hen, she's shown herself to be capable of dirty deeds. She must be playing for high stakes to resort to kidnap. And if she's somehow mixed up with the thugs that broke into your man's house . . . what are you going to do if you find her and she just keeps you prisoner too? Let's face it, Liam would not be an easy person to contain if he wanted out. You're not aiming for a nice place to be, lassie."

"I have no choice. It's what I have to do."

He nodded, and then, slowly, a new idea lit up his face.

"You have to go, aye, that's a given. But you don't have to go alone!"

"Sorry?"

He straightened up, chest puffing out, fist thumping down on the bar in astonishment at the brilliance of his plan. "I can come with you!"

"Oh, Harley, I couldn't possibly. . . ."

"I beg of you, hen, do not tell me you couldn't put me in danger, couldn't risk my delicate wee neck. I have so wanted to travel with you, from the very beginning, as well you know. And now we know you can take someone with you. And you need someone. And"—he glanced at the ceiling, as if visualizing his wife in the apartment above—"and now I have a way I can help you. Annie can go to Scotland. I can say I've decided to stay here and oversee the workmen. Actually, I don't trust the lazy creatures, so it would all be very believable. And no, I don't like the idea of lying to her, but . . . hell's teeth, hen! This might be my one and only chance. And you need me. Can you deny that?"

Part of her wanted to. Wanted to say that she was fine, she could manage, she had new people to help her, she didn't need him. Not just because of her pride, but because she had already led one dear friend into danger and was in no hurry to do it again. But another part of her felt a surge of gratitude and of relief. Gratitude that Harley should step up so willingly, so bravely, knowing as he did the very real risks involved. Relief that she would not arrive at Lydia Flyte's home on her own, possibly, as Harley had so accurately pointed out, to become another prisoner, unable to contact Erasmus and Elizabeth for help, and useless to Liam.

Harley saw her hesitate. He watched as she weighed up the options.

"Give me the chance to help you and Liam, hen. Give me the chance to go on what might just be the biggest, maddest, un-bloody-believable-est adventure of my whole entire life!" He could not resist banging the bar with his mighty fist again, making the bottles on it rattle. He smiled at her, his best, brightest, most hopeful smile.

She found herself smiling back. She looked him up and down critically.

"What?" he asked. "Are you thinking I'm too fat, too slow, too old? Let me tell ye, lassie, I can put on a turn of speed when called upon to do so and—"

"I'm thinking, Harley, that we are going to have to pull out all the stops to pass you off as a Victorian gentleman, and if we're going to do it we'd better get started."

He took in the meaning of her words and let out a whoop of sheer joy, swiftly followed by a mumbled apology. He started prattling on about a pair of steampunk goggles he could dig out and a bowler hat and an old tweed deer-stalking jacket that had belonged to an uncle from the Highlands until Xanthe had to shush him.

"Harley, I'm sorry to burst your bubble, but listen to me. We will get your costume sorted out, somehow, but the first thing you have to do is go upstairs and lie to your wife."

She watched the fun drain from his expression, the seriousness of what he was doing taking hold. The price he would have to pay being asked of him not at some vague time in the future, but there and then.

He tugged his leather waistcoat a little straighter over his large tummy. "Right you are, lassie," he said calmly. "Right you are," he repeated as he marched toward the stairs to the apartment.

10

BEFORE SHE LEFT, XANTHE AGREED TO A PLAN WITH HARLEY. HE WOULD SEE ANNIE OFF in the morning and then come to the shop, where she and Flora would kit him out. By that time, she hoped to have decided which object belonged to Lydia. That meant she had the evening and the night to figure it out. As she crossed the high street she saw her mother and Stuart walking together, arm in arm, in the direction of Flora's favorite wine bar. She felt a surge of affection for her mother and a gladness to think that maybe her broken marriage was at last behind her and that she might find happiness again. Xanthe went straight to her room again and took the treasures from the shelf. She sat in her little window seat, the warmth of the early evening air drifting in from the garden, cooling the attic room. She thought how different were the sounds and smells of her own home compared to that of Elizabeth and Erasmus's. It was strange to think of them living their lives in another time and yet waiting for her. She rubbed her temples briefly, staving off a threatening headache. It was wonderful to think Harley would be traveling with her, but it did mean there was lots to do before they could leave. Right now she needed to concentrate on the two antiques in front of her. She heard Erasmus's words in her head: *focus is all.*

She picked up the hatpin. It was a particularly lovely one, all silver, with a large blue stone set into a filigree-worked finding. The lapis was shot through with threads of gold, making it glitter as she turned it to catch the light. The point of the pin was still sharp, and the whole thing had clearly been cared for, but there were a few signs of wear. The top of the setting for the stone was slightly dented and the middle of the long stem was worn a little flat, no doubt from years of rubbing against all manner of hats and bonnets. She could hear the familiar high notes of its song, and the silver became uncommonly warm as she held it. There was a definite connection there. She thought of Mistress Flyte, picturing the old woman in her mind, trying to visualize her wearing the pin. She could imagine it, but no vision came. No vivid glimpse of a real moment in the past. Setting the hatpin down, she picked up the brooch and tested the weight of it in her hand. The quantity of gold alone made it a valuable piece. It was about three inches wide, oval, the gold a deep, rich color. The setting was not elaborate, but rather relied on the burnished beauty of the metal for its charm. Behind the glass, the picture woven from human hair was both exquisite and slightly disturbing. The background was an ivory color, and might well have been a piece of carved tusk, or possibly mother-of-pearl. It was hard to be certain, as so much of it was covered by the intricate picture of a tiny tree with its branches reaching out over a casket. Even if the brooch had not called to her, she would have found it moving. The thought of the loss and grief of the person who commissioned and wore it had a powerful impact. She looked at it with her antique dealer's eye. She was completely certain now that it was not Victorian, and that her earlier assessment of it being much earlier was correct. The style suggested centuries earlier, in fact. The singing of the brooch was more discordant than that of the pin, and had an eerie edge to it. The gold did not become warm against her skin as the silver had, but vibrated. The tiny movements created a small, stuttering rhythm, which she realized, with some disquiet, mimicked a heartbeat. It was as if she were feeling the pulse of a person long gone, but whether it belonged to the deceased loved one or the grieving relative she could not tell. She resisted the urge to drop the thing. This was an important connection, a visceral one, and a chance, perhaps, to know more. This was not the time to pull back. Again she attempted to picture in her mind Lydia Flyte, this time wearing the brooch, imagining it pinned to a gown that was vaguely early eighteenth century, pale blue, which she seemed to favor, outdoors somewhere, perhaps a garden. Again she succeeded in creating a passable picture in her imagination, but it was not reinforced by the singing of the object. No true vision came. She was on the point of giving up and trying something else when she had the alarming sensation that everything was going dark. She blinked, confused, looking around her. The light in her bedroom was still on, but it was as if the edges of her sight were dimming and darkening, as if a sort of blindness was descending upon her. She told herself not to panic. Singing objects each had their own very specific ways of communicating with her. She held her nerve and waited to see what would happen next. The depth of the darkness increased. The noises from the brooch seemed to recede a little. Suddenly, without further warning, there came a nerve-shredding scream, as loud as any she had ever heard, full of rage and despair, a howl of pain and anguish. It was so unexpected and so shocking that she dropped the brooch and leaped from her seat at the window, staggering backward across the room. The sound diminished in an instant, silence replacing it, interrupted only by the frantic thudding of her own heartbeat echoing against her eardrums. She stood still, waiting, listening, fearing what more might come. When nothing did, she stooped down and picked up the brooch from the floor. It trembled less than it had done and its singing was quieter, as if such an outburst had drained it of its psychometric energy somehow. Gradually, Xanthe's sight regained its light and its clarity. The room came back into focus. The scream lingered in her memory. It was a woman's, she was certain of that, but which woman she could not tell.

"Well," she said aloud, as much to calm herself with the sound of her own voice as to articulate the thought, "that was terrifying but unhelpful. Looks like I'm going to have to try something else."

She decided her next course of action was to seek help in the *Spinners* book. Not wanting to move away from the brooch, and unhappy with the idea she might drop it again, she pinned it to the lapel of her dress. It seemed more settled there, its song softer and its vibrations slower. She sat on the bed and opened the book on her lap. As always she experienced a scintilla of excitement as the pages began to reveal their secrets. Portraits of mysterious Spinners, as yet unknown to her, swam into focus. Intricately detailed maps of strange places emerged from nothing to show themselves upon the thick, dry paper. Pages of poems and prayers and incantations formed as she watched, shifting and adjusting to fit in a top corner here, a lower half there, a central position further on in the book, all seemingly gently jostling and competing with one another for their place in the book. When she lifted the tome up a little for a closer look at a map of ley lines she became aware of the brooch reacting to the proximity of the book. Its song grew slightly louder again with higher notes. It occurred to her then that the special treasures were influenced by *Spinners* in a similar way to that in which they were affected by the blind house. The thought flashed through her mind that she might be in danger of triggering a journey. She had always used the blind house, but who knew what powers lay within the covers of the magical book. Her first instinct was to unpin the brooch and move it a bit farther away again, just to be on the safe side. After all, this was not the moment to make an unplanned trip: she did not yet know if this was the object she should be following. True, it had produced a particularly strong demonstration of its need of her, but still she could not be certain that it would lead her to Lydia Flyte. She fought against this reaction, however, as a different thought came to her. However important *Spinners* was, however much she needed it, *she* was the Spinner. *She* was in control and had to hold on to that thought. She turned another page. There was a recipe this time, apparently for a beef tea to restore health after a long illness. She could not see the relevance of the thing, so continued on. Next there was a beautiful picture of some honeysuckle, all painted in glorious colors, and accompanied by the glorious scent of the blooms. She turned one more page. Now writing began to appear, as if written by an unseen hand, the ink flowing from a nib that she could now hear scratching its way left to right with great haste. This was a fleeting revelation. The words disappeared almost as quickly as they appeared so that she had to read what was written quickly or miss the message. She followed the letters with her finger, the surface of the page rough yet fragile as she trailed the transient words. She soon realized it was not a diary entry or an instruction of any sort but part of a story.

—

The bell above the entrance to the silversmith's sounded as the young woman entered and closed the door behind her. Bertram Myers, for such was the name of the proprietor, looked up from his desk. The hour was late. He had been on the point of closing his business for the day but had not yet pushed home the heavy bolts, turned the impressive key, nor fixed in place the sturdy oak shutters that would secure the premises. He was not an old man, but nor did he enjoy good health, and his bones had started to ache. His mind was, therefore, more than a little drawn toward sitting by the fire and sipping hot milk laced with a generous tot of rum to ease his discomfort. He was not best pleased, therefore, to see a customer stand before him. Particularly when the evidence of his eyes suggested the maid was of no account, and therefore unlikely to make a purchase of any significance. He removed his glasses and set them down on the desk, rising somewhat creakily to his feet.

"Good day to you, mistress. How may I be of service?" he asked, his words solicitous, his voice not entirely able to disguise his lack of sincerity.

"I wish to commission a piece." While evidently not a woman of substance, the customer was well-spoken, both her voice and manner cultured and refined.

Mister Myers rallied himself. A customer was a customer, after all.

"I should be delighted to oblige. What had you in mind? Shall it be a gift for another? Or a precious stone to celebrate an occasion, mayhap? I have this very day taken delivery of some pearls of the highest quality."

"I will not require pearls," she told him, taking from beneath her kirtle a simple leather purse which she placed upon the desk. Carefully, with dainty fingers in neat cotton gloves, she untied the ribbon that laced it and took out a tiny wooden box. This she opened and turned around so that the smith might view the contents.

Mister Myers needed only a glance to know what it was he looked upon, for there is a singular luster to the golden hair of a small child. He arranged his face in a countenance he believed to be both somber and consoling.

"Ah, my sympathies, madam," he said, lamenting the fact that the woman's gloves had not allowed him to see a wedding ring. He quickly reassessed her as a client. Here was a bereaved mother, no doubt reeling from the body blow of the greatest loss imaginable. Somewhere there would be a husband, grieving also, but no doubt keen to ameliorate that suffering by looking to future babes. A memento, a pretty piece that would both commemorate the dead and bring a modicum of solace to the living, was a thing worth a fair purse of any man's money.

The woman closed the box and pushed it across the desk toward him, though she could not bring herself to let go of it. "I desire a picture of serenity. Of peace. Have you someone who can fashion such a thing?"

"The very best! An artist, no less. His work is very fine and highly sought. I promise you he will produce a most fitting and most beautiful memorial."

"The setting shall be gold. Neatly and plainly worked. A broad brooch with a pin. Nothing ostentatious, you understand."

"It will be tasteful and modest, I assure you, madam. However, gold . . . at such a size . . ." Here he faltered. His acumen for business, his need to capitalize on each and every bargain struck, rubbed up against his compassion as a father of small children himself, and chafed his conscience.

Evidently anticipating his query, the woman retrieved a second purse, this one from a pocket set into her fine woolen skirt. The simplicity of the purse gave no hint as to the contents, for from it she brought forth a large, gleaming gold coin. She set it before the silversmith, who, on glimpsing the thing, had already snatched up his spectacles and positioned them in front of his eager eyes. For this was no ordinary coin. It was a rare and powerful thing. Not only was it one of the largest gold coins ever struck, its weight considerable, its metal pure, but it bore upon it the likeness of a king no longer in possession of either throne or head. Mister Myers's hand trembled slightly as he picked up the coin, the better to gaze upon the expertly wrought visage of the late King Charles, last of the Stuarts to rule before the country (in his secretly held opinion) lost all reason and stood by as the parliamentarians committed regicide in chill, brutal daylight.

"This is to be for the setting," the woman told him.

"Well . . ." he managed to say as he sought for something more eloquent. Then, realizing what the woman intended, he gasped. "You mean to melt it down? This coin?" When she merely nodded he cast about for a way out of the situation. "But madam, forgive me, such a piece, such a rarity, 't'would be a shame, nay a waste, I cannot conceive . . ." Here caution returned to temper his astonishment. He had lived half his life in dangerous times, and the other half in fear of them. It was, even still, impossible to know which side it was safest to support. Allegiances and fortunes changed with the tides of the Thames. Was this woman from a family of Royalists who had kept the coin in loving memory of their lost monarch? Or was she a passionate advocate for Cromwell, with her simple clothes and plain airs? It was safest never to assume anything.

While the smith wrestled with the best way to serve his conscience, make a living, and save his own neck, the woman dipped into the purse and, to his amazement, took out a second Triple Unite gold coin. It was, if anything, in even better condition that the first.

"This one," she said, "will pay for the work. Will it not?"

Now it was his turn to merely nod, emphatically.

"I wish there to be an inscription," she told him.

"Of course!" He took up his pen and found a fresh page in his ledger of works.

"My daughter's name only," she said, the slightest break in her voice betraying the emotion she held in check. "Amy. Just that. It means 'beloved.' She was named for her father."

He wrote it down, letting her see it so that there might be no mistake about the spelling.

She nodded. "Yes," she said, and then repeated the word in little more than a whisper, "Beloved."

—

The words stopped. The story came to a halt. Xanthe waited, hardly daring to move, but the book would reveal nothing more. She quickly unpinned the brooch and examined the back of it closely. The metal was worn smooth and she couldn't see an inscription at all. She went to her bedside table and found one of the magnifying loupes she and Flora relied on. She put it to her eye and looked again, turning the brooch beneath the light. She was now able to make out what could possibly be the bottom loop of a "y."

"Amy," she said to herself. "So, the brooch matches the story. And in the story the young woman had lost a child. But was that woman Lydia?" The description fit as far as it went; elegant, refined, small delicate hands. It might be her. Or it might not. The coin, and the silversmith's reaction to it, meant the story took place soon after the execution of Charles the First. Erasmus had told her that he and Mistress Flyte had their origins in the sixteenth century, but as they were both Spinners the date was less than helpful. She needed something else, something more definite to be sure she was following the right call. She rubbed her thumb over the glass that covered the picture. Knowing the story behind it made it somehow less creepy and more poignant. She racked her brain to think of anything else she had just read that could be helpful. She recalled the woman saying the child was "named for her father" because Amy meant "beloved." A word she had repeated at the end of the tale. Was it the pet name the woman had for her husband? Where was he in the story, anyway? The way she spoke of him suggested he was dead, or at least gone. And she hadn't actually called him her husband, just the girl's father. An idea came to Xanthe and she snatched up her phone, typing in a search for the words "beloved" and "boys' names." She scrolled through the less helpful-looking links until she found one that seemed reasonable. She was disappointed to see a long list of names that had the same meaning. Some were Greek, some Hebrew, others Italian, so that they were not listed alphabetically but in groups according to their origins. At last she saw it and her heart skipped a beat. There it was. Boy's name, from the Greek, meaning "beloved": Erasmus.

Early the next day an overexcited Harley arrived at the shop. He had waved Annie off to Scotland, overcome his guilt at having lied to her, and put on his best attempt at a period-appropriate costume.

Xanthe let him in, raising an eyebrow at his outfit as they went into the vintage clothing room.

"What do you think, hen? Have I got the Victorian vibe going on here, d'you reckon?" he asked, tugging at the edges of his tartan waistcoat in an effort to make them meet over his ample stomach.

"If I'm honest, it's a little more steampunk than authentic."

He looked crestfallen. "D'you not think my hat is quite the very thing?" he asked, adjusting the angle of his bowler. "I rather liked it," he said, catching sight of himself in one of the antique mirrors.

"The hat we can use, definitely. The waistcoat . . ."

She was saved saying anything further as Flora and Pie could be heard coming down the stairs; crutches and slow steps combined with the scrabbling of whippet claws on wood.

"Mum, come and cast your eye over Harley," she called out to her.

On seeing him, Flora's face registered surprise. She stifled a giggle as she said gently, "I think we've a little work to do."

For the next half an hour Harley endured being undressed and redressed, forced into one or two ill-fitting items, discarding others as too bright or too modern, wriggling in and out of all manner of trousers and boots until Xanthe was satisfied with the way he looked. He ended up with a pair of dark brown woolen trousers with wide leather braces over a pale blue shirt; a dark red silk cravat; a tweed jacket; his own black leather boots; the bowler hat of which he was so proud; and a dark blue silk waistcoat that was a better fit in all respects than the one he had shown up in, its brass buttons fastening with room to spare. The finishing touch was a pocket watch on a silver chain with a carnelian fob. His own beard and moustache looked a little wild for the time, but were just about acceptable. His shaggy hair would pass for authentic, particularly when swept off his face and beneath his hat.

Xanthe and Flora stood back to admire their handiwork.

"Not bad," Flora decided. "If a little rough around the edges."

"I've been called worse," said Harley.

"I think he looks pretty good," said Xanthe. She had been about to say more but the bell on the shop door clanged. She glanced at Harley's watch, making a note to tell him to take it off. It was too early for customers so she had not bothered to lock the door when she let him in. Seconds later, Gerri stepped into the room.

"Oh," she said, taking in the scene in front of her. "Harley! Look at you. What have I missed?"

There was an awkward pause. Harley was struck dumb, and Xanthe could think of no explanation to offer. It was her mother who filled the questioning gap.

"Harley's going to surprise Annie with a fancy dress party, and . . ."

"No, Mum, don't." Xanthe put a hand on her shoulder. She looked at Gerri, in her lovely 1940s dress, with her expertly applied lipstick that never smudged, her hair in victory rolls, her bright smile, none of it revealing the struggle and challenges of her life as a single mother running her own business. Here was a friend. Here was a person who deserved better than being lied to.

"Gerri," she said, moving to take her arm, "we need to talk. Can I treat you to tea and the best lemon drizzle cake in town? I know a place not far from here."

Gerri gave a light laugh but clearly picked up on the fact that something important was going on. "Sounds like a great way to start a Tuesday," she said, allowing Xanthe to lead her out of the shop and across the cobbles to her own tearoom. "Take a seat," she suggested, "I'll ask

Wendy to bring us a tray out. It's warm enough to sit outside, don't you think?"

"Wendy?"

"Work experience girl from the high school. A true entrepreneur in the making. Very keen!"

Xanthe waited for Gerri to return and sit on the little wrought-iron chair opposite her. It was a pretty morning, and a light breeze caused the colorful bunting around the doorway to flutter. She had no real idea of what she was going to say, but her friend mattered to her. She had to try to be honest with her. At last, Gerri was in front of her, setting down a tray of mismatched vintage china.

"I'll be mother," she said, "and you can tell me what's going on." When she noticed Xanthe hesitate, she added, "Is it Liam? Have the two of you fallen out?"

"What? Oh, no. Then again . . . it's hard to know where to start."

Gerri poured tea into cups. "How about explaining why Harley was in your shop looking like a member of the local amateur dramatic society?"

She accepted the cup and dropped three sugar cubes into it.

"Now I know it's serious," Gerri said, raising her own black tea to her lips. "You never take sugar."

Xanthe sat back in her seat with a sigh. "OK, I'm just going to come out and say stuff. And it will only be half a story, because right now that's all I think I can share with you. And some of it will sound crazy and some of it will make no sense . . . I just, didn't want to hide things from you. Or lie to you. And, I know I can trust you—"

"Xanthe—"

"I know, sorry, just get to the point! OK." She fortified herself with a sip of tea, grimacing at the sweetness of it. "Basically, Liam has been kidnapped and Harley is going to help me rescue him. And no, the police can't help. And it was my fault he was taken in the first place. And, well, me and Harley need to . . . disguise ourselves, if the rescue plan is to work. And Mum knows what we're doing, and she's OK with it. Annie doesn't know, and I'm sorry about that."

To her credit, Gerri did not shoot back a volley of questions. She sat for a moment, drinking her tea. When she seemed on the point of forming some sort of query, Wendy arrived with the cake. The girl was indeed enthusiastic, placing the plates on the table with a flourish and explaining that the cake was organic and made on the premises before arranging napkins and silver forks. Xanthe fought the desire to speak up to hurry her along, wishing the girl would just leave them alone. When she finally went back into the tearoom, she leaned forward on the little table, too anxious to even try the cake, despite the delicious lemony smell beneath her nose.

"Gerri, please, say something."

"OK, so it's too early for you to have been drinking, and even Harley looked completely sober. You say Flora's in on all this, and as far as I can tell she's a sane and reasonable woman."

"But you're not so sure about me?"

"Kidnapped? Rescue plan? Disguises?"

"I know!" She pushed her hair off her face. "I know it sounds ridiculous, but seriously, Gerri, Liam needs us."

"And the police can't help why?"

"Let's just say he's being held . . . out of their jurisdiction."

Gerri nodded slowly. "So what are you and Harley going to do, exactly?"

"We are going to where he's being kept. We're going to talk to the person who has him there. And we are going to bring him home." She held up her hands. "I am sorry, it's half the story, and one day, I promise, I *promise* I will tell you everything. Once we have Liam home, safe and sound, I'll tell you all of it. But right now . . . it's not the moment. Can you just trust me? Please?"

"Of course I trust you, Xanthe, but that doesn't mean I'm not worried. Are you sure this is safe? For any of you? What have you got yourself mixed up in? Is it to do with the band, or the shop, or the pub, or that flaky ex-boyfriend of yours?"

"It's none of those things, really."

An awkward silence joined them at the table. From the high street came sounds of shutters being rolled up as shops opened for the day. The church clock began to strike the hour.

Gerri reached across the table and placed her hand over Xanthe's. "Be careful. For heaven's sake, from the little you've told me . . . it sounds dangerous. But, well, you will have Harley with you."

"He's the brains of the operation," she said, making Gerri laugh out loud, breaking the tension of the moment. "I will be careful," she assured her. "And I will tell you everything eventually."

Gerri smiled, picking up her fork and waving it at the cake. "I'll hold you to that. In the meantime, if we don't do this lemon drizzle justice, we will have Wendy to reckon with. Come on, tuck in. I do have one question for you, though?"

"Oh?"

"What era exactly were you going for with Harley?"

"Mid-Victorian."

"The clothes are pretty good, but please, for the love of all that's holy, let me sort out his whiskers!"

The day after the visit to the house of Dawlish and Brook-Morton, Liam went downstairs in search of Mistress Flyte. He was surprised to find the small sitting room empty. There was neither fire in the hearth, nor food on the table, as if the old woman had not yet risen from her bed, even though the plain wooden clock on the mantelpiece showed it to be gone nine o'clock. After a moment's hesitation, Liam pulled the bell rope to summon the maid. She arrived on swift and silent feet.

"Ah, Millie. Can you tell me if your mistress is up? I had expected to find her here."

"She had a bad night, sir," said the girl. There was something in the way that she said it that suggested to him that this was not an unusual occurrence.

"I am sorry to hear that. I had hoped to speak with her."

"She will be down directly, I'm sure, sir. Can I fetch you tea while you wait?" The young girl seemed so eager to please that he did not want to disappoint her.

"Tea would be very nice, thank you, Millie."

As he waited he thought about what Lydia Flyte had said. How time travel could only stave off the aging process to an extent, and how she was weary of it. Could it be that she was more debilitated than she had let on? He had so many questions about the "proposition" the men had put to him the previous day. He had tried to question her on the carriage ride home, but she had put him off, saying she was too tired but promising answers in the morning. He wandered around the room picking up objects, trying again to understand how his curious hostess's mind worked. She seemed to be a collection of contradictions, one minute showing herself to be a friend to Xanthe, the next an enemy. One moment seeming to be a powerful Spinner, the next a frail old lady.

At last the door opened. One thing about Lydia Flyte that remained consistent was her ability to present herself as elegant and dignified. If she was unwell she did a fine job of covering it up. Her dress, however simple and inexpensive, was immaculately clean and as tightly corseted as ever. Her hair and makeup were done to perfection. She walked gracefully with a straight back and head held high. Even so, scrutinizing her a little differently now, Liam thought he detected a stiffness to her movements and a tension about her features that could indicate she was in fact in pain. She took a seat by the unlit fire, smoothing the skirts of her dress with the flat of her palms.

"Well now, Mister Adams. You have questions for me."

"You're right about that," he said, taking the chair opposite her.

The door opened and Millie appeared with a tray of tea things. They waited until she had placed it on the table and left the room.

"Before you interrogate me," Mistress Flyte spoke up, "I wish to thank you for your cooperation yesterday."

"You pretty much gave me no choice but to cooperate."

"Be that as it may, our endeavors are more likely to be successful should we present a united front."

"*Our* endeavors?"

"As I have said, your compliance will work for the better of all of us. Xanthe too. I know that is important to you. And because of your regard for her, you are able to accept that her work is of value. And that she has a calling to answer."

"That doesn't mean I want to see her walk into danger because of it. Or because of me. The way you've brought me into the moneymaking scheme of your friends . . . it pulls her into a situation I can only see as dangerous."

"They are not my friends."

"All the more reason not to get her, or me, tangled up with them!" Liam felt his hold on his temper slipping. "For all their champagne and posh graces, those men are ruthless. They will do whatever it takes to get what they want. I know, I've already been on the blunt end of some of their less gentle persuasion. The other night, when I went out for a walk, they tried to abduct me."

"They?"

"Oh, not Dawlish and his flashy sidekick. They wouldn't get their own hands grubby. Sent one of their thugs to do their dirty work."

"You made no mention of this to me."

Liam frowned. "Excuse me for not letting my actual kidnapper know about my would-be kidnappers."

"Can you be certain it was their man?"

"I saw him at their house. As we were leaving. He must have thought he was keeping out of sight but I saw him slipping down the servants' outdoor stairway into the kitchens. I don't know why you're surprised. They are playing for high stakes. You think if I say no to them they'll just leave it there, and what, let me go? No way. You've used me to gain entry to their little club to pay for a comfortable old age, and you have no control over what happens to me. You are out of your depth, Mistress Flyte, Miss Flyte, whatever I'm supposed to call you these days. You've taken on more than you can handle, and I'm not going to let Xanthe be the one who pays the price for that." He stood up.

"Please, sit down, perhaps some tea . . ."

"Seriously?" He had been about to say more on the subject of what he felt about the old woman's scheming and planning but the sight of her pulled him up short. The color seemed to drain from her as he watched and her hand went to her heart. She let out a little gasp, her breathing shallow. "Are you unwell?" he asked. When she did not answer but leaned forward in her chair as if she might pitch out of it he instinctively knelt in front of her, gently easing her back so that she was not at risk of falling. Whatever his opinion of her, he could not stand by and watch her suffer. "Shall I ring for Millie? She could fetch a doctor."

She shook her head, her breathing steadying a little.

"Some tea?" he suggested, having no real clue what he was supposed to do but sensing whatever had overcome her was now passing. When she nodded he fetched a cup, poured in Darjeeling, which he cooled with a little milk, and added plenty of sugar, which he recalled being good for shock. Her hands were shaking, so he held the fine china to her lips so that she could sip. It was a slow process, but eventually she had taken in half a cup. She relaxed, the distress past, nodding her thanks. Liam set down the cup and sat in the chair opposite her again.

"I think it's time you told me exactly what is going on, don't you?" he asked.

Mistress Flyte looked up at him, her bright blue eyes awash with tears.

"Yes, young man," she said quietly. "I believe you are right."

11

THE BLIND HOUSE HAD SEEMED TINY WITH HARLEY IN IT. XANTHE HAD GIVEN HIM CAREful instructions before they started their journey, making sure he understood the importance of holding on to her. After her experience of losing Liam while trying to travel home, they were both very aware of the dangers. The result was he encompassed her in an enormous bear hug, and that was how they arrived in London in 1878.

"Harley, you're on my foot," she told him quickly as she tried to step back so that she could take in their surroundings.

"Sorry, lassie . . ." He shifted his weight, unprepared for the dizziness that had descended upon him so that he staggered and lurched against the brown brick wall of the building next to them.

"Steady," she said gently. "Take a moment. We're OK here."

They had arrived not in an alleyway or side street as had often been the case, but in an enclosed yard. It appeared to be at the rear of some sort of warehouse. There was a cart parked up, its shafts resting on the ground and empty flour sacks stacked upon it. There was a high wooden fence on three sides, forming an enclosure with the wall of the storehouse itself and that of a stable. A bay horse, no doubt sensing humans, came to stick its head over the stable door, its mouth still full of hay. Apart from this benign presence, the place was empty. Xanthe noticed that the large double doors, which were barred by a heavy plank, had a smaller door set into them. She looked at Harley.

"How are you feeling?"

"Like I've got the grandmother of all hangovers without having gone to the trouble of drinking anything."

"It can be a bit unsettling. You'll feel much better in a few minutes."

"Aye, I'll feel more settled when yon building stops spinning." He straightened up, still keeping a stabilizing hand against the brickwork.

"It gets easier the more you do it."

"Not so much like a hangover then."

"Can you walk?"

"Oh, aye." To demonstrate, he let go of the wall and strode toward the other side of the yard. He had only gone a few paces before he wobbled perilously and veered to the left, grabbing hold of the old cart to keep himself upright. "Maybe another minute . . ." he said a little shakily.

"It's OK." She straightened his cravat for him and put his hat on properly. "You look great, by the way."

He managed a smile and twirled the ends of his moustache that had been so expertly shaped and oiled by Gerri before they left.

"Take some deep breaths," she told him, "and eat a couple of these." She pulled a paper bag of Jelly Babies out of her leather satchel and offered them to him.

Harley chewed on a handful solemnly before nodding, his eyes at last properly regaining their focus.

"Better?" she asked.

"Like a new man."

"Right. We'll use the small door. Stick close, in case we have to travel back in a hurry. Try not to gawp at everything. I know you'll feel like it but it marks us out as newcomers, you know."

"Hen, I am not the complete innocent abroad."

"No. Sorry."

"When we get out there, what are we looking for?"

"The treasure always brings me to within sight of the place where I'll find the person connected to it. I don't think this yard is it, it's too enclosed to see anything much. I'm hoping to get a better idea once we are on the other side of that door. Basically, we just go looking."

He nodded again and followed her to the door, which proved to be easily opened. They stepped out onto a broad, noisy street. She closed the door behind them. He was all for marching on, presumably trying to look as confident and local as possible, but she took hold of his arm.

"Easy, tiger," she whispered. "The place we need will be close by."

He slowed to an amble, doing a fine job of hiding his astonishment at the full-blown Victorian scene he now found himself a part of. The first thing that was obvious to both of them was that this was not a smart area of the city. The stink from the river reached them before they were able to see water, rank and sour with a hint of the sea borne in by the ships at anchor. She took in the tall buildings, the laden wagons, the rough types milling in and out of taverns, the gaudily dressed women on street corners, the poor quality of the houses, the shouts from the waterside, and the ragged children darting about among the trade taking place.

"We're in the docklands," she said. "This is not what I expected."

"Hell's teeth, hen. Here was me thinking I'd play the part of a gent in a grand house or two. Looking around us, I feel more like I'm back in the rough end of Glasgow thirty years back. Or would that be a hundred years forward?"

"Which is exactly why I need you," she said. "You know what to watch out for while I get on with finding the right place."

"Aye, I have your back, don't worry about that," he assured her, glancing over his shoulder to glare at a teenager who seemed to be sizing them up for possible victims of pickpocketing. As the boy took another step toward them, Harley raised his hand in a manner that left no doubt as to what would happen if he came any closer. The youth melted back into the bustle of the street.

Xanthe felt a pull to her right and turned, for a moment dropping Harley's arm so that she could move between fruit barrows and parked carts. He followed close behind. A little farther along the road she saw a row of tall town houses, all nondescript, each one of them wanting a coat of paint on their woodwork and repairs to their sagging roofs. Her skin began to prickle. She heard first a chiming, then a high note. The brooch was close. She might not be able to see it, but two more strides told her which house contained it.

"That one," she said to Harley, briefly pointing so that he could be clear which one she meant. She turned her back on it. "Don't stare. We might be seen from the windows. Come on. Let's move farther up the street." She led him to an upturned rowing boat, where they stopped to talk.

"You're sure?" he asked. "It's not much of anything, is it?"

"I'm sure. The brooch is in there, and I'd put money on Lydia Flyte being in there too. Which means Liam. Or at the very least, the person who knows where he is."

"Right you are, hen. Stand by, Liam lad, we're coming to get ye!" Harley tugged his jacket straight and was all for barreling directly through the front door.

"Wait, no!"

"But, if she's there, and—"

"If she's there she won't be alone. Think about it, Harley. Like you said, it'd take more than one old woman to keep Liam somewhere he didn't want to be. We don't know how many henchmen she has with her."

He looked frustrated by the thought that he was to be denied the chance to prove his worth and free Liam himself, but he could hardly argue against the very reasoning he had given her only the night before. "So, what's our plan, then?"

"We go to Erasmus," she said, finding the street sign and making a mental note of the name.

"What? And leave the house unguarded? She could decide to move him to somewhere else while we are not watching her front door."

"She could, but she won't."

"How can you be certain?"

"Because she wants me to find her. She's using Liam to get to me. She might prefer to work to her own schedule, but, ultimately, it's me she wants." She put her hand above her eyes to shield them from the blurry sun as she scanned the river up and down. "I know where we are, more or less. We can walk to Holborn from here. Won't take more than half an hour. We need to let Erasmus and Elizabeth know what we know. That this is where she is. That way we have their support if we need it. Then we organize a rendezvous, OK?"

Harley looked at the house and then back at her with a sigh of acceptance. "When did you get to be so bloody sensible, lassie?"

She grinned, taking his arm again and wheeling him west, hoping to give the impression to anyone who cared to look that they were a well-to-do couple about their legitimate business in a town they knew and understood. As they walked away from the house she felt a pang of longing for Liam. It wasn't easy to leave him, not now that she was so close. If she understood Lydia Flyte at all she believed she would keep him near her. He was in that house, she was certain of it. Before they turned a corner at the end of the street she looked back over her shoulder one more time, wondering if Liam was at one of the windows, wondering if he had seen her, and if he had, what he would make of her apparently abandoning him? She shook off the heavy feeling, putting her head down and allowing Harley to help her weave through the pedestrians, stevedores, and tradesmen who seemed largely intent on bumping into them.

As they moved away from the docklands, not only through a less rough area but also away from the possibility of being observed by anyone who knew them, Xanthe noticed the tension in Harley ease a little. As she held his arm, his gait became less of a wary walk and more of a swagger, the joy of the adventure clear on his face as he looked about him. She was pleased for him. Happy he was there to share it with her. At the same time, their reason for being there would bring him into possible danger, and she felt a weight of that responsibility toward him. Despite the fact that he was there to protect her, she could not put from her mind the fact that he would not be there if it wasn't for her needing him, and that she was the only one who could get him home to Annie again.

"Here it is," she said at last, stopping on a quiet part of the street, pointing at the bookbinder's establishment on the other side of the road.

"Will ye look at that!" Harley let out a low whistle. "Just as you described it, hen. And your friendly Spinner lives there? Even now, with all this"—he waved his arm in an expansive and expressive gesture—"'tis hard to believe I'm about to meet another Spinner."

"This one's a Time Stepper. Try to keep up." Grinning, she led him to the front door. Erasmus and Nipper were both in the shop. Xanthe was under no illusion that this had anything to do with the business of creating books but everything to do with security. She was greeted with warm smiles and effusive welcomes that quickly turned to astonishment when they realized where her companion had come from.

"This is my good friend, Harley," she told them. "He has known about me being a Spinner right from the start. Anything you want to know about ley lines and the history of all things peculiar in Wiltshire, he's your man. He volunteered to help me."

Erasmus shook his hand enthusiastically. "You are most welcome, friend," he said.

"Anything for Xanthe. And young Liam. It's a fine place you have here," he said, gazing at the rows of beautifully bound books and the samples of leather and paper on display.

"A good business, and one Nipper will take over from me before too long. He has learned the craft well," he added, his pride in his son plain for all to see. "But there is another business that occupies my mind now. And it is to this that all our talents must be put."

Harley nodded at Nipper's bruised face. "I hear we've some new acquaintances who like to throw their weight about. Well, I've plenty of that myself. They might be persuaded to change their ways."

"We are able to deal with them ourselves," Nipper put in, a little too quickly.

Xanthe sensed it was his pride talking and directed her words to him.

"I could not do any of this without you and your family, Nipper. But it can't hurt to have an extra pair of hands, can it?"

"Father and I know the city. We know these types. We do not need more brawn."

To his credit, Harley resisted putting the youngster in his place, settling instead for an eloquent raising of his bushy brows.

Erasmus quickly defused the situation. "We will each of us be tested, and each must play to our strengths. Xanthe, have you identified the whereabouts of Mistress Flyte?"

"I have. We have just come from there. A shabby little town house in Litham Street."

"The East End?"

"Yes, right on the waterfront. I admit, I was surprised."

"As am I. Lydia had always a refinement about her that would not fit well in such an area."

"A good hiding place then."

"Possibly," he agreed, sounding unconvinced, his expression suggesting he was running through alternative explanations in his mind.

Harley was confused. "I'm bewildered by the woman's behavior so far. From what Xanthe has told me, it's hard to know if she's trying to hide or wants to be found."

"That's what was driving me crazy," Xanthe said. "And now, we don't have to wait for her. We can make our move."

"I'm ready. Just say the word," said Harley.

"Xanthe will find a person of more use if they know the city," said Nipper, giving Harley a look that was unmistakably insolent.

"Now, just one minute, laddie—"

"It's OK, Harley." Xanthe put a hand on his arm. "Nipper's just trying to help. And you can both relax, for a bit at least. The first thing I have to do is write a letter."

The two men looked deflated at the sound of this somewhat tame course of action.

"You will write to her?" Erasmus asked. "To what end?"

"To arrange a meeting. Cards on the table time. Find out what she wants. And make it clear she's getting nothing from me until I've seen Liam for myself. Erasmus, can I trouble you for ink and paper?"

"In that department we are exceptionally well equipped!" He smiled as he fetched her what she needed.

Nipper leaned back against the counter. Harley moved over to the window, not missing the chance to emit a low growl as he passed the youth.

Xanthe wrestled with the ink pen, tutting at herself when she let blobs and smudges infect the pure page as she wrote.

Erasmus could not resist reading over her shoulder.

"You are suggesting going to her house! Do you think that wise? I had imagined neutral ground of some sort. A public place . . ."

"The sort of things we will be discussing are not chats to be had with lots of other people around. Besides, I doubt she'd be persuaded to bring Liam with her. And I am going to see him and talk to him or there's no deal. I will meet her at noon. And I must be permitted to speak to Liam alone."

Erasmus interrupted. "She'll never agree to that! You could simply spin home, taking him with you."

"But how can I know if he's really OK otherwise?"

"My dear girl, I fear you are not viewing the situation from Lydia's perspective. She cannot agree to this demand."

Harley spoke up. "Strikes me, lassie, that you and Liam know each other pretty well. If there's a trap or something he can't speak freely about, you'll pick up on it."

Xanthe thought about this. He was right, they had become close enough to be able to communicate at least the importance of what they needed to without words. This realization, and the fact that it was obvious even to Harley, caused her to experience a fresh wave of longing for Liam. She had to get this right. "OK," she said, returning to the letter. "I won't insist on us being alone." She finished writing the note and let Erasmus fix it with a blotter. He folded it expertly, sliding it into a cream envelope and using his own seal to secure it. Xanthe wondered how reminders of their past love would affect him and Lydia. She was uncertain as to whether their history was a help or a hindrance in everything they were trying to do. No doubt time would tell. Since reading in *Spinners* of how the woman had commissioned the mourning brooch, she knew that she had borne and lost a child of which Erasmus was the father. Had he known about the baby's existence, or its death? The fact that he knew nothing about the mourning brooch suggested he did not. It was not going to be an easy thing, to find the right moment to tell him what she had learned. She put the matter from her mind for the time being. She would tell him: he had a right to know, she believed. But such personal revelations would have to wait. She turned to Harley.

"I need you to come with me," she said.

Nipper stepped forward. "Will not we all be coming?"

"What? No, Nipper, it's really important that the book be guarded. Think about it; if Lydia is in any way connected to the men that broke in here, they will know of the rendezvous once it is arranged. Us all being out of the house would be the perfect time for them to try to take it again." To make her point she took it from her satchel. "I need you to protect it for me. I know you will guard it—"

"With my life!" he assured her, looking at the book almost reverently.

She turned to Erasmus. "He shouldn't be here alone."

He nodded. "I will stay with him. Your mission does not require a mob. Now that we know where you are, if you do not return by, say, six, we know where to come. Nipper, before you take up your duties as guardian of the Spinners' bible, would you be so kind as to step outside and find a boy to take the letter?" he asked, handing his son the note.

"You know, I still have no idea what she wants," said Xanthe. "Why has she forced me to come here like this? Is it to do with the book? Is she really like Fairfax and just after *Spinners* for herself? She might not even be able to read it."

Harley, listening, shook his head. "Surely she would have tried to take it the last time she saw you, without having to go to these lengths. . . ."

Erasmus agreed. "Others want the book, that much is evident. As to Lydia's motives, I am as much in the dark as you. She was always a woman who kept her emotions in check and remained inscrutable much of the time. Even to those close to her. But be certain of this: she does nothing without good reason and without good planning. She is neither impetuous nor reckless."

"Whatever she wants," said Xanthe, "she needs me to do it. And she's prepared to sacrifice our friendship and her own integrity for it."

"It cannot then," Erasmus said plainly, "be an insignificant thing."

After the letter had been sent they shut and locked the shop and joined Elizabeth upstairs in the drawing room. The tension that accompanied the wait for a reply had everyone on edge. Elizabeth produced an herbal tea she insisted they all drink to soothe their nerves. The men of her family were clearly used to such things and drank it without complaint. Xanthe drank it to quench her thirst and oblige her host and was pleasantly surprised at the taste and the calming effects. Harley sniffed it suspiciously and drank it down in one gulp out of good manners, unable to stop himself grimacing as he did so. At last the doorbell rang and Nipper went to answer it. He returned with a note addressed to Xanthe. She tore it open and read the brief lines written in a flowing if somewhat shaky hand.

She looked up at the others.

"Well, lassie?" Harley could not contain himself a moment longer. "Don't torture us further."

"She says yes. Noon. And Liam will be there waiting for me."

—

After a bite to eat—during which Erasmus paced the room and kept up a recitation of caveats and instructions for the rendezvous—Xanthe and Harley prepared to leave. Elizabeth took hold of both her hands.

"You are courageous, child," she told her. "Temper that bravery with caution today. You do not yet know what it is the old woman wants from you."

"I'm too much of a wimp to be brave," she replied a little self-consciously.

Elizabeth looked wistful. "I had a brother once thought the same, and I will tell you what I told him: There is no courage in being fearless. To know fear and yet act, well, there is bravery."

She felt the warmth of Elizabeth's hands as they held hers and fancied she detected something more. Some strength, some tremor of energy that seemed to pass between them. She looked up and met the woman's unwavering gaze and saw in it a brightness, a light of such quality that it made her gasp. Not for the first time she wondered about Erasmus's strange and beautiful wife. There was something extraordinary about her. She knew she should not be surprised. A Time Stepper would need someone extra special to share his life with, after all.

"I will be careful," she said. "And I have Harley," she added, smiling.

Overhearing his name, her friend straightened his bowler hat. "Right you are, hen. Ready and able to retrieve young Liam."

"I need you to hold back a bit, Harley. This is not a time to start a fight."

He clutched his heart dramatically. "Me? *Start* a fight? I'm wounded that you think me capable of unprovoked violence, lassie."

Erasmus stopped his pacing to add his thoughts. "There may be provocation aplenty. And indeed, your strength might be vital to the success of the mission. But, Xanthe is correct when she recommends a restrained approach. At least, in the first instance." As if instinctively, Erasmus's hand went to the hilt of the dagger he wore at his hip.

Elizabeth frowned at him. "Husband, you are the last person to instruct another on self-restraint in such circumstances."

"'Tis true," he agreed somewhat sheepishly, "I have been known to rush in and earn myself the name of fool. But in the best of causes. So it may be I am in fact the very person to understand your character, Harley. And for that reason, you might heed my words."

"Rather than those of a woman?" Xanthe asked.

Erasmus did not know her well enough to be certain she was teasing him, so he simply bowed and took a step back before saying carefully, "I give way to the young Spinner, for she is the one called, and she must do as she thinks best."

Elizabeth agreed. "Indeed she must, yet I will have Nipper hail a cab and will brook no refusal. We shall happily pay, rather than have you march across half of London for a second time this morning."

The hansom made swift progress due to an expert driver and a well-nourished horse. It seemed to Xanthe only a matter of moments before they had left the comparatively wealthy part of Holborn and arrived at the gritty area of the docks. They made the short journey in silence and she was glad of it. However light she had kept the conversation at the bookbinder's, now that they were almost at their destination she felt nervousness grip her stomach. She was not so much afraid of what might happen to her as much as she was afraid of failing. She gave herself a silent pep talk, focusing on how far she had come in such a short time as a Spinner and taking Elizabeth's words of encouragement to heart. Mistress Flyte was not a complex and challenging opponent, but she was a match for her. It was she the *Spinners* book had chosen to reveal its contents to. She, who was now the more competent Spinner. She would hold that thought.

By the time they stepped down from the carriage in Litham Street the chill damp of the morning had evaporated beneath strong sunshine. She felt hot in her tightly fitted jacket and skirts and more than a little claustrophobic inside all the buttons and layers. However gorgeous the outfit was, it was heavy and the unforgiving cut restrictive. It passed through her mind that running would be a challenge. She took a breath and told herself there would be no running.

Harley offered her his arm. "Are we ready, lassie?"

She nodded, hoping he could not feel the speed of her pulse as she slipped her hand through his arm. "Just remember—"

"I know, I know . . . restraint and patience, aye."

When they reached the shabby front door it was Xanthe who lifted the dull brass ring and knocked firmly. Seconds later the lock was turned and the door opened. A whey-faced young maid peered out at them.

"We are here to see Mistress Flyte. She is expecting us. My name is Xanthe Westlake."

The maid did not question her and let them in. She offered to take their hats but both refused, unwilling to part with them in case they had to make a swift exit. They followed the girl across the meager hallway and into a small sitting room at the front of the house. With a quick glance, Xanthe took in the worn and humble furnishings illuminated by sunlight falling through the long window that gave onto the street. The room was clean, but there was no disguising the lack of money that had gone into its dressing and upkeep. Her eyes went to the chair by the fireplace. Of course she recognized Mistress Flyte at once, but she was shocked to see the woman so changed. Not only did she look older and frailer, but her skin had about it the pallor of someone unwell, and her movement, when she rose from the chair, was stiff, suggesting pain. As ever, though, she remained poised and refined, smoothing her skirts carefully as she turned to greet her visitors.

"I am happy to see you again, Xanthe," she said calmly.

"I wish I could say the same. Truly I do."

"Ah, you are angry with me. That is to be expected. Yet I hope it will not be a barrier between us."

"You kidnapped someone who means a great deal to me. You put him in danger. You brought him here, to a place and a time he doesn't belong, without his consent. Your actions forced me to spin through time when perhaps I should be helping someone in real need elsewhere. You surely don't expect me to be anything but angry."

Mistress Flyte inclined her head in a bow of acknowledgment. "Please, be seated. Shall I send for refreshments for you and your . . . companion?"

"We are not here to take tea."

"You are anxious, no doubt, to discover the reasons for my actions."

"I am anxious to see Liam."

"All in good time."

While Xanthe took a breath to steady her temper, Harley could keep silent no longer.

"Maybe we don't wish to wait any longer," he said. His tone was calm, but there was a firmness to the way he spoke that was intentional and clear.

Mistress Flyte took her seat by the fire again. "I would prefer to avoid the unpleasantness of violence," she said with a sigh. "Rest assured, however, I am prepared for it, should the necessity arise."

Harley and Xanthe exchanged glances. It was impossible to tell whether or not the old woman was bluffing. The maid who had answered the front door was hardly going to stop anybody doing anything, and they had seen no henchmen or guards. So far. Xanthe gave him a small shake of the head as she placed her hand briefly on his arm. They had agreed they would be patient. They would follow their plan. She walked to the other side of the fireplace and took her seat there. Harley came to stand, pointedly, beside her, solid, silent, and determined.

"Very well," she said. "I will listen to what you have to say if you give me your word that Liam will be brought here and I can speak to him directly afterward. Do we have a deal?"

"We do."

"OK, let's hear it."

Mistress Flyte nodded, pausing for a moment as if to decide how best to explain herself. When at last she spoke her voice was measured and her words chosen with care. "As you know better than most, there are those who abuse their talents as Spinners. We should not, alas, be surprised by this, for where there is money or power to be had, there will be those who take it, regardless of the consequences of their actions—"

"Oh, aye," Harley could not resist interrupting, "says the woman not above a bit of kidnapping when it suits her."

"I am unable to defend myself against your accusation, sir, beyond perhaps claiming that there are occasions when the end justifies the means."

Xanthe could not help gasping at this statement. "I never thought I'd hear you, of all people, sounding like Benedict Fairfax! Let's wait and see, shall we? Maybe we won't all agree on the truth of that premise."

Mistress Flyte waited to see if anyone had more to say. When she was content that the interruption was over she continued with her story. "Such people—the unscrupulous, the greedy, the arrogant, the wicked—they are guided only by their own avaricious natures. What matters to them is that they succeed, with the least risk to themselves, in achieving their goals."

"This is not news to me. I fail to see how, just because others behave worse than you, what you do is justified."

"I have heard some reason that, as they were granted the gift of spinning time, it is theirs to use as they see fit. Indeed, on more than one occasion I have been told it would be an insult to the skill, to the magic of the talent, not to use it to its fullest potential. I might even agree with them on that, though of course I disagree on what that potential could or should be. As I think you will know, Xanthe, should you search your heart for your memory of our friendship, I am a woman of integrity. I support those who deserve my help. I will not stand by and see an injustice perpetrated on another if it is within my power to stop it." She paused again, waiting, Xanthe presumed, to see if either of her visitors would choose to take issue with this statement.

Xanthe fought the impulse to do so, determined that she could allow the old woman her say, so that she could get to Liam. The more she and Harley challenged her, the longer this whole thing would take.

"You are also aware that I was, in my time, an active Spinner. I moved through time, just as you do now, to answer the call of treasures, to right a wrong, to give assistance where it was most sorely needed. Alas, a Spinner's powers dwindle with the years traveled. I have lived my life out of sequence, and it has taken its toll on my body. Which is why, even though I have been able to settle and resettle in various times in order to support your own endeavors, I have, until this point, restricted myself to one place and a mundane and gentle lifestyle."

"The chocolate house and the tea shop in Bradford."

"Precisely. However, it came to my attention that something truly dreadful was being done by two talented Spinners. Something that goes against the code of our brethren, that twists our true purpose and calling that, frankly, shames any who would call themselves Spinner. These men have set themselves up in the business of selling their talents to the highest bidder. They move through time in order to gain valuable information which they pass on to their clients, who are all members of an elite club—the Visionary Society—and this they do without regard to anyone who suffers as a result of their selfish actions. My investigations revealed that they abide here, in London, in this time. These men must be stopped, and that is why I am here. That is why you are here."

Xanthe sat forward in her chair. "If what you say is true, why did you not just ask for my help? Why resort to dragging Liam here to make me follow you?"

"I could not take the risk that you might refuse to assist me in this."

"Why would I refuse? You know that I've answered the call of the things that sing to me. You've seen me do it. Couldn't you just have explained all this to me when I was in Bradford-upon-Avon at your home?"

"As I say, it is too important a matter to risk your refusal."

"You can't think much of me if you believe I would have turned you down. From what you've said these men are acting in a way that is completely the opposite of what every Spinner believes. They go against everything in the *Spinners* book. You knew how much I would hate that."

"True, but I also know how conflicted you are regarding your own life in your own time. You have a mother about whom you care deeply. A business which I understand she would struggle to continue were you not there."

"My mother is more than capable of holding the fort while I'm away."

"But could she stand to lose you forever?"

The bluntness of the question took her by surprise. When she had first traveled through time she had thought a lot about the possibility of not being able to return home, and about what that would mean for her mother. She would have been left on her own, heartbroken, grief-stricken, unable to make sense of her only child's disappearance or to do anything about it. As she had got more adept at spinning she had thought less about this possibility. She had persuaded herself she knew what she was doing. She was cautious and methodical and had the *Spinners* book to help her. She would always be OK and she would always return home. Now she was being asked to consider anew the thought that she might, by spinning, be abandoning Flora for good. While she processed this idea, Mistress Flyte went on.

"The facts of the matter are these: the Visionary Society is not only the business of two ruthless men, both of whom are expert Spinners, it works to the furthering of the interests of a company of powerful people. Many of whom have earned their wealth and positions by dubious or even explicitly illegal means. They will not have their endeavors thwarted. They care not for those they trample in their stampede to take what they desire."

"I dealt with Fairfax."

"This is not the same!" she snapped, frustration telling in her tone. Frustration and, Xanthe was surprised to notice, fear. "Fairfax, for all his money and position, was one man. And a poor Spinner, at that. These men are immeasurably more dangerous." She took a moment to calm herself, the agitation clearly taking its toll. "What is more, they guard themselves and their position. They are sufficiently clever to know that there will be those who seek to stop them. In point of fact, others have tried. Two acquaintances of mine, fellow Spinners, attempted to expose the club as a sham and its founding members as charlatans in order to disgrace them and turn people from wishing to use their services."

"What happened? Did they go to the newspapers? Did they get the police involved? I mean, they couldn't tell them the truth, obviously, but they could have accused them of, I don't know, shady business practices? Tricking people out of their money, something like that?"

"They made the mistake of underestimating the reach of these fallen Spinners. Their clients are few but they hold immensely powerful positions. They did not want the means for their own enrichment to be taken from them. My friends did their best, they were brave men—"

"Were?"

The silence that followed was more eloquent than any explanation Mistress Flyte could have given. Again, Xanthe thought how frail the old woman looked. The loss of her fellow Spinners had clearly had an impact on her already failing health.

"So you see," she continued, "the task ahead is a perilous one. There is not one victim at the center of it, but many. Not one adversary, but a cabal. The risks are great and very real, and anyone opposing these men must understand that success and, indeed, survival cannot be guaranteed. I know you, Xanthe Westlake. You might be willing to take such a risk for yourself, but for your beloved mother? Would you be willing to risk her future, her health, her happiness?"

"So you took someone else I care about. Someone you knew I would come for."

"I regret such a course of action because there is cruelty in it. I am sorry for that. But I do not regret my plan. I did what I had to do. For I believe you are the only Spinner left who can stop these people. I have no one else to whom I can turn. No one I can trust."

Xanthe shook her head. "How do you think I can stop them? I mean, be realistic, I'm one woman, one Spinner. This is not my time. I'm lucky to have Harley to help me, but as you say, people like that will be well guarded. What makes you think I can possibly succeed where your friends failed, even assuming I agreed to help you?"

"To take your second point first, I believe you will agree to help me first because you know it is the right thing to do as a Spinner, and second because it is the way you will secure Liam's freedom. On the first matter, I know that you will not be facing these men alone. Of course, you will have what support I can give, and I am pleased to see you have brought such an . . . able assistant with you." Here she made a small gesture in Harley's direction, causing him to puff up his chest a little with pride, his waistcoat straining at its buttons. "More than that, I am certain you will have the help of your newfound friends."

"The Balmorals. Of course, you know that they are already helping me."

"It is as I had hoped."

Xanthe stood up, finding herself employing Erasmus's habit of pacing up and down the room to order her thoughts.

"Let me get this straight. You knew I would find Erasmus. You knew I would go there first and then come here, so that by the time you told me all this, I'd have his support."

"And that of his remarkable wife," she agreed.

"But how could you know that? How could you know I'd find the treasure to take me to him first?"

"The writing slope, I believe, belongs not to Erasmus, but to Elizabeth."

"And the mourning brooch brought me here afterward. What was your plan, to sit around and wait with Liam chained up in the cellar for as long as it took for the found things to sing to me?"

Mistress Flyte gave a light laugh at this. "Trust me, my dear, your friend has enjoyed his freedom during his stay here. My home is modest, it's true, but he has not been ill treated. No cellar. No chains."

"I'm very glad to hear that but it doesn't answer my question. How long were you prepared to wait for me to show up?"

"Sadly, the Visionary Society is very active. Time is of the essence.

I could not merely stand by and allow the treasures to find their way to you in their own time."

"So what did you do?"

"I did what all good Spinners have done through the centuries and what I am, in fact, doing by bringing you here. I called upon one of our brethren for assistance."

"Another Spinner?"

"Yes. There are not many of us, alas, but I am acquainted with most who still live. An advantage of my own great age."

Xanthe felt the fine hairs on her arms begin to stand.

"Who was this Spinner? How did he help?"

"He made certain that you came into contact with the found things as soon as possible. I knew that once they sang to you, you would answer their call."

Xanthe's mouth opened and it was a moment or two before she found her voice. "The old man who sold me the treasures? He was a *Spinner*?"

"That is correct."

"But, he didn't reveal himself to me. If you'd contacted him and asked him for his help, he must have known everything about me. He told me he was a retired antiques dealer."

"And so he is."

"He lives only a few miles away from my home. If he's a Spinner, why hadn't he made contact before? He could have helped me when I was starting out in all this, when I was learning . . ."

"My dear girl, he has been watching over you since the moment you arrived in Marlborough. More than that, it was because of him that you moved to start your new life there."

"I don't understand. . . ."

Mistress Flyte allowed herself a small smile. "You were understandably agitated and distracted when you went to his home to buy new stock. And of course, having more than one object sing to you took your attention entirely. Do you remember, I wonder, the name you wrote on the bill of sale?"

Xanthe did remember. And as she did so, things fell into place like so many pieces of a complicated and dazzling puzzle. When she spoke again it was a whisper of understanding and astonishment. "Morris," she said. "His name was Mr. William J. Morris."

Mistress Flyte nodded. "And where, pray, have you heard that name before?"

"The vendor of The Little Shop of Found Things. The previous owner was a Mr. Morris!"

"There you have it. One and the same."

"But, we were told that he had died, that the business was being sold to settle his estate."

"I think you'll find, if you speak to your mother about it, you were allowed to assume such to be the case. No one ever, in point of fact, told you that he had died."

Xanthe sat back down again heavily. She and Harley exchanged stunned looks. "He was a Spinner!"

"Like me, he reached the end of his traveling days. Also like me, he was . . . indeed he is . . . aware of your importance. Did you never consider it a coincidence that you, with your gift of psychometry, should come to live so close to such an important blind house on a crucial intersection of ley lines?"

"Well, yes, but . . ."

"There is, I am sure you have concluded for yourself by now, no such thing as coincidence."

"Mr. Morris . . ."

"Saw to it that your mother was the only person who viewed the property. The only one who could, in fact, buy it."

"But, my parents' marriage broke down. If that hadn't happened, we wouldn't have left London. He couldn't have relied on that happening!"

"Had your parents' marriage continued he would have found a way to present the business opportunity to both of them, as a new venture extending their existing auction house business. He would have found another way."

Mistress Flyte got to her feet and rang the bell to summon the maid. "And now," she said simply, "I believe it is time for you to be reunited with your friend. He is as anxious to see you as you are to see him, and we have kept him waiting long enough." When Millie appeared at the door, the old woman instructed her to take Xanthe up to his room. Xanthe was just processing her own surprise at this when she spoke again. "But first, I must ask something." She held out her hand. "Would you be kind enough to give me your gold locket?"

Her hand instinctively went toward the precious necklace, stopping just short of touching it. It was clear Mistress Flyte knew it was the means by which she could travel home. Without it she could not suddenly leave, possibly taking Liam with her. Without it, she was as much a prisoner of the old woman as he was. Her hand still waiting, the elderly Spinner added, "I know its value to you. It will be safe with me but will remain in my keeping until the time comes for you—for all of you—to return to your own time. This, I have to tell you, is a condition of your seeing Liam, and I will not be moved upon this point."

Xanthe looked at Harley, who gave a shrug as if to say she had no real choice in the matter.

"Very well," she said, reluctantly undoing the clasp. She made a point of neither looking at it or thinking of home as she did so. As she let the chain slip through her fingers when she dropped the locket into Mistress Flyte's palm she felt a shiver of apprehension run through her. Her disquiet was not improved as she watched her tuck the necklace into a buttoned pocket in her skirt. She turned back to Harley. "Will you stay here?" she asked him. "As long as Mistress Flyte has my locket, she doesn't leave your sight, OK?"

"You can count on me, lassie," he said, stepping closer to their hostess's chair.

She nodded, satisfied, and followed the maid from the room.

12

AS SHE CLIMBED THE STAIRS TO THE TOP OF THE NARROW HOUSE, XANTHE FELT excitement bubbling up inside her. She achieved her aim of finding Liam and getting to see him alone, and therefore being several important steps closer to taking him home. She had scarcely allowed herself to acknowledge how much she missed him. By the time the maid opened the door to the low-ceilinged attic room she was aware her own breathlessness was only partly due to the steepness of the stairs and the speed with which they had scaled them.

And then there he was. Standing in the middle of the sparse bedroom, dressed in what appeared to be authentic but somewhat shabby clothes of the day, his face lit up by his habitual easy smile at the sight of her, for all the world as if he had been waiting for her only a few hours, rather than a distance of more than a century. The maid left, shutting the door softly behind her. For a brief moment the two of them stood there, grinning. She started to ask him how he was at the same moment he began speaking. They both laughed. She tried again.

"You OK?"

"Aside from having to wear underclothes that are apparently made of horsehair and not having had a decent pint in, oh, a dozen or so decades, I'm good, yeah. You?"

"I'm fine. Better than fine, now I know you're safe."

"The old bat may be a few sandwiches short of a picnic, but she's treated me OK."

"She's told me why she took you . . . why she brought you to this place, this time."

"Then you'll know all about the Visionary Society and their plans for me."

"Plans for you? Hmm, she left that bit out." Xanthe nodded at the small bench seat beneath the window. "Let's sit over there. We need to talk. I'll fill you in on what she's told me she wants and you can tell me what you've heard while you've been here. OK?"

"Sure," he said as she took a step forward, and then quickly, "To hell with that." In two strides he reached her. Before she had a chance to say anything more, he took her in his arms and pulled her close, kissing her with undisguised passion.

After a fleeting moment of surprise, she felt herself responding to him. She loved the way his strong arms held her, safe and close. His mouth felt sweet on hers, his kiss deep and filled with longing. When at last he pulled back a little he still held her tightly.

"I thought I might never see you again," he whispered.

"Oh, Liam, I am so sorry."

"Really? Kiss that bad?"

"What? No!" She laughed. "I'm sorry about what happened, about what I let happen to you. . . ."

"Hey, no one ever said time travel was without its risks. You explained that to me, remember?"

"Yes, but—"

He silenced her with another kiss. This one was slower, lighter, filled with tenderness. After the kiss he rested his brow against hers.

"I feel better already," he said.

"Liam, we have so much to sort out. So much to talk about."

"I know. Need to stay focused."

She nodded, kissing him this time, reveling in the moment, not wanting it to end. "Plans to make," she muttered. "Really important things we have to do."

"Yup," he agreed, kissing her again.

"There's things you need to know," she murmured.

"I'll tell you what I know," he said quietly. "I know that being away from you . . . not good. Didn't like it. Not at all."

"Better not do it again then."

"Better not." He noticed her glance at the narrow brass bed against the far wall of the room.

"How long have we got?" he asked.

She smiled but pushed him gently away then, slipping out of his arms and taking his hands in hers. When he held them tightly, searching her face, she whispered, "Rain check?"

"Deal," he said simply, then let her lead him to the seat by the window where they hurriedly attempted to fill each other in on all that they knew about Mistress Flyte's plans. In a tumble of words he told her how he had been attacked in the street and saved by a man who ran bare-knuckle fights. She told him of Erasmus and Elizabeth and Nipper. He told her how Mistress Flyte had used him to gain a place in the Visionary Society and what Brook-Morton and Dawlish wanted him for. She explained that Mistress Flyte's motives were honorable: that she wanted to put an end to the society's nefarious actions and stop the two Spinners from abusing their gifts so wantonly and dangerously.

"I'm relieved to hear that," he said, still holding her hand as they sat on the worn wooden bench. "I really thought she wanted into the club to make money for herself."

"Quite the opposite. While I still don't agree with what she did to you—to us—well, her intentions are good. She doesn't want money for herself."

"She certainly doesn't seem to have any of it," he said with a glance around the spartan room. "How does she expect you to stop them? I mean, I'm your biggest fan, Xanthe, but they are not going to be pushovers. That house of theirs looked pretty secure, and, well, I've met their musclemen."

"I hate that she used you to get into the club at all. Bad enough her bringing you here . . . what if they'd wanted you to spin with them straightaway? You could have ended up anywhere. I might never have found you."

"Oh, somehow I think you would," he said with such firm conviction she knew it was what he truly believed. The thought comforted her. He had never given up on her coming to find him. He had known that she would.

"Oh, I forgot to mention. I didn't come alone," she told him.

"You brought one of your new friends with you?"

"No, I mean, I didn't come back to this time alone." She got up and pulled him to his feet. "Come on. I'll show you our secret weapon."

In the little sitting room she found Harley and Mistress Flyte just as she had left them; her friend warily guarding the old woman, who was still sitting in her chair by the unlit fire looking frail and tired. At the sight of Liam, however, Harley broke into beaming smiles.

"Liam, lad! Still in one piece, I see." He stepped forward and slapped him heartily on the back. "No ill effects, eh? You look right enough, skinny as ever, mind you. Though I'll admit you're stronger than you look."

"Great to see you too, Harley." Liam grinned. "You scrub up pretty well."

"Do you think so? Aye, I'm pretty pleased with the outfit myself. Might just adopt it as my new look, what d'you reckon?" he asked, arms akimbo, doing a slow twirl. As he did so he caught sight of Xanthe's raised eyebrows and remembered where he was and what he was supposed to be doing. With a quick clearing of his throat he stood still once more, rearranging his features into a more serious expression only with some difficulty.

Xanthe moved closer to Mistress Flyte. "These people, this society, from what Liam tells me, they are well defended."

"That is true," she agreed.

"And from what you tell me, they are good at getting what they want and ruthless with it. Which means, if we're going to put a stop to what they're doing, we are going to need all the help we can get."

The old woman's eyes widened. "Then you agree to assist me? You will do as I ask?"

"As a Spinner, knowing what I now do, I can't stand by and let them carry on breaking every rule there is about what we do and how we do it. They have to be stopped, you're right about that. But we do this on my terms."

For an instant, Mistress Flyte looked perturbed. She sat up in her chair a little straighter but quickly regained her composure. "And what might those be, pray?"

"First, Liam is no longer your prisoner."

"I assure you, he never was."

"I was allowed to come and go," he said with a shrug, "so not exactly locked up."

"Second, neither he nor Harley are to be put in any unnecessary danger."

At this both men began to protest, Harley being the loudest. "Hell's teeth, hen, I came here to be of use! Don't sideline me now."

She held up her hands. "Is either of you a Spinner?" When they both had no answer to this she continued. "This is Spinners' business, our mess, our risk. Yes, we will need your help, guys, but you are here because of me and I'm going to see that both of you get home once this is sorted out. OK? We will, however, need the help of Erasmus. Mistress Flyte, you are going to have to put aside any awkward history between the two of you; we can't do this without him. Or Elizabeth."

At this Harley bridled again. "You'll let your man's wife step up but not us?"

"Please try to understand. You and Liam will have your parts to play, I promise."

"But she isn't a Spinner," he pointed out.

"No, she's not. But she has been married to one for a long time. They have traveled together to stop people like this before. And besides, she's . . ."

The assembled company waited to hear what Elizabeth was that made her so important and useful. Xanthe struggled to find the word, uncertain still exactly how to describe the woman she knew to be different, to be special. In the end she said simply, "Elizabeth is part of the team and that's that. So, Mistress Flyte, what I need you to do now is write down all the details you have about the Visionary Society. Everything from the names of the men who belong to the club to how it works. I'll take the letter to Erasmus, and we will decide on a course of action." The old woman nodded and she saw again that she was struggling with pain of some sort. However badly she had behaved, it still troubled Xanthe to see the person who had helped her when no one else would, suffering so. "And while you're writing," she added more brightly, "perhaps we could all have some of that tea we were promised." She took it upon herself to pull the bell rope to summon the maid and ignored Harley's mumbled suggestion that something a little stronger than tea might be a better idea.

—

An hour later both tea and letter were finished. Liam had helped Mistress Flyte to write by prompting her with some of the details he had gleaned about Brook-Morton and Dawlish. Xanthe was touched by how patient and gentle Liam was with the woman who did not deserve his sympathy. When it came time to leave she was not entirely surprised that he volunteered to stay with Mistress Flyte.

"Your friends will have a houseful with you and Harley as it is. Besides," he lowered his voice, "she's really not well."

"I noticed the change in her."

"She had some sort of turn yesterday. Could have been a heart attack. I know she's broken your trust, but you are right when she said she did what she did for the best of reasons."

Xanthe hesitated, reaching out to put her hand on his chest. "About that rain check . . ."

"It's fine. Thought I'd try playing hard to get, now you're keen. Actually, the maid here is a bit sweet on me—"

She moved her hand and pinched his arm hard, making him yelp before walking over to the table where Mistress Flyte was drying the wet ink on the paper with a blotter. "I'll talk to Erasmus," she said, taking the letter and tucking it into her skirt pocket. "Once we've decided what to do we'll meet up again. Liam will stay here with you."

The old woman registered surprise. Before she could say anything Xanthe went on, picking up the pen from the table as she spoke. "I'm writing down Erasmus's address. If anything happens, if they contact you wanting Liam to go there or anything like that, you'll know where to find us."

"I confess," she said quietly, "I was aware of Erasmus's location."

Xanthe gave her a stern look. "I know that. This is for Liam. He has volunteered to stay here to help you. That doesn't mean I entirely trust you yet."

Mistress Flyte nodded. "Perhaps this will help toward regaining that trust," she said, taking the gold locket from her pocket and handing it to her.

Xanthe took it quickly, relieved to feel it in her hand again but taking care not to hold it too tight or too long, fastening it around her neck before her thoughts could be drawn to it or to home. The last thing she needed was to inadvertently spin back at that moment. She looked at the old woman.

"I will do what needs to be done," she told her.

"I know you will," she replied. "I have always known that it would be you."

This seemed to Xanthe a curious choice of words. "What does that mean?"

"Your destiny as a Spinner was clear to me the very first time we met, even though you were struggling to accept it yourself."

"Everything was new to me then. Now, things are different. I'm not that beginner anymore."

"Indeed. You are moving closer to what you were always meant to become."

"A Spinner, yes. I know." She frowned. There was something else the old woman was alluding to but she failed to see what and would have liked to press her further on the subject, but time was short. She needed to get back to Erasmus. There was no telling when the Visionary Society might call upon Liam to spin through time with them. Whatever they were going to do, it had to be done soon.

Liam took the paper with the address on it from Xanthe. "You know, something's occurred to me. Mistress Flyte bought her way into the society using me."

Harley gave a chuckle. "Who knew you were so valuable, laddie?"

"Price beyond rubies, apparently. Anyway, my point is, once she had an in to the club, well, we were inside the house. Able to mingle, move about between rooms, rub shoulders not only with our dodgy hosts but all their precious clients too."

"So?"

"So, if we could get Erasmus and you an invitation?"

"Wouldn't work"—Xanthe shook her head—"they know what he looks like. He had to tackle the henchmen who broke into the house, remember, I told you?"

"OK, but that was just their thugs. Doesn't mean the main men know what he looks like."

"It's too much of a risk. And one of those thugs followed me and Elizabeth when we were out."

Harley put in his thoughts on this. "I recall you telling me of it, hen, but did you not say you only saw him when you turned because you sensed another Spinner?"

"Yes, that's right."

"Well, strikes me a thug is a thug. Those two Spinners gone to the bad who think so highly of themselves are not going to have another Spinner working for them in such a lowly position now, are they?"

"So who was he?" she asked.

"Who knows? Who cares? Right now we've got to concentrate on getting as many of us as possible inside that house."

"OK, so there might have been another Spinner following me, I mean one not connected to the society. That's something I need to think about, but right now I'm prioritizing Dawlish and Brook-Morton."

Liam nodded. "And Harley's right, we need to get as many of us as possible inside that house. Let's assume they don't know what Elizabeth or Harley looks like. If we could get them invited to the table, and me and Mistress Flyte went because of me, that would be four of us inside. We could let Erasmus in. And you, Xanthe."

"And Nipper," she added, ignoring Liam's question as to who that was. "You know, it could work. Or at least, it would if we had any money. Mistress Flyte, how much would it take?"

"There is an initial joining fee of five hundred pounds," she told them.

Harley whistled. "That's a fair sum now, hen, but I have it in the till at The Feathers. Shall we nip back and fetch it?"

"You're forgetting the currency, Harley. Nice idea, but I think pictures of a queen who hasn't been born yet might not get us very far. We could bring back some silver and try to sell it but it would all take too long. And anyway I'm not sure we've got enough of the right age. No, we need to get our hands on the money here, and quickly."

Lydia Flyte raised a point. "Might Erasmus have access to funds?"

"I will ask him, but somehow I don't think he and Elizabeth are the sort of people to have a small fortune squirrelled away."

Liam broke the thoughtful silence. "Actually, I might just know a way to make a fair bit of cash." Everyone in the room turned to look at him, waiting to hear what he had to say. "I mentioned how I was saved from being dragged off by some musclemen when the guy who organizes fights scared them off? Well, he offered me the chance to take part."

"In a boxing match?" Xanthe asked.

"You, laddie?" Harley was astonished.

Liam protested, "He saw how I handled myself. Recognized a bit of natural talent."

"You?" Harley repeated.

Xanthe shook her head. "Liam, are you sure?"

"Why is nobody prepared to believe I could be any good at it?"

"You're strong enough and fit enough, of course, but . . . don't you need a killer instinct to get in a ring and beat someone else? I mean, that's not the Liam I know," said Xanthe as tactfully as she could.

"All due respect . . ." Harley said.

"Which is what people say when they are about to insult you," said Liam.

". . . we want to *win* money. I can't see backing you in a ring against some burly East End fighter being a safe bet."

"OK." Liam held up his hands. "I confess, I'd be rubbish at it. But that's the whole point."

"Sorry, you've lost me," said Xanthe.

"This fight organizer—Albert Taverstock his name was, even gave me his card—he saw me land a lucky punch. That's all it was, a fluke, but it wiped the other guy out. Only he thought I knew what I was doing. He thinks I've got skills and would make a good opponent for someone. Put up a good fight and probably win. He would talk me up.

Make a good draw, a dangerous unknown contender. Don't you see? The betting will be on me. All we need is a few quid to put on me to lose, which I will, and we can rake it in."

Xanthe started to protest, but Harley was muttering that the plan had merit and might possibly work. Eventually she shouted him down by pointing out that they still needed the stake money, which none of them had. To make it worthwhile it would still have to be quite a bit. It was at this point that Mistress Flyte spoke.

"I would be willing to pawn this," she said. As the others watched, she walked to the mantelpiece and opened a small, plain wooden box, from which she took the beautiful, shining, gold mourning brooch. She turned and handed it to Xanthe, who flinched at the shrillness with which it was now singing to her. "An appropriate measure to take, don't you think?" the old woman asked, her face sorrowful as she regarded the poignant piece of jewelry that trembled in Xanthe's hand.

—

The next twenty-four hours saw a great deal of activity all round. Xanthe and Harley returned to Holborn and showed Erasmus and Elizabeth the letter. After much discussion it was decided that Harley and Nipper should go with Liam to talk with the fight organizer and agree on a time for a match. Erasmus would take the brooch to the pawn shop. Elizabeth would see to it that Harley had evening wear appropriate for a man of means for when they would present themselves at the Visionary Society, assuming Liam's fight went as planned and they had the money they needed. Xanthe decided that, while they could not be certain who had broken in to try to steal the *Spinners* book, she would present herself as the daughter of Elizabeth and Harley. If Brook-Morton and Dawlish knew who she was they would no doubt reveal the fact and she might be able to use it to her advantage. If there was another Spinner involved, it would seem he was unknown to the pair. In which case, better to face him on her own terms and in a public place, with the help of her team around her. Elizabeth announced she would work to cloak the fact that Xanthe was a Spinner, something she had been able to do for Erasmus many times. It was this point that drove Xanthe to seek out the unusual woman later that same day, hoping to have the chance to speak to her on her own. The men were all busy with their various tasks, and Elizabeth was in the kitchen. When Xanthe found her she was straining herbal infusions from a copper pan through a piece of muslin cloth into a stoneware pitcher. The room was filled with the sweet smell of lavender and comfrey. On the dresser, pristine blue glass bottles stood waiting. She noticed the care and precision with which Elizabeth worked, her movements practiced and deft.

"Can I do anything to help?" she asked.

"You can write some labels for me. There is pen and ink there on the table."

Xanthe sat in front of the prettily bordered pieces of paper, which she could imagine Erasmus had made especially for his wife's produce. "What shall I write?"

"Half a dozen with tincture of lavender. The rest simply comfrey. I make oils and other distillations of lavender, but only this infusion of comfrey flowers, so there's no need to specify further. And the date, of course."

She smiled. "You will have to remind me what that is."

"We are in the year of our Lord 1878 and this is the twenty-eighth day of July. Almost Lammas Day. I have fond memories of so many festivals and celebrations of this time. From fierce fires at Beltane, glorious sunrises at the summer equinox, and then the joy of Lammas itself . . . my sister's favorite, though of course we were not able to publicly observe the customs and traditions connected to the date, as such festivals were frowned upon when she and I were young."

"Really? When was that?"

Elizabeth glanced at her and then said without so much as the slightest alteration in her casual tone of voice, "My sister died when she was eight years old, taken by the plague. That was harvest time, in 1628."

The atmosphere in the room crackled.

"But you are not a Spinner?"

"Nor am I a Time Stepper, though I have accompanied Erasmus on many missions since I married him."

Xanthe waited for her to volunteer an explanation but she simply carried on pouring the fragrant liquid through the straining cloth, her gaze entirely directed at her task. At something of a loss as to how to ask impossible and personal questions of this enigmatic woman, she cast about for safer ground. "What are these for?" she asked, gesturing at the infusions.

"They are both very much staples in the pharmacopeia of any healer," Elizabeth explained. "Lavender is the one herb no medic down the centuries could have managed without. It is a powerful antiseptic, a helpful remedy for insomnia, and particularly good for the reduction of scarring. This one," she said, lifting the jug of strained comfrey, "has a more specific function. Its old name is knitbone, and every goodwife and grandmother grew it in her garden, knowing its matchless ability to speed the healing of broken bones and lessen the chance of bone fever."

"I've heard of lavender pillows to help people sleep, but the rest is news to me. Fascinating. And do you regularly make new batches of your oils and things like this?" she asked, looking up at the rows of jars and bottles of all shapes and sizes on the dresser.

"I would never be without either of these, but there are others just as important and useful. Some should be made at the most advantageous phases of the moon, naturally, but, on this occasion, I am preparing for what might be needed imminently." When Xanthe still looked blank she said, "I might have added that lavender is also very effective at reducing bruising."

With a lurching stomach Xanthe realized she was preparing to heal

Liam after his fight. "I'm not happy with the thought of what he's going to do," she said, momentarily distracted from trying to find out more about her hostess. "He could get really hurt."

"I think we should be reassured by the fact that he is not required to strive to triumph over his opponent, only to give a convincing display of someone losing."

"Even so . . . I'm going to make him promise he won't let pride get the better of him and try to drag the thing out. The second round will be time enough to guard against accusations that he's thrown the fight."

"It is a brave thing to do. Am I right in thinking he is a willing participant in our plan because of his feelings for you?"

To her own amazement, Xanthe found herself blushing. "He does care for me, yes."

"And are his feelings returned?"

"We started out as friends, good friends, but . . . well, yes, we've grown very fond of each other."

Elizabeth set down the jug and turned to look levelly at Xanthe. "Dear me. Did any man truly ever act so out of fondness? Certainly he must love you."

She thought about this for a moment and then smiled. "Yes. Yes, I think he does love me."

"And though you might try to deny it, the glow in your eyes tells me his feelings will not go unrequited."

"Oh, I don't know . . . we haven't known each other very long."

"In my experience, though true love may smoulder for a lifetime, it has its beginning in a spark. And a spark exists in the quickest of instances. Its brightness cannot be mistaken for anything else. So tell me, young Spinner, do you love him?"

Xanthe seized the moment. "I will answer that," she said, "if you will first tell me how you come to be over two hundred and fifty years old."

Elizabeth placed the empty jug in the sink and came to sit on the chair opposite Xanthe. She clasped her hands in front of her on the table and said with just the hint of a smile, "It seems strange to me that in all your spinning through time, you have not yet encountered a witch."

13

"OK, YOU ARE GOING TO HAVE TO BE A LITTLE BIT MORE SPECIFIC," XANTHE SAID AS calmly as she could. "I mean, I grew up in a time when sane people believed a chunk of crystal could cure a headache, or a smelly oil could lift depression, and there's a whole heap of people celebrate the summer solstice at Stonehenge every year, and some of the same people call themselves witches. They tend to wear velvet and tie-dye, and a lot of them are vegetarian, and one or two of them have been my good friends and all-round lovely people. But not one of them is centuries old."

"You don't imagine there is only one kind of witch, surely?"

"Not anymore."

"I'm surprised at your somewhat narrow view, Xanthe. Surprised and a little disappointed. Would you like to be so dismissed if you told someone you were a time traveler?"

"Honestly, most people in my time would think I had lost my mind if I told them half of what I do."

"And yet you know it all to be true."

"It's happened to me, hasn't it? That's the difference."

"So you would require proof of someone else's claims to the extraordinary and supernatural, even after discovering the extent of your own gift? A gift, I might point out, that you have always had."

She thought about this. "I do remember the way some of Mum's friends reacted when I was little and she would tell them about treasures singing to me," she said, a little shamefaced. "And really, I'm happy for people to believe what they want, anything that helps and doesn't hurt anyone else is fine by me. I think maybe it's a matter of scale. I mean, I'll admit I find the smell of lavender in this room right now truly relaxing. And yes, having discovered I can journey through time has changed the way I see things. But . . . you don't spin or step. You say there are different types of witches, so I'm assuming your type is very long lived. . . ."

"As a matter of fact, my being a witch is not particularly linked to my longevity. That has more to do with the influence and designs of another person. Like you, I grew up with certain talents that set me apart. My mother was a herbalist and a healer and she taught me these valuable skills, but I had something other than that in my being. Something that enabled me to affect and influence things, a communication with the elemental, if you like, which extended to an ability to communicate well with species other than my own. But I see by your expression that I am going too fast and only telling you things that require further explanation. Perhaps it would serve our purposes better, given the current demands on our time, if I gave a demonstration of some sort. If I provided the proof you so desire. Ordinarily I object to being made to perform tricks to explain my existence, but I am prepared to make an exception. For you."

Xanthe waited, not wanting to say anything that might make Elizabeth change her mind. Elizabeth sat quietly for a moment as if weighing up possible options, possible ways to demonstrate the truth of her identity. Then, with slow deliberation, she directed her gaze to one of the small blue bottles on the table between them. Without touching it, she caused it to move. Just a little, but there was definitely unmistakable movement. After a short pause she made it move again, farther this time. Xanthe's smile began to broaden. Suddenly the bottle skidded the length of the table at some speed. Instinctively, Xanthe grabbed it before it shot off the end.

Laughing, she looked at Elizabeth. "Wow," she said, "it feels hot. Like a found thing sometimes does when it's talking to me and I hold it."

"Everything is energy, after all," Elizabeth said in a matter-of-fact way. She made a second bottle move, this time having it describe a circle on the table, a third bottle joining in to follow it. The candles in the candlesticks suddenly acquired flames, causing Xanthe to gasp. Next, Elizabeth took in the dresser with a graceful wave of her arm, causing all the jars, vials, and bottles to spin, and the eggs in the basket to rotate. Soon all the shelves seemed to teem with life, everything on them turning or jiggling in some way. Glass against glass set up chimes, with beats against the wood of the dresser, so that there was music to accompany the dance. Elizabeth stood up. She raised her arms, holding them out wide, her eyes bright with love of her craft, the magic shining out of her as she too slowly turned around. As she did so, the chairs, the candlesticks, the plates in the wooden drainer, the bunches of herbs tied to hooks in the ceiling beams, all started to wriggle and vibrate or twist and spin until it seemed that the whole kitchen and everything in it was part of the performance. Xanthe leaped to her feet as two wooden spoons flew past her and three more began to beat an increasingly frantic rhythm on copper pots and pans. The faster Elizabeth turned, her head flung back, her smile wide, her joyful laughter filling the air, the wilder the dance until there was not a thing that sat still or did not join in the music of the spell. And then, just like that, it stopped. Everything dropped back to its own allotted place. Bottles became quiet and still again. The flames of the candles extinguished themselves. Elizabeth stood calm and motionless in the center of the room.

"Well, young Spinner? Is that proof enough for you?" she wanted to know.

—

At about the same time that Xanthe was being instructed in the ways of a near immortal hedge witch, Liam was standing in front of a broad, sturdy door in Cotterall Street. The same street from which he had, only a few days before, met with the thugs who had attempted to abduct him. This time, however, he was not alone. To his left stood Nipper, his face unable to conceal the wariness with which he regarded his new acquaintance. To his right was Harley, whiskers freshly oiled, standing tall, ready for whatever might be asked of him. Liam was grateful for the company and assistance of both men. He knocked hard upon the door and after a short while a small shuttered window set into it was opened. A heavily browed face peered out.

"I'm here to see Mr. Albert Taverstock," Liam told the owner of the face.

"Is he expecting you?" came the gruff response.

"He gave me his card and asked me to call," he said, holding up Taverstock's business card for the man's myopic inspection.

After another grunt the window was slammed shut. Bolts were drawn, and the door pulled open on stiff hinges. Liam stepped over the threshold with an outward confidence that did not match the slight churning of his stomach. He knew his plan could work, and he was happy to see it through, but that did not stop him harboring a small but real anxiety about what would be required of him. Harley and Nipper kept close behind him as they followed the doorman along the passageway of the old building. Instead of taking them to the main room at the back, where Liam had seen the boxing ring and a fight taking place within it, he led them up a creaking stairway to a room on the first floor. It was furnished with a seemingly random selection of pieces; a desk in front of the single window with a leather chair behind it, a chesterfield sofa from which horsehair was escaping through the missing buttons on its back, a cabinet with a glass front housing bottles of whiskey and an assortment of glasses, and, in pride of place, a birdcage on a stand housing an enormous green parrot. At one end of the room there was a bed, piled high with mattresses and bedcovers. The light in the room was not bright, coming only from the sunshine that struggled through the grime of the windows. So it was that it took a moment for Liam to realize that the bed still contained a rotund person, and that person was Albert Taverstock himself. He was not asleep, but sitting up, nightcap still on his head, coverlets pulled up to his chin, gnawing on what looked like a chicken bone. This he waved at his visitors by way of greeting, clearly not prepared to actually rise from his nest of quilts and blankets to talk with them.

"Ah, the young lad with the splendid right hook! Quite something to see, it was. Quite something. All shyness and reticence overcome, I see? No more denials of your prowess now, then. Appraising the venue and opposition, perhaps? Understandable, indeed, understandable. Welcome to you, young sir. And your friends. Step in, step in, do, let us close the door. McBride will have me catch my death, for the drafts in this building will kill a man quicker than a jab to the jaw, sirs, a jab to the jaw!"

They moved farther into the gloomy room. McBride shut the door and stood, arms folded, barring it. He was a solid-looking fellow, and had a mean expression he had evidently perfected over time, but Liam highly doubted he could have prevented them leaving had he been called upon to try. In fact, the rank odor emanating from him was sufficient to keep them from wanting to push past him.

Taverstock, sensing money to be made, shifted in his bed to sit a little straighter, not for a moment relinquishing his grip on the platter of meat he held on his lap. "Are you come to make your fortune, young man? For there is gold in that swift fist of yours, gold for the taking.

Are you brave enough to grasp it, that is the question, is it not?" While the man spoke, still chewing chicken, his gaze swept over Harley and Liam, no doubt assessing them as possible trouble or possible sources of further income.

"The pertinent question," Harley replied, stepping forward, "is what terms would you offer, and what sort of opponent would you find? I am the lad's manager, and you will direct all matters of business to me. My man is a prizefighter. He won't fight any ragtag flotsam washed up on the dockside. He has a reputation to keep," he assured him.

"Has he? A reputation, you say? And yet when we met he declared he was not a boxer, no sir, not at all."

"I was about personal business that night," Liam told him. "I did not wish to have my profession brought into it."

"You did not? You would rather spy upon my establishment." He tapped the side of his nose knowingly. "I see, I see." He turned back to Harley, asking, "And what name does this champion fight under, just so I might be sure I give him all due respect."

"This is none other than Rabbie Bearpaw. If ye've ever ventured from this . . . palace and ventured north enough to escape the stink of London, you'll have heard of him right enough. Scotland is where we hail from, for that is where such men are born and made."

Taverstock fought a battle within himself, affronted at the slight on his home, not wishing to be thought small or unworldly, tempted to make some sharp remark, but pulled toward the possibility of using the newcomer to line his own pockets. If he had not heard of him, nor would others have, but that need not stand in the way of a lucrative match.

"What use have I for traveling to Scotland, when Scotland so readily comes to me?" he replied, treating Liam to a gappy smile. "If your lad be a prizewinner, we can find him a worthy opponent, do not fear on that score, Mister . . . ?"

"Harley. Of Glenawer."

"Mister Harley. Of Glenawer." He paused to wipe grease from his mouth with the uppermost bedcover. "In point of fact, I have just such a contender in mind, would suit very well indeed. A little heavier than your boy, a little taller, maybe a few years more experienced, but slower with it. He should put up a good fight, give the crowd what they want, but I fancy your lad might be up to him."

Harley looked convincingly insulted. "What? You'd offer us some old lag? A lump past his prime? My lad is at the top o' his game. If you've no one more fitting, we'll be on our way." He turned, gesturing at the others to do so, and the three of them made as if to leave.

McBride blanched, but, to his credit, stood firm.

"Why so hasty?" called Taverstock from his bed. "Gentlemen can always agree on terms. Let us say I was to find you an opponent you deem worthy for your prodigy—and I grant you his talent appeared to me to be prodigious—how much of the prize money would you be financing?"

At this Harley gasped and then scowled. "What? Not content with insulting my lad, you ask for us to provide the purse! Hell's teeth, man, the ways of you southerners are not to be tolerated! I offer you the pride of the north! The one to beat to make any man's name! Such an opportunity walks into your . . . *establishment* and yet you ask for prize money? Come, Rabbie, my boy, let us waste no more time here." He took a purposeful stride toward the door, jaw set, eyes murderous. McBride balked and stepped aside. Harley wrenched open the door.

At last, Taverstock was compelled to leave off feasting. "Stay! Mister Harley, again I urge you not to act in haste, for we are both about the same purpose here, are we not?" The stout little man heaved back the covers, revealing a nightshirt that was as worn as his cap, and swung his bare, bandy legs out from their hiding. Filthy toes protruded through the holes in his hosiery. Whatever money the entrepreneur made from the pain and exertions of others, evidently he did not spend much of it on his clothes. He pushed those same feet into napless velvet slippers and became a most solicitous host. "Come, sit, be at ease. I promise you, an arrangement can be made to the satisfaction of all concerned." Here he pulled out dusty chairs from their random stations.

Harley paused for effect before nodding at the others. He and Liam seated themselves, while Nipper remained standing, marking McBride in a very obvious way, much to the doorman's dislike.

Encouraged by this cooperation, Taverstock opened the cabinet and pulled from it a decanter containing a golden liquor. "Not Scotch, I confess, but the best the Irish have to offer, I assure you. A sweetener, this was, from a happy manager, a man such as yourself, yes, such as yourself. A fine lad he brought to London, and fortunes improved all round. Here, you will try a glass? If only to compare it with your own . . . ?"

Harley nodded. "Aye, let's see what watery beverage those Irish can manage to muster from their peat bogs."

Beside him Liam winced, not sure whether to be impressed or appalled at how easily and how quickly Harley was able to take on the sensibilities of the time. He leaned close to his friend and whispered in his ear, as they had earlier agreed he would do when the moment was right.

Harley nodded again as he took the smeary glass from Taverstock. "Rabbie wants to know, how soon can ye arrange a fight? He's a sweetheart back in the Highlands he's pining for. We'll stay no longer than we must."

"Well, now, once we agree on our second player in this game, I can move forward swift as a hare before a hound, I promise you that. Let me see, if it's someone younger you want, a true match . . ."

"Aye, that . . ."

"I've a fella comes to mind might suit. He is a little untried, but the coming thing, word is."

"People hereabouts will know of him? I'll have no nameless boy."

"Oh, he's known. His father was a fighter before him, and his brother too. The family is held in high regard in and out of the ring. The name of Wilkes always draws a crowd, and a crowd with money to wager."

"Ha! Let them come. Let them think they can beat my lad!" He turned to give Liam a rather too hearty slap on the back. "We'll have a surprise for them, that I guarantee."

"Your boy is gifted, I will not argue different, no I will not, sir. But mark my words, a Wilkes will not go down easy. A Wilkes will test him. Test him hard."

"He is not afeared of some southern whippersnapper! Let them meet, I say! We'll show them what a Highland man is made of."

"Do we have an arrangement, then?"

"If you can have them toeing the line by tomorrow night we do."

"Tomorrow! That leaves precious little time for spreading the word. . . ."

"Such a match? Surely word will travel like salts through the belly!"

"Quite so, quite so. Then yes! I will put up a purse sufficient to tempt the Wilkes and his clan, we will pull plenty who will wager grandly, and you and I will split the proceeds of the door, what say you to that?"

"I say we drink to seal our arrangement! No, not for the lad. Do not spoil him." He batted away the glass Taverstock was offering to Liam. Nipper, holding his position, was seen as muscle only, clearly, and not part of the proceedings.

Taverstock raised his glass. "To a fine match, and an even finer haul," he said, a gleam of excitement lighting up his ruddy face.

"I'll drink to that!" Harley agreed, tipping his glass to down the whiskey in one swift gulp.

Liam watched him closely. He could detect a slight bulging of his friend's eyes and a swift intake of breath, but he withstood the rough liquor well enough. However harsh it was, he found himself wishing he had the chance of at least some of it, as the realization of what he had just been put up for hit home. Whatever Harley's thoughts about him being spoiled, when the time came he would not be stepping into that ring without a decent helping of Dutch courage.

14

ALONE IN HER ROOM AT ERASMUS'S HOUSE, GETTING UNDRESSED, XANTHE AT LAST HAD time to process recent events and prepare herself for what was to come. Her relief at finding Liam had freed her mind to focus on the mission she had been called to by both the writing slope and the mourning brooch. Since Elizabeth had revealed her true identity to her, the writing box had taken on a new significance. She was still buzzing from the thrill of seeing real magic performed in front of her. A thrill that was heightened by the knowledge that she and Elizabeth had so much in common. She herself might not be able to cast spells and move objects without touching them, but being a Spinner, and connecting with the hidden histories of treasures in the way that she had all her life, was a very real kind of magic. As Elizabeth had been quick to point out. This shared aspect of their natures, this overlap of their talents, made her feel strongly connected to her new friend. Was that why the writing box had summoned her? To allow them to meet so that she should have a new ally? If so, there had to be a specific purpose to their meeting beyond a helpful friendship. Xanthe knew that found things only sang to her for an immediate and particular reason. She was meant to do something with Elizabeth's help that she could not do without it. From what Lydia Flyte had told her, the Visionary Society Spinners were to be challenging adversaries. It seemed likely, then, that she would indeed need Elizabeth's special talents to be successful in her task. For the society had to be stopped, defeated, disbanded forever. The mourning brooch had helped her find Liam, but as far as her duties as a Spinner went, it had led her to Mistress Flyte. She was still struggling to organize her thoughts regarding the old woman. She had been so hurt when Mistress Flyte had betrayed her, and that betrayal was not easily forgiven or forgotten. But, as seemed to be the case, if Lydia's sole aim had been to get Xanthe—and therefore Erasmus and Elizabeth—to halt the actions of the Visionary Society, how could she hold a grudge? Mistress Flyte was right; Brook-Morton and Dawlish were the very worst kind of Spinners, who had to be stopped, not only to put an end to their own dangerous exploits, but as a warning to any others who might think to abuse their gifts that this would not be tolerated. She wanted to forgive her old friend, to repair that friendship, but she doubted she would easily trust her again. And that thought saddened her.

There was another factor that niggled away at her reasoning. Mistress Flyte's health. It was obvious to Xanthe just by looking at her, and reinforced by what Liam had told her, that the old woman was seriously ill. In fact, now that she formed the thought calmly and sensibly, she knew that the elderly Spinner was dying. Which would go some way to explaining, perhaps, why she had taken such drastic steps to ensure Xanthe would step up and deal with the society. She hadn't the luxury of time to persuade her gently, or wait until such time as suited her. The mourning brooch, then, had called her to the shabby dockland house as part of the mission to confront Brook-Morton and Dawlish. This seemed to make sense, and yet there was something not quite right about it as an explanation. It felt like she was forcing a piece of the puzzle into a space that wasn't a proper fit. She was missing something, and for the life of her she could not see what it was.

As darkness deepened over London, she climbed into the brass bed and snuggled beneath the patchwork quilt that covered it. Outside she could hear church bells chiming the house. She recalled the nursery rhyme of her childhood and wondered which towers the great iron bells were swinging in.

Oranges and lemons, say the bells of St. Clement's,
You owe me five farthings, say the bells of St. Martin's.
When will you pay me, say the bells of Old Bailey?
When I grow rich, say the bells of Shoreditch.

The sounds were muffled by distance and by the heavy atmosphere of the city, but she could make out at least three different chimes. The ringing was strangely comforting and made her sleepy, putting her in mind of Flora and her bell-ringing sessions back home in Marlborough. How far away home seemed at that moment. She had traveled greater distances in time before, but on this journey felt somehow more disconnected from her own time and her own life than ever. While the pull of family, of the familiar, of her own home, would always be there, it was not as strong as it used to be. Why was that? Could it be that with Elizabeth and Erasmus she had found a second family and that in some way softened the way she missed those she loved? Or was it because she had Liam there with her, in Victorian London, an important part of her mission? She had taken him with her before, of course, but now things had changed. Now, after their reunion, and after the way Elizabeth had questioned her about her feelings for him, there had been a shifting in his importance in her life. Because now, at last, she had admitted, at least to herself, that she was in love with him.

Forcing herself to push this enormous thought to one side, Xanthe brought her mind to bear on the plan that she and Erasmus had been developing. Liam having offered to take part in a fight was not something she was happy about, but the money could not be found quickly any other way. With the brooch pawned, they had their stake. Erasmus, not being known to the boxing fraternity, would buy a ticket for the fight and place his bet. Harley and Nipper would be there as

Liam's manager and second, and would help make sure Erasmus was allowed to leave the premises with his winnings safely. Elizabeth and Harley would present themselves as husband and wife buying their seat at the table of the Visionary Society's next meeting. After much debate, Xanthe had convinced them to take her as their daughter. Erasmus had argued that they would detect a Spinner, to which Elizabeth had replied that she could cloak her so that she would not be discovered. But Xanthe had her own idea. She considered it best to wrong-foot the men. Let them expect to impress new clients and take their money, and then see how unsettled they were when they realized they had another Spinner in their home. If they already knew who she was—which would confirm they were connected to the Spinner she had seen following her and Elizabeth—it would be one more question answered. If they did not, they had to keep in mind that there was someone else, someone whose identity they had no knowledge of, who knew of her existence and, more important, knew about the *Spinners* book, its importance, and where it was being kept. It was also agreed that Mistress Flyte and Liam would attend the meeting, dangling the prospect of his agreeing to cooperate with their spinning as a way to get him into the building and add a further distraction for Brook-Morton and Dawlish.

The second part of their plan relied on those of them who had legitimately gained entry into the society's headquarters doing two things successfully. They had to find the talismans or treasures that the men were using to help them travel, and they had to make sure that Erasmus and Nipper were let into the building. Fairfax had needed his astrolabe to travel. Xanthe needed her found things to travel and her locket to return home. It seemed to her reasonable to expect these Spinners would also have artifacts or devices that they used to journey. As with Fairfax, she saw it as her task to remove these precious treasures from them. To destroy them, preferably. After that it was very much a matter of playing things by ear, which was not a tactic that had found favor with either Harley or Elizabeth but no one could improve upon it. Xanthe made the point that they must keep their main goals in mind: to stop the men in their work, remove their ability to spin through time ever again, and permanently disband the society. As long as they kept to the brief of their mission, with so many of them there to help, they stood a good chance of succeeding.

Her mind still whirring, she was at last lulled to sleep by the clocks chiming the quarter hour. Her sleep was peopled with strangers and disjointed stories, with snatches of conversations and moments of darkness so that nothing made any sense when she woke again only three hours later. She sat up and used one of her own matches to light the candle beside her bed. She fetched the *Spinners* book from its hiding place beneath the false floor of the oak wardrobe and climbed back under the covers, shivering against the cool night air that seeped through the thin glass of the window. She had no specific question for the book's authors this time; she knew only that she was drawn to communicate with those Spinners who had gone before her. That she needed to feel that kinship, that connection, so that she could most effectively complete the tasks she had been called upon to do. As she opened the book, leaning its weight against her knees, she heard again the whispered voices of people like her who had, in their own time, followed the path of a Spinner. She turned the pages, studying the maps, charts, portraits, and sundry images that revealed themselves to her.

She soon realized that the book was behaving a little differently to what she had come to expect. Instead of mostly blank pages among which stories and illustrations gradually appeared, the book was full. There was not an empty page to be seen. Every leaf was covered in flowing script or colorful images. She did not have to wait for writing to materialize on the paper; it was there already. Where before there might have been modest line drawings or faded charts, now everything was displayed in fabulously rich colors, illuminated with gold lettering, bordered with vibrant reds and greens, each page more beautiful and more detailed than the last. Flowers and vines trailed up the margins, overflowing each page, bursting into bloom and perfuming the air with sweet scents of orange blossom and lily of the valley and honeysuckle. All the contents of the book were laid bare for her, and with it the voices of those who had inscribed their stories, or penned their incantations, or printed their own likenesses, or given the gift of a man or plan. She sat up straighter. The covers fell from her, but she wasn't cold. She was enveloped in the warmth that emanated from *Spinners.* She was overwhelmed with the feeling that she would never know loneliness again; that she would always and forever have the companionship and support of her brother and sister Spinners. It was an utterly joyous moment of revelation and she felt both humbled and elated.

"Thank you!" she whispered in reply to the many voices that filled the room with their welcomes and greetings. "I won't let you down, I promise!"

She gently closed the book and sat quietly for some time, allowing herself to process what had just happened. She believed she had been given the full approval of her fellow Spinners, and that now she had to reward their trust with the success of her actions. Beyond rescuing Liam, the reputation of all Spinners was at stake, as well as the need to put an end to the damaging work of the Visionary Society. A great deal depended on what she did next. Instead of feeling a burden of responsibility, however, she felt empowered, strengthened, and reassured. At last, knowing she would not get back to sleep, she returned the book to its hiding place. She shrugged on a warm brocade nightgown Elizabeth had lent her and pushed her bare feet into her own boots, grateful for the familiar feel of the old worn leather and the firmness they added to her step. She decided to go down to the kitchen and attempt to make herself some tea. The kettle was always on the range, and Elizabeth labeled all her supplies with great care, so it should not prove beyond her. It was still dark, so she took the bedside candle in its brass holder, rather than tackle the gas lights that made her a little nervous.

As she descended the stairs she noticed the flicker of more candlelight coming from Erasmus's workshop, the door of which was ajar. She stepped into the room, raising her candle, which had the unhelpful knack of illuminating herself rather than what she was trying to see if she did not hold it at precisely the right height. She saw Erasmus, still dressed, sitting at his workbench. The shutters of the windows were open, but the room was too high in the building to benefit from the streetlights, and he had only a stub of candle beside him, so that he sat mostly in shadow.

On seeing Xanthe enter the room he lifted his head.

"Ah. Another who cannot find sleep?" he asked, though it was clear to her he had not even been to bed to search for it himself.

"Can I join you?" she asked.

"But of course," he said, pulling another stool out from beneath the bench.

She sat beside him, setting her own candle down on a space between the rulers, snippets of leather, and paper samples in front of her. She noticed then that there was a heavy purse of coins on the workbench next to Erasmus and knew at once that it was the money he must have obtained for pawning the mourning brooch. She wondered what he had understood of it. As difficult as such a conversation might be, she could not put off telling him what she knew about Lydia's child any longer. It was hard to know how to begin such a subject. She started carefully.

"You were a Spinner before you became a Time Stepper, Erasmus. I'm curious, did you use treasures to travel? Was there something in particular, or did different things call to you?" she asked.

"My experience of traveling as a Spinner was similar to your own in as much as I was often found by certain objects and I would follow where they led. I did not have a personal talisman as such in the way that some do. As for finding my way home, well, that talent seemed given to me free from the necessity of any totem. Perhaps that is why I was able to make the transition to the work of a Time Stepper without difficulty. I would answer the summons of those who needed me and then simply return to my own time when my task was completed."

"Like when Elizabeth needed you?"

"Like when Elizabeth needed me, yes. Though of course on this occasion we traveled to my own time, and here we have settled. Thus far."

"Did you . . . did you sense anything in particular when you held the mourning brooch?" she asked.

At this question he turned to look at her and as he did so the pale light of the gray London dawn found his face. Xanthe's heart constricted as she saw that he had been crying.

"I confess," he said, his voice breaking, "it was not an easy thing, to hand that treasure over to the pawnbroker."

"Would you like me to tell you what I know?"

"If you would be so kind," he said and nodded, looking away from her again now, appearing to steady himself for what he was about to hear.

And so she recounted to him the story that had been revealed to her in the *Spinners* book. She told him how she had seen a young woman take valuable coins to a goldsmith and have one melted down to make the brooch. How she had given very specific instructions as to the way the brooch should be made, from its style, to the use of the lock of the child's hair, to the inscription bearing the name Amy. "To mean 'beloved'—the same meaning as the name of her father," she explained.

Erasmus made no reply but sat in silence for a while. She knew it was likely he had worked out the story for himself just from having the brooch in his possession and knowing who it belonged to. Even so, to hear the truth must have been hard.

When he spoke his voice was steadier but still soft. "Did you discover the age of the child when she died? I should like to be able to imagine her, yet I cannot decide if she lived beyond infancy."

Xanthe shook her head. "I'm sorry, I don't know. If it's any help, the lock of hair was quite long. She could not have been a baby."

"And there was no reason given for her death?"

"Not that I can recall."

After another short silence he said, "Lydia must have known—when we parted for the last time—she must have known that she was with child. And yet she chose not to share that golden knowledge with me."

"I don't presume to know about the love the two of you shared," she said, "but, don't you think her not telling you shows just how much she put being a Spinner before everything else? I mean, if she'd told you about the baby you might have stayed. You might have put personal happiness before the clear path you saw you had to tread to become a Time Stepper. You thought she let you go because she wanted to remain a Spinner and join those who would spin time for their own gains. But she knew what you had to do mattered more than your being together. She would not hold you back, even for the child she was carrying. I believe that the woman you fell in love with, the woman I counted as a true friend, is every bit the wonderful, fine, selfless person we always knew her to be. She sacrificed her own happiness for the good of the Spinners. She let you go so that you could police them as no one else would."

"And the sad irony is, when the child died, she too took up that work."

"Which is why she helped me defeat Fairfax. Which is why she brought me here, to help you do what you have to do."

"Ah, there you and I hold opinions which differ, young Spinner. It is I who am assistant to you, not the other way around."

"There's something else," Xanthe said, anxious now to discuss a matter that had been playing on her mind. "Lydia is not well."

"Yes, you mentioned that. I am sorry to hear it."

"Erasmus, I think she's dying."

He reached forward and picked up a workaday awl. The wooden

handle of the bookbinder's essential tool fitted perfectly into the palm of his hand, its surface worn smooth and gleaming by years of repeated use. The iron spike it held tapered to a fine, sharp point, perfectly designed to pierce neat holes in fine leather ready for stitching. Without looking up from it he said, "The toll that spinning takes from a person varies between individuals. There is no standard measure, yet there is always a price to be paid for the manipulation of time. For time is a jealous mistress and will have her due. We all of us will know that reckoning. What we cannot know is when that day will come."

She was shocked by his words. From the very first occasion she had spun through time she had been worried that she would upset the correct order of things, until she had come to understand that her work maintained that very order. She had never stopped to consider what journeying back and fore through the centuries might do to herself. Hearing that her gift, her calling, her work, that it could have a detrimental effect on her health and ultimately shorten her life, it was a lot to take in. She wanted desperately to question Erasmus on this. She needed to know more. But this was not the moment.

"Do you want to see her?" she asked. "I can arrange a meeting for just the two of you, if that's what you'd like. If you think Elizabeth would be . . . OK with that."

"Elizabeth?" He looked puzzled for a second before understanding Xanthe's meaning. "Oh, you need have no concerns on that count. My wife and I do not have secrets from each other, aside, perhaps, from the few we have not yet had time to share." He smiled then, some of the sadness leaving his handsome face. "She and I have also led long and busy lives. No, she would not begrudge me a farewell with Lydia. And yet . . ." He put down the awl and stood up, his manner suddenly more businesslike, his more usual energetic demeanour returned, though clearly by an act of will, it seemed to Xanthe. "I do not believe it would serve either of our purposes to revisit painful times. Lydia did not make such a sacrifice only to see us falter at such a crucial moment in the history of Spinners and Steppers alike. No, we will be reunited in a common cause, and that cause is the one that brought us together all those long, winding years ago. There is a pleasing symmetry to that, do you not agree?" Before she could answer he offered her his arm. "And now," he said, with a brief, courteous bow, "I recommend we go to table. The days ahead are long and will test us. What restoration we have foregone by way of sleep, let us make up for with hearty food."

Xanthe slid from the stool, took his arm, and paused to blow out the candles before the pair made their way down through the house to the kitchen, soft morning light accompanying their descent.

15

THE SMALL YARD BEHIND LYDIA FLYTE'S DOCKSIDE HOUSE WAS NORTH-FACING, SO THERE was no sunshine to lift the dreariness of the space. Liam thought briefly of the beer garden behind The Feathers back home. On this occasion, however, he had not stepped outside to sit and drink. Harley had insisted he coach him a little in boxing before the fight. When Liam had argued that he had only to lose, his friend had reminded him that the whole event had been agreed upon the understanding that he was a prizefighter. He had to at least give the impression he had stood in a ring before. In the yard, he wore breeches and a loose white shirt.

Harley came out of the house carrying a jar in one hand, a sack of flour casually slung over his shoulder. Not for the first time Liam wondered if it wouldn't have been better to volunteer him as the contender.

"Right, laddie," said Harley, swinging the sack to the ground. "Let's have your hands."

Liam held them out. Harley plucked the cork stopper from the stone jar with his teeth and spat it to one side before sloshing the cold liquid over Liam's knuckles.

"Vinegar?" he exclaimed, recoiling from the smell.

"Aye, given the lack of time it's the best we can do to toughen up these delicate paws."

"They're not that bad," Liam protested, watching as Harley rubbed the vinegar into each knuckle in turn. "Might get the last of the engine oil out, I suppose. I seem to remember pickling conkers as a child to make them harder."

"You'd likely have baked those too, but we are not about to do that. Now, let's see fists."

Liam did as he was asked, holding up his best effort at fighting fists in a boxing stance. Harley's face was a picture of dismay.

"Hell's teeth," he muttered, stepping forward to alter his position. "That's . . . shocking."

"Think it'd terrify my opponent?"

"There is a danger he could die laughing! For the love of God, not like that. Here, this hand up higher, protect your jaw. This one in close to it. OK. Now, feet further apart. You look like a strong sneeze could blow you over. . . ."

"Oh come on, it's not that bad, I work out."

"Maybe . . . take your shirt off."

"It's pretty chilly out here." Seeing the murderous expression on his coach's face, Liam nodded and removed the shirt. His tattoos were helpfully edgy for the day, and the truth of his working out was plain to see in the definition of his muscles. He was lean, but not skinny. His frame muscular enough to give an opponent cause for worry.

"Aye"—Harley nodded—"you look the part now. That'll help. Could you maybe try to do something with your face?"

"What?"

Harley put his hands on his hips and spoke somberly. "Liam, lad, you are stepping up to fight a boy from a fighting family. A youngster who knows what he's about. There's not Queensberry rules here. This is bare-knuckle. The clue is in the name. It hurts to hit and it hurts even more to be hit. There will be a deal of money riding on the outcome. He's not going to mess about. You've been talked up as a contender." He paused, not so much, Liam thought, for effect, more because he wasn't sure what he was going to say was helpful, but it had to be said. "He'll kill you if he has to."

"Good to know."

"Seriously, all I can do is show you how to protect yourself. Your best bet is going to be to keep moving. Don't let him land a punch."

"Shouldn't I be trying to hit him too?"

"It would help, but we can't have you leaving yourself open and being knocked out in the first few seconds."

"The being knocked out bit does not sound good, no."

"Your man Taverstock will smell a rat. If he works out you're no boxer, he could cry foul."

"Then we won't get our money."

"Then we'd be lucky to leave with all our teeth, never mind money. You just need to keep going into the second round. Show a bit of style. Let's see that famous hook of yours. Wait while I set this up." Harley used a length of rope to string up the sack of flour from an iron lamp hook on the side of the house. "Hit it from here," he said, pulling Liam to stand to one side. "Away from the wall."

Liam paced around a little, swinging his arms to loosen them and warm up a bit. He jogged on the spot for a while, then tried to take the position Harley had shown him. From there he swung his right fist as hard as he could into the sack. There was a disappointingly small puff of flour and dust.

Harley rolled his eyes. "Is that what Taverstock saw you do? The man's eyesight must be even shorter than his legs."

"When he saw me I was being attacked. I was fighting for my life."

"And that's what you'll be doing in the ring, laddie! Ye have to believe that. When you stand in front of your opponent, you have to see in him every danger you've ever faced. Every person who's ever threatened you. Go again."

Liam focused, casting his mind back to how he had felt in that alley, how fear and anger had driven him. He threw a second punch. A little out of breath, wincing from the harsh contact with the surprisingly unyielding flour sack, he turned for Harley's reaction.

"Better"—he shrugged—"but I don't see murder in your eyes yet."

"I don't have murderous experiences to draw on."

"There must be something makes the red mist descend."

He thought for a moment and a recollection of Fairfax threatening Xanthe flashed before his mind's eye. He thought also about how her loathsome ex-boyfriend had mistreated her. He thought about how he would feel if anyone laid a finger on her. With a growl, he attacked the flour sack again, first with a right hook, then swiftly a left uppercut and another right, following it up with a series of fierce jabs, one after the other, again and again. At last he stopped.

Harley let out a low whistle.

"Good enough?" Liam asked.

"Remind me never to piss you off," said Harley.

Liam grinned. "As long as we get the money Xanthe needs."

"She's lucky to have you on her team," Harley told him.

"She came to find me. It's the least I can do."

"She feels responsible. For you being here. And for me. For getting both of us home safely."

"I know. And she's got a job to do. It worries me, you know? That she's trying to do something really difficult and dangerous and all the time she's worrying about us, when we should be looking after her."

"We will, laddie. Don't you worry. We will."

At that moment the back door to the house opened and Nipper appeared. He took in the sight of Liam, shirtless, in boxing pose, and narrowed his eyes at the tatty flour sack. He slowly folded his arms and leaned back against the doorframe.

"You know, do you not, that your opponent is a skilled professional? You think he and his people won't know a fraud when they see one?"

Harley turned to face him. "That's why we're putting in some work, laddie. We're doing what we can in the time we've got."

"Might it not be better if you learned how the fights work? Furnished yourself with knowledge of the rules?"

Liam looked surprised. "I thought there weren't any. Isn't that the point?"

"Naturally there are rules!" Nipper straightened up and strode toward him. "You think us uncivilized, I know. You look down on what you see as our old-fashioned ways."

"No, really . . ." Liam protested.

"You think I do not see it? The way you regard me? Even my father, who knows more of life and humanity than you ever will should you live to be a hundred! You act as though you and you alone brought about all the great advances and scientific miracles you are all so proud of in your own time. How many diseases did *you* cure? How many great houses did *you* build?"

"OK, none, I admit," said Liam, holding up his hands with a smile, not wanting to rile the young man further.

"How many mechanical devices have you yourself created?"

Harley could not keep quiet. "Point of fact, laddie, young Liam here is a talented mechanic."

Nipper ignored him. He was standing close enough to Liam to prod him in the ribs now. "Were I to have been born in your day I would have matched your knowledge, your position, your wealth. Do not convince yourself otherwise."

"Wouldn't dream of it," Liam said, not appreciating being goaded physically now as well as verbally. He stood his ground. "If you'd been brought up in my time you might have learned some manners too."

At this, Nipper bridled and drew back his hand. Whether to retreat or throw a blow it was hard to tell. Liam grabbed his wrist and the two glared at each other.

Nipper scowled. "You know nothing about what it means to be a boxer, here. Now. In *my* time. *My* city. Yet you are too full of pride to think to ask me what I know."

Harley stepped in, gently putting a hand on the youngster's shoulder. "Aye, you've a point there. Maybe we should have come to you. My mistake. I was eager to try to at least show Liam how to avoid getting that pretty nose of his broken."

Nipper kept his eyes on Liam, who still had not relinquished his grip on the youth's wrist. "Or getting himself killed," he said baldly.

"Aye, that too," Harley agreed. "So how about you tell us what you know." He waited and then added, "Xanthe needs all of us to help her right now. All of us."

Nipper considered this and snatched his hand free of Liam's grip. For a moment he did not speak and Liam wondered if he would sulk rather than be of any use. At last, Nipper broke the uneasy quiet.

"He will need mufflers," he said.

"Mufflers?" Harley had no idea what he was talking about.

"To wrap his hands. There will be no gloves, it's true, but linen wound around the palm and knuckles will protect the hands a little. Don't expect the blows to be softened, though." He paused to lean closer to Liam again, as if enjoying the point a little. "Mufflers only make a good boxer strike all the harder."

"OK." Harley nodded. "We'll fix him up with some of those. What else do we need to know?"

"The rounds are not timed, so don't think there will be a bell to save you."

"How does that work?" Liam asked.

"You fight until one of you goes down. The man on his knees has thirty seconds to get back in the ring and come up to the mark—"

"The mark?" Harley asked.

Nipper used his foot to draw a line in the fine layer of flour that covered the cobbles. "There's a line in the center of the ring—which may or may not have a rope."

Liam recalled the one he had seen on his first encounter with Tavistock. "They were using straw bales, I think."

"Yes"—Nipper nodded—"that's more likely in such a match as this. So, the referee will ask the fighters to come to stand toe-to-toe on the line. He will remind you of the rules . . . no wrestling, no biting or gouging, no hitting below the waist, no striking a man when he is down . . . then he will instruct you to fight. A man's seconds may help him only while his opponent's time is being counted. If a man is struck down and cannot come back to the line within the given time, he forfeits the match. If he is able, the fight continues."

"Until?" Liam wanted to know.

Nipper looked at him as if he had asked a stupid question. "Why, until one man is no longer able to fight. The other will then be declared the victor. You must not be defeated too quickly."

"Or they will smell a rat and work out I'm not really a boxer. I know, I get that bit."

"Not only that," Nipper explained. "Most of the betting is done while the fight is in progress. Odds change by the moment, depending on how the men fight. If you don't give the organizers and the opposing team time enough to make their money . . . well, we will have a bigger fight leaving the place unscathed, all of us, never mind collecting our winnings."

"In that case," Liam said, summoning up a smile, "you two had better both teach me all you know."

For a further hour the three worked on Liam's technique. Nipper's frosty demeanour slowly thawed as he became more and more hopeful about Liam's chances of success. For his own part, Liam was thankful he wouldn't have to hold out for very long. Even so, he knew he had to make a convincing show of being a real fighter, while at the same time protecting himself. And then there was the fact that Xanthe would be watching him. He told himself he didn't want her to feel scared on his behalf, but in truth there was more than a little pride involved. The thought of having the woman he loved watch him being thrashed was not an appealing one.

Harley's voice brought him properly back to the moment. "Now we're getting somewhere! That's more like it. Again, with that left jab, just as you did before."

Liam repeated the move, keeping in his mind the importance of what he was doing.

"Elbow in," Nipper corrected him. "Hands closer when you protect your chin. Yes, like that!"

"Aye, there you go."

Liam pounded the flour sack, determination and focus driving him now. When at last he stopped he found the two men staring at him.

"Well"—Harley grinned and twirled his whiskers in the manner of one pleased with his own work—"I do believe we might have something of a boxer on our hands after all. What say you, eh, Nipper?"

Nipper nodded slowly, his own expression showing a mixture of surprise and relief. "I think we just might," he agreed, finally allowing himself to smile.

—

Xanthe spent more time that morning studying the *Spinners* book in the quiet of her bedroom. She delved deep into its pages, absorbing all the wisdom she could, listening to the voices that were now not only clearer, but familiar, so that she felt she knew those who spoke to her down the years. She began to realize that most of them were no longer living, but every now and again one would appear on a page or speak to her with a different vibrancy, with more vigor and resonance, and she would know they were living still. Somewhere. Some when. She had no concept of how long she had been immersed in the book, so she was surprised when Elizabeth knocked on her door to tell her it was nearly two in the afternoon.

"It is a beautiful day," she told her. "Would you join me on the roof? I have made lemonade and ginger biscuits."

"That sounds lovely, thank you."

The two women made their way up through the house, out of the low door, and onto the narrow roof space where Elizabeth had her favored viewpoint. She had taken up cushions, and the refreshments were already laid out.

Xanthe smiled. "I don't think I've ever had a picnic at such a height before," she said, sitting on a velvet cushion, tucking her feet beneath her, and taking the glass Elizabeth was offering.

"The view at nighttime, with the city illuminated, is rather magical," said Elizabeth as she poured the lemonade, "but there is something splendid about the same place bathed in such sunshine, wouldn't you agree?"

She took in the vista. Gone was the smog, replaced by bright sunlight. London was no longer a place of grime and gloom, but transformed into a gleaming metropolis. She could see for miles in all directions, landmarks such as the dome of St. Paul's and the distant spires of Westminster clearly visible. Instead of streetlights and the lamps of thousands of houses burning into a nighttime cityscape, this was a vision of man's ambitious reach, of regal buildings, of monuments to God, of the aspirations and achievements of people who dared to dream and strove to realize those dreams. Instead of dirt and toil and air thick with smoke, a gentle summer breeze blew through the streets and chased between walls and roofs, purging the town of its filth, replacing stale, fetid air with fresh, as the sunlight seemed to polish stone and brick to a new shine. And through it all, the silver pulsing artery of the Thames, not rank and cold this time, but sparkling, light dancing off the washes of small boats and barges that plied their trades up and down its teeming shores. She thought about the stereotypical modern image of Victorian life in a large city. Yes, there were slums, and when the weather was wet the air was toxic, but on a fine day the place looked beautiful, serene, elegant, and prosperous. The trees that lined the broad avenues were in full leaf. The rose gardens in the parks in full bloom. The residents dressed in their summer finery. It was a place that suggested what could be, even if at times it fell short of that potential. Even if for many, the reality was much harsher. Even the beggars and paupers would benefit from such a bright day and such clean air blowing through the city.

Elizabeth took her place on the cushions next to Xanthe.

"It is refreshing to see London revealed in loveliness, is it not?"

"Are you a mind reader as well as a witch?" she asked, only half jokingly.

"Alas, no. Though, on reflection, I would not wish to be. To eavesdrop on the secrets of others . . ."

"Sometimes I feel as if that's what I'm doing. When I read what is in the *Spinners* book. Or when I listen to the cries of people calling me through the blind house. Like I'm looking deep into the souls of people I've never even met. It's a very . . . intimate connection."

"Such personal insight is a rare privilege as well as a burden. You will not abuse that trust."

"How can you be sure? I don't mean to be rude, but you hardly know me. How can any of you know I won't get my head turned by the power of it all? I might be tempted one day to, oh, I don't know, use spinning to make a huge sum of money. Buy a yacht and sail away to somewhere with turquoise seas and skies to match and endless tropical cocktails."

Elizabeth shook her head. "Your body might thrive in such a place, but your soul would shrivel at the price you paid to get there."

Xanthe sipped her drink and helped herself to a ginger biscuit. They were still warm and their aroma made her mouth water before she had even taken her first bite. "Do you think Erasmus ever feels like that?" she asked. "I mean, you and he are settled here now. You have Nipper. I can't imagine what he does—not just time stepping, but chasing down Spinners who have gone to the bad—well, that can't be easy when you have a family."

"We work as a team. That was ever my aim when we decided to make our lives here. And of course, he already had his business, this house.

And this is where Nipper belongs. This is his time." She paused, her face suddenly more serious. "But, as you well know, things do not stay the same for as long as we would like them to. He would never admit to it, but Erasmus is not as young as he was. He finds the stepping more and more taxing. And of course, the nature of his work being what it is, that means every encounter with an adversary becomes increasingly dangerous."

As she paused to sip her drink, Xanthe watched her closely. Erasmus would no doubt have told her of Lydia Flyte's failing health. Was that what was starting to happen to him now? How long would it be before it happened to her?

"Will he ever be persuaded to stop?"

"Ah, that is the question. In fact, circumstances may contrive to bring about alterations, whether he wishes it or not. We cannot remain here, in this time and place, for very much longer."

"Why not? Surely you both have the perfect cover here, with the bookbinding business. Normal work that Nipper and Erasmus can do when he's not summoned."

"You forget I have history of my own, and, alas, that history places its restrictions upon our present and our future if we are to be together. When I was a much younger woman, I lived a lifetime here in London. I worked as a young doctor, a rarity then. I was fortunate enough to be in the employ of a fine surgeon, Professor Gimmel. He taught me a great deal, and I admired him immensely. By time stepping with Erasmus, I arrived at a point mere decades before that time, and now it is approaching again. You will know that an object cannot be duplicated in the same time period. That is why none of your found things, the ones that call to you, ever travel back with you to their places of origin. They are already there. Well, it is just so with people. I cannot stay to inhabit the years in which my origins locate me in this place. I must leave before that can occur."

"How long have you got before that happens?" Xanthe asked, thinking at once how hard it would be to give up the life she and Erasmus and Nipper had together.

"Two years. Three at most. We have always known that day would come. We have prepared for it. Nipper will take on the business. We may, on occasions, be able to visit him. Erasmus and I will return to the life I had nearer your time."

"The twenty-first century? Wow, I find it hard to imagine Erasmus there!"

"Mine was a quiet, rural existence. I believe he will adapt, in time."

"And Nipper knows this is going to happen?"

"Of course." The older woman reached up and took the pins from her hair, shaking it with a sigh, letting it fall about her shoulders. It was a glorious color, a rich chestnut, with barely a touch of gray, save for the broad white streak that swept back from her left temple. "There are times," she said with a small smile, "when I miss the freedoms and advantages of your era. It is true there is much trouble in the modern world, but it was ever thus. You have made so many advances in medicine. So many lives can be saved now that would have been lost at this point in man's journey. You can communicate with people a thousand miles distant. You can travel up to the stars to view the very planet on which we sit. You can share all the wonders of the world without leaving your own home. You can create art to lift the soul, and music to soothe it, and food to transport you to foreign lands. You need look no further than your fingertips for millennia of knowledge and wisdom. I believe Erasmus will find much to his liking."

"You make it sound wonderful," Xanthe murmured. "It's strange how we romanticize the past but get caught up in only seeing the bad stuff in our own time. Like how much inequality there is, how divided people feel, how much we are all wrecking the planet. It's easy to forget the good things."

Elizabeth waved her hand to indicate the city spread out beneath them. "As with all things, it is often a matter of perspective," she said simply.

—

The fight was slated for eight o'clock that evening. As Xanthe and Erasmus sped through London in a cab, dusk was falling and the lamplighters were about their business. Elizabeth had elected to stay behind. They still had to be on their guard in case another attempt was made to steal the *Spinners* book. She had promised to stay in the drawing room with it hidden among the hundreds of other books on the shelves. The doors, front and back, were firmly locked, with extra barricades in place. She would cast a spell for protection and await their return. Erasmus and Xanthe would present themselves as a bohemian wealthy couple enjoying the thrill of watching a fight. It was rare for women to attend, but it was accepted that certain ladies enjoyed the proximity to violence and displays of such manliness while enjoying the protection of their escort. Their money was as good as anyone else's, after all, and such people liked to place large wagers. Erasmus carried the purse of coins from the pawned brooch buttoned into the inside pocket of his jacket. He wore a top hat for the occasion and a cape with red satin lining, and carried an ebony walking cane, which was in fact a sword stick. He would not go into such a rough and rowdy place without the means with which to protect both Xanthe and himself. Elizabeth had lent Xanthe another outfit, this one a dark green velvet dress with matching hat. They made a striking couple, the idea being to hide in plain sight, their connection with Liam and the others being unknown to anyone else who would be present. If the cab driver was surprised at the insalubrious drop-off point for his fare, he did not show it, aside from the speed with which he steered the narrow carriage away from the dingy street. There was no crowd, only a line of dark figures threading their way through the mean portal of the workaday building.

Erasmus offered Xanthe his arm.

"Shall we?" he asked. Light from the solitary streetlamp fell upon his handsome face to show a reassuring smile. "All will be well," he told her.

She did her best to smile back but inside she was in turmoil. She knew what they were doing was necessary, but that didn't make her any less anxious about it. It seemed so unfair to ask such a thing of Liam, after all that had already happened to him because of her.

They followed the others inside. As they made their way along a low-ceilinged corridor, the very nature of the air altered. Gone was the comparatively fresh air of the summer evening, replaced by something warm and fetid and heavy with the smell of drunken men. They emerged into the main space of the building, where the ceiling was a little higher at least, but the atmosphere was similarly unpleasant. Xanthe was determined not to show anything of how she was feeling. Elizabeth had warned her that any display of disgust or upset would mark her out as a newcomer to the situation. She and Erasmus were to give the impression attending boxing matches and betting on the outcome was an occasional diversion for a wealthy couple, and one they were accustomed to. When they arrived, a different match was already underway. There were four bouts on the card, Liam's fight having top billing and being scheduled last. The crowd shouted abuse and encouragement at the boxers with equal fervor. As Erasmus led her through the press of people to a bench near the ring they garnered curious glances, and in her case several lascivious ones, but nothing more. The men were far too busy with the fate of their favorites and their fortunes to worry about a pair of toffs in their midst. Xanthe took her seat, doing her utmost to keep her focus on the ring so as to avoid making eye contact with anyone who was staring at her. Watching the men fight, however, was no easy task.

"Flatten 'im!" yelled a thin spectator from the other side of the ring, which was formed using straw bales, his own fist raised as if to demonstrate to his chosen champion how he should be doing his job. "Go on with ye . . . put him down!"

Around him others roared their approval of this instruction. The more the boxers lunged at each other, swinging blows, the louder the crowd shouted their encouragement and the more colorful the language became. Every time one boxer landed a punch there was a collective roar that rattled the rafters of the room. To the stink of ale and sweat and urine came the sickly sweet odor of fresh blood. Xanthe noticed Erasmus check his pocket watch. She peered over his arm to see the time. It was almost eight o'clock. Presumably the punctuality of the bouts depended on how quickly one or the other of the contestants succumbed to their beating.

As if on cue, there came a bellow from the ring as the heavier of the two men hurled himself forward, driving home a singularly weighty punch that found its target on the side of his opponent's jaw. The lighter man was lifted off his feet by the force of the blow, describing a shallow arc through the air before landing, unconscious and awkward, legs crumpled beneath him, upon the filthy floorboards. The referee went through the formality of counting the man out, but it was already clear to all present that he was not going to be able to continue. As he was carried, still senseless, from the hall by his seconds, the referee raised the bloodied hand of the remaining fighter and declared him the winner. Among the spectators there was a great deal of excitement with some voices raised in anger, others in triumph. Bookmakers were pounced upon for winnings. A desultory worker pushed a broom through the detritus, causing more smears than clean patches. A short, stout man with an outlandishly feathered top hat stepped into the ring and raised a hand for quiet. He had the look of a shabby ringmaster in a down-at-heel circus, such was the faded grandeur of his extravagant clothes and somewhat raddled state of his complexion.

Erasmus whispered, "That is Albert Taverstock. Do not be deceived by his appearance; from what I have learned, he is a man of some position in these circles."

"Gentlemen! Gentlemen . . . and lady!" he sang out, pausing to direct this last at Xanthe, who was indeed the only female in the room. The crowd gave a bawdy response to her presence. Smiling, the patron of the establishment continued with his announcement. "At last we come to the top billing on this evening's card! A match that will in every way possible reward your turning out this night, and handsomely reward your investment, should you place your wager wisely. And why would you not? For looking about me now I declare I have never seen a wiser collection of men in all my long life. No, sirs, I have not!" This was met with peals of laughter. Now that he had their attention, Taverstock got to the business of the day. "Without further ado—for who am I to stand in the way of money being made and sport being appreciated by such fine fellows as your good selves?—I give you, all the way from bonnie Scotland, a young man with Scotch whiskey in his blood and the granite stone of the Highlands at his heart, Rabbie Bearpaw!" He paused for a cheer, which was more polite than enthusiastic. He had evidently expected this and had a plan to whip up enthusiasm and, more important, wagers. "What?" he cried, his expression incredulous, his tone one of astonishment. "Have you not heard, gentlemen? Does the reach of your knowledge of the best and most upcoming fighters in the land fall so short? I am astounded! Young Rabbie is the one to watch, I assure you. But, no matter, for I know you will judge quality when you see it. Here . . . Rabbie Bearpaw!"

Somewhere a drum was beaten in a haphazard but effectively dramatic fashion. From the back of the crowd another door opened, the throng parted, and the contender and his seconds marched the short distance to the ring. There was a murmur of excitement as everyone craned their necks and jostled for position to get a better view of the newcomer.

Xanthe felt her stomach lurch at the sight of Liam stepping into the newly scattered sawdust of the ring. He had his jacket loose over his shoulders. His feet were bare, and he wore close-fitting white breeches. Harley stood beside him, apparently giving him last-minute instructions. Nipper took his jacket from him and Liam bounded into the center of the arena, arms aloft, acknowledging the crowd.

Erasmus gave a small gasp. "Well, well. Your young friend looks the part, I'll give him that."

And she had to agree that he did. Liam's muscular frame, honed on his own set of weights in his garage, stood him in good stead. His tattoos gleamed under the low light, and his height and long legs made for an imposing figure. She felt her heart race. For fear. For love. As Liam circled the interior of the ring, smiling his most charming, most confident smile, the crowd warmed to him. His apparent confidence and his athletic physique were winning them over. Xanthe saw a flurry of activity as people laid their bets, liking what they saw, hastening to make their wagers before the odds shortened. As he passed the place where she and Erasmus were sitting, Liam saw her. She expected him to ignore her, going along with their plan that they two were unknown to each other. But he had other ideas. When he was sure that all those watching had noticed him see the only woman present, he made a point of stopping. He bowed low before her in a gesture of exaggerated chivalry. The crowd cheered. Xanthe tried a haughty smile. He clutched at his heart dramatically. Thinking quickly, she took a lace handkerchief from her pocket and held it out to him. Smiling, Liam stepped forward and took it, holding it up for all to see. The crowd loved the showmanship and more and more people raced to place their bets in his favor. At last, Liam tied the handkerchief into one of the mufflers wound around his hands and blew her a kiss. His performance over, Taverstock introduced his opponent.

Harley had relayed to Xanthe all that Taverstock had told him about the Wilkes boy, but nothing had prepared her for the fearsome figure who now stepped into the ring. He looked to be a similar age to Liam, but there the points in common ended. He was a good head taller, with the broadest, most muscular shoulders she had ever seen. She had hoped for someone large and slow, but young Wilkes looked every bit a fighter, from his sinewy arms to his flattened nose, and the raw danger in his eyes. She felt Erasmus take her hand in his and was grateful for the gesture. Suddenly, the risk of Liam being seriously hurt in this unregulated, ungoverned environment seemed terrifyingly real.

16

"SHOULDN'T WE GET OUR BET LAID?" SHE WHISPERED TO ERASMUS. SHE KNEW THAT they had to appear to make their decision based on what they saw. Looking at the Wilkes boy, as soon as he started fighting the odds on Liam being thrashed would begin to shorten.

"Can't appear too keen," Erasmus replied. He squeezed her hand.

They had discussed tactics with Liam, hence his showmanship. The more he could get the crowd to back him, the better. This also meant, however, that he would have to attempt to keep the fight going as long as possible.

"I think we should just do it now," she murmured.

Seeing her anxiety, Erasmus nodded. "I shall return. Be at ease," he said, getting up and heading over to the most prosperous-looking bookmaker.

He was still waiting to make his transaction when the referee called the two men to come up to the line. Wilkes stood like a rock, staring down his new opponent. Liam danced from one foot to the other, shaking out his arms, still smiling. He was doing an impressive job of hiding the very real fear Xanthe was certain he would be feeling at that moment.

The referee raised his voice to give the rules of the fight and suddenly the bout was underway. The shouts of the crowd seemed to bounce off the walls of the hall, the sound sickening in its bloodthirstiness.

Whatever Harley and Liam had discussed by way of strategy, however much information Nipper had been able to give him on how such fights worked, now Liam was on his own. He was the one in the ring. Xanthe found herself holding her breath and forced herself to let it out. She glanced over at Erasmus, who had still not placed his bet. The two boxers circled each other warily as the crowd egged them on. Wilkes maintained a surly, fierce expression. Liam, continuing to smile, suddenly darted forward and threw a swift right hook; the very punch Taverstock had been so impressed by. To Xanthe's astonishment, the blow sent Wilkes reeling. The favorite spun round, staggered two paces, and fell on top of the bales. The crowd roared. Wilkes was visibly dazed and for one awful moment Xanthe feared he might not make the count. But he was a seasoned fighter. He spat a little blood from his mouth, his expression even more murderous than before, and stormed back to the line. Liam jigged lightly as the referee made them stand toe-to-toe once more before instructing them to fight. Wilkes slung fierce blows at Liam, who nimbly dodged them, taking time to jog around the ring in order to save himself but also to put on a show and wind up his opponent. Beside her, Xanthe saw two men hurry to place bets on Liam to win. She saw Erasmus hold back, waiting for the odds to improve again, as they surely would, as long as Liam kept dancing. Wilkes was becoming increasingly maddened. His seconds were shouting at him to stop letting his opponent slip beyond his reach. He evidently heeded their advice and succeeded in stepping in front of Liam in a way that quickly pinned him against the bales. With terrifying speed, he threw two punches, one to Liam's chest, then an uppercut catching his jaw as he was doubled over. Liam tumbled sideways, hitting the floor heavily.

It was all Xanthe could do not to shout out his name. Erasmus rejoined her.

"The wager is made," he told her. "Fear not. Our boy is equipping himself well."

"You think so?" She did not share this opinion as she watched Liam take most of the allotted thirty seconds to get back to his feet and into the center of the ring. The men flew at each other once more. Wilkes missed this time, and a wild haymaker from Liam found its mark on the end of the other man's nose. Wilkes roared in rage as blood poured from his nostrils. Barreling forward, he threw his arms around Liam and the two crashed to the ground. The second they landed, Wilkes began raining blows onto his opponent, who was now trapped beneath him. The referee attempted to intervene but Wilkes was not listening. It took Harley and Nipper to leap in and haul him off. Wilkes turned on Harley and for a moment Xanthe thought he would strike him. Harley, to his credit, stood his ground, his fury at the unfairness of the fight no doubt lending him extra courage. The referee stepped between them and berated the young man for foul play, warning against it happening again. Nipper led Harley away and the fight resumed. It was clear to Xanthe that, while Wilkes had been bloodied, Liam was hurt. The heavy blows to the chest he had sustained could easily have cracked a rib. He continued to move about as much as he could but she could see pain etched on his face and the thought of it tore at her heart.

"How much longer?" she murmured, letting Erasmus take her hand for a second time.

At that moment, Liam stumbled. Whether through fatigue or pain it was hard to tell, but he missed his footing, meaning that instead of dancing away from Wilkes's punches, he stayed within range for a crucial couple of seconds. Again he took a blow to the ribs, and again the second punch sent him to the ground.

"Stay down!" Xanthe whispered. "For God's sake, Liam, stay down."

The crowd's shouts grew louder and more urgent. Liam raised himself from the ground and onto one knee, then, with a noticeable wobble, he stood again. Xanthe was horrified to see he intended to step up to the line again. His supporters urged him to do so. Wilkes sneered at him from the other side of the ring. It was then that Liam's somewhat dizzy gaze found Xanthe again. He smiled at her. She wanted to shout at him to stop but she knew she could not. Then, as if reading the anguish in her face, he teetered and sank to his knees once more before toppling over, facedown, onto the bloody sawdust and the grimy boards of the floor. The referee finished the count, snatched up Wilkes's hand, and declared him to be the winner.

The spectators erupted into shouts of delight and rage in equal measures.

"Quickly now." Erasmus took Xanthe's arm and steered her through the increasingly wild crowd. He went straight to the bookmaker, who was less than pleased to see him. He was a dark-eyed man with a wild beard and smelled powerfully of whiskey. Erasmus silently held out his hand. Xanthe admired the way he kept so calm amid all the chaos around them. She turned back, trying to see what had happened to Liam, praying that he was not unconscious. She saw Harley and Nipper bending over him and then, to her enormous relief, lifting him to his feet. Nipper placed his jacket around his shoulders and they helped him stagger from the room. The bookmaker grudgingly handed over the winnings. Xanthe was keenly aware that around them strangers had noticed the large amount of money that was changing hands. She turned to stare at them. They had not come this far, and Liam had not suffered so much, only for thugs to take what was rightfully theirs. One of the men melted back into the crowd but another spat throatily at her feet. She did not flinch but held his gaze.

"Come," Erasmus said softly to her, buttoning the money inside his jacket.

Together they left the room as quickly as they were able, given the excitable state of the spectators and the general level of drunkenness. Fortunately, the Wilkes family's celebrations provided something of a distraction. Even so, Xanthe saw Taverstock frowning in their direction, not best pleased with the result and quite probably looking to recoup some of his losses. She and Erasmus slipped out of the front door and onto the street. It was mercifully empty of anyone who might try to mug them, but also empty of cabs.

"We must make all haste to Lydia's house," he told her. "I think it inadvisable to search for a hansom. We will be too vulnerable. Are you content to walk?" he asked.

"No," she said, hitching up her skirt and pinning it at her waist with the special clasp. "I am content to run. Come on!" So saying, she broke into a fast jog, Erasmus falling into step beside her. She was thankful for her leather boots with a low heel that enabled her to run across the cobbles without twisting an ankle. From behind them came shouts and sounds of heavy footsteps. Erasmus paused to draw his sword from his sword stick.

"There are too many," she protested. "We have to outrun them!"

And so they fled. Along the seemingly endless alley, out onto another deserted street, into yet another where only drunkards and harlots lingered in the shadows. Only people who would stand by and see them robbed or worse. They ran on, the heavy footsteps behind them getting closer, until at last they came to the dockside. Here the commerce of the night continued, so that even though the hour was late, stevedores and sailors and merchants were going about their business. Xanthe led Erasmus into the center of the street where the lamplight was strongest and they were most visible. She turned and checked. Their pursuers hung back, defeated, hesitating for only a moment before melting away into the gloom of the narrow street again.

Her heart pounding, her breath ragged, she took Erasmus's arm as he returned the sword to its hiding place, and together they walked the rest of the way to the house of Lydia Flyte.

—

An hour later, as Xanthe sat with Liam in the soft light of the small sitting room in Litham Street, she wondered if she would ever be able to forgive herself for the injuries he had sustained. Nipper and Harley had done their best to patch him up, but when she reached the house and saw him for the first time after the fight, she had been shocked by the state of him. The left side of his face was swollen and bruised, one eye closed from the swelling. There was a cut above one eyebrow that refused to stop bleeding, making him all the more gory. He had taken several powerful blows to the ribs, which were causing him pain with every breath. Despite the mufflers, both hands were bruised and bleeding, and it looked as if at least two of his fingers might be broken. Erasmus and Nipper had taken a cab back to Holborn immediately. Erasmus would stow the money away and remain to guard both it and the book. Nipper returned with his mother, he and his father having insisted that she was needed to tend Liam's wounds. Xanthe had wondered briefly how awkward the meeting might be between Elizabeth and Lydia Flyte, but there were more important things to worry about. The old woman had taken herself off to the kitchen to help the maid prepare soup. Liam was in a chair beside the fire. Xanthe sat on a footstool next to him. Harley and Nipper had managed to get him out of his dirty clothes, had washed the worst of the blood from his wounds, and helped him into a clean white shirt. His hair was still matted with blood and sawdust, however, and he still wore the breeches he had fought in.

"God, Liam," she said, reaching forward to touch his left hand as gently as she could, wary of causing him more pain. "Sorry."

"You weren't the one hitting me. No need for you to be sorry. Anyway, you should see the other guy," he joked, his smile making him wince as the expression stretched his bruised face.

"It was so brutal . . . I never imagined . . ."

"Me neither, which is just as well or I might have chickened out." When he saw that his jokes were not working he lifted his hand and put it under her chin, tipping her face up to look at him. "I'm OK," he said calmly. "Nothing that won't heal in a few days."

"Watching you go through that . . . watching him beat you . . ."

"It was worth it. We have the money we need. I will be fine, I promise." And then, still looking straight into her bright blue eyes, he said suddenly, "God, you're beautiful."

She smiled then, her fierce affection toward Liam lifting her spirits again. "Well, you look terrible," she said, taking hold of his hand and lightly kissing it.

They sat in silence for a while, the atmosphere between them charged, the tension and excitement of the night's events slowly fading to be replaced with a deep and powerful desire for each other.

From the hallway came the sound of the front door knocker and the maid going to answer it. Moments later Millie showed Elizabeth into the room.

Xanthe got to her feet. "He's a bit of a mess," she said.

Elizabeth set her doctor's bag down on the floor and took in the condition of her patient.

"I will need boiled water and lots of it. Fresh cloths. And better light. If nothing else is available, have the maid bring more candles."

Xanthe hurried to do as she was instructed, returning to help Elizabeth in her work. At the start of his treatment, Liam tried to keep up a cheerful banter, until Elizabeth firmly told him to keep quiet, reserve his strength, and let her see to her tasks without interruption. She knelt before him and scrutinized each injury before cleaning and dressing them with great care. Xanthe noticed that she appeared to use a combination of what was the conventional medical treatment of the time in tandem with more ancient and natural remedies. She gave Liam a little laudanum before stitching the cut above his eyebrow. She lightly rubbed a homemade ointment of comfrey onto his ribs before strapping them tightly with broad, clean bandages. She used iodine to clean his hands, but applied a soothing balm that smelled of lavender before dressing the wounds. She declared three of the fingers on his right hand broken and used small wooden splints to make sure they would set properly. The bottom layers of the strappings were soaked in a comfrey infusion. The top layer of bandages she sewed in place so that they would not allow the splints to shift. When she had finished she stood up and addressed them both.

"The ribs will no doubt cause you the most discomfort, but it is your hand that must be tended with the greatest care. If the bones are not encouraged to knit and knit straight, you will lose much of the mobility in your fingers. Also, the breaks are from impact and were sustained when the knuckles were flexed. There may be bone fragments adrift in your bloodstream, so we must be vigilant for signs of bone fever. I will leave more laudanum for the pain. Use it sparingly, unless you wish to add opium dependency to your troubles. The strappings on your ribs can be removed after twenty-four hours; they are there to give a little relief in the short term. Ribs must heal while moving, that is the painful truth of it. I will return to inspect your hand again tomorrow," she said, snapping shut her leather bag.

"Thank you"—Xanthe put a hand on her arm—"I really appreciate you coming here."

Elizabeth smiled now, her stern manner a result of focus and concern, her more habitual good nature returning. "Liam has done well to emerge with no more serious injuries, by the sound of it. We should be grateful for that."

"Trust me, we are," said Liam a little woozily.

"Are you going to stay here with him?" Elizabeth asked.

"Yes, I think I should, don't you?"

"See that he eats something," Elizabeth went on, nodding her agreement. "And once he has, you may wash his hair."

Xanthe was about to ask more questions regarding the care of the patient when the door opened and Mistress Flyte entered the room, followed by Millie, who was staggering somewhat under the weight of a tray of soup bowls. Elizabeth stood, bag in hand, tall and dignified. Lydia Flyte, who walked with the aid of a stick, stopped at the sight of her. For a moment she seemed thrown but quickly regained her composure.

"Mrs. Balmoral, I have heard so much about you. I have long harbored a hope that one day we might meet," she said, holding out her hand.

Elizabeth stepped forward and took the proffered hand. She did not so much shake it as simply hold it, warmly, it seemed to Xanthe. "Our meeting is overdue, I feel," Elizabeth replied.

"We are fortunate to have your assistance," said Lydia. "All of us."

"As a healer, naturally I go where I am needed. As the wife of a Time Stepper, I have always understood my calling to be to support my husband in his work."

"Quite so. And now that work calls upon all of us to do what we can. Alas, I have little left to offer."

Xanthe thought Elizabeth might dispute this, if only out of politeness, but she did not. Instead she remained holding Mistress Flyte's hand, regarding her with a gaze so intense it was unsettling to watch. At last she said, "We are all, I believe, ultimately measured by the reach of our love."

At this, Lydia gave a small, thoughtful nod. "Thank you," she said quietly.

Elizabeth let go her hand and turned. "Xanthe, perhaps you would show me out?" she asked.

In the hallway she paused and took a small blue vial from her bag. "Give three drops of this to Liam before retiring," she told Xanthe. "And three more in the morning upon waking."

"Is it a painkiller?"

"In a manner of speaking. It will help you both," she said, holding up her hand to fend off any questions on the subject. "I have to tell you, Mistress Flyte is gravely ill."

"I know. I've seen her deteriorate even during the short time I've been here. I think she should have more help, someone here to take care of her after Liam and I leave."

"She will have no use for anyone then."

"What?"

"If there is anything you wish to learn from her, do not wait."

"You really think the end is that close? Is there nothing you can do?"

"Alas, there is not."

"But you are such a skilled physician. I've seen you work. And . . . if not medicine, can't you help her with, well . . ."

"Magic?" Elizabeth shook her head slowly. "To influence the health of a time traveler, be they Stepper or Spinner, when it is that very travel that has taken its toll, is beyond even my ability, either as healer or witch. There is a price, ultimately, to be paid for what you all do, child. Lydia needs to settle that account now. There is nothing anyone can do." She pulled on her gloves then, her manner suddenly businesslike. "Now, I must get home. And your patient needs you." She patted Xanthe's hand and smiled at her then. "Until tomorrow," she said, and then left.

On her return to the small sitting room, Xanthe found Lydia sitting at the table, where the maid had set down the soup bowls.

"Millie, kindly prepare a bed for our guest. Miss Westlake will be staying to oversee Liam's care tonight."

"That won't be necessary," Xanthe told them. "I plan to sit up at his bedside. There is a perfectly comfortable chair already in the room. Elizabeth warned me to watch for signs of bone fever. It's better he's not alone. Millie, if you could bring a blanket I would be grateful."

The maid bobbed a curtsey and went to carry out her instructions. Xanthe took a bowl of soup over to Liam. She sat on the stool next to him again and dipped her spoon into the broth.

"It's OK, you don't need to do that," he protested. "I can feed myself."

"Oh really?"

She waited for him to sit up a little straighter, which he did with some effort and a fair amount of wincing. He could not take the bowl, as his broken hand was useless. When he attempted to get hold of the spoon the swollen joints on his other hand made him clumsy, so that he could not grasp it properly. He let out a sigh of frustration.

"Sorry," he muttered.

"Don't be daft. Here, eat up. It smells quite tasty." Slowly she fed him the soup. It was a curiously intimate thing to do. There was no room for conversation, and she had to time the spoonfuls just right. She was surprised to find there was a fundamental pleasure to be found in such a nurturing act. After he had devoured half of the bowlful, Liam held up his bandaged hand and she stopped.

"Thanks," he said. The single word sounded so weary, Xanthe realized his injuries must be more painful than he was letting on.

"You look exhausted," she told him. "I'm going to have my soup and then get you to your bed."

He nodded. "Sounds good. Though, actually, would you mind helping me with this first?" he asked, gingerly touching his filthy hair. "I'm not sure if it's my blood or Wilkes's. Either way, I'd feel better if we could wash it off."

It took Xanthe and Millie a full ten minutes to assist Liam in climbing all the stairs to the top of the house. She felt stupid for not suggesting a room on the ground floor, but it was possible there was none, and it would have been difficult to set up a bed anyway. At last they reached his room. She had Millie place a wooden chair near the washstand and bring hot water, a jug, towels, and soap.

"Can you tip your head back?" she asked him.

Liam did as she asked, flinching but not complaining.

"Is it hurting?"

"No, it's fine," he assured her.

She positioned the blue-and-white china bowl behind him and carefully poured the steaming water over his hair so that it ran off into it.

"Not sure how good this soap's going to be," she said, "but it smells divine. Sandalwood, I think." She gently massaged the soap into his hair, rinsing with more water and then massaging his scalp again.

Liam groaned.

"Am I hurting you?"

"No, you're doing a great job." He sighed. "I feel better already."

When she had finished rinsing she cautiously rubbed his hair dry, leaving it shaggy and clean.

"You look almost human again," she said, smiling at him. Then, remembering what Elizabeth had told her, she took the small blue vial from the pocket of her skirt. "Here, you need to drink this."

"What is it?"

"Elizabeth said it would help you. I didn't ask for details. I think we can agree she knows what she's doing. Half now, half in the morning."

Liam awkwardly took the bottle from her, determined to do it himself. He swallowed three drops of the liquid and grimaced. "Yuck! She could work on making her medicines taste better."

"Don't be a baby. Right, let's get these off you," she said, unbuttoning his breeches.

"Blimey, Xanthe, you chose your moment!"

"Ha-ha," she said dryly. "Don't read anything into it. I am here in the capacity of a nurse, remember? You can't sleep in these filthy things."

With some difficulty she succeeded in removing his trousers, his cracked ribs reminding him of how he had spent the early part of the evening every time he tried to bend or take a deep breath or use the muscles in his torso. Next, she helped him into the bed, leaning him back gently against the freshly stacked pillows.

"How's that?" she asked.

"Better," he said. "Actually, much better." His face brightened. He lifted up his left hand and bent and straightened his fingers, an action that only minutes before would have been nearly impossible. He shifted his position in the bed a little, waiting for pain to shoot through his body again. But it did not.

Xanthe reached forward and tenderly stroked his swollen jaw. "Does that hurt?" she asked.

"No, but I can feel it. I mean, it's not numb. Whatever was in the bottle Elizabeth gave you is some strong medicine! It's weird, it's not working like a painkiller, is it? In fact, do that again."

"What?"

"Touch my cheek."

"Like this?" She ran her fingers lightly over his cheekbone and along his jaw.

"Mmm," he murmured.

"What does it feel like?"

He grinned. "Well, not like something a nurse is supposed to make you feel!"

She drew back her hand quickly.

Liam sat up, reaching out with his left hand to touch her cheek. "Xanthe . . ."

"You're all broken and battered. Elizabeth said you were at risk from bone fever . . ."

"Elizabeth gave you that special stuff. What did she say it would do?"

"She just said it would be helpful. For both of us."

Liam gave a knowing smile by way of response to this information.

Xanthe was confused. "She is a healer. She wouldn't give you some sort of . . . what . . . drug to make you feel . . ."

"Just to be clear, the way I feel now, is exactly the way I always feel when I'm with you. No magic potion required."

"Magic potion!" She laughed, but, knowing the truth about Elizabeth, she had to admit to herself that it was quite possible Elizabeth had used her craft as a witch, rather than a doctor, to effect such a change in Liam's levels of pain without rendering him senseless. She took both his hands in hers and examined them closely.

"Don't they hurt anymore?" she asked, turning them over, inspecting the bruising on his unbandaged one, astonished to see the skin already returning to a more normal color.

"It's difficult to say about the one in the splint because I can't move it. But no, the other one doesn't hurt. Nor do my ribs, watch," he said, turning and twisting his body first one way and then the other. "See? Not so much as a twinge."

"That's amazing. Don't overdo it, though. It's bound to wear off eventually. You mustn't make your injuries worse."

"My broken fingers are protected by the splint. My cracked ribs are already cracked anyway, and the strapping's pretty tight. I don't think we can do any serious damage."

After a beat, in a voice that was a little breathless, she asked, "We?"

Liam pushed a stray lock of hair from her face before reaching up and removing the pins that were keeping her bun in place. She sat motionless as he released her heavy curls, letting them fall about her shoulders.

"You have the most glorious hair of anyone I've ever met," he told her softly. "And you are so damn beautiful. Have I said that before?"

"You have mentioned it."

"Good. You should be told. I want to tell you. I've wanted to tell you lots of things for a long time."

"How long?" she asked, enjoying the feel of his fingers combing lightly through her hair.

"If we're allowed to count backward as well as forward, several centuries."

"That is a long time."

"Isn't it? Especially when I've also wanted to kiss you. Like this," he said, leaning forward and planting the softest of kisses on her lips. "And like this," he said, kissing her again, a little more firmly this time, with more urgency. "And like this," he told her, this time wrapping his arm around her waist to pull her close while his free hand still cupped her cheek. He kissed her deeply then, so that she felt his hunger.

She kissed him back. Months of wondering, of being cautious, of waiting to see. Weeks of becoming aware of the way her feelings toward him were changing, growing stronger, shifting to something altogether different. And then, more recently, days of missing him, of fearing for his safety, of yearning for him, of longing for him.

He stopped kissing her and looked into her eyes, searching her expression for a clue to her true feelings.

"What else have you wanted to do?" she whispered.

"How long have you got?"

She smiled slowly, her heart beating so loudly she was certain he must be able to hear it. "All night," she said, wrapping her arms around his neck and pulling him toward her so that she could kiss him properly, passionately, finally letting go, ready to give herself to him and show him exactly how much he meant to her.

17

HOURS LATER, XANTHE FELT HERSELF BEING SHAKEN GENTLY AWAKE. OPENING HER EYES, she blinked against the stark brightness of a single candle in the otherwise deep darkness of the room. As her vision corrected itself, she saw that it was Millie standing over her. Even in the limited illumination, the distress of her face was noticeable.

"Beg pardon, miss, but it's the mistress . . . she's asking for you." The girl choked back a sob. "She's awful poorly," she added.

"I'll come at once," she said, slipping carefully out of bed, not wanting to disturb Liam.

At any other time, the maid might have been embarrassed to find two unwed guests sharing a single bed, but her concern was for Mistress Flyte now. She stepped back a little, holding up the candle so that Xanthe could find her shift and underskirt to step into, and wrap her shawl around her bare shoulders. The two made their way quickly down one flight of stairs and Millie led the way into the old woman's room. The bed was a simple brass affair and there was a lamp alight on the bedside table. The ailing Spinner was propped up against pillows, looking small and fragile and so alone it pulled at Xanthe's heart. She leaned over her and took hold of her hand. The old woman's eyes were closed and her breathing labored.

"Mistress Flyte? Lydia, can you hear me?"

Her eyelids fluttered open.

"Ah, my dear child," she said, her voice thin, the effort of speaking making her breathing yet more ragged. "Sit. Sit, I have much to tell you."

She perched carefully on the edge of the bed. "You must not exert yourself. Shall I send for the doctor?"

She shook her head. "There is nothing a doctor can do for me now." She smiled a little then, her bright blue eyes focusing on Xanthe's face. "Do you recall the time you summoned a doctor for me at the Chocolate House?"

"Yes, of course. You had taken such a beating. I wasn't sure you would survive it."

"I had a highly competent young nurse, and I'm certain you prevented that bumptious quack from doing me more harm than good."

"I couldn't let him bleed you."

"You sent him away with a flea in his ear."

"Edmund was horrified."

"Edmund? Yes, I remember him, too. Such an earnest lad. He had a good heart. So many people. So many lives that have come and gone while I have continued to zigzag my way through the centuries."

"Can I get you anything? Elizabeth left some laudanum for Liam. . . ."

"You have a powerful ally in Mrs. Balmoral. She will play an important part in the work that lies ahead."

"She and Erasmus have both proved themselves to be true friends already. I am confident that with their help, we will put a stop to the Visionary Society."

Mistress Flyte nodded. "I believe you will. Though you should not rely too heavily upon Erasmus. He and I are, after all, of the same vintage."

Xanthe thought about what Elizabeth had told her of her own origins and wondered if Lydia knew the whole truth about her. She missed the moment to question her on the subject, however, as the old woman moved on.

"Vanquishing the society will be but one of your tasks. Dawlish and Brook-Morton are not the only Spinners to abuse their gifts, as you know better than most. There will be others. Indeed, there already are."

"Here in London? In this time? Elizabeth and I were followed the other day. . . . Erasmus thought it was Dawlish's men, but I wasn't so sure. Do you know of someone else who might be trying to get *Spinners* from me?"

"The book is of paramount importance. There will be many who wish to claim it for themselves. Some might even have the ability to see some of its hidden wisdom. Others may seek to compel you to reveal its contents. Either way, your guardianship of the *Spinners* book puts you in perpetual danger, and you must be ever alert because of it."

"Don't worry. I will see that it is always safe. I nearly lost it once. I'm not going to take that sort of risk with it again, I promise."

"More than this, you must now accept your ordained place as protector of the Spinners' creed."

"I'm sorry, I don't understand."

Mistress Flyte fell to coughing and for a while was unable to speak. Xanthe slipped her hand beneath the old woman's neck and helped her lean forward while she held a glass of water to her lips. After a few sips she sank back onto the pillows. Xanthe waited as long as she dared before questioning her further.

"Lydia, what do you mean, 'protector'?"

Taking another breath, she spoke again. "Your work as a Spinner to this point has been, aside from guardianship of the book, to answer the calls of those in distress and to right the injustices that have befallen them. You have already proved yourself to be a courageous, resourceful Spinner, and those qualities will help you to continue in this important aspect of your work, but . . . that is not all." She paused, seeming to summon up another vestige of strength from a dwindling resource.

"For many years, Erasmus has done his best to police the Spinners, and in recent times he has had Elizabeth to help him. Yet, it is not to him that I must pass the baton of protector."

"From you?"

"Yes, from me. I was not always the old woman you have known me as. And yes, I gave up spinning through time in the way that you do a long while ago. By which I mean, I no longer followed the call of treasures to assist those in need. There were others who could do that."

"Others like me."

She nodded. "I took on the work of protector when the group split."

"When Erasmus left you to become a Time Stepper?"

"We each must follow our hearts, tempered by our consciences. We both did what we thought best for the good of all time travelers and the work that we do. Our paths diverged, though our objectives were in fact the same."

"You gave up so much, both of you."

The old woman looked wistful then. "Of course you know about the child. Have you told Erasmus?" Seeing Xanthe nod she said, "He had a right to know. Our babe sickened and died. The outcome would have been the same even had he been with us. But still, I regret that he never had the chance to see his daughter."

Xanthe squeezed her hand. "Without the mourning brooch I might never have found my way to you. So she is still playing a part, isn't she?"

Lydia smiled again, the lamplight glistening in the tears that rolled unchecked down her pale cheeks. "Such a beautiful child. Alas, much is asked of a Spinner. Be careful where you give your heart, my dear, for not all will withstand sharing you with such a calling."

"I still don't understand. If you were the protector, and you . . . can no longer do your work, why wouldn't you pass the title to Erasmus? He has so much more experience than me. He is so much better equipped."

"First, he is no longer a true Spinner. I cannot pass the responsibility to a Time Stepper, however well intentioned. Second, he is aging, almost as swiftly as I. The role demands youth. Experience will come with the doing of it."

"No, really, I'm not the right person . . ."

"Child, do not think that this choice rests with me alone. I have waited a long time to find my successor. When first we met I had hope but was uncertain. Over time you have proved yourself. More important, the *Spinners* book has chosen you. Do you not see that?"

She started to protest again but then remembered how the book had behaved only the day before. How differently it had communicated with her. How completely and marvelously it had laid bare to her all its secrets and wisdom. It was true, she had felt a shift, not only in the level of the book's acceptance of her, but in herself as a Spinner too.

"What will it mean?" she asked. "What will I be expected to do?"

"You will continue to answer to the song of the found things, as you have been doing. But, above and beyond this, your responsibility will be to seek out those who would ill use their gifts as Spinners."

"But, how will I know about them? I'll be living in the twenty-first century, getting on with my own life . . . they are hardly going to call to me like the people who need my help, are they?"

"They will not, but their deeds vibrate down the invisible arteries through which time flows. Those vibrations, that disruption to the intended order, that is what will summon you, in a way similar to the cries for help that you sense."

"In things, do you mean?" Xanthe found she disliked the idea of treasures being connected with people such as Fairfax himself rather than people in urgent need of her help.

"Just so. It will be up to you to travel to wherever and whenever they are and to put a stop to their actions, for left unchecked they would not only besmirch the reputation of all Spinners but their deeds could cause real and dreadful damage to future lives. I know that you understand this, and—" She broke off coughing again, a sound so painful and so wretched that Xanthe could hardly bear to listen to it. She offered her old friend more water, but Lydia waved it away. When she was able to speak again her voice was little more than a whisper. Xanthe leaned closer in order to hear. "It is vital that you understand. We are not discussing some nebulous wrong, some vague notion of morality twisted, or codes broken. The results of their actions can have devastating effects for thousands of people. For example, it has come to my attention that one of the members of the Visionary Society is a man called Heinrich Moeller. He is one of a group of thinkers who follow an alarming and dangerous creed. A ruthless one, that unchecked, will see many, many dead in its name. I don't expect you to have heard of him, as he has not yet benefited from the services of Dawlish and Brook-Morton."

"But if he did? I mean, if they get him what he wants . . . ?"

"Then he will be rich beyond imagining. And such wealth will grant him and his cohort immense power, not now, but in years to come, shoring up their cause, bolstering their following, helping them equip an army that would be almost impossible to defeat, such would be the limitless funds available to them."

Xanthe felt a chill sweep over her. "How many years later would they come to power?" she asked, fearing that she already knew the answer.

"Sixty or so."

"The nineteen thirties," she murmured, hardly daring to voice what was in her mind.

"Precisely." Mistress Flyte paused again, not, this time, to recover her breath, rather to allow Xanthe time to understand what she was telling her. When she tried to speak again, however, she fell to another fit of coughing and it was some time before she could find her voice. Seeing the look on Xanthe's face she said, "Do not grieve for me, child. There is not time for fancy mourning. Surround yourself with those you can trust. Those whose integrity and steadfastness are beyond doubt. I see such qualities in young Liam. You cannot do your work alone." She lifted her hand then and laid it upon Xanthe's head, almost as if she were bestowing a blessing. "Travel well, young Spinner. Time is at your behest; use it wisely." So saying, her eyes closed again.

"Lydia?" Xanthe clutched at her hand. "Oh . . . Lydia," she said softly as she watched her mentor take her last shallow breath and finally lie still and silent.

—

Millie was too distressed to help prepare Mistress Flyte for her final journey, so it was Elizabeth who came to assist. Xanthe had never dressed a body for the grave before. The two women worked silently, taking infinite care to ease the frail remains of the Spinner into her best gown; to comb and dress her hair; to secure a smart bonnet. To her surprise, Xanthe did not find the task at all uncomfortable or upsetting. Instead she felt she was doing the right thing for her friend, a simple act of respect and intimacy that she deserved. When they had finished, Elizabeth rubbed fragrant oil into Lydia's hands before folding them across her chest. The room smelled sweetly of orange blossom.

"I think we are ready," she said at last.

Erasmus was fetched. He looked very dashing in his seventeenth-century clothes. He wore dark breeches and a close-fitting short jacket with a russet cloak thrown over one shoulder, pinned at the neck with a silver knot-work clasp. His hair was swept back beneath a wide-brimmed black felt hat with a silver band and buckle. At his hip was not only his ever-present dagger, but a fine sword. He dipped a low bow to Xanthe.

"You wish to step through time, Mistress Westlake?" he asked her solemnly.

"I do."

"Then I shall gladly take you, and together we shall accompany Mistress Flyte on her final journey down the centuries." He moved to the bed and laid one hand on Lydia's shoulder. "Come, take my hand," he said, reaching out to Xanthe.

She did as he instructed. Elizabeth had helped her cobble together an outfit that would pass for correct in the late 1600s. It felt curiously clumsy and coarse, with its homespun kirtle, starched collar and cuffs, and thick underskirts. The white cap sat tightly pinned to her tamed and coiled hair. At the last moment, Elizabeth had pointed out they did not know what the weather would be doing, and so draped a floor-length black woolen cape about Xanthe's shoulders, fastening it with a simple chain at the neck. She glanced at Liam, who now stood in the corner of the room watching the proceedings. They had scarcely had a chance to speak since Lydia's passing, but the look of longing that passed between them told Xanthe all that she needed to know and reassured her about what their future might be. Elizabeth stood next to him. Nipper and Harley were still at the bookbinder's guarding the *Spinners* book. A spot of time travel had not been in the plan they were expecting, but the death of a Spinner was not something that could be put to one side. Erasmus had explained that there were promises to keep and rituals to observe when a time traveler died. It fell to him and Xanthe to attend to Lydia's needs. The simplest mode of travel would be for him to act as a Stepper summoned by her. She felt safe with Erasmus, but even so, having someone else responsible for her spinning felt strange, and gave her an insight into how Liam and Harley must have felt.

She became aware of Erasmus muttering an incantation. His voice was too low for her to be able to discern the words. He did not close his eyes, but kept his gaze firmly on her, his concentration intense. Then, with shocking abruptness, everything went black. There was no light at all, and no sound, no smells, nothing she could feel except Erasmus's hand in hers. She did not experience the sensation of falling that often accompanied her own spinning. Instead her body felt as if it were traveling at a terrifying speed, forcing its way through time at such a rate that they must all surely crash to their deaths at the end. To her relief, she detected a gradual slowing in their movement, until at last they seemed to softly land at the time and place of Erasmus's choosing.

When her vision returned to her, she saw that it was twilight, and that they were in a small field in a pretty stretch of what looked like English countryside. Erasmus had told her they would travel to the church Lydia had attended when she was a girl. It was where they had met, only a few miles outside the town of Bradford-upon-Avon. As Erasmus lifted Lydia's body from the ground and cradled it in his arms, Xanthe peered through the gloom. A few yards distant she could make out a low stone wall and some tall trees. Yews, she decided. And where there were yews, there was invariably a church.

As if reading her thoughts, Erasmus told her, "That is St. Mary's, at the bottom of the hill. The sexton dwells in the cottage behind it."

"Is there a vicarage?"

"We need not trouble a priest," he said as he strode past, carrying his erstwhile lover as if she were no heavier than a child. Within moments they arrived at a tiny house built in the shelter of the churchyard wall. Xanthe knocked on the door and a wiry little man opened it, squinting out at them suspiciously. On seeing Erasmus and what was evidently a corpse he was not shocked, but somehow reassured. Xanthe thought this reflected the times, when it might be an ordinary event for someone to request a secret burial, and less alarming than strangers come to rob the man of what little he had. She explained their situation, telling the sexton that they were returning the old woman to the place of her birth, that she had no relatives living, but that they believed she had one in the churchyard and it would be fitting for her to join them. The man listened, scratching his bristly chin. It seemed he was undecided, so Xanthe took out the silver coins she had brought for the purpose, and these convinced him of the legitimacy of their claim. He directed them to the relevant corner of the churchyard, shrugged on a shapeless coat, and told them he would fetch a gravedigger and meet them in ten minutes.

St. Mary's was a modest place of worship, already more than three hundred years old, built of the peach-colored stone of the region, with a short, square tower and small arched windows on three sides. Erasmus carried Lydia behind Xanthe as she scoured the headstones, searching for one in particular, reminding her of the time she had conducted a similar, heart-wrenching search in St. Cyriac's Church in Laybrook only a few months before. On that occasion she had been looking for Samuel's grave. How long ago that seemed. How distant her time with him was.

"It will be small," Erasmus reminded her, bringing her back to the moment. "Nothing ostentatious. A short inscription."

She searched on. The light was fading fast, so that she was forced to take out the small torch she always traveled with to enable her to read the words on the tombstones. They walked to the farthest point from the church, a lowly place, home to humble headstones, rather than the fancy marble edifices nearer the church door. At last she found it. Erasmus tenderly set Mistress Flyte down, taking off his cloak to cover her.

Xanthe read out the words inscribed on the curved stone. "Beloved Child, Taken into God's Care, 1648. Forever in the hearts of those who loved her." She hesitated, glancing up at Erasmus before reading the name, "Amy Margaret Balmoral." She felt rather than heard him gasp, the sharp intake of breath his only reaction to discovering that Lydia had given their child his name. Not just a first name to allude to his own, but his surname, so that everyone would know whose child this was. And everyone would also have known they had not married before he disappeared.

"She risked a great deal to do this," he said, a slight catch in his voice.

Xanthe reached out and touched his hand. "She did the right thing," she said simply.

The sexton returned with a slightly drunk gravedigger and the two of them set about opening the grave. Xanthe retreated to sit beside the body of her friend, the smell of the freshly dug soil stirring her senses. Erasmus stood, still as one of the gravestones, watching two strangers unearth the coffin of his lost child. With the poignantly tiny box removed, they continued to dig until there was also room for an adult body. At last the grave was ready. The men went to move the coffin again, but a barked warning from Erasmus stopped them. With great tenderness, he placed Lydia, still wrapped in his cloak, into the grave. Next he lowered the wooden casket into the dark space in the damp, peaty soil, positioning it so that Lydia held their child once more. In the branches of a yew tree, an owl hooted, its mournful song answered by another a short way off, and yet another farther off still. In a way that Xanthe had never heard before, a choir of owls set up a low chorus, the sonorous notes filling the air. The gravedigger was unnerved and hastily shoveled earth back into the grave. When the digging was complete, Erasmus paid both men, giving extra to the sexton. "This is for the mason," he told him. "He is to add, 'And her mother, Lydia Flyte.'"

"And the date?"

"No. No date. She was not a woman to be constrained by a calendar. Mark my words. Be sure to have it inscribed as I tell you. I will return to check in a month and will look to you if it is not as I wish."

Grumbling about how people who steal up in the night and raise a man from his fireside to inter a person without a priest ought not to be so demanding, the man gave a stiff bow and followed the gravedigger down the church path and out of sight.

Erasmus and Xanthe stood at the graveside. The owls at last fell silent. A chill wind had got up, tugging at her cloak and stinging her eyes. Whether it was this or emotion that caused Erasmus's eyes to glint in the moonlight she could not be certain.

"She was a good friend to me," she said. "When I thought she had betrayed me I couldn't understand it. Now I know why she did what she did. Now it all makes sense."

"Lydia was ever sensible," he said.

"I will miss her."

"And I." He paused and then asked, "When she spoke with you, last evening, did she tell you of your destined path?"

"To be protector? Yes, but, how did you know?"

"It was obvious to me that you would succeed her. The more I heard of what you have already done as a Spinner. The more you told me of how the book speaks to you. And the fact that Lydia herself set such store by you. It is no small thing, the position of protector. Do you accept?"

She thought about this. Had she ever felt she had a choice? It hadn't seemed like that when Lydia had told her what she wanted her to do. But, even if it had, even if she had been given the chance to refuse, she would not have done so. "Yes," she said calmly. "Yes, I accept."

He nodded, satisfied if not surprised. Turning his attention back to the freshly filled grave, he removed his hat, holding it a little too tightly, and spoke as if to Lydia. "You have found your journey's end. In God's arms you are reunited with our child. All is as it should be. The order of things restored. You have made your final journey, you're traveling over. Rest well. Spin no more."

They stood in silence for a moment, only the soft moaning of the wind through the yews disturbing the quiet. When it became too painful to stay longer, she put her hand on Erasmus's arm.

He turned and smiled at her then. "Do you wish to step through time again, mistress?" he asked her.

"I do. For Lydia has left us work to do, hasn't she?"

"Indeed. Then let us go to it." And with that he took her hand, not allowing an instant more to pass before together they made the leap forward through time, leaving Lydia and her babe to sleep in peace together.

18

ON RETURNING FROM THE SEVENTEENTH CENTURY THERE WAS MUCH TO BE DONE. Together they composed a letter, written by Erasmus for style and authenticity, but ostensibly from Harley, to be delivered to Dawlish and Brook-Morton, requesting membership in the Visionary Society. Harley introduced himself as an industrialist who had made money somewhere vague in the north and now wished to establish himself in London. He saw great opportunities in manufacturing, but wanted to gain an edge over his competitors. He had been given their name by a mutual friend, and here he named Mistress Flyte. At the same time, Liam sent a note claiming to have considered their proposal and requesting a further conversation, preferably when he would have the chance to meet other society members. The hope was that they would both receive invitations to the next gathering.

Erasmus had returned Xanthe to Mistress Flyte's house, as it was their point of departure. After he left to go home, she took the chance to spend a little time with Liam. Before they could be alone they had both been an hour with Millie, reassuring the girl that a future post would be found for her. They had explained that her mistress's body had been taken to be buried in a family grave, which successfully staved off further questioning on the matter. Millie was, understandably, saddened by the old woman's passing, but more pressingly anxious that she would be out on the street. Only after extracting a promise from

Liam himself that this would not happen did she calm down and return to her duties in the kitchen.

"Poor thing," he said after she had left the sitting room. "Her whole world has just fallen apart."

"Must have happened to so many people in service. Girls in particular. I don't suppose Lydia thought to leave her a reference. She'll find it hard to get a new position without one."

"Elizabeth volunteered to vouch for her," he said, going to sit in one of the fireside armchairs.

She had noticed that since Elizabeth's special medicine had come to an end he was suffering from his injuries again, despite more conventional pain relief. His ribs, in particular, were affecting his mobility and though he did not utter a word of complaint, she could see he was putting up with more than a little discomfort.

"Can I get you anything?"

"No, just you," he said, holding out his hand. When she took it, he pulled her onto his lap.

"Careful! Your ribs."

"Are fine."

"No, they're not."

He leaned forward and kissed her throat. "Trust me, they are feeling better by the minute."

She smiled at him, taking his face in her hands and kissing him slowly, comforted by the sincerity and deep affection she felt, confident that he felt the same.

"I don't think I'll ever get used to seeing you vanish like that," he told her. "Even though I've traveled with you myself. It's like . . . I dunno . . . losing you."

"But I came back. I will always come back."

He kissed her then, and she sensed a passion in that kiss that told her how real his fear of her one day not returning was. She thought about what Lydia Flyte had told her; of how many personal sacrifices she, and Erasmus, had made. How any Spinner would be challenged to question their right to involve a non-Spinner in their lives. Did she have that right? Would it be fair to let herself fall completely in love with Liam, for them to become a couple, when she would always have to put her duty as a Spinner first? Especially now. She had not yet explained to him how she had taken over the role of protector. There was so much to think about, so much else going on. And, if she was completely honest with herself, she didn't yet know how she felt about it. Sitting there, with Liam, wrapped in his arms and his love, it was hard to imagine pushing him away. Hard to envisage herself putting an end to a relationship that had just begun. And one she knew in her heart would be wonderful for both of them, were it not for her other life.

"Penny for them," he said, noticing she was becoming distant.

She shook her head. "Not sure my thoughts are organized enough to be worth good money."

"All the same, I'd like to know what's going on in that head of yours. I might be able to help."

"I'm sure you would, I just . . . need a little time to work out . . . stuff."

"'Stuff'?"

"Told you a penny was overvaluing them." She slipped off his lap and walked about the room, once again falling into Erasmus's habit of pacing to order her thoughts. "Well, one thing that's bothered me is how I should present myself at the Visionary Society's place," she told him.

"What, you mean in a killer dress with borrowed jewels, perhaps?"

"Yes, but no. We'd thought I'd tag along as Harley and Elizabeth's daughter."

"Yeah, let me just digest that idea again. It takes some doing."

"It does, for us, but that's not the point. If I'm going to act as a diversion, something to really distract Dawlish and Brook-Morton, keep their attention while Harley and Elizabeth let the others into the house and do what needs to be done, well, I don't want to arrive with them, do I? How much better would it be if I went as your plus one?"

"I'm liking the sound of this already."

"It would be a surprise because they'd be expecting you to know no one in this time other than Lydia. They might assume she would accompany you . . ."

". . . as they don't know she's dead."

"Exactly. What they won't be expecting is someone who is not only from the modern day, but is also a Spinner, as in, me."

"You'd definitely distract me."

"More to the point, I can protect you. If things get really bad I can use the locket to spin us home, take you back to Marlborough. I can return here straightaway to help Erasmus carry out our plan."

"No way are we doing that!"

"Liam, we have to keep it as an option."

"No."

"You're hurt. You've done enough for this task, and now you're injured."

"Thanks for your concern, still no."

She stopped pacing and put her hands on her hips. "Has anyone ever told you you're stubborn?"

"No, but I get the feeling they're about to."

He smiled at her then, and her heart melted just a little bit more.

"Am I always going to have trouble saying no to you?" she asked him.

"I hope so." He grinned, flinching as his jaw objected to the movement.

It was then that Xanthe remembered what else Lydia had told her; that she must surround herself with people she could trust completely. That she could not carry out her duties alone, so she would have to choose others whose integrity was beyond question and whom she could rely upon without a single doubt.

Liam took her silence as agreement. "So," he said cheerily, "that's settled then. No pinging back home for you and me until we've sorted out Dawlish and his cronies once and for all. Where you go, I go, agreed?"

"Be careful what you wish for."

"Do we have a deal, Miss Westlake?"

"We do," she said at last.

"Excellent. Then I think we should seal it with a kiss, don't you? You're not going to make me get up out of this chair, are you?"

"Oh, *now* you want to play the injury card!"

"It's my poor body that's battered, my brain is working just fine," he said, reaching out to grab her hand and pull her to him.

—

By noon, Harley and Liam had received responses to their letters. Both were the same, and both caused a fair amount of excitement among the team. Instead of the anticipated notes inviting them to another soirée, footmen delivered crisp white cards requesting their presence that coming Friday to attend a grand ball. Xanthe could not help feeling excited at the prospect but had to reassure Liam that the dancing would not be a problem. Harley was openly thrilled at the thought of the chance of witnessing such a spectacle. Elizabeth had been unimpressed, noting only that suitable outfits would have to be found for everyone. Erasmus had suggested the bigger the occasion, the busier their hosts were likely to be, which could only help their own purposes. Nipper had declared himself relieved at not having to "parade around with a collection of self-important exhibitionists, all competing to show off their wealth" and had even offered, unprompted, to lend Liam his clothes. It fell to Millie to give Liam and Xanthe dancing lessons over the next two days, which greatly cheered the girl. If she was puzzled that neither of them knew the steps, she didn't show it. They quickly mastered the waltz but failed miserably at the fox-trot, so decided to stick with just one dance. Elizabeth arrived with two gowns for Xanthe to try. Once she had made her selection, Elizabeth took the dress away to make the necessary alterations. There was, despite losing Mistress Flyte, and despite the seriousness of what lay ahead of them, a general air of excitement about the ball. She told herself that everyone had earned a little fun, and that it would be churlish not to celebrate and make the most of the enjoyable bits of being a Spinner. It was good to be reminded that her calling was a blessing as well as a responsibility.

The evening before the ball, Erasmus came to the house wanting to speak with her alone. Liam took himself off to the kitchen to help Millie.

"Let us sit at the table," Erasmus suggested, "for I have items I wish to show you, and the light is better there."

Xanthe took the chair beside him at the small, bare wooden table. From the bag he had brought with him he took out, first, the *Spinners* book.

"As you requested."

"Thank you," she said, taking it from him, holding it close and feeling the warmth of its greeting through the leather cover. She knew it had been safely hidden and protected at the bookbinder's but she felt much happier having it in her possession. The more involved with the Spinners she became, the more she hated being parted from it. That said, it was impracticable for her to try to take it to the ball. Having it with her now at least gave her the opportunity to study it more before they confronted the Visionary Society. She would be grateful for any wisdom she could glean from her fellow Spinners. They had agreed on a hiding place in Mistress Flyte's house and Erasmus had already secured the services of a trustworthy pair of strongmen who would guard the house while they were out without asking awkward questions.

"Though I myself might not use a talisman or a treasure with which to travel, I do have items I rely upon quite heavily the better to do my work." Erasmus spoke as he pulled more things from the old leather bag "My dagger I think you are familiar with," he said, pausing to remove it from his belt. He placed it on the table and Xanthe experienced a shiver, as if picking up on some of its violent history. "It is as well to be armed for our work. Have you considered carrying a weapon yourself?"

"I..."

"As I thought... which is why I brought this." Next to the dagger he placed a second knife. This one had a carved bone handle and a short, broad blade, about four inches long. "It is of little use for attack as such, but at close quarters would serve well in the way of defense. It has the added quality of being easily concealed about one's—" he paused and looked at Xanthe, waving vaguely at her body "—person."

"Erasmus, really, I don't think..."

"Then, of course, there are things I recommend for their usefulness. Here." He continued to pull items from the bag. A pair of pliers, a loop of wire, a box of matches, a purse of silver coins, a length of string, a bandage, folded notepaper, and a surprisingly modern pen. "These are all things I have gathered during my journeys and which I have ever been grateful for. As you are to spend increasing amounts of time spinning, it behooves me to see that you are suitably equipped. Now, if you don't care for the knife, might I suggest a small firearm?" Here he held up a tiny gun, stout and shiny and small enough to fit in the palm of the hand.

She looked at him and spoke in what she hoped was a kind but firm tone of voice.

"Erasmus, first of all, thank you for thinking of me. Of my safety, and of my work. I appreciate it, truly I do, but, well... I have been spinning for a while now. I have a bag of my own, and, like you, I have collected things that I've found really useful. Things I would not like to do without. My experience may be less than yours, but I have learned from it, I promise you."

Erasmus considered her words and looked suddenly crestfallen. "Of course. Forgive me, I should have taken into account all that you have already done." There was an uncomfortable silence and then he started hurriedly sweeping the objects off the table and back into his bag. "I was overreaching myself . . . it really is not my place . . ."

"Please, don't take offense."

"Not at all, not at all. You are quite correct. I have acted in the manner of a fussy parent. . . ."

"And I'm grateful for it, really I am," she said, reaching across the table and placing her hand on his.

He stopped what he was doing and looked at her. "I only sought to be of assistance to you. It is no small thing, to have the responsibilities of both guardian of the *Spinners* book and protector of the creed."

"I know. I'm astonished, honored, and just a little bit terrified."

He smiled at this, his handsome features relaxing. He pushed back his silvering hair, his eyes flashing once more, showing Xanthe how easy it must have been for Elizabeth to fall in love with him. "You will be a worthy successor to Lydia," he said as he slipped the dagger back into its sheath at his hip. "I am certain of it."

"I still think it should have been you."

"No, my decision to become a Stepper, all those years ago, put me forever outside the inner circle of Spinners. We are cousins, if you like. Spinners are your brothers and sisters. Even so, I wish you would at least take the gun." He picked it up and handed it to her.

It felt surprisingly heavy. She turned it over, examining it closely, trying to imagine herself pointing the thing at anyone in earnest. She could see how useful it might be as a defense, but would she be capable of pulling the trigger? Of killing someone? Fairfax had been responsible for his own death. She had not yet been called upon to take the step of ending the life of another, however dangerous they were, however wicked their actions. Would this be something she would have to do in her new role? Could she? She passed it back to Erasmus.

"I'm not quite ready for that," she said. "And maybe I'll regret not taking it. All I can say is, someone once told me to follow my heart, but temper my actions with my conscience, and I think that's pretty good advice, don't you?"

He nodded then. "I can imagine the manner of person who would give such advice, and I would be the last one to disagree with it," he told her, both of them enjoying the unspoken but shared understanding that these were Lydia's words. "Rest assured," he added, "I will always be at your service. Whenever you have need of me, you have only to call and I shall find you. You have my word."

"That is a great comfort, believe me. As long as Elizabeth can spare you."

"My dear, our partnership is more than merely matrimonial. My beloved wife will always support me in my work. So, you see, you have us both to aid you."

Xanthe nodded and then said, "And I have a small team of my own. They are not Spinners, or Steppers, or witches, but they will never let me down. I know that."

"We all of us started out as beginners. Their loyalty to you will be their spur, but their adventures will school them." He leaned back in his chair, evidently content that she had what she needed. "You will do well, young Spinner, you and your curious yet stalwart companions."

Laughing, she replied, "I can't wait to tell them you called them that!"

—

After another dress fitting and too few dancing lessons, the moment of the ball arrived. It was agreed that Liam and Xanthe would arrive first. This would allow her to speak briefly with their hosts, hopefully piquing their interest without having to give too much away. With guests still arriving both men would have to wait until later in the evening to question Liam more about his companion. A short while later, Harley and Elizabeth would make their entrance as wealthy industrialists with money to spend and allegiances to form. The strategy would be to keep the men occupied, either together or separately, so that whoever was freest could slip away and search the house for what they knew must be there: Talismans. Treasures. Sacred objects. Xanthe and Erasmus had agreed upon this. Most Spinners required something with which to spin. And these items were precious beyond rubies. They would be kept somewhere away from the main activity of the house. Somewhere quiet and secret, yet accessible to the Spinners when they needed them. She had no way of knowing what they might be, but they were accoutrements and essential possessions of time travelers, and things that they could not do without. Elizabeth and Xanthe would then cause an incident which would enable them to descend to the kitchen. They would send a note for their footman—Nipper—who would be waiting in their hired carriage in the road. Erasmus would be the driver. The two would then enter via the kitchen when summoned. As soon as they were unobserved, they would go to the room identified as the one they needed, and the others would join them when they could. The final part of the plan was the most dangerous. Brook-Morton and Dawlish would be lured to a room where they would be confronted directly. Xanthe and Erasmus had agreed no further details could be decided upon until they gauged the men's reactions to being told the game was up.

Getting ready took Xanthe more than an hour, and she could not have done it without Millie's help. They started with her hair, and the maid proved to be adept at smoothing her naturally tight curls into smoother coils with a pair of rather frightening tongs. She then twisted these up on top of Xanthe's head, pinning them into place with a fistful of pins and grips. The result was a sophisticated updo, softened by tendrils teased out to frame her face. The dress itself was in fact a two-piece, made of the most glorious pale golden silk. It was cut quite low at the front, the borders and edges finished with intricately stitched braid of a deeper gold. It had off-the-shoulder capped sleeves that gave a glamorous yet decorous sweep to the neckline. She was, by now, familiar with the layers—combinations in light cotton, which incorporated bloomers to the knees; a long-boned corset, tightly laced but surprisingly comfortable; a bustle pad and petticoat, mercifully without a cage; a fine cotton corset cover, which Millie explained was to soak up the sweat when she danced; the flounced and ruched skirt; an overskirt; and a boned bodice. There were also stockings held up with garters, and white satin gloves that came up over the elbows. The biggest differences between the ball gown and her daywear were the weight of the fabulous silk and the quantity of fabric, due to the ruffles in the skirt and the heavy train. She stepped into a pair of dainty white silk and leather pumps.

"Oh!" Millie clapped her hands. "It suits you very well indeed, miss. Perhaps you might try a little walk?"

Xanthe took small steps around what had been Lydia's bedroom, to the accompaniment of rustling silk. She caught sight of herself in the looking glass and gasped. "I didn't know I could look this shape!" she said, turning to view herself from the side and peer over her shoulder at the elaborate bustle and skirt. Elizabeth had explained that the Natural Form fashion of the day was only natural at the front and sides, with the corset cut to allow a curved stomach, and the line smooth and narrow over the hips. At the rear, all was exaggeration and flounce. It felt surprisingly comfortable and allowed a reasonable stride, but the train felt heavy and cumbersome as it swept along behind her. "How will I ever dance in this?" she asked.

Millie hurried forward. "Here. Before you step onto the dance floor with your partner, you take hold of this ribbon at the hem, like this, see? And then slip the loop around your wrist. Try."

She did as she was told. "But, I can't hold my hand in the air to keep it up all the time."

"You won't need to, miss, because your hand will be held by your dance partner, or placed on his shoulder while you dance." Not for the first time Millie regarded her new mistress with a puzzled expression, clearly wondering how little the young woman knew about what were, to her, everyday things.

She turned back to study her reflection again. She wore no jewelry other than her gold locket, which went perfectly with the color of the gown. The silk gleamed under the low light of the room. She recalled the beautiful dress Petronella had loaned her when she had traveled to the early 1800s, but this was glamour on another level. Whether it was the fabric, the cut of the gown, or the whole look, she couldn't be sure, but she felt transformed. She suppressed a giggle at the thought of how Liam might react to his plus one.

"Right," she said, smiling at Millie, "I think I'm ready."

"Oh, not quite, miss. You can't go without this," she said, opening a drawer in the chest by the window. She took out a fan and handed it to Xanthe.

"How lovely!" It was made of mother-of-pearl and lace and was quite the prettiest example of its type that she had ever seen. She opened it with a flick of the wrist, practicing fanning herself and holding it up in front of her face, making Millie laugh out loud. "What? Am I doing it wrong?"

"Why, no, miss, if you don't mind inviting all the men in the room to request the next dance!"

"Good grief, how have I done that?"

With great patience, Millie took the fan from her and explained how it could be used to signal things. It turned out that twisting it to the left suggested "we are being watched," dropping it indicated a person was interested only in friendship, and drawing the fan along the cheek meant "I love you."

Promising to keep the thing as still as possible and avoid eye contact while she was using it, Xanthe at last went downstairs. She found

Liam waiting for her in the narrow hallway. Even with such a plain and simple staircase, she was aware of making something of an entrance, dressed as she was. She saw Liam's face light up at the sight of her.

"Wow," he said, grinning. Then, after taking her offered hand when she reached the bottom stair, he remarked, "Just bloody wow, Xanthe. Is this one of those occasions girls go hunting for a husband? Because I think you are in danger of finding one. Or maybe several."

"I'll leave it to you to fight them off." She smiled before kissing his cheek lightly. "You look terrific, by the way," she told him. He was wearing a black suit with tailed jacket, a broad scarlet cummerbund, and a starched white collar and tie. He had been forced to forego the matching white gloves because of the splint on his hand, but otherwise looked every inch the part.

"Good of Nipper to lend me his suit. Of course he's a little narrower in the shoulders, a little skinnier in the arms . . ." He pretended to have to tug the sleeves to make adjustments.

"Nonsense. It fits you perfectly. Now, come on, we are on a tight schedule."

"Says the one who's kept me waiting twenty minutes."

"You try getting into this lot."

"I very much hope to, later on," he murmured, causing her to pinch him playfully as they left the house.

It wasn't until Xanthe saw the burly men standing on the pavement that she was reminded of the reality of what she was about to do. She was glad Erasmus had hired them to watch the house and protect the *Spinners* book. She silently chided herself for being so girlish about the evening. There was serious work to be done, and dangerous work at that.

By the time they arrived at the imposing Georgian house of the society, it was properly dark. The driveway was lit with large, dramatic caged torches, and smartly liveried footmen attended the carriages that queued to deposit their passengers. From all the tall windows of the house, golden light fell, and within it the sound of an orchestra already playing. Footmen, postilions, and drivers dashed hither and thither to assist the illustrious guests as they stepped from their conveyances and up the short, broad flight of steps to the entrance of the house. When their hansom cab drew up into place, Xanthe squeezed Liam's good hand.

"Ready?" she asked him.

"Ready. And by the way, you are beautiful, did I mention that?"

She smiled as the footman opened the door and offered a gloved hand to assist her down the step.

As they entered the building, she found herself comparing this grand occasion to those she had attended at Corsham Hall when she had been called by the wedding dress to help Petronella. Whereas the Regency home of the Wilcox family had been a statement of wealth and position in itself, its decor was restrained, delicate, underplayed. This venue, however, while classical in its exterior lines and crisp white stuccoed walls, was all about extravagance and ostentation. As they walked through the marble hallway, even Liam was moved to comment on the interior.

"Looks like somebody went to the more is more school of design, wouldn't you say?" he whispered as he handed his hastily written card to the butler who stood at the double door of the ballroom.

The pair stepped forward, and they were announced.

"Mister Liam Adams and Miss Xanthe Westlake," he declared, his sharp, slightly nasal voice rising above the music and the general hubbub.

It was in the ballroom that the commitment to lavish decoration reached its peak. The entrance was slightly elevated, so that newcomers were clearly visible, and so that they might better take in the splendor before them. The room was huge, with chairs placed in groups at either end and along the sides. It was already warm, the air thick with cigar smoke and perfume. Glancing up, Xanthe saw that, unusually, there was a mezzanine, upon which the orchestra was seated. She could not see the musicians from the doorway, but she could certainly hear their expert and energetic playing. The great height of the ceiling could easily accommodate this extra stretch of floor, and provided excellent acoustics. The ceiling was gloriously patterned plasterwork, its intricate repeats picked out with what must have been a small fortune in gold leaf. With a quick glance, she counted six fabulous chandeliers, each made of hundreds of teardrops of crystal, and supporting maybe thirty candles each. She could only imagine the trouble and risk to life and limb that several servants must have gone to when replacing and lighting all those candles. And the heat they gave off was not inconsiderable. The walls of the room, originally fairly ornate with gilding describing swags along the plasterwork and pretty pale blue and gold wallpaper, was further embellished with garlands of white and pink roses, threaded with what looked like faux pearls and silver bells, hung in festoons the length of the room. Every table or other surface was similarly covered in matching blooms and decorations. With the addition of so many fabulously dressed guests, the overall effect was one of dizzying color and grandeur.

Xanthe and Liam stood a little stunned, momentarily forgetting their mission, so dazzled were they by the spectacle before them. She became aware of someone standing too close to her. She turned to her left and found a man with a painstakingly oiled moustache and gold-framed monocle staring at her. Liam saw him.

"Ah, Dawlish. Quite the occasion you have going here. Allow me to introduce my friend, Miss Xanthe Westlake."

They had earlier agreed that presenting her as a friend would be helpfully vague.

Dawlish clicked his heels together and gave a rather perfunctory bow of the head, snatching up her hand to kiss it.

"*Enchanté!*" he gushed.

Xanthe was glad to be wearing gloves. Even so, the pressure of his lips on her hand was unpleasant, a little too forceful, and a little too lingering to conform to etiquette. She wondered if he was trying to confirm to himself through touch what his other senses must be telling him: that they had another Spinner in their midst. She followed the plan and merely smiled her acknowledgment of his welcome. Dawlish looked at her then and removed all doubt. He knew. The barely concealed excitement on his face, the widening of his eyes, the slight coloring of his already drink-reddened face, all told her that he knew what she was. He quickly gathered himself, clearly a person long practiced at deception, and addressed Liam. "We have much to discuss," he said baldly.

"Indeed we do," Liam agreed. "But first, my friend and I are thirsty." Before his host could reply to this, Liam led Xanthe down the two carpeted steps and along the side of the dance floor to where punch was being served. "How am I doing so far?" he asked her as they smiled at other guests left and right.

"Spot on," she whispered back, dipping a curtsey to a regal old woman who had sufficient diamonds in her tiara to build her own ballroom.

"You've certainly got Dawlish's attention. And look, he's telling Brook-Morton all about you. They're over there"—he nodded, raising his glass of punch in the direction of the two men who were indeed in earnest conversation.

She made a point of letting them see that she knew they were watching her, and that it did not bother her in the slightest. She wanted their attention on her. She imagined their surprise at having a Spinner simply walk into their home. They may have sensed her presence in the town, but to have her present herself publicly, in their very house, that introduced a whole different level of possibilities. She sipped her drink and casually engaged in light conversation with the nearest guests.

Liam leaned close and said into her ear, "They won't be able to resist talking to you for long."

"Well, they'll have to wait, won't they. Anyway, they'll be busy, look who just showed up."

Liam followed the direction of her gaze just as Harley and Elizabeth were announced.

"Mr. Dougal Fitzwilliam-Harley and Mrs. Elizabeth Fitzwilliam-Harley!"

"Fitzwilliam?" Liam muttered.

"He said he wanted something a bit grand," she explained.

"Well, that would be fitting. They are quite something, aren't they?"

The pair did indeed present a spectacle to rival anything in that splendid room. Harley, his whiskers expertly oiled and groomed into shape, his bushy hair tamed and swept back, was resplendent in a frilly-fronted shirt, red-and-black tartan kilt, and all appropriate regalia. His knee-high socks had tassels at the garters. His sporran was positioned exactly right. His matching tartan sash crossed his shoulder at the perfect angle. His black-and-scarlet jacket matched the whole outfit perfectly. He even had what looked like a ceremonial sword at his hip. He looked like the proudest man in the room, and well he might, for the woman on his arm was a vision. It was the etiquette of the day that unmarried women should wear simpler dresses, more modestly cut, with fewer jewels. Married women, however, were under no such constraints, and Elizabeth had clearly enjoyed this small freedom. She had also eschewed the rule that for balls ladies should choose gowns in pale colors. Elizabeth, Xanthe decided, looking at her anew, was not a pale color kind of woman. For this occasion, she had chosen a dress made in the richest ruby red Xanthe had ever seen. It was not so bright as to be garish, nor so dark as to be somber, but was the perfect shade, set off beautifully by deeper versions of itself at the hems, ruffles, and neckline. Elizabeth wore her glowing chestnut hair in a high, elaborate bun, the distinctive white streak woven through the coils, gaining even more inches of height by the addition of three artfully placed peacock feathers. Xanthe remembered reading that they were considered bad luck by some, but that they were beloved of witches. Her gloves were black, long, and sleek. At her throat were what looked convincingly like rubies strung with jet, though Xanthe knew they would be paste. Having paused to ensure the whole room had seen her, Elizabeth expertly flicked open a black fan, working it effortlessly to keep cool, and descended the steps with Harley.

"That is quite an entrance," Liam said.

Xanthe noticed Brook-Morton and Dawlish making a beeline for the new arrivals. Harley promised to be an important source of income, and that would start with the money he had agreed to bring with him. As she watched, the men greeted the couple with great bonhomie before gently leading them away through a side door, presumably for the purposes of that vital first payment.

"Come on." She took Liam's punch from him and put it down. "They're busy now. We need to find their spinning room."

"You don't think they'll have taken Harley there?" he asked, following as she threaded her way through the crowd.

"No. He thinks they get their information through séances. If anything they'll have some tacky clairvoyance table set up, just to impress him."

They succeeded in leaving the ballroom through another side door but found themselves back in the hall again. A footman sprang from nowhere and asked if he could be of assistance. She told him the heat had made her a little faint and they were searching for some air, whereupon the servant helped them through a door onto the terrace at the rear of the house. When he had gone, Liam gave a shrug.

"OK, not quite where we wanted to be, but it's very nice out here."

Everywhere the garden was illuminated with the same fiery torches that had lit the drive at the front of the house.

"It's definitely a statement look," Xanthe agreed. "Not your usual pretty lanterns. A bit more . . . well, masculine. Gothic? Almost threatening, somehow."

"Maybe the interior designer doesn't do gardens and they were left to their own devices."

"Maybe. I think it's more than that. Like a small but deliberate nod to how powerful they are, and how much they will protect that power."

"As with a ring of fire?"

"Sort of thing." She turned to look up at the rear aspect of the house. "Most of the important rooms would be on the first floor. Houses like this were designed to give a better view of the gardens, and to allow the occupants to look down on everyone else."

"Nice."

"They couldn't do it with the ballroom, though. Everyone would come through the floor. So, the room we are looking for is most probably on that floor. We need to get up a level."

"You make it sound like a video game."

She looked at him seriously then. "Trust me, this is no game. These men, Liam, they will protect what they have with anything and everything."

He raised his splinted hand. "It's OK, I got schooled in risks quite recently. OK, let's just brazen it out, then. Straight up the main staircase, dismissing all offers of help from flunkies, taking on the attitude of people who are used to doing what they want without question."

"That's actually quite a good idea," she said.

They went back inside and headed straight for the grand staircase. First a maid and then a footman attempted to stop them, but all that amounted to was solicitous offers of help or queries as to their state of health. Xanthe found they were easily brushed aside with a "thank you, no" or "we require no assistance" or even just a haughty look. She used the ribbon attached to the train to lift it so that she was able to climb the stairs. They quickly reached the first floor, where there were no more servants to slow their progress.

"That was easy," said Liam quietly.

"They may go and fetch someone with more authority. We must be quick."

They hurried along the corridor, pausing to open one closed door after another, peering into a variety of luxurious rooms. They reached the end of the landing.

"Nothing," Xanthe muttered.

"Where next? This house goes up and up."

She thought about Erasmus's second-floor workshop, and Elizabeth's love of the roof, and of Fairfax's observatory, and even her own attic window seat with a view of the townscape. There was something about being in a high place. Something that perhaps suggested a safe distance from unwanted interruptions and uninvited guests. The design of the house did not suggest a glass roof anywhere, or a rooftop terrace that would not be exposed to the elements, which wouldn't quite work. "It must be in the attic," she decided.

"Isn't that where the servants live?"

"Ordinarily. But there are often rooms in the basement too. And let's face it, these are not ordinary circumstances or ordinary people." She lifted up her skirts again and they moved quickly to the stairwell, continuing their climb beyond the next floor, which appeared to house bedrooms, and up to the attic level. Here the degree of opulence was significantly diminished. The boards were bare. The walls plainly painted with only a scattering of small oils or watercolors. The sideboards and tallboys were utilitarian rather than decorative. Even the air seemed different, with an aroma of furniture wax and mothballs rather than silver polish and fresh flowers. The corridor was narrow, and myriad doors were set into it, each looking as workaday as the next. Just visible halfway along was the top of another, far more humble stairway, that would inevitably lead down to the kitchens and the servants' quarters.

"Hard to know where to start," said Liam, trying the first one and finding it locked. "Ah, maybe that's a clue. I mean, if you had important stuff you'd probably keep it locked up, wouldn't you?"

"Maybe," Xanthe agreed, but all the same she began walking away from him. The temperature on this floor was considerably cooler than in the ballroom, but it was not the chilly air that was making her skin break into goose bumps. Every part of her Spinner being was telling her that she was close to treasures; ones with significance and power and stories to tell. She began to hear whispers, snatched words urging her to come closer, calling her in a way she could not refuse. She moved purposefully toward the door at the very end of the gloomy hallway. It looked no different than all the other drab doors, but she knew that she had found the right place.

"Here," she said to Liam. "Everything they use, everything that enables them to spin through time . . . it's behind this door."

Liam stood beside her. Xanthe reached out her hand to take hold of the door handle.

"Mr. Adams, Miss Westlake! Are you lost?" The voice cut through the moment, making both of them jump and swing round. Walking down the hall came a broad-shouldered, hefty man. His clothes were not those of a servant, but nor were they the finery of a guest.

Liam whispered to her urgently. "Dawlish's henchman! The one who attacked me in the alleyway."

She stepped between Liam and the man, reasoning a fight was less likely with a woman in the way. She forced herself to dampen down her frustration at being so close to what was calling her, yet not being able to answer that call. "I fear we have indeed lost our way," she replied brightly. "Such a lovely house, we could not resist exploring."

"Mr. Dawlish would like to speak with you both. Allow me to show you the way back to the ballroom," he said, stepping aside with a sweep of his arm, his meaning clear. They must go back and they must do it at that moment. He would not take no for an answer.

Smiling politely, Xanthe took Liam's arm, and together they walked past the man and permitted him to escort them back to where they were supposed to be.

In the ballroom, the dancing was in full swing.

"Oh, a waltz. Liam, I believe I promised you the first dance," Xanthe said, letting go of his arm and offering him her hand.

"But, Miss Westlake, if you would step this way, Mr. Dawlish is waiting . . ." The thug was thrown by this.

"I am certain our host would want us to enjoy ourselves. He would surely not begrudge me my first dance!"

Without waiting for him to protest further, she and Liam stepped into the gathering of dancers as the floor began to fill up, drawn to dance to the joyful, rhythmic Viennese waltz. Liam frowned as he concentrated on getting his hands in the right position and leading with the correct foot.

"Smile," she told him, "you're supposed to be having fun."

"It's smile or dance, I can't do both. I'm still counting one, two, three in my head," he said as he fairly deftly steered her around the room.

She felt herself able to relax into the dance, finding it an instinctive movement after all their lessons with Millie. The music was so uplifting and so pretty, and the novel experience of dancing in a room full of beautifully dressed men and women, all clearly enjoying themselves, was a marvelous experience she would never forget. For a moment she questioned her own sense. How was she able to go from a heightened situation as a Spinner and only minutes later be reveling in some new activity time travel had afforded her? Shouldn't she stay more focused? It was an instant of personal revelation, then, to discover that the two things were one and the same. All Spinners, from whatever era, must eventually travel to times not their own and find themselves in new and bewildering circumstances. How could they not wonder at the magic of what they were doing, even when facing difficult challenges with uncertain outcomes? As they whirled about she caught a glimpse of Harley and Elizabeth dancing with quiet concentration. Liam saw them too and they contrived to dance close to one another. When the piece of music came to an end, the four steadfastly ignored the stares and hailing gestures of their hosts at the side of the room and swapped partners. Liam would tell Elizabeth what they had found. Xanthe would get the chance to speak with Harley. Mercifully, the waltz was so popular it was requested again, so the orchestra played it for a second time.

"Harley, I'm impressed."

"Thought I'd have two left feet, did ye? I've many hidden talents."

"So it seems," she said, surprised when he added a sudden dip to the steps.

"Steady on! Leave me enough breath to speak. We've found the room where they keep everything. I'm convinced their talismans are in there; things on the other side of that door were singing to me the length of the hall. It's at the top of the house."

"They're a couple of smooth bastards, I know that much. Took our money right enough, and promised us all manner of ways to cheat and make ourselves richer. No mention of who they were going to have to trample on to do it, just some bollocks about talking to the dead."

"Most of their clients are in it for money. I don't think they usually care about the *how*, just the *how much*," she said.

"Aye, that's the truth of it."

"Now that we know where to send Erasmus and Nipper, Elizabeth and I are going to do what we agreed so we can get to the kitchens. You and Liam stick together and don't take your eyes off Dawlish and Brook-Morton. We don't want them going upstairs before we're ready. Can you make a good job of pretending to be a bit drunk, d'you think?"

Harley raised his bushy eyebrows. "Lassie . . . do ye not know me at all?" he asked, before giving her a wink. For the next minute or so he made a point of dancing somewhat erratically, giving vent to the odd whoop or guffaw. As expected, people started to look in his direction. Xanthe played her part by looking embarrassed.

When the music stopped again the dancers cleared the floor for a short interval. Liam fetched everyone more punch while Xanthe spoke with Elizabeth.

"We don't have long. I can see Dawlish heading this way."

"Be calm, my dear, all will be well," she said gently.

Harley loudly challenged Liam to down his glass of punch in one, demonstrating to everyone that he himself was more than capable.

"Have you no fire in your belly, lad? Here, give me another. This stuff is weak as spring water. Is there no decent Scotch to be had? You, there!" He snapped his fingers imperiously at a footman, who came trotting to him. "Fetch me whiskey and quick about it. I've reason to celebrate, and 'tis an insult to try to do it with yon gnat's piss!"

Around him guests were frowning, one or two of the men steering their women away, others watching, amused by the entertainment this drunken stranger was providing. His antics were all the more noticeable while there was no music playing. Dawlish reached them just in time to see Harley swallowing a large whiskey in one gulp. He attempted to politely contain the situation.

"I am pleased to see you so happy to be a part of our society, Mr. Fitzwilliam-Harley."

"'Tis a grand club ye have here, Dawlish. Fine work you are about for us, a fine place, fine . . . people." Here he openly leered at a particularly buxom middle-aged woman to his left. The woman flicked open her fan with an expression of disgust and hid behind it. Xanthe noticed she didn't try to move away, however.

Elizabeth put a hand on Harley's arm. "Husband, so much excitement might not be advisable for your dear heart. Perhaps a turn around the garden for some air?"

"*Air*, you say?"

Xanthe stepped forward, needing to put herself in the mix. "Or a bite to eat, perhaps? That can have a . . . calming effect."

Dawlish smiled at her. "A wise suggestion, Miss Westlake. There are refreshments to be had in the morning room. We might go there together, with Mr. and Mrs. Harley," he suggested. He had a smooth, controlled manner of speech that made Xanthe feel uneasy.

"I'll not eat!" Harley objected strongly to the idea, snatching up the decanter of whiskey from the tray the hapless footman still held nearby. "Not while there's passable whiskey to be had and dancing to be done!" he insisted, pouring himself another generous measure.

"My dear," Elizabeth spoke softly and did well to give the impression of a long-suffering wife accustomed to her husband's excesses, "come, I would like a bite to eat. It would be a pleasant way to pass the interval. And it seems to me a short while sitting down could benefit you—"

"Sitting down!" Now Harley was roaring. "Hold your tongue, woman! I am not a child to be sat on a chair and spoon-fed," he declared, draining his glass again. "Do not write me off as in my dotage just yet."

"Husband, I assure you I see you as neither babe nor old man—"

"And yet ye see fit to treat me as such!"

The disagreement was now reaching farther around the room so that more and more people were watching. Brook-Morton came hurrying to help quell the rumpus. Their clients were no doubt used to a certain level of behavior at their events. Xanthe reasoned that even for the wealth their hosts had, a ball was quite an investment, and they would not want the evening soured. But Harley was in his stride now, to such an extent that she worried he might actually be drunk.

"I'll have you know I fought the French for six years straight. And I served in the Fourth Regiment of the Scots Dragoons in the Crimea! Where I was decorated for bravery and my swordsmanship was second to none!" To underline his point, much to the horror of those standing close to him, Harley reached to his side and drew out his sword, which he brandished with a flourish. Three women screamed. One fainted. Several men swore and two of the bolder ones drew their own swords.

"I say, sir!" Dawlish was bold enough to step forward. "Sheath your sword at once!"

"This is not to be tolerated!" Brook-Morton declared, though he stopped short of doing anything about it.

"Hush, my dear . . ." Elizabeth stood very still as about her Harley swiped and swooshed with his sword, determined to demonstrate he had lost nothing of his youthful talent.

"I will not be hushed!" So saying, he made one terrifying downward stroke that was so close to his wife that it caused her to leap backward, arm raised. This in turn emptied her glass of punch over Xanthe's dress, the rose-red liquid spreading down her bodice in an alarmingly dark stain. One or two of the onlookers clearly thought it was blood and more shrieking ensued.

Harley gave the impression he was appalled at what he had done and at last stopped his cavorting, putting away his sword and, chastened, mumbling words of apology.

Liam stepped in between Harley and Xanthe. "Have a care, man!" he told him, before turning to her. "Are you hurt?" he asked.

"No, thank you, only, my dress . . ."

Elizabeth took her arm. "Forgive my husband, I beg you, he is a little exuberant when in his cups," she said.

"Exuberant be damned!" exclaimed Brook-Morton.

Elizabeth continued to make excuses for her husband, assuring their hosts that he would soon recover his manners and his good humor. "If we might retire to the kitchens for a moment. I am certain your housekeeper will be able to help repair the dress."

"But my gown is ruined!" Xanthe complained, fairly convincingly she decided, judging by the reactions of onlookers.

"I promise you, it can be saved," Elizabeth assured her. "And I have a spare chiffon shawl in my carriage outside, so your evening need not be at an end. Come, let us throw ourselves upon the mercy of . . . forgive me, Mr. Dawlish, what is the name of your housekeeper?"

"Mrs. Stanton."

"Let us ask for Mrs. Stanton's help. Dougal, dear, please say you will accompany us, as it was your overenthusiastic demonstration of sword craft which resulted in poor Miss Westlake being so inconvenienced."

Harley gave a harrumph but managed to look both guilty and drunk at the same time. "Aye, fair enough. You have my apologies, lassie."

Dawlish appeared to be on the point of objecting, but melted under the warmth of Elizabeth's most dazzling smile as she led the others away. "We will return shortly, and all the more civil for a short break, I promise," she told them.

Their arrival in the kitchen caused quite a stir among the servants. It was not an everyday occurrence to have guests enter the domain below stairs, but, as Elizabeth had known she would, the housekeeper sprang into action, leading the visitors to her office. This was a cheerfully furnished, tiny room to one side of the main part of the kitchen. It had a glass wall, so that Mrs. Stanton could keep a critical eye on the staff when the head butler was not able to do so.

"Do not be distressed, miss," she said to Xanthe, "I will fetch water and Epsom salts and we will have your beautiful gown good as new in no time. No time at all."

"Thank you so much," said Xanthe, sitting on one of the small, tapestry-cushioned chairs by the housekeeper's desk. Harley stood in the center of the room swaying slightly, still giving the appearance of someone the worse for drink.

Elizabeth spoke to the housekeeper as she reached the doorway. "I wonder if there is a boy who might take a note to my footman. My carriage is parked in the street. I would like him to bring my shawl so that Miss Westlake might have the benefit of it, and—" here she hesitated, glancing over her shoulder at Harley before continuing in a conspiratorial tone "—I will ask for my driver, also, in the hope that my husband might be persuaded to return home with them. He is, I fear, no longer in a fit state for dancing. Better he leave quietly. They may bring the carriage back for me later."

"You will be without your husband for the rest of the evening?"

Elizabeth sighed. "Alas, it would not be my first choice, but, needs must. I am sure an experienced housekeeper such as yourself is aware of the sacrifices we women must sometimes make."

Mrs. Stanton grew at least six inches. She nodded, delighted to have been taken into the confidence of someone so glamorous and obviously important as Elizabeth. "You need not say another word, ma'am. I will send a boy to your carriage. We will have all arranged to everyone's satisfaction in no time at all. No time at all," she said again.

19

WITHIN MINUTES, NIPPER AND ERASMUS, CONVINCINGLY ATTIRED AS FOOTMAN AND driver, were in the kitchen. Xanthe declared herself delighted with Mrs. Stanton's efforts to clean the worst of the punch from the dress, and the chiffon scarf was adroitly tucked into her décolletage, overflowing in just the right amount to hide the remaining stain. By now several of the downstairs maids had come to stand around the entrance to the housekeeper's office. It was rare for them to get a glimpse of the glamorous guests. The butler and his troupe of footmen were all engaged in their duties in the ballroom.

Harley beamed. "There ye are, lassie! Good as new, ready to be the belle of the ball once more." He waved his arms about expressively.

Elizabeth spoke calmly but firmly to him. "My dear, it is late, as Thomas is here and the carriage available, why not return home with them? The dancing will not continue longer, and I know how conversation bores you. I can follow on later, so as not to offend our hosts."

Xanthe watched the faces of the servants closely. If any of them knew anything of what their masters were about, they would think it odd that a new society member would not stay to discuss important matters after the dancing. It was clear to her that the girls, and even the housekeeper, were ignorant of how their employers made their luxurious living. Harley made a show of being about to argue and then accepting that this was an attractive idea.

"Aye, maybe you have something there. I'll go along now, if you'll make my excuses."

"I will," she said, giving him a brief farewell kiss. If Erasmus disliked this part of the performance, he succeeded in hiding his feelings. Harley's delight, however, was obvious. The men began to move slowly out of the room as if to go to the back door. Right on cue, Xanthe stepped forward to do her bit to distract the staff. She had to keep them in that room and keep their attention long enough for the men to turn left instead of right at the end of the kitchen corridor and sprint up the back staircase to the attic.

"What would we have done without you and your staff, Mrs. Stanton?" she asked. "You've all been so kind. I wish there was something I could do in return."

One of the bolder maids spoke up. "It's lovely to see your beautiful gown, miss. You look so very pretty."

Mrs. Stanton said, "Just go back and enjoy the dance, miss. We are happy to help."

The maid muttered, "Oh, imagine dancing in such a dress!"

"Do you like to dance?" Xanthe asked her.

"Oh, yes, miss! But I don't go to balls. I like the music hall. We get a Saturday off once a month and we always go and listen to the newest song, don't we, Betty?" She turned to her fellow maid, who nodded enthusiastically. "And then we go to a tea dance after." She fell silent, noticing the disapproving stare from the housekeeper.

"I like to sing," Xanthe told them, "and I've been told I have a tolerable voice. Would you let me sing for you? As a thank-you. I have made extra work for you when you are already so busy."

After initial protests from Mrs. Stanton that they couldn't possibly ask such a thing, it was agreed. The maids shuffled round to allow her a little more space. She asked them which were their favorite songs, relieved when they mentioned one she vaguely knew. "Do please help me with the words if I forget them," she said, before taking a deep breath and beginning to sing. It was a light moment in what had already been a tense evening. Singing soothed her, and the obvious joy it brought to her tiny audience was very rewarding. More important, from where she stood she had a clear view through the windowed wall of Erasmus, Nipper, and Harley darting down the hallway and up the stairs. She sang on, a popular music hall tune of the time, encouraging the maids to join in when, as she knew she would, she faltered with the words. The tune was easy and lilting and the lyrics so charming that it lifted everyone's mood.

The boy I love is up in the gallery,
The boy I love is looking now at me.
There he is, can't you see, waving his handkerchief,
As merry as a robin that sits in a tree.
Now, if I were a duchess and had a lot of money,
I'd give it to the boy who's going to marry me.
But I haven't got a penny, so we'll live on love and kisses,
And be just as happy as the birds on the tree!

When she had finished her song the girls clapped enthusiastically and she and Elizabeth said their goodbyes and returned to the ballroom. Dawlish and Brook-Morton were waiting for them and somewhat bewildered to hear Harley had left. Before they were able to question Elizabeth further about why he had not stayed to discuss further business, Xanthe distracted them by saying she wished to dance, as the orchestra had struck up again. Seeing a chance to find out more about the Spinner in their midst, Brook-Morton readily offered to be her partner. Xanthe disliked the feeling of his arm around her waist but at least as they were both wearing gloves she did not have to feel his skin against hers. There was something inescapably creepy about the man. He was, it turned out, an accomplished dancer, and steered her expertly around the dance floor, more than capable of holding a conversation while doing so.

"We are intrigued to have such an interesting guest," he told her. "I was unaware Mr. Adams had acquaintances in this time, beyond Mistress Flyte, of course."

"Who says I am of this time?" She smiled as she spoke, so that to the rest of the room they presented the perfect picture of a happy dancing couple.

"Of course, we know that you are not," he replied levelly. "How is it that you come to be here. In this place and this year?"

She felt certain that news of Mistress Flyte's death had not reached the society. "I came here for Liam. To take him home to his own time. Which is exactly what I intend on doing."

"Indeed? You are very sure of your own capabilities, Miss Westlake."

"I am very sure you will try to stop me."

"I have to tell you, Mr. Adams is far too valuable to us to be simply given up. I should warn you we have no desire to be talked out of keeping him."

Around them other dancers stepped and whirled, silk rustling, expensively shod feet tapping against the polished boards of the dance floor as the musicians played on. The heat of the room had only increased with time, not least because of the excessive amount of candles. To the smell of perfume, cigar smoke, punch, and candle wax was now added the sour odor of perspiration. Xanthe felt Brook-Morton's fingers digging into her waist. She was grateful for the protection offered by her boned bodice and corset. The man's breath was malodorous, unmistakable halitosis unsuccessfully masked by peppermint and red wine.

She put to one side how repellent she found the man. "And I have to tell you," she said, "that not only will I be returning Liam to his rightful place . . . oh, and by the way, he never had any intention of working with you . . . not only shall I be making sure he gets home safely, I will also be putting an end to the Visionary Society."

At this Brook-Morton gave a bark of laughter. It was an unattractive, joyless sound.

"My dear girl, I understand that modern women have quite a high opinion of themselves, but a young Spinner as yourself might do well to temper such confidence with caution. Instead of pitting yourself against us, why not consider how best we might help one another? There is much to discuss here, do you not agree?"

At that moment the waltz came to an end. The dancers stopped, a little breathless now, bowed to their partners and applauded the musicians. Xanthe immediately dropped his hand and took a step back.

"I do. But I won't talk to you more here. If you want me to hear what you have to say, it will have to be in that very special room of yours at the top of the house. Oh, and my good friend Elizabeth Balmoral will be coming with us."

Brook-Morton struggled to keep his composure as he realized that not only did Xanthe know about the Spinners' room, but that Elizabeth was not who she claimed to be, but the wife of a known Time Stepper. He recovered his composure quickly, however.

"I see no need for us to include one who is not a Spinner in our conversations."

"She comes with me, or we talk here. I'm sure your guests would be fascinated to listen in on our discussion." She stood in front of him, using her fan in a way that suggested she would stand there as long as it took for him to agree to her condition. He evidently recognized the truth of this in her stance and expression.

"Very well," he said with a bow, allowing Xanthe to lead the way.

Elizabeth fell into step beside her as she passed, with Dawlish following suit. As they left the ballroom the orchestra started playing a Polish mazurka this time; faster, more urgent, more chaotic in its rhythm. The unsettling music followed them as they mounted the stairs. Xanthe was also aware of Dawlish's henchman catching them up. She offered up a silent prayer that the men had found their way into the room and done whatever they could. In a few more moments they had reached the top of the house. Dawlish stepped forward and turned the handle, throwing open the door and inviting the ladies to step inside.

Whatever Xanthe had been expecting, however many ideas she had entertained concerning the treasures and unique objects these Spinners might have kept for their work, nothing she had thought of remotely resembled what she found in their precious room. Apart from a grandfather clock placed against one side wall, the room was entirely empty. Empty of things. Three people stood who had been waiting for the door to open, looking in equal measures perplexed and determined. Xanthe gave Liam an incredulous glance. In response he shook his head slowly and gave an eloquent shrug. To his left, Harley stood, drawing himself up to his fullest height and size. To his right, Erasmus remained silent, calm, but with a dangerous look in his eye that made Xanthe relieved they were on the same side. Behind them, along the length of the far wall, was a row of closed doors. She counted eight. They were identical, unremarkable, and solid-looking. A sense of desperation began to take hold of her. If the clock was the crucial item in their travel, it could be easily dealt with. If, on the other hand, it was the doors they used, how on earth were they going to get rid of them? And what if only some of them were important? How would they know which ones to focus on? Clearly all these thoughts had already occurred to the men, who had not had time to form an answer or take any action before Xanthe had brought the Spinners to the room.

It was Dawlish who broke the tense silence.

"I see we have underestimated you, Mr. Adams. And I now better understand the eagerness of your Scottish friend to join our society."

Brook-Morton was less reserved in his opinion. "Damn your eyes for liars!" he spat.

Erasmus leaned back against the frame of one of the doors, giving the impression of a man with not a care in the world. "Come, come, sir, to bandy about such a word hardly seems reasonable, given your own dark practices."

Dawlish defended himself. "We offer a service. For which we are paid handsomely, I grant you, but we enter into a contract with our clients and fulfill the terms of that deal."

Xanthe turned to him, stepping backward into the room as she did so, drawing Elizabeth with her carefully. "You really have convinced yourself you are nothing more than businessmen, haven't you?"

"There certainly is a demand for membership of the society, you must see that."

"Of course there is," she replied. "There will always be people ready to make easy money. But you don't tell them the truth of what you do."

"My dear girl," Dawlish's tone was infuriatingly patronizing, "we could hardly speak to them of traveling through time now, could we? It is not necessary for them to understand the details of our working practices."

"No," she agreed, "not necessary. Because if they knew that you act without regard for the consequences of what you do—the consequences for others, people who have no choice in the matter—if they knew that your actions distort the order of things . . ."

"Ah, such fine Spinner sentiments." Dawlish smiled. "Such a shining conscience as yours must be a dazzling thing to live with."

"It is more than a matter of conscience. The rules of the Spinners are there for good reason. What you do does not disrupt some theoretical thing. Yours is not a victimless crime. People's lives are changed forever. Their given paths destroyed. Their hoped-for futures crushed. Sometimes their very lives. It is these people who pay for your gain. And it stops now."

Brook-Morton sneered at her. "If you believe a couple of women and a ragtag collection of fellows—one of them a drunkard—are going to take away all that we have worked for, you are very much mistaken."

Harley took exception to this. "And if you think I could get drunk on that bitter bilgewater you call whiskey, you are completely deluded." So saying, he drew his ceremonial sword and held it as if to strike at the grandfather clock. "Now, you'd better be telling young Xanthe here which door is the one you use for spinning, before I reduce yon timepiece to a pile of kindling."

Dawlish was all for negotiating a way out of their situation. "Now, surely we can find a way forward that would work to the advantage of all of us here," he said. He might have had more to suggest, but Brook-Morton was having none of it. Even as his partner spoke, he reached inside his dinner jacket.

"He has a gun!" Liam shouted, flinging himself forward at the man. He connected with him in a low rugby tackle, sending Brook-Morton backward against the wall. His wounded hand hampered him, however, so that he wasn't able to keep his target pinned down. Harley started hacking away at the clock in a bold attempt to draw attention from Liam. Erasmus was fully engaged with tackling the henchman who had entered the fray. He threw his dagger, which found its target in the heavy man's arm, causing him to cry out and stagger to one side. Dawlish seemed rooted to the spot. Xanthe tried to grab at Brook-Morton as he shook Liam off and rose to his knees, but he was already firing the gun. Elizabeth shouted at her to stay back. Brook-Morton swung round and fired at Harley but missed as Xanthe pushed him forward with all her strength. The man pivoted as he fell forward and fired again, aiming directly at her. Later, when Xanthe would play that moment over and over in her mind, she would never be entirely certain what happened, or if she could have prevented it happening. So many things occurred at once, and with such speed, that even when she discussed it with the others who were there, events were unclear. What she knew happened, what was indisputable, was that Erasmus, having thrown his knife, leaped to tackle Brook-Morton in an attempt to get the gun from him or at least prevent him shooting Xanthe. But the furious Spinner was too quick for him and fired off four more shots in quick succession. One harmlessly hit the ceiling. One grazed the skirt of Xanthe's gown. The others hit Erasmus. The room was filled with noise. There was a cry of agony from Erasmus, a scream of despair from Elizabeth, and a roar of rage from Nipper, who was intercepted by the henchman. Amid it all, Xanthe could hear the calling of lost souls and people in need of her help from behind the locked doors. For a few terrible moments there seemed to be nothing but confusion and fear and pain. Somewhere in it all more shots rang out. Only then did Xanthe see that Liam was holding the small gun Erasmus had offered her. He had pointed it at Brook-Morton with his left hand, being unable to hold it in his splinted right one. The two shots he fired both hit the man full in the chest and he fell heavily to the ground, motionless and silent. Dawlish chose that moment to turn and run. His henchman gave up the fight and fled after him. Nipper scrambled to his feet and ran to his father, where Elizabeth was already trying to staunch the flow of blood.

"Lie still," she told him, slipping at once into the role of medic. "Nipper, your cravat, give it to me." She used the starched cloth to plug the wound in his belly. "Place your hand here," she instructed her son. "We must turn you onto your side, Erasmus. The exit wounds are bleeding profusely."

Xanthe was horrified at the growing pool of crimson blood that was spreading out underneath him. Liam came to kneel beside her, putting an arm around her shoulders. She was aware of him finding where the bullet had cut through the silk of her dress and that he was making sure she had not been hit, but she was too appalled at Erasmus's wounds to speak. Harley had stopped slashing at the clock and stood watching.

Nipper held his father in his arms as his mother worked to save him, but it was evident to all of them that he was bleeding too fast, that his injuries were too catastrophic. Erasmus knew it too. Elizabeth would not give up. Xanthe saw her expression change, as if she had made an important decision.

"Nipper, sit him up a little now, in your lap, yes, support his head, that's good. My love, do not be afraid," she said, placing a bloodstained hand tenderly on his cheek, looking deep into his dark eyes.

Erasmus managed a small smile. "Since you came into my life, my sweet Elizabeth, I have known not a moment's fear," he said, placing his hand over hers.

Elizabeth nodded, sitting back on her heels, gently withdrawing her hand. She paused, taking in a long, slow breath. Xanthe could see she was about to try something that was not in any nursing manual, that she had not learned when she'd trained to be a doctor, that she had not practiced in her years assisting a surgeon. She was about to draw on something more ancient, something altogether from another realm.

It was Erasmus who stopped her.

"No, my dear. Do not trouble yourself . . ." he said, closing his eyes briefly in a grimace of pain, coughing as he did so.

"Let me try," she begged him. "I can help you. The bleeding is fast but I can at least slow it, I'm certain of it. Perhaps then I might mend the damage . . . and with time and care . . ."

He was shaking his head. He opened his eyes again and reached for her hand. She gave it to him, blinking away tears.

"Please!" she begged him. "Let me try."

"My love . . . forgive me . . . I would not leave you for all the world," he gasped, paused, and then carried on. "I am, after all, a Time Stepper," he said gently, pulling her hand to his lips to bestow upon it a shaky kiss. "I am closely acquainted with the passing of moments and the arrival of points in time that are of significance. It has been my life for so very long. Too long, in fact."

"Husband, you are not so very old. . . ."

"Ah, but I have lived more centuries than is good for a person, we both know that, my love. I of all people should know when my time has come. I am not afraid. I go to my brethren. I am only sorry to leave you, my darling wife."

"Oh, Erasmus . . ." Elizabeth's voice was a whisper filled with heartbreak.

He looked up at his son. "For all my traveling, being father to you was the work of which I am most proud, Thomas. Know that."

"Father!" was all Nipper managed to say.

Erasmus's breathing became rapid. As his chest heaved and he began to cough scarlet blood, he found the strength to address Xanthe. "Godspeed, young Spinner," he said, and then the light went out behind his eyes forever.

Xanthe felt rather than heard Elizabeth draw in a long, shocked breath. The heartbroken woman battled to contain the grief that looked as if it might burst from her violently. Xanthe could sense the zinging energy coming from her.

"Oh, Elizabeth," she said softly, "I . . . I am so, so sorry . . ."

She turned to look at Xanthe then, her beautiful face stern with barely contained rage. "Stop him," she said levelly. "He must be stopped!"

Xanthe nodded and started for the door, Liam and Harley following as Elizabeth rose to her feet.

Nipper stayed cradling his father in his arms. "We can't leave him. Not here!" he said.

Elizabeth nodded. "Take him to the carriage. He must go home."

Xanthe put a hand on Liam's arm. "Help him," she said. "Go with him."

"But . . ."

Harley stepped in. "Go on, laddie. We will see to yon bastards." When Liam offered him the gun, he held out his hand to take it but Xanthe stopped them.

"No," she said. "No more guns."

She and Harley helped Nipper and Liam to lift Erasmus. Elizabeth leaned forward to plant a kiss on his cold brow.

"Right." Xanthe strode from the room. "Let's finish this thing."

Harley and Elizabeth hurried after her. They descended the main staircase in time to see the nameless henchman stepping back into the shadow of a doorway, clearly hoping to see rather than be seen.

Harley let out a bellow of rage. "There's the thug! There!"

People in the hallway turned to see what the shouting was about. The man sprang from his hiding place and sprinted from the door. Harley showed an impressive turn of speed, jumped the last few stairs, ran after the man, and, with a perfect rugby tackle, brought him crashing to the ground.

Several guests shrieked or shouted for help. Two footmen came running and caught hold of Harley, dragging him off the man on the floor.

"The man's gone mad!" the thug told anyone who would listen, clambering to his feet. "He's raving!"

"Let me go! He'll get away!" Harley cursed as he shouted at them. But the footmen knew the man to be in their masters' employ and were inclined to believe him over what they considered to be a drunken stranger.

It was not until Xanthe, keeping her composure as best she could, spoke up, that they doubted him.

"That man," she said, pointing directly at the henchman, "just killed Mr. Brook-Morton! Shot him dead!" When the onlookers gasped she went on. "He's in the attic, lying in his own blood. If you don't believe me, look at my poor friend, the wife of the man you are now unjustly restraining!" She stepped aside. There were cries of horror at the sight of Elizabeth, the guests and servants not knowing that the blood she was covered in was in fact that of Erasmus. "At least hold him until you have checked," Xanthe told the footmen. Other servants had arrived, including the head butler. At the thought that his master might indeed have been slain he instructed three of his staff to take hold of the man she accused. He struggled so fiercely, protesting his innocence, that she worried he would get away or change their minds about Harley. Fortunately, her friend had his own ideas about how to deal with the situation and strode forward to deliver a hefty punch to the man, which put him out cold. The butler took another servant with him and ran upstairs. Harley stayed to make sure that when the man woke up he would not get away, while Elizabeth and Xanthe rushed on into the ballroom.

The mood of the evening had noticeably altered. The music was more up-tempo, the dancing wilder, the condition of the guests in most cases more inebriated. Xanthe spotted Dawlish attempting to shield himself with his visitors, threading his way among the dancers in the center of the ballroom. She set off toward him, having to step around dancing couples as she did so, her progress being frustratingly slow. She had no clear idea of what she would do when she reached him. She had no weapon. She seemed to be alone now, with no one to help her. All she knew was she could not let him get away. Then a plan came to her. She was a Spinner, and she would use her skill to trap him. All she had to do was get close enough to grab hold of him, then she would use her locket to return home to her own time, taking him with her. He would be lost in the modern world, penniless and friendless. What she would do with him next she had no clue, but there would be time to figure that out and others to help her do it. She pushed on, but every time she felt she was gaining on him she was swept aside by the increasingly frenzied dancers.

Suddenly, she heard a shout, a cry of warning. She followed the direction of the desperate gestures of those who had raised the alarm. Looking up, she saw that the hundreds of candles in the chandeliers were burning in a dangerous and unnatural fashion. Their flames, instead of being small and pretty and harmless, had grown into great tongues of fire, leaping ever higher, growing as they watched. Within seconds, molten wax began raining down. The dancers screamed and ran in all directions, desperate to get away from the scalding liquid.

The orchestra stopped playing and began to hurry from the mezzanine. When she looked up to see them flee she saw a single figure, standing at the galleried edge of the high platform, ignored by the terrified musicians in their haste to leave.

"Elizabeth!"

She watched as the woman, who had only moments before been a woman struck almost dumb with the shock of grief, revealed her true nature, her real identity, her elemental self to be that of an ancient, powerful witch. Still in her evening finery, the rich red fabric stained darker with the blood of her beloved husband, her hair had come loose from its bun and not only fell about her shoulders but seemed to billow as if conducting the fearsome energy within her. She held her arms up and out and her attention was entirely concentrated on the chandeliers.

At every door there was an agitated crush of people trying to get out. Here and there one of the braver men attempted to stamp out the flaming wax that was beginning to set light to tablecloths and cushions and even some of the clothes of the guests. Dawlish dashed toward the main entrance to the room but saw that there were too many people in front of him and so changed direction. Xanthe sprinted after him, cursing the weight of her dress as she did so. He tried another exit, only to be shoved back by a furious man who was attempting to get his dance partner to safety. All the while more and more wax dripped onto every surface, increasing amounts of it burning as it fell, so that fires were springing up all around the room. Now people were screaming and scuffles broke out at every possible exit. Two of the footmen courageously battled to open some of the enormous windows so that more guests could escape. At last all the frightened men and women had found a way out of the ballroom. All except Dawlish, Xanthe, and Elizabeth.

Seeing a chance, Dawlish sprinted for one of the open doors, but before he could reach it, it slammed shut, directed by a wave of Elizabeth's hand. All other exits likewise closed themselves, and each resisted his desperate attempts to open them.

Xanthe noticed that the wooden balustrade of the mezzanine, and indeed the very staircase that led up to it, was ablaze. Layers of varnish covered in years of polish ignited in a moment, the sound of splintering wood and crackling flames replacing the earlier music.

"Elizabeth! Elizabeth, come down! The stairs! You will be trapped, you have to get out now!" She shouted as loudly as she could but her words were all but lost in the roar of the fire that now encircled the room. At that moment, Dawlish made a dash across the center of the dance floor. Xanthe saw her chance and sprang in front of him, just as a nearby table went up in a frightening ball of fire as the punch bowl sitting on it ignited.

They stopped, facing each other, each trying to read what the other's next move would be.

"Out of my way, you little fool!" Dawlish glanced at the curtains, which had now been engulfed in flames. There was no longer any chance of getting out via the windows or the doors to the terrace, or the doors back into the house, due to the spread of the fire. With a crash that caused the whole room to shudder, one of the chandeliers plummeted to the floor, exploding in a lethal burst of broken glass and burning candle wax.

Xanthe stood her ground. She knew that, one by one, the escape routes had been cut off and she could feel the terrible heat of the fires around her. She shouted at Dawlish.

"The only way out of here now is with me!"

"No! Don't touch me!" he spat at her as she snatched at his arm. He drew back, tripping over broken glass as he turned, stumbling away from her but losing his footing. He fell onto the glass-strewn floor, shouting oaths as he floundered about, his hands cut and bleeding, the tails of his jacket singeing.

Xanthe heard the sound of more exploding glass and a creaking noise. Looking up, she saw that a second chandelier was about to drop, the plasterwork around its fastening weakened and burned, the wooden joist to which it was fixed now ablaze.

"Dawlish, you have to move!" she yelled. "Get up. Here, take my hand!"

She reached out toward him but he tried to get farther away, twisting upon the cruel shards, flapping at his now burning clothes. "No!" he shouted again. "No!"

And then the great crystal light fell. It plummeted to the ground so close to Xanthe that she had to fling herself backward, the awful sound of it smashing on impact with the wooden dance floor not completely masking Dawlish's terrible screams.

The whole room seemed filled with fire and smoke and heat. As the fumes from all that was burning started to make her cough and splutter, Xanthe took hold of her gold locket. She opened it, blinking through the smoke to focus on her mother's dear face, forcing herself to think only of home, willing herself to spin through time once again.

20

ELIZABETH WAS SITTING ON THE TURKISH RUG ON HER ROOFTOP HIDEAWAY, STRAIGHT backed and still, gazing out at the sunset over the cityscape. Xanthe leaned against the tall chimney stack a few strides from where her friend sat. The prettiness of the sky, with its hot pink and scarlet streaking the deepening blue of the dying day, seemed at odds with the mood of the house. The past few days had been draining in the extreme and had taken their toll on all of them, but it was Elizabeth who was suffering the most. It was as if in losing Erasmus she had lost a part of herself. After the events of that terrible night, she had been subdued, her expression one of contained pain, her words spoken slowly and with care, as if at any moment she might reveal the true depth of her heartache and then not be able to regain her composure. Xanthe was still uncertain what skills her friend had used to escape the fire, but she had emerged completely unscathed. The rest of the household—all servants and guests—had also got out of the house unhurt, as had Nipper and Liam, who had managed to carry Erasmus's body to their carriage. By the time the summoned fire brigade had arrived, bells clanging, the blaze was out of control, the house beyond saving. All present could do no more than stand and watch the spectacle of such a grand and powerful building being reduced to ashes and rubble. Dawlish's and Brook-Morton's bones lay among the ruins of their home, their Spinner doors consumed along with them.

Xanthe had used her locket to leap to safety but had not lingered at home. In fact, she had not so much as left the blind house, but had picked up the writing slope and used it to return immediately. She had been anxious that it might stop singing to her at any moment. With Lydia's brooch now silent, it was the only remaining treasure to take her back to Liam and Harley. To her huge relief, she had found herself back in the narrow street opposite the bookbinder's house, arriving less than an hour after the others had returned there. Liam had been beside himself with worry and refused to leave the remains of the house, terrified that she had not escaped. She had used a cab to go directly to him. At the sight of her stepping from the little carriage, disheveled, bloodstained, with a gunshot hole in her dress and burn marks to her hem, he had enfolded her in his arms, kissing her hair and face over and over, telling her he would never leave her to do something so dangerous without him again.

They had held a swift and private funeral for Erasmus. She had worried that he might need to be taken back to his original era, but together they had agreed that nowhere and no time was ever more home to him than the years and the place he had shared with Elizabeth and Nipper. She came to see that it was Elizabeth she had been called to, in fact, rather than Erasmus. While he was important, it had been the two women who had ultimately defeated the Visionary Society.

Something else that had surprised Xanthe was that the writing box had fallen silent the moment Brook-Morton, Dawlish, and the Visionary Society itself, ceased to be. She had noticed this the moment she returned to the bookbinder's house and heard nothing. When she went to investigate, the treasure neither vibrated nor sang. Which meant that she had successfully spun back to a place and time of her choosing without having a found thing calling her. When she had mentioned this to Elizabeth she'd pointed out that, as both guardian of *Spinners* and protector of the creed, she was now of the highest order of time travelers. Just as Lydia Flyte had been able to move through the years without anything to call or guide her, so, now, could Xanthe.

With her work done, she was free at last to take Liam and Harley and return home. She had been surprised to find herself reluctant to leave, however. The bookbinder's shop, Erasmus's workshop, Elizabeth, even Nipper after their shared experience of the night of the ball, all exerted a tangible pull on her. Beyond that, she felt comfortable in the time. She had grown accustomed to the clothes, now that she had learned how to move in them. She liked the absence of modernity in the city. True, it was dirty, and the air could be toxic at times, and there was poverty all around, but it felt real somehow. As if, in fact, her own day was equally dangerous, divisions equally unjust, the only difference being that these things were more hidden. Climate change only really impacted somewhere far off, something to be worried about but not felt, at least, not yet. Concern about poverty could be managed by donating to a food bank or buying charity Christmas cards, enabling a person to get on with their own busy life, their conscience salved. In 1878, with the liberal social vision of her twenty-first-century upbringing, Xanthe could clearly see the inequalities. She could feel the grit of those dangerous factories in her eyes and taste the pollution on her tongue. The shoeless child holding out its hand in the street had no safety net but was her responsibility. That connection, that exposure to the truth, it was something that spoke to her. Perhaps, she thought, it was because she was a Spinner that she felt this way. After all, her duty was to right wrongs, to go where an injustice needed to be addressed. She promised herself that when they had a quiet moment she would quiz Liam about it, to see if he, a non-Spinner, shared these feelings.

She was pulled from her thoughts by the sound of Elizabeth's voice.

"I am sorry," she was saying, "if my actions frightened you."

She experienced a vivid flashback to the blazing ballroom, the sounds of the fire, the shattering crystal, and Dawlish's screams. It had been frightening, but at the time her only real fear had been that he would get away. That she would fail. "I couldn't have stopped him without you doing what you did," she said.

"Oh, I think you are more resourceful than you know, my dear." Elizabeth got up and came to stand beside her, both of them gazing out at the psychedelic sky. "You would have found a way. Just as Nipper must now find his way forward without his father."

"He will make an excellent job of the business. Erasmus taught him well."

Elizabeth nodded. "And he will see looking after me as part of his job too. Which is why it is really a good thing that I cannot stay beyond next summer."

"He knows? That you have to leave because of having existed in this time before?"

"He has always known the day would come. We had all expected that Erasmus and I would make the journey to my old home together." She gave a sigh and the light wind that moaned between the chimney stacks and rooftops seemed to answer her. "But that was not to be. And I shall do well enough. The cottage is a special place."

"Tell me about it."

"It is a cheerful house. Someone once told me it looked like a face, with windows placed just so for eyes. I like that. It has a charming sitting room and warm bedrooms, but the place where I will spend most of my time is the kitchen. There is an antique dresser—you would appreciate its quality and rarity, I'm certain of it—and it is perfect for all the oils and tinctures that I will make again. The garden will no doubt be in dire need of attention, but it is sheltered and sunny and there is room enough for all the herbs and plants I require for my recipes." She paused and looked at Xanthe. "It is less than thirty miles from Marlborough, did I mention that?"

"No! I would love to see it. I could take a trip out there, between now and when . . . when we meet again. Is there anyone living there now?"

"I believe it is currently unoccupied. Tegan continues to travel the globe learning her craft. But, that is not to say she will not have returned before my homecoming. I should like that very much," she said, smiling properly for the first time since losing Erasmus.

"When you need to leave here, leave now, I will come for you. It will be a job I will gladly do, because then we will meet again," Xanthe said. They had discussed how Elizabeth could be taken to the modern day and Xanthe had come to realize that she was now quite able to move about without a treasure if she needed to. While she would not be taking up Erasmus's work as such, she could fulfill his duty on this occasion, for Elizabeth could not be left to inhabit the same point in time as her earlier self. She smiled at Elizabeth. "Erasmus said he was the luckiest of men to have you as his wife. I am the luckiest Spinner to have you as my friend."

Elizabeth looked away again then, still struggling to hide her feelings. "Well, did not Erasmus and I prove that a time traveler and a witch make a good team? Come, let us go down. The others are waiting."

They found the men in Erasmus's workshop. Although everyone was making an effort to keep the mood light with easy conversation, there was a tension in the air and a sadness that accompanies such partings that they were all inevitably feeling. Liam's hand was still in a splint, but his other wounds had healed well. He smiled at Xanthe as she entered the room and she felt her heart skip just a little, despite the melancholy moment. They had a future together, she knew that with such a reassuring certainty that it made her love him even more. Harley was making the most of the last moments of wearing his Victorian outfit, his moustache oiled and twirled to perfection, his hat brushed and worn at a rakish angle. Nipper shuffled from one foot to the other, a little embarrassed at the intensity of the situation. Xanthe offered him her hand, not to kiss, but to shake.

"Thank you, Nipper," she said. "I landed in your family uninvited and caused mayhem and yet you made me feel welcome."

"You were doing the work my parents have done all my life," he said with a shrug. "And besides, you needed me. I was glad to be able to assist you." He nodded at Liam. "To assist all of you." He held out his hand and Liam shook it gratefully.

Xanthe turned to Elizabeth and the two women embraced.

"I am so glad you were able to take Millie in," Xanthe told her. "She will be happy here, I know it."

"I think perhaps it was time for me to have a little help," Elizabeth said. "Someone else to cook and so on. Someone to support Nipper when I am no longer here."

A poignant silence joined the party. Xanthe knew that she could put off leaving no longer.

"Well, gentlemen," she said, pulling the strap of her satchel over her shoulder, the *Spinners* book tucked closely into her side, "I believe it is time for us to depart."

—

Arriving back in the blind house encircled by the arms of two of her very favorite people was quite an experience for Xanthe. It was not just the emotional upheaval of leaving Elizabeth that affected her so strongly as her eyes adjusted to the gloom of the little stone building, it was the overwhelming relief of seeing that she had brought her friends home safely at last. The three of them took a moment to steady themselves and clear their heads. Harley, in particular, seemed groggy after the time travel and staggered against the rough wall.

"Careful," she said as she put an arm on his shoulder. "Give yourself time."

"I'll be right as rain, hen, don't fret."

Liam located the writing box and picked it up. "Here," he said, "it looks fine. Just a bit damp. Has it . . . has it stopped singing to you?" he wanted to know.

"Yes. It has. Which is sort of sad, but also good. It means I've done my job. Actually," she corrected herself, "*we've* done my job!"

"I can't find the brooch," he said, groping around on the gritty floor, warning Harley to be careful not to tread on it with his size twelve feet.

Xanthe leaned down and, without looking, was able to locate the keepsake instantly. Nipper had gone to retrieve it from the pawn shop after his father's funeral and had been distressed to find it had already been sold. She had reassured him it was on its own journey; the path it had been meant to take. She knew it would find its way back to her and be waiting in the blind house. She picked it up, holding it carefully. She felt anew the significance of the treasure but there was no vibration. No song. Its silence was not unexpected, but it touched her, reminding her that her final connection with Lydia Flyte was gone. She would always share the experience of being a Spinner, of course, but the personal link that the memorial brooch had offered had quietened and faded. Now it was no more than a pretty memento. She slipped it in her pocket, knowing that whatever its value, she would never sell it.

The three emerged from the old jail into the soft light of a summer afternoon. Everything was reassuringly normal and homely. The flower beds and borders were still a tangle of fragrant rambling roses, butterfly bushes, and leafy shrubs. Flora's tubs and hanging baskets were still filled with color. The lawn was still as much weed as grass and in need of a mowing. House sparrows flitted about in the branches of the little apple tree, and a robin sang its heart out from the top of the high brick wall. Into this moment of calm, Pie came bounding at full tilt, tail wagging, emitting curious noises of greeting that were somewhere between barks and howls. She tore around Liam's legs before leaping up at Xanthe, who caught her in her arms.

"Yes, we're pleased to see you too, Pie," she assured the wild creature. "Have you been a good dog? Have you?"

"Xanthe!" Flora appeared in the doorway and waved one of her crutches in greeting. "And Liam! You're all here. Oh, welcome home!" She hurried across the lawn to properly greet them. "It's so good to see you. I've been so worried."

"Mum . . ."

"You'd no need to worry, Flora," Harley reminded her, "she had me along, after all."

"I know, and I know you know what you're doing, love," she said, giving her daughter an extra hug. "But I'm a mother. Worrying about possible catastrophes, however unlikely, is written in my job description somewhere. Oh, it is good to have you home! Now, I want to hear *everything*. Come on, let's all go inside. I've got wine in the fridge."

"That sounds great, Mum, but honestly, we're all just a little bit exhausted. I don't know about the others, but I for one could do with a long soak in a hot bath and then bed."

"Sounds good to me," Liam said with a grin.

Xanthe shot him a look.

Harley gave a loud yawn. "Have to admit to being a wee bit knackered myself, hen. This time travel business, it takes it out of a person. Who'd have thought it?"

"Of course, silly of me," said Flora. "We'll catch up with each other's news tomorrow, when everyone's rested."

As she stick-stepped her way back to the house with the others following, Xanthe asked quietly, "Each other's news? What's been going on here, Mum?"

"Oh, nothing important. Nothing that can't wait until later," she said evasively. It was clear to Xanthe she was bursting to tell her something, and the small smile that lit up her face was a good indication that it was something nice. She thought at once of Stuart and how well the two of them had been getting on.

Liam took her hand. "I'll see you tomorrow," he said, a statement, not a question. "Will you be OK? I mean, Erasmus was important to you. . . ."

"I'll be fine." She leaned in and gave him a light but lingering kiss. "See you tomorrow," she said as she smiled.

As Harley went to pass her she threw her arms around his neck.

"Hey, lassie! What's all this about?" he asked, giving her a hug.

"I am so grateful to you, Harley. Honestly, you were such a help," she said, slipping from his arms to smile at him, both of them suddenly a little self-conscious.

"It was the most exciting thing I've ever done in my life. But don't tell Annie," he teased.

"Thank you," she said again.

He touched the brim of his bowler hat, made the smallest of bows, all the more effective for being less showy and more authentic, proving if there were any doubt, that he really was a changed man after his bit of spinning through time. "Good night, hen," he said, and followed Liam out of the front door.

—

Xanthe slept dreamlessly and peacefully for the first time in what felt like forever. She awoke to birdsong, accompanied by the slightly less tuneful sound of her mother in the kitchen singing along to the radio. She allowed herself a moment or two and then got up slowly, not entirely surprised to find herself bruised and stiff after the particularly physical demands of her time in Victorian London. She pulled a fluffy jumper over her vintage cotton nightdress and pushed her feet into her Dr. Martens boots, the cool leather familiar and comforting. When she reached the kitchen she found her mother had already descended to the ground floor, so she followed the sound of her singing. Pie heard her footsteps and came to greet her on the stairs, tail wagging in a blur.

"That you, Xanthe, love?" Flora called from the shop.

"It's late, you should have woken me," she said, seeing the hands of the ormolu clock showing past ten o'clock.

"We tried," Flora told her. "You didn't even stir when subjected to whippet kisses, so I thought you'd better sleep on. Now that you're here give me a hand with this, would you?" She patted the eighteenth-century bedroom chair, taking hold of the back of it. When Xanthe lifted the other end Flora directed her to the space she had made in the window. "There. Very nice. Thought it was time for a new display. Like it?"

"It's good, Mum." She nodded, looking around at the shop. "I can see you've changed a few things while I was gone. I like the pictures up there."

"Yes, well, I couldn't sit and twiddle my thumbs."

"The escritoire is new, isn't it? Where did that come from?"

"Oh, I saw it in the small ads, Stuart picked it up for me. Those Renaults have really roomy boots, you know."

Xanthe detected the subtle change in her mother's voice.

"Been seeing quite a bit of Stuart, have you?"

"Oh, now and again," she said vaguely, busying herself with an arrangement of Royal Worcester teacups. "We've had extra rehearsals at bell ringing because there's a wedding coming up. And then as I was on my own, and he is on his own, we went out to supper. At that Italian place you and Liam like. How is Liam after his adventures, by the way? You haven't told me what things were like for him."

"He's fine, just a little battered around the edges. And don't change the subject."

"Did I?"

"Mum, this is me you're talking to. So, Stuart . . . ?"

"He used to have a framing business, did I tell you? He's very handy. Helped me fix a cupboard I was trying to up-cycle. Very stubborn hinges, but he sorted them out in a jiffy. And he likes walking, so of course Pie loves him. He's taken her out a few times, given her a good long walk, which I can't quite manage."

"Sounds like he's been a really good friend."

"Yes. He has."

She waited. When her mother didn't offer anything more she probed a little further.

"Maybe more than a friend?" she asked.

"Perhaps." Flora's answer might have been evasive, but the color that came to her cheeks spoke volumes.

Xanthe gave her a hug. "I'm so happy for you, Mum. You deserve to have someone kind and good in your life."

"You make him sound like a vicar!" Flora laughed. "He's not spending time with me because he feels sorry for me."

"Of course not! I didn't mean that. It's just that, well, after Dad was such a . . ."

"Stuart makes me laugh. And we have a lot in common. And, in case you hadn't noticed, he's got a particularly nice bum."

"Mum!" It was her turn to laugh now. The two women giggled, Flora's eyes brighter than she had seen them for a long time. It occurred to her that her mother wouldn't need her so much now. If she really had found a new partner, she could leave her without worrying that she was having to cope with the shop and everything that went with it on her own. In fact, there was every chance that Flora would want a little more space in the future.

"And what about you and Liam? At least tell me how that's going?"

"Sorry, Mum, I know I haven't filled you in on anything about our trip yet."

"You will, when you're ready. I can wait. What I really want to know is, are you two an item or not? I mean, you've been keeping him dangling for ages. . . ."

"Dangling!"

"Poor boy."

"Mum, he's not a boy. And he knows how I feel about him."

"Oh?" Her mother stopped positioning chintz-patterned saucers and turned to lean on one of her sticks, head tilted, waiting for more.

Now it was Xanthe's turn to blush. "Let's just say I'm very happy to have him back."

"How happy? On a scale of finding-a-fiver-on-the-street-pleased to Christmas-morning-when-you were-eight-years-old-ecstatic?" she asked, using an old family measure.

She grinned, only now able to admit to herself, let alone anyone else, how she felt. "Christmas and birthdays all rolled into one," she said, causing her mother to beam. "Something else that might interest you," she went on, steering the conversation onto less emotional ground, "Mr. Morris is alive and well and living in a bungalow near Devizes."

"What? Our Mr. Morris? The one used to own this place?"

"Yup."

"Not dead?"

"Not last time I saw him. He's the one who sold me the three found things that sang to me. And, you might want to sit down for this bit . . . he used to be a Spinner."

Flora sank down into the chair they had just repositioned.

"Good grief!" She shook her head slowly, taking it all in. "I think you'd better make us both a cup of tea and then tell me the whole story, right from the beginning, don't you?"

As if agreeing that this was a good idea, Pie jumped up onto Flora's lap and curled into a tight ball, ready for a doze.

—

A week later, Xanthe was still finding it difficult to settle back into normal life. While it was lovely to be home, to enjoy the comfort of family, the familiarity of the little town, the shared purpose of the shop, she continued to feel distant. Disconnected. In a way that she had not experienced after her previous time travels. It was as if she had changed gears. As if now, with her new responsibilities as a Spinner, she was not able to fully engage with her old existence. Or at least, she was not able to completely put aside her other, more compelling, more mysterious life. She was aware that Liam and Harley were having similar problems picking up the rhythm of their more usual lives. Harley had

thrown himself into the task of getting the pub beetle-free and ready for business with such gusto that the work was already finished. Annie was due to return at the end of the week, and the pub would reopen that weekend. Tin Lid were booked as the first live music event, scheduled to play on Saturday. Liam had been delighted that the band would be performing together again, and had mentioned to Xanthe how he felt it would help them both move forward. She was cheered at the prospect of singing, and of making music in such a friendly venue with an easy, appreciative audience of regulars. Even so, she doubted it would be enough to settle her completely.

The shop had been quiet all that Wednesday, the hours passing slowly without the distraction of many customers. After an early supper with Flora, she texted Liam and Harley. Half an hour later, she picked them up in her black cab and they headed out of Marlborough toward the white horse. The car purred along the main road as the light began to fade. The long summer days were reaching their peak, and soon the solstice would turn the year toward autumn again. Liam and Harley talked about the new beer that was to be served on tap at The Feathers. Xanthe knew they both enjoyed a good ale, but she also knew pointless chatter when she heard it. It was as if they were all preoccupied with things that were really too complex to talk about, too confusing to set straight in their minds, let alone when spoken aloud. After a few more miles, Xanthe swung the car into the small parking place reserved for visitors to the chalk hill figure. The only other vehicle there was just on its way out. She found she was pleased to think they would have the place to themselves.

As they made their way up the footpath, Liam fell into step beside her, taking her hand in his. They had not been able to spend much time together since their return. Liam had had plenty to do to catch up with business at the workshop, and she had wanted to be useful in the shop and getting more stock.

"You OK?" he asked her as they walked.

"I'm good. You?"

"Great, yeah."

Harley, walking behind them with quite a lot of puffing going on, gave a grunt. "Listen to the two of you," he said. "'OK.' 'Good.' 'Great.' Aye, bollocks!"

Xanthe and Liam stopped and stared at him but he simply kept walking, overtaking them and pressing on toward the top of the hill. They followed. By the time the path opened up onto the enormous white horse, the sun was dipping over the distant horizon, and all three of them gasped at the colors of the sunset. She was immediately taken back in her mind to that final evening with Elizabeth, up on the roof, watching the sun go down over the city. How long ago and far away that seemed, and yet the pull she felt toward both time and place was fierce. She stood beside the great head of the ancient effigy, Liam to her right, Harley to her left. The day was cooling but there was no wind, and they were sufficiently far from any roads for there to be no traffic noise. All the farm machinery had stopped work for the day. A gentle silence enveloped them as they stood and watched the tangerine dream that tinged the whole landscape as it fell away at their feet, spreading for many miles in all directions. She could feel the unspoken thoughts of her friends. She knew that they too were experiencing that curious, irresistible pull from the past. They had been forever changed by their recent experiences. It was not, for them, a sense of duty as it might be for her. It was that, having stepped into such magic, having been taken out of the everyday and the here and now in such a supernatural and fascinating way, they could not simply fall back into step with the modern world. Xanthe thought about the hatpin then. About how it still sang to her. Still called out from an unknown time, letting her know that she was needed elsewhere. Else when. As she would always be needed. She recalled how Lydia Flyte had told her there were other Spinners to be watched. Others who were corrupted by the power of their gift. Like the ones who had followed her and Elizabeth as they had walked through the city. Like the ones who had broken into the bookbinder's and tried to steal the Spinners' book.

Liam squeezed her hand and they exchanged a warm smile. She turned to Harley and in his expression saw joy at the wonder of what they all shared. She knew there would be more injustices to address. More adventures to be had. Treasures would sing to her, calling her to action. And she knew that, together, the three of them would answer that call.

ACKNOWLEDGMENTS

Huge thanks, as ever, to the whole team at St. Martin's Press. With special mentions, of course, for my tireless editor, Pete Wolverton, and his supremely organized right-hand woman, Lily Cronig. Where would I be without you all?

City of Time and Magic is a pandemic book. The second I have worked on. I enormously appreciate all the hoops jumped through, leaps of faith taken, and extra miles trudged by everyone in order to bring it into being. At the time of writing, we still have a way to go before anything that could be called normality is in sight. It is my dearest wish that the world will have righted itself once more by publication day. I look forward to hearing how readers have strolled into bookshops, browsed at their leisure, found *City of Time and Magic*, and taken it from the shelf. That's surely a lovely kind of normality.